Praise for *Skullsworn*

'Staveley has quickly become one of my favourite fantasy authors . . . *Skullsworn* is a brilliant new chapter' V. E. Schwab

'Visceral action scenes and memorable characters bring this tale to life. Despite the outsize aspects of this adventure, it still feels remarkably intimate, right up to an epilogue that casts the book's events in a whole new light' *Publishers Weekly*

'This is a pleasantly grim and emotionally complex *divertissement* that will give pleasure to fans . . . an accessible entree for new readers, who will undoubtedly go on to consume the rest of the series' *Kirkus*

'*Skullsworn* is a fantastic standalone book with a very satisfying conclusion' *The Book Bag*

'A highly engrossing fantasy world' *Fantasy Book Review*

'Brian Staveley deftly weaves a fast-paced and compelling tale filled with excellent characterization, vivid world-building, and high personal stakes, making this one an outstanding novel on every level'

SKULLSWORN

After more than a decade teaching history, religion, and philosophy, Brian decided to write epic fantasy. He now lives on a steep dirt road in the hills of southern Vermont, where he divides his time between fathering, writing, husbanding, splitting wood, skiing, and adventuring – not necessarily in that order.

His blog, *On the Writing of Epic Fantasy*, can be found at bstaveley.wordpress.com and you can see his other social media haunts below.

Twitter: @Brianstaveley
Facebook: facebook.com/Brianstaveley
Google+: Brian Staveley

Also by Brian Staveley

THE CHRONICLE OF
THE UNHEWN THRONE

The Emperor's Blades
The Providence of Fire
The Last Mortal Bond

SKULL SWORN

BRIAN STAVELEY

TOR

First published 2017 by Tom Doherty Associates, LLC

First published in the UK 2017 by Tor

This paperback edition published 2017 by Tor
an imprint of Pan Macmillan
20 New Wharf Road, London N1 9RR
Associated companies throughout the world
www.panmacmillan.com

ISBN 978-1-5098-2298-0

1 3 5 7 9 8 6 4 2

A CIP catalogue record for this book is available from the British Library.

Typeset by Palimpsest Book Production Ltd, Falkirk, Stirlingshire
Printed and bound by CPI Group (UK) Ltd, Croydon, CR0 4YY

Visit www.panmacmillan.com to read more about all our books
and to buy them. You will also find features, author interviews and
news of any author events, and you can sign up for e-newsletters
so that you're always first to hear about our new releases.

For Jo,
who shows me the notes

ACKNOWLEDGEMENTS

As always, I'm tremendously grateful to all the people who contributed to this book in ways large and small, general and particular. It takes a village to tell a story, and I worry that if I started listing the villagers I would never stop. There are, however, five people who have read the manuscript all the way through, several times over in each case. Suzanne Baker and Gavin Baker are a formidable mother/son team, absolutely indefatigable in reading draft after draft, generous in their praise, keen and unflinching in their criticism. I've always thought it's better to be lucky than good, and I'm about the luckiest writer alive to have Hannah Bowman as my agent and Marco Palmieri as my editor. Finally, this book, like all the others, wouldn't exist without Johanna Staveley, who believed in it and me more powerfully than I did.

SKULLSWORN

PROLOGUE

This is a story I never intended to tell. I thought, when I finally walked away from you all those years ago, that I was taking the tale with me. I thought, because it happened to me, because I seemed to stand at the center of everything, that it was *my* story—but that's not how stories work. A tale belongs only partly to the teller—even the wildest fabrication needs a listener, and this is no fabrication. It is the truth—or as close to the truth as I can come, so many years later—and there are other characters in it. This story is theirs as much as it is mine, but since they are dead, the telling falls to me. You were there, of course, the only other person who survived straight through to the end, but you didn't know what was happening. You couldn't. I should have told you a long time ago, but it wasn't until much later that I realized this story is yours, too. It's late, but I'm telling you now.

I went to Dombâng for love.

And yes, to kill seven people in fourteen days, sure, but I wasn't worried about the killing. I grew up in a place where women wear vests ribbed with stilettos, where each priest has a dozen knives, steel traps, needles so fine you can slide them beside the eye into the brain and out again without leaving a mark. I watched my fellow priests die by fire and iron, sometimes quickly, leaping from the tops of the sandstone cliffs, or slowly, by dehydration's intimate degrees. By my fifteenth year, I had set to memory a thousand ways to offer a woman or man to my god's sure unmaking. I wasn't concerned about my piety or my ability to make the sacrifice.

Love, though. Love was tricky. By the time I turned twenty-five, I'd had lovers and laughter, long nights in the high desert peaks learning the ways of my own body, alone or in the hot clutch of another. And yet love had eluded me.

To the uninitiate, this will not seem strange. *How can love,* you might demand, *take root in the stony heart of a Skullsworn? How can Ananshael's knives know love?*

I'm not offended. For most people, my god—like the death he brings—is all mystery and terror. You have not been to Rassambur, have not heard our choruses beneath the new moon, have not enjoyed the sweet fruit of the trees espaliered against our sandstone walls. How could you know the first thing about the men and women you call Skullsworn? How could you know if I don't tell you?

Maybe we could start with the word itself. It's wrong.

I don't swear on skulls, not *on* them, not *to* them, not *around* them. I haven't seen a skull for years, in fact. A bit of blood-smeared bone through a torn-open scalp, perhaps, but an actual *skull,* wide-eyed and jawless? What in the god's name would I be doing with a skull?

"Drinking the blood of innocent children," seems to be a common notion, so I'll set that little misconception to rest, too: I do not drink the blood of children, either guilty or innocent. I do not drink the blood of humans or beasts. I did have a blood sausage in Sia once, a thick black slab perched on a mountain of rice, but I ate it off of a normal plate, not out of a skull, and everyone else there seemed to be eating the same thing.

I should also clarify that I do not bathe in cauldrons of blood. I get bloody enough going out into the world to do the work of the god. The whole point of the bath is to scrub the blood *off.* The priests of the God of Death bathe in hot water, just like every other sane person on either side of the Ancaz. Back in Rassambur, I sift a little jasmine and ground sage into the boiling water. I like to be clean.

A few other clarifications, in no particular order:

I have no garments made of human skin. I prefer silk, although it tends to be easier to scrub the blood out of wool.

I have never fucked a dead person. I'm not sure who's going around sizing up the erections of the hanged, but I can promise you, it's not me. Most men are confused enough in bed already without the added disadvantage of death to slow them down. I like my lovers like I like my baths—warm, clean, and, if at all possible, good-smelling, although I'm willing to compromise on the last two.

I understand, of course, how people make these mistakes. If you're seeing a skull, or a barrel full of blood, chances are good that my god has come, unmade a creature, then disappeared. Surely as a strong dawn wind kicks up dust and bends the branches of the trees, Ananshael leaves blood and skulls in the wake of his passage, but blood and skulls are not death any more than a bent branch is the wind.

Death resists all comparison and simile. This is something I learned in my first year at Rassambur. To say death is like a land beyond the sea or like an endless scream is to miss the point. Death is not like anything. There is no craft analogous to Ananshael's work. The truest response to his mystery and majesty is silence.

On the other hand, to remain silent is to encourage the fantasies of the uninitiate—skulls brimming with blood, graveyard orgies, infants dangling like impractical chandeliers from the ceilings of candlelit caverns—and so maybe an imperfect analogy is better than none at all.

Take a grape.

The purple skin is muted, as if by mist or fog. Polish it, or not, then pop it into your mouth. The flesh is firm beneath the cool, smooth skin. If you find yourself becoming aroused, stop.

Start your imagining over. The grape is a grape. Imagine it properly, or this will not work.

Now. What does the grape taste like?

A grape tastes like a grape? Of course not. Until you bite the grape, it has no taste. It might as well be a stone lifted from the cold current of some river in autumn: a smooth, chill orb, reticent, flavorless. You could hold it trapped between your palate and tongue forever, with only the faintest hint of juice at the tiny breach where it was plucked from the stem.

You are like that grape—plump with slick, rich sweetness, with wet purple life. The truth of life is the grape's truth: only when jaws bite down, when the skin splits, when the sun-cold flesh explodes onto the tongue does it matter. Without the moment of its own destruction, the grape is just a smooth, colorful stone. Without the foreknowledge of the woman who holds it in her hand, her anticipation, before it even passes her lips, of the mangled skin and the sweet life draining over the tongue, the grape would hold no savor.

The Csestriim and the Nevariim were like this, if the chronicles are true—immortal, unbroken stones, incapable of joy, either the feeling or the bringing. Of course, my god was young when they walked the world, his strength more meager in the age when they were made, meager enough that for thousands of years and longer they escaped his touch. They might have continued forever that way—immortal save in those rare cases when the body was so broken by violence that my god could finally slide his fingers inside—but the Csestriim overreached. In their dust-dry desire to catalogue the world, to know it so they could bend it to their will, they pushed the Nevariim too far, and finally, the Nevariim pushed back.

They lost; the Csestriim wiped them from the world, but my god learned much in the conflict, and in the long millennia that followed, he grew stronger, strong enough that when *we* came—humans, women and men wandering the unforgiving earth—he could end us with a flick of his infinite fingers. He never learned the trick with the Csestriim, but it didn't matter. We were there to help him, to pry open that immortal flesh with our bronze and let him in. The Csestriim were stones, but we shattered them, scrubbed them out as they had scrubbed out the Nevariim.

We are not stones. Our human skin is thin, the life inside us bright. And death? The god I serve? He is the jaw locked around us, the promise of a sweet purple destruction without which we would be no more than so much polished rock.

My brothers and sisters in the faith understand this better than most. We devote our lives to this truth. And so, within the walls of Rassambur there is no shortage of joy, of delight, of music, and yes, of love. I have watched old couples step hand in hand from the bloodred cliffs, linked even in the moment of their unmaking. I have seen wives pour the poisoned tea for their husbands, hold the clay cup to the feeble lips themselves, offer the final release when the pain of one disease or another grew too great. I have witnessed the glee on the faces of younger couples as they sneak away, even felt a hint of it myself, a little shiver of ecstatic bliss when my lips met other lips.

But not love.

Not that it bothered me. I was young, strong, alight with my own devotion and the fellowship of my sisters and brothers. Love was a pleasant afterthought, something I could experience later, more slowly, when I was finished being young.

Then came the Trial, and with the Trial, the song.

My god is a great lover of music. Not the still, finished forms of painting or sculpture, but music. Music is inextricable from its own unmaking. Each note is predicated on the death of those before. Try to hold them all, and you have madness, cacophony, noise. A song, like a life, is all in the letting go, in the knowing, the moment you begin, that it will end. And of all music's variegated forms—fiddle and drum, harp and horn, plangent or joyous—Ananshael loves the human voice, the sound of the instrument giving song to the knowledge of its own impermanence.

It was no surprise that the test concluding all my training would begin with a song, but of all the melodies I'd heard at Rassambur, this one had been kept from me, as it was from all the acolytes, until just before the Trial. Listen, and you will understand the fierceness of my sudden need to love:

> One who is right, and one who is wrong,
> A singer snared in a web of song—
> Deliver them, deliver them
> Into his million-fingered hands.
>
> Deliver to him a dealer of death,
> Severed from life, shorn of breath.
> Deliver a mother, ripe with new life.
> Find the kindness in the sharpest knife.
> Deliver to him a giver of names;
> There are no words in his domain.
>
> When these are safe inside his hands,
>   One more remains,
> One more remains—
> Give to the god the one who makes your mind
> And body sing with love
>   Who will not come again.

I don't know who composed the music, but it is perfect, polyphonic, one melody the naked blade, the other the warm skin in the moment before it parts. Ela and Kossal sang it for me—it fell to them as my Witnesses in the Hall of All Endings, a vault-roofed, windowless sandstone cube just a dozen paces across. Not so much a hall as a room, really. Twin candles lit the space, ivory pillars as thick as my thigh set into sconces in the wall. There were no altars. Their singing bodies were the altars, their music the offering, brimming in the lambent space until it seemed almost liquid, her voice throaty, rich; his spare

and unadorned as old iron. I cried, listening to them, cried first
for the sheer beauty of the thing, and then again, a moment
after, when my mind moved from the music to the words, and
I realized what it meant: I was going to fail. I had already failed,
fallen short of my great exercise of devotion even before it truly
began.

The song is a list, obviously, a list of those that each acolyte
must give to the god before becoming a full priest of Ananshael.
From the first offering to the last, the would-be priestess is
allowed fourteen days. Fourteen days for seven offerings. Not
such a daunting task—not for one raised and trained in
Rassambur—but an impossible one for someone, like me, who
had never been in love.

The words trembled in my mind even after the singing was
over: *Give to the god the one who makes your mind and body
sing with love.*

Ela saw my shock first, but she misunderstood it.

"I know," she said, sliding a strong, gentle hand over my
shoulders. Her fingers were warm in the cool night air. Even
without the notes, her voice still sounded like song. "I know."

Kossal had already turned to the candles. Those twin flames
gave the room its only light, but he was halfway to snuffing
them, reaching for the first wick with his calloused fingers, ready
to pinch the flame.

"Give her a moment, you old goat," Ela said.

The priest paused, turned. Despite his age, he didn't stoop.
He carried himself—that whole tall, sinewy frame—like a man
forty years younger, though his face—olive beneath the graying
stubble—looked like something carved, each line and wrinkle
scored into the flesh. Candlelight glinted, needle-bright, in each
eye.

"She can have all the moments she wants. In the dark."

"And what if she wants a little light?"

Kossal shifted his eyes from Ela, whistling tunelessly through
a gap in his teeth as he studied me. "She wants to be a priestess,

she ought to get acquainted with a little darkness. Besides, we're wasting wax."

"We've wasted worse than wax," Ela replied. "I'll snuff the candles when we leave."

The old man watched me a heartbeat longer, looked back to the candles as though there were some answer there, then shook his head. "That you and I keep working together, Ela Timarna, is a mystery I cannot fathom."

Ela's laugh was a silver bell. I'd seen her put a fist through a thick block of sun-baked clay, watched her take a dying goat by the horns and snap its neck, but she carried her strength lightly. The muscle and sinew knitted beneath her brown skin looked built for leaping or lounging, not slaughter. Everything about her seemed light: her hair—a tumble of tight black ringlets—seemed to bounce with every movement; her hands were forever floating up as she gestured about one point or another; even her lips were always on the verge of turning up into a smile.

"We keep working together," she replied, shooting me a wink as she answered the priest, "because you have a weakness for young women."

Kossal grunted. "Funny thing about people: you give 'em enough years, and they stop being young."

"And how many years," Ela asked, spreading her arms as though offering an embrace or inviting the older priest to hazard a punch, "do you figure that takes?" She cocked her head to the side, smiling, her teeth bright in the candlelight. "Have I stopped being young yet?" She turned in a slow circle, graceful as a dancer, pausing fractionally when her back was to him, then completing the rotation.

Kossal kept his eyes on her. His gaze was frank, open, appraising, but utterly uncovetous, utterly scrubbed of lust's sticky need. I found myself wanting someone to look at me that way: not just to look at me, but to *see* me. The priest's eyes, however, were only for the older woman.

"Not yet," he conceded finally.

Ela smiled. Both of them stood still, but a draft tugged at the candles, making their shadows shiver. "I'm glad. I can't tell you how demoralizing it would be if you were younger at seventy than I am at thirty-five."

Kossal shook his head. "I quit being young a long way back. Never did suit me."

"I'll be the judge of what suits you."

The old priest grunted again, then turned to me. "I'll give you a piece of advice, kid. Might come in handy if I don't have to kill you at the end of your Trial."

Ela draped an arm over my shoulder, gave me a conspiratorial squeeze, then leaned close to mock-whisper in my ear. "Pretend like you're listening. His advice is terrible, but it makes him happy to give it."

Kossal ignored the gibe. "When you give the god *the one who makes your mind and body sing with love,* make sure you get it right. Otherwise," he went on, nodding to Ela without breaking eye contact with me, "she'll be there to bother you the rest of your life."

"As I said," Ela murmured, still loud enough for Kossal to hear, "his advice is terrible. I was ten years unborn when he had his Trial."

"Should have waited," he said, half to himself, shaking his head, then moving toward the door.

In a movement so fast I didn't understand it until after, Ela twisted away from me and pivoted toward the older priest, aiming a sparring blow low between his ribs. She was fast, as fast as any priestess I'd seen at Rassambur, but it wasn't her speed I marveled at later, over and over, but the perfect ease with which Kossal blocked the blow, catching her wrist, holding those stiffened fingers inches from his side. Ela glanced down at her hand, shook her head ruefully, smiled, then leaned in to kiss him lightly on the brow.

"Would you really have strangled me in my crib?" she asked.

The words were warm, private, as though she'd forgotten I was there.

"Would have been easier," Kossal replied, letting her wrist go.

"Easier than what?"

The old priest just shook his head. "Snuff the candles when you're done. A little light's all well and good, but when the wax is gone, it's gone."

Kossal stepped into the night, and the cedar door swung shut quietly behind him. Ela watched it for a while, lips pursed, as though she were about to whistle the first few bars of an old tune. She looked totally relaxed, but I could see her heartbeat testing the vessel in her neck; not fast, exactly, but faster than before. Her breath was faster, too, her chest rising and falling beneath her robe, whether from the short struggle with Kossal or from something else, I didn't know.

"He loves you?" I asked stupidly.

Ela turned to me, then smiled. "That old fool doesn't know the first thing about love."

"He must have, once."

"Once?" The priestess cocked her head to the side, then nodded. "Ah. His Trial."

"He passed. Which means he loved someone. He had to have."

"Perhaps," Ela replied, then shrugged. "Enough about him. He's half in Ananshael's hand already. This is what *you're* worried about, isn't it? Making that last gift to the god?"

I hesitated. The truth made me feel small.

The priestess turned me until I faced her. She kept one hand on my shoulder, then lifted my chin with the other, until I was looking into her dark eyes. The fog of her hair caught the candlelight until it seemed to glow, while her face was lost in shadow. She was only a few inches taller, but in that moment I might have been a child all over again, wandering a warren of emotions barely known to me.

"They're always hard," she said, "the song's last lines. Even Ananshael's priests forget, sometimes, that we belong to him. Love, meanwhile, is a sneaky, beguiling goddess. She makes you believe."

"Love . . ." I said, then trailed off, unable to manage more than the single syllable.

Ela nodded. "Whoever it is, you think you can keep her. Or him." She traced the line of my chin with her thumb. "You can't."

Suddenly it was too much. I could only shake my head, the tears hot in my eyes, before pushing open the heavy cedar door and stepping out into the night's chill, leaving behind the warm light of the twin candles for that other, older, colder light of the innumerable stars scattered overhead. All around me, the pale sandstone halls and houses of Rassambur glowed in the moonlight. Women and men moved between them alone, in pairs, or in small groups, chatting, laughing, silent. Shards of far-off song etched the darkness. I ignored it all, walking away until there was no more walking to be done, to the very edge of the mesa, where the only choice was between stopping and falling.

From the cliff's brink, I stared down into the great gulf that surrounded all of Rassambur. I'd been beyond that gulf, of course. I was born beyond it, raised to the age of ten beyond it, and in the fifteen years since, I had crossed dozens of times over the delicate sandstone span linking Rassambur to the mountains, to the rest of the world. For all the remoteness of our fortress, our devotion is evangelical, ecumenical, not monastic. Where there are people, there is our god, pacing silently in the marble corridors of power and the rankest alley alike, visiting the solitary cabin in its forest clearing, the bustling harbor, the camp aswarm with soldiers. His justice is equal and absolute, and so, as ministers of his justice, we must go out into the world. For every year in Rassambur, I had spent one year abroad, sometimes to the west of the Ancaz, sometimes to the east, always living among people, learning their ways, their hopes and fears, their needs. I had lived in Sia and Freeport, in the sprawling maze of Uvashi-Rama and a tiny town on the east bank of the Green Cataract. I had friends, acquaintances, and fondly remembered lovers scattered across two continents, and yet . . .

I didn't hear Ela approach, she moved too quietly for that, but I could smell her scent—jasmine and smoke—on the cool desert breeze. She stood half a pace behind me. When she spoke, her voice seemed to hang in the air all around.

"You'd think I would be used to it by now," she murmured. Her voice was warm with some humor I didn't understand.

"Used to what?"

"My own obtuseness."

I shook my head but didn't turn around. "I don't understand."

"No," Ela replied. "You understand just fine, about your own interesting . . . predicament, at least. I didn't see it." She chuckled. "Our lives blind us, and I've always fallen in love so easily."

I blew out a long, uneven breath, stared down into the abyss. It was steadying, somehow, to know the drop was there just a step away, to look down into it. It was like seeing the marvelous, million-fingered hand of my god, patient and waiting.

"How is it possible," I asked, half to Ela, who stepped up quietly to my side, half to myself, "after all these years, that I haven't . . . that I don't . . . ?"

"Love anyone?"

I nodded, dumb.

"Perhaps you are more discriminating. Discrimination isn't a bad thing, Pyrre—take it from me. I fell in love with a farmer from just outside Chubolo, once. He reeked of rutabaga. Had short, rough little fingers, like crusty sausages. If he ever said more than five words in a row, I never heard it."

I turned to stare at her, trying to imagine the lithe, smooth, deadly woman at my side with a rutabaga farmer. It was like

trying to picture a lioness sliding her golden flank along an old
pig's bristly hide.

"Why?" I asked.

Ela laughed again. "Well, that's the question, isn't it? Eira's
a goddess, and that makes her a tyrant, no matter what anyone
tells you. Lady Love doesn't explain her ways to me."

"But there must have been something. . . ."

"I suppose. Maybe it was watching him move that stone."

I shook my head, baffled.

"I was on the road," she went on, her voice slipping into the
rhythm of memory, "and he was clearing a field. There was a
stone. Must have weighed ten times what he did, maybe
twenty—I don't know, I've never made a study of field clearing.
The point is, it was huge, impossible to move. Or so I thought.
He worked at it all day, digging it out with those stubby fingers
of his, laying down the logs to roll it, shifting the weight a little
at a time. I never saw anyone so slow, so patient, and I thought
to myself, 'He might not look like much, but a man who can
move a stone like that is a man I need to get to know.' I needed
to see what he could do with all that slow, undeniable, relentless
patience. I wanted to be that stone."

We both stared into the darkness. The sky overhead was clear,
the stars excruciatingly sharp, but off to the north, a hundred
miles distant, the spring winds had pinned a thunderstorm up
against the higher peaks. Every few heartbeats, blue-white lightning shattered the cool bowl of the night, though we were too
far away to hear the thunder.

"So what did you do?" I asked, glancing over at Ela just as
the next bolt hit, watching her face go from blackness to brilliance, then back again.

"Spent six months with him. At his farm."

"Six months?" I tried to imagine it—noticing a strange man
working his field, then deciding that very day, on no better
information than his stone-shoving capacity, to pass half the year
in his home. The whole story seemed like just that, a story, the

kind of thing you might read in a book or hear over a campfire, the fabric of the tale spun half out of lies and half for laughs. Only, Ela wasn't laughing, and I couldn't think of a reason she might lie. I felt dizzy, suddenly, as though the flat top of the mesa were lifting by imperceptible degrees to tumble me into the abyss. Ela put a steadying hand on my shoulder, pulling me back.

"How?" I asked, when I regained my balance.

She shrugged. "It was easy enough to keep my eyes off his fingers, to breathe only through my mouth."

"Averted glances and mouth-breathing don't seem like a sound foundation for love."

The older woman chuckled. "And just what do you think love *is,* Pyrre?"

I shook my head stupidly.

"As I said," Ela continued after a pause, "it comes easier to some of us than others. The goddess makes us in endlessly different ways. Our struggles are no more the same than our faces."

It was impossible, when I replied, to scrub the bitterness from my voice. "And yet, Ananshael sets the same Trial for all of us."

"Anything less would be unjust."

I bit my lip so hard I could taste blood. "Why didn't anyone *tell* me? All these years . . . I can kill a woman thirteen different ways with a wooden bowl. I've memorized poisons that no one has seen since the Csestriim wars, poisons as old as the Nevariim, if the Nevariim ever even really existed. I can hang upside down from a rafter for hours, or pop the glass pane from a window without making a sound. All the time I thought I was getting ready, and now . . . none of it matters."

Ela squeezed my shoulder. "Oh, it matters. You've got six other people to give to the god, all questions of love aside."

"But the questions of love *aren't* aside. Even if I offer up everyone else on the first day, I'll still fail."

"Not necessarily. You can take the place of that last sacrifice yourself. Kossal and I will see to it."

The words were level, even encouraging, but I couldn't find any comfort in them. It wasn't that I was afraid to die. Anyone raised in Rassambur comes to peace with the notion of her own unmaking. Ananshael's mercy and justice extend even to us. Especially to us. A priestess unwilling to make an offering of herself is no priestess at all, but a mere murderer. I understood that even then. It wasn't the prospect of my own death that bothered me, but of my failure. So much about Ananshael's art had come to me so easily for so long; it seemed unfair that I should come up against such an abrupt, unexpected impossibility.

"Who's the judge?" I asked quietly.

"Judge?"

"Yes, the judge. About love. Who decides?"

"Ah." Ela turned from the immensity of the night to face me. "Kossal and I will decide in concert."

"And if I lie?"

The priestess tsked. "Generally, we hope for a little more piety from those approaching the Trial."

"The piety will be the pile of bodies," I replied grimly. "It's something I've always admired about our god—he abides no lies. When the life goes from a woman, it is gone. Love, though . . ." I blew out a long, frustrated breath. "Anyone can fake it. Fakery is built into it."

"Spoken like a girl who has never been in love."

"How will you know?" I insisted. "If I find someone, if I say I'm in love, if I *insist* on it, how will you know?"

"There is a shape to love, a pattern to the way it moves in us, through us. Between us."

"What are you? A priestess of death, or a 'Kent-kissing poet?"

I regretted the words even as I spoke. Ela was only ten years older than me, only ten years clear of her own Trial, but she had already become half a legend in Rassambur. At the age of twenty-eight, following one of our god's inscrutable commands, she had traveled to Badrikâs-Rama, found a way inside the ancient, unbroken walls of the Palace of Evening Waves, slipped past the Dusk Guards, and strangled the oldest Manjari prince. It was an act of devotion that many had deemed impossible. Then, the next night, she went back and killed his brother. This was the woman whose piety I had impugned; I half expected her to shove me from the ledge. Instead, she chuckled.

"I'd like to think a woman can be both. She can be more. The nights I've spent tangled in someone else's arms don't diminish my devotion to the god. You can hold a knife to a woman's throat . . ." she began, and then, in a motion so fast I could barely follow, her knife was free of its sheath and pressed against my skin. Her dark eyes sparkled starlight. ". . . And, if you were so inclined, you could kiss her at the same time."

For half a heartbeat I thought she intended to do just that. For half a heartbeat it felt as though we weren't standing at the edge of the mesa but hanging just beyond it, buoyed up by the dark, or not buoyed at all, but already falling, the night air so soft against my skin that I hadn't noticed. This is one of Ananshael's truths—we are all dying, all the time. Being born is stepping from the cliff's edge. The only question is what to do while falling.

Ela's eyes seemed to offer an answer, but it was one I couldn't understand. Then, quick as it came, the knife was gone, slipped back into the sheath at her belt. She hadn't stepped back, but she felt farther away, as though some bond between us was suddenly broken. I could have left it there, could have nodded and walked away.

But I've never been good at walking away.

"I'm not you," I said quietly.

Ela nodded. "Nor should you be."

"The thing that you call love might not be love to me at all."

"Your hands," Ela said, taking my wrist, holding the hand up to the moonlight, "are not my hands, but they're still hands.

Your love won't be mine. This doesn't mean I can't see it, know it."

"And if you're wrong? What if I fall in love and you don't even recognize it?"

She took my other hand, then. We stood like lovers at the edge of the cliff, facing each other. I got the sense that she was making her face grave for my sake, the way an adult will feign attention for a furious child. "Then, when I come to kill you, Pyrre, you should fight back."

1

The creatures of the Shirvian delta are fluent in the language of my lord. Even the smallest have not been made meek. A millipede coiled around a reed can kill a woman with a bite. So can the eye-spider, which is the size of my fingernail. Schools of steel-jawed *qirna* ply the channels, each fish more tooth than tail; I've watched people toss goats to them—an old offering to forbidden gods; it is like watching the animal dissolve into blood and froth. There are crocs in the delta half as old as the Annurian occupation, twenty-five-foot monsters that have lurked in the rushes for a hundred years or more, the most deadly with names passed down from generation to generation: Sweet Kim, Dancer, the Pet. The only thing in the delta that can kill a croc is a jaguar, a fact that might offer some solace if that great cat, too, didn't feast on human flesh. There are ways to avoid crocs and *qirna*. Jaguars, though—it's hopeless. Like trying to hide from a shadow.

Ananshael's first servants were the beasts. Long before we came, blood-hungry carnivores stalked the earth, each claw and tooth, every twisted sinew a living tool fashioned to the same absolute end. Before the first note of the first human song, there was music: a howl launched from some hungry throat, the rhythm of paws quick through the brush, over the hard-packed dirt, a bright, final squeal, then the silence without which all sound means nothing. The devotion of beasts is crude and unchosen but utterly undiluted.

A fact of which I was reminded when the causeway over the delta, the causeway upon which we'd been walking for the better part of twenty miles, a causeway that had been safely suspended on wooden pilings fifteen feet above the rushes, groaned with a strong gust of wind. Until that moment, the day had been still as a painting, the bridge like bedrock beneath all the thousands of feet. When it shifted, the people around us—travelers and muleteers, tinkers and wagon drivers—glanced uneasily down at the swirling currents. A worried mutter sprang up like new fungus after a rain. Some people stopped in their tracks. Others moved faster, hurried unknowingly into Ananshael's waiting arms.

"Does it always do that?" Ela asked, turning to me. She didn't look concerned. During the whole thousand-mile trek from Rassambur, she had not once looked concerned. Although we'd been marching down the causeway since dawn, she looked like a lady out for a summer stroll in her light sandals and bright silk *ki-pan*, a parasol of waxed red paper tossed idly over her shoulder to keep the sun off. During the first days of our trip, her packing had struck me as impractical. Soon enough, however, I'd come to envy her sartorial choices—on hot days, those short dresses looked enviably cool; when storms came, the parasol kept her head and torso dry while the rain ran harmlessly down her long legs and off the sandals.

"I don't remember," I confessed. "It's been more than fifteen years since I was here."

The wind gusted again, raking the rushes, making the great, tar-soaked posts of the causeway creak. Beneath my feet, the wood shuddered.

Kossal ignored it, just kept stomping along in his bare feet and gray robe exactly as he had every day since Rassambur, indifferent to rain or hail, washed-out sections of roadway, or even the immensity of the Shirvian delta spread silently beneath and before us as far as the eye could see.

"These people," Ela said, waggling a finger at the crowd around us, "look nervous."

She was right. A few paces in front of us, a basket-packer bent almost double beneath his load had quickened his pace, muttering something that sounded like a prayer. Beyond him, a woman was urging her husband to walk faster, pointing vaguely toward the east, where hot white clouds scraped over the sky. I felt my own pulse quicken, which was strange.

I'd made peace, during the long years in Rassambur, with my own impermanence. My god's mercy and his justice didn't frighten me. I had learned to face the prospect of my own unmaking with equanimity, even with joy. At least, I thought I had. I discovered, standing on that pitching, swaying causeway, that coming back to the place where I was born had rekindled something inside me, some childhood instinct deeper than any epiphany. My mind might have been calm as the people around us mounted panic's swaying ladder, but my body knew we had come back, my bones and blood recognized the thick reek of mud, the hot salt air.

"I will confess," Ela went on, "that I will be vexed if this marvel of Annurian engineering suddenly becomes less marvelous."

Kossal shrugged. "We live until we die."

"And yet," Ela added speculatively, "the best beds and finest plum wine in Dombâng wait at the end of this causeway. It would be a shame to miss out."

"You do understand," the old priest replied, glancing over, "that Rassambur's coin is not for the spending on frivolities and idle luxury."

"*Life* is an idle luxury, Kossal. Before I go to the god, I intend to enjoy wine and a soft bed at every available opportunity, hopefully in the company of someone very beautiful and very naked."

Then, before he could respond, as though in rebuke to Ela's hopes, the wind kicked up again, and the world lurched. Women and men hoisted their screams into the air, ten dozen bright pennons flapping madly above us as the quarter-mile span on which we stood twisted, shrieked, broke away from the causeway at either end, listed toward the west, and then, with a snapping of old wood, collapsed.

It was a soft landing—all water or mud—which somewhere else might have been a comfort. Not here. When the fishers of Dombâng who ply the delta channels talk about someone who has died—died in any way, alone in bed, at the tavern, stabbed in some back alley—they always use the same expression: *he flipped the boat.* To be boatless in the waters of the delta, the wisdom goes, is to be dead.

Of course the wisdom isn't quite right. Funny how often that happens. The Vuo Ton live in the delta somehow, well beyond the boundaries of Dombâng. Occasionally, someone from the city itself survives. I remember Chua Two-Net walking out of the delta, bleeding but alive. It doesn't happen very often.

All of which might suggest that the Shirvian delta would be a terrible place to build a city, but that, after all, was the point. According to the stories, Dombâng's first settlers—the women and men who arrived among the house-high reeds thousands of years earlier—didn't come for the fishing or the sunsets; they came to hide. Harried by the Csestriim near the end of those ancient wars, they fled into the rushes. The Csestriim—some of whom had lived five thousand years and more—died trying to follow. It could have been the snakes or crocs that killed them, the *qirna* or the spear rushes, but those earliest settlers told a different tale, one of gods built like humans but faster and stronger, impossibly beautiful. It was these, the story goes, that killed the Csestriim, and so it was to these that the human survivors, eking out their tenuous survival deep in the delta, began to offer sacrifice. For thousands of years something seemed to guard the people of Dombâng, shielding them as the hamlet grew to a village, the village to a city, something in the delta promising death and protection both.

Then the Annurians came.

When the empire invaded, it did so with its typical mixture

of breathtaking vision and plodding determination. Instead of trying to thread the hidden path through the delta's hundred thousand deadly channels, the Annurian legions arrived on the north bank of the delta, established their camp, and started building.

A million trees were felled to build the causeway, some hauled from a hundred miles off. Ten thousand soldiers died—some taken by disease, some bitten by snakes or crocodiles, some devoured by schools of *qirna,* some simply . . . gone, lost in the shifting labyrinth of reeds and rushes. Not for nothing did the people of Dombâng believe that the gods of the delta would protect them once again. To the city's horror, however, the Annurians accepted their losses and simply kept on building. When the Annurian commander was told the causeway would be the largest structure in the world, he shrugged and said, "One more reason I've never been much impressed with the world."

In the end, the gods failed.

When all the bodies had been burned or washed away, when Dombâng's ancient worship was finally crushed, when the old ways had been nearly scrubbed out by the invaders, the causeway remained, a forty-mile spear lodged in the city's heart. Wagons and muleteers replaced soldiers on the huge wooden bridge. A tool of war became just another piece of infrastructure. Built more than a dozen feet above the water and the rushes below, it provided the only safe passage for travelers mounted or afoot over the deadly morass.

Safe, that is, as long as it didn't collapse.

Unlike most of the people trapped on the failing span, I'd waited until we were halfway down, then leapt well clear of the railings, the falling bodies, and the limbs of the panicked, thrashing beasts. I would have landed well, had the ground been solid. As it was, both feet plunged into the mud, and I found myself mired well past my knees. I tried to pull free. Failed. The panic of all trapped things slid a cold feather down my spine. The air was ablaze with screams, broken people and beasts of burden writhing their way deeper into the mud while those who were still whole tried to help or flee, clawing their way through the water and mud toward loved ones or safety.

I forced myself to watch as one man, stuck hip-deep in the channel, thrashed and thrashed and then collapsed, crumpling as though he were made of paper.

Don't be like him, I told myself. *If today is the day you meet the god, then go with grace.*

The thought steadied me. Whatever childhood terror ached in my bones, I was no longer a child. Death held no sting, so why should any of the rest of it?

I turned my attention back to my own predicament. This time I tested each leg slowly, deliberately. They were stuck fast, but I found I could slide inside my leather pants just slightly. I loosened my belt, managed to writhe another few inches free before the hilts of the knives strapped to my thighs snagged on the inside of the fabric.

Behind me, the chorus of screams found a new pitch. I glanced over my shoulder to see half a dozen crocs floating silently up the channel, backs and eyes just breaking the silty water. As I watched, one of them slipped below the surface, and a moment later one of the women who had been churning up the channel with her own panic offered a final, baffled scream before being yanked out of sight.

Slowly, I told myself, sliding a hand down inside my pants, pulling the knives free one at a time, then laying them on the mud in front of me. *Slowly.*

With the knives clear, I could move once more. I leaned forward, dug my fingers into the sloppy mud, then dragged myself free gradually as a snake molting last season's skin.

Free, of course, was hardly the same thing as safe.

The broken section of causeway had dumped more than a hundred people into the swamp when it collapsed. At least half of them were stuck, thrashing, bleeding, screaming—doing everything necessary, in other words, to attract the delta's most eager predators. If I'd been alone, I might have tried to creep slowly through the mud toward safety. With the crocs already circling, however, and the snakes tasting the air with their flicked, forking tongues, there was no time for creeping. Already the sluggish water of the channel a dozen feet away was turning russet with blood.

The way out was obvious. The causeway had collapsed onto its side, snapped pilings stabbing sideways like broken legs, what had been the western railing buried in the mud and the wreckage of the rushes, eastern railing suddenly horizontal, like the scaffolding of a walkway robbed of its planking. I'd landed about fifteen feet from the wreckage, but if I could get back to it, get on top of that railing, I could follow it a hundred paces or so to where it had ripped free of the rest of the causeway. The wood was snapped and broken in two dozen places, but it would beat slogging through the mud or trying to swim the swirling channels.

As I ran my eyes along the span, searching for the best way up, I realized my Witnesses were already atop it, Kossal standing on the railing, arms crossed over his chest, Ela straddling it, open parasol on her shoulder, shielding her face from the sun, sandaled feet dangling as she kicked her legs. The older priest pointed toward me, Ela narrowed her eyes, then smiled and waved. They might have been at a picnic, or an open-air concert, the horrified screams spangling the air no more than the discordant music of musicians tuning their instruments.

Ela waved me over gaily. I could barely hear her voice above the clamor: "What are you *doing,* Pyrre? Come on!"

I retrieved my knives, sheathed them against my bare thighs. My drawers had stayed on when my pants slipped off, but they'd offer almost no protection against snakes or crocs. The safest thing was to get out of the mud as quickly as possible, which meant moving straight through a knot of men and women stuck between me and the causeway.

Two crocs had closed in on them from the south. One of the women—slender as a reed, but fierce—was using a four-foot spar of shattered wood to smash at the beasts over and over while two men struggled to drag a fourth companion free of the murk. For the moment, the wood-wielder had managed to hold the two beasts at bay. It was obvious, however, that she wouldn't hold them much longer. Already, the smaller of the two crocs had started to slide to the side, flanking her. Worse, she stood up past her knees in the bloody water, so focused on the crocs she had forgotten the other dangers posed by the delta.

I skirted behind her, aiming for the closest section of the fallen causeway while also giving the group an ample berth. I didn't want to get pulled into the chaos of their struggle. As I neared the wrecked wooden structure, however, I realized for the first time how high above the mud the railing hung. The causeway had been easily wide enough for two wagons to pass, which meant that, tipped on its side, even buried in the mud, it presented a vertical wall more than twice my own height.

Off to the west, screams crescendoed. I glanced over. Two men were lumbering through the water, trying, like me, to reach the safety of the causeway. Just behind them, a third had fallen to his knees, his mouth torn open in a horrified howl. Around him, something boiled the water to a red-brown froth.

"*Qirna,*" someone screamed, as though the announcement could do any good.

The first victim clutched pointlessly at his companions, who hadn't spared a look back, then collapsed into the soaked violence of his own unmaking, screams swallowed in the greater chorus. A moment later the next man in the channel stumbled, then the other, devoured before they could cross to the mud-bank beyond.

Luckily for me, I didn't have a channel to cross to reach the causeway. Of course, that still left me confronting the wooden wall. A few paces down the wreckage, some planks had sprung free during the collapse, offering jagged and unreliable holds for hands and feet. Less luckily, these were immediately beside the woman doing battle with the crocs.

"Pyrre!" I glanced up to find Ela grinning at me from beneath the sun-drenched halo of her parasol. "Are you coming up here, or what?"

"You could throw me a rope."

She laughed, as though I'd made the most delightful joke. "I don't have a rope. Besides, what fun would that be?"

"You do realize," Kossal interjected testily, "that we still have fifteen miles to walk today. We could have skipped all this if you'd stayed on the causeway."

He offered this last crack as though staying on the causeway had been an obvious option.

"Feel free to go on without me," I said. "I'll catch up."

Ela shook her head. "Don't listen to him. We're happy to wait. It's a gorgeous morning."

The poor fools a pace away didn't seem to agree. In trying to drag their friend out of the mud they had succeeded mostly in further miring themselves. One of the men—long-haired, square-jawed, narrow-waisted—caught my eye as he strained on the girl's wrist.

"Please," he gasped. "Help us."

He was up to his knees in the mud and sinking deeper by the moment. Just over his shoulder, the woman with the stick was losing her battle. Despite the ferocity of her attacks, the crocs had backed her all the way into her companions, snapping at the shard of wood whenever it came close. She was beginning to flag, propped up at this point mostly by her desperation.

"Pyrre," Ela called down from above. "This is the work of the god."

I stared, frozen for just a moment, at the four people battling for their own lives.

"No," I replied after a moment, shaking my head. "Not yet, it's not."

What I did next may seem like a strange decision for a servant of Ananshael. The truth was, I wasn't bothered by the weight of my god gathered in the air around us. Ananshael is everywhere, always. Nor did I have anything against the crocodiles, which seemed magnificent beasts, more than capable of the god's message. It was the intervening moments that troubled me; not the struggle itself, but the pointlessness of that struggle. When one of our priestesses takes a life, she does so quickly, cleanly. If these men and women were going to die, I wanted them to die. If they were going to fight, I wanted them to fight. Instead, they occupied an awful middle ground, a hopeless territory that did not belong to Ananshael, but to fear and pain. I remembered fear and pain all too well from my childhood. It was to escape them that I had first turned to my god.

"Lie down," I said, gesturing toward the mud in front of the trapped woman.

The man stared at me, baffled.

"Lie down," I said again. "You're sinking because your feet are small. Your body is large. Lie down and let her use you to climb out."

It took him a moment to understand, then he nodded, dragged his own feet from the mud with great sucking sounds, and hurled himself down before the woman. The other man wrenched himself free, sat on his friend's back, and from that more stable platform managed to begin hauling the trapped woman, inch by agonizing inch, from the delta's grip.

Behind them, the woman with the stick lashed out, landing a blow squarely on the nose of one of the crocs, forcing the beast to retreat. The other, sensing a shift in the fight, subsided a few feet into the water.

"Is she *out*?" she shouted without turning. "Is she fucking *out*?"

"Almost," gasped the man lying in the mud. "Are you all right, Bin?"

The woman with the stick—Bin, evidently—had doubled over, hands on her knees, sucking air. For a moment she couldn't respond.

"*Bin!*" the man bellowed, his voice ragged with sudden panic. "Are you *all right*?"

He couldn't see her from where he was, face shoved down into the mud.

"She's fine," I said. "She's forced them back."

"There!" shouted the second man, sitting back in the mud as the trapped woman came suddenly free. "She's out, Bin. She's *out. Come on.*"

"This way," I said, gesturing toward the causeway.

They stared, lost, each one, in the private labyrinth of their own panic. There was no time to explain.

"Follow me," I said, turning to the wooden wreckage and beginning to climb.

My feet and hands were slick with mud, making even the most generous holds treacherous. There were spots where I had to hold on by the tips of my fingers. Twice, the board I was holding ripped free with a furious shriek; each time I managed to catch myself. When I looked down, I could see the first woman, the one who had been stuck, following me up, eyes wide as saucers, the tendons of her neck and back straining. I doubt she'd ever climbed anything more strenuous than a ladder, but her fear made her strong, and each board I tore free offered a more secure handhold to those that followed.

"You're close now," I called down to her.

She met my eyes, nodded, and kept climbing.

We almost made it. Or maybe that's not quite the right pronoun.

I *did* make it, as did the woman who'd been following me, and the man after her. While they climbed, the other two—the man who'd thrown himself down in the mud and Bin—held off the crocs, lashing out with their sticks every time the creatures got close. They weren't going to hold them forever, but they didn't need to. They just needed time for their companions to get clear, and then the woman was climbing while the man, a jagged length of wood in each hand, battered the beasts. The crocs backed off a few feet; he hurled his meager weapons at their faces, turned, and began to climb.

I watched from the railing above, chest heaving with the recent effort.

"Well," Ela said, draping her arm around my shoulders. "For a servant of Ananshael, you've made some curious decisions today."

I just shook my head, wordless, unsure how to explain.

Below, the crocs gnashed their teeth, churned the water with their tails.

"Come *on,* Vo," bellowed the man beside me, reaching down through the railing toward his companions. "You're almost there. Come on, Bin, keep climbing!"

She was close, close enough to reach a hand toward him. When she did, the board she'd been holding tore free. She seemed to hang there a moment, caught on an invisible line; then she fell backward, trailing her scream behind her. She landed badly, leg lodged in the mud, bent all wrong. The crocs turned, their movement so graceful it might have been choreographed.

"Make way," Ela murmured, "for the million-fingered god."

The other climber, Vo, turned. I caught a glimpse of the horror carved across his features.

"Get up, Bin!" he pleaded. "Get up!"

Then, when it was obvious she wouldn't be getting up, he jumped.

"That seemed ill-advised," Ela mused.

Kossal grunted. "We're not going to get to Dombâng any quicker for watching this nonsense."

"Since when," Ela asked, turning on him, "is the work of our lord *nonsense?*"

"The work of our lord is happening everywhere," Kossal replied. "All the time. You plan to stop every time some insect expires mid-flight? Whenever we have the chance to see a few fish hauled up in a net?"

"This," Ela said, nodding to the scene below, "is more interesting than fish."

Kossal glanced down, then shook his head. "Not really."

Ela elbowed him in the ribs. "Don't be dull. It's instructive, at the very least."

"I don't need instruction on how to die in the jaws of an oversized lizard."

"Not for you, you old goat, for Pyrre." She nodded toward the long-haired man, who'd managed somehow to get his footing in the deep, treacherous mud. "That," she said, smiling contentedly, "is love."

"Stupidity," Kossal grumbled.

Ela shrugged. "It's a fine line, sometimes, between the two."

If it was a fine line, the painters and sculptors down through the ages had managed to stay on one side of it. Artistic depictions of love tended to focus on softer subjects: lush lips, rumpled beds, the curve of a naked hip. Fewer crocodiles, certainly. Far less screaming.

"Would you fight a crocodile," Ela pressed, elbowing Kossal again, "to save me?"

"You are a priestess of Ananshael," Kossal observed tartly. "When the beast comes, I expect you to embrace it."

"Doesn't seem to be working for him," Ela pointed out.

Vo, too, had landed badly. While he seemed unbroken, the twin pieces of wood he'd used to hold off the beasts had disappeared. The nearest of the two creatures was bearing down on the injured woman. No weapon to hand, a scream of defiance hot in his throat, the man leaped. He landed on the croc's back, somehow avoiding those massive, snapping jaws. The beast thrashed, churning the muddy water to a froth with its tail, while Vo clung on, arms wrapped around the crocodile's neck, face pressed against the wet, glistening hide.

"That's how they do it in the fights," I said. "Get behind the thing, get on its back. Get an arm around the neck, then go to work with the knife."

"He doesn't have a knife," Ela pointed out.

Bin had managed to tear herself free of the mud, to drag

herself a few feet along the channel's bank, away from both the churning fury of the crocodile and the causeway itself. Beside me, her companions were screaming.

"I'm going to give him one," I said, slipping a blade from the sheath on my thigh.

"Waste of a good knife," Kossal said.

"I've got others."

The knife landed with a wet *thwock* in the mud, blade down, well within reach of the desperate man. Locked in his battle with the croc, he didn't notice. Afternoon sun gleamed off the steel, but his eyes were squeezed shut. Bin, blind with terror, blundered into the water. In fact, no one at all had noticed my throw. All eyes were fixed on the struggle below.

"I take it back," Kossal said.

Ela broke into a wide smile. "That might be a first!" Then she narrowed her eyes. "Just what is it, exactly, that you're taking back?"

Kossal gestured to the man as the croc thrashed back into the water and rolled. "It is excellent instruction in the ways of love."

"Love," Ela explained patiently, "was in the jumping off the causeway to protect the woman."

"Love," Kossal countered, "is hurling yourself onto a deadly creature, then realizing once you get hold there's no way to let go. Either you die, or it does."

He didn't look at the woman as he spoke, but Ela threaded her arm through his. "Surely I'm a good deal more attractive and obliging than a crocodile."

"Marginally."

The creature stayed below for three heartbeats, five, ten. The water roiled where it had disappeared, as though someone had kindled a great fire below the surface. A few feet away, Bin stumbled to her knees, then her screams broke into an entirely new range. A moment later, a red stain bled through the mud-brown water around her.

The crocodile rolled upright, hurling the man from his back onto the bank. He was obviously exhausted, bleeding from his scalp and shoulder, his shirt half torn away, but he hadn't given up.

"I'm coming," he shouted, gesturing to the woman. "Just get to the causeway and you'll be all right."

"No," she screamed. "They have me. *They have me.*"

I shook my head. "I'm ending it."

Kossal turned to study me. "The beasts of the land and of the water were the god's servants long before our order."

"And this is the Trial," Ela reminded me. "There are rules to observe."

Both my blades were in the air before she finished speaking. One took the woman square in the chest. The other sliced through the man's throat before splashing into the water beyond.

Kossal turned to me, old face grave. "The offerings of the Trial are prescribed by the song. To go outside of them is to fail."

I shook my head, pointing. "She said they had her: *One who is right.* He said he was coming: *One who is wrong.*"

Kossal raised an eyebrow. Ela just started laughing.

"I expect this will prove a delightful trip."

Staring down into the blood and mud, listening to the screams shaking the air around me, hearing my own pulse thudding in my ears, remembering all the old feelings I'd thought long banished or forgotten, I wasn't sure I agreed.

2

"I consider the whole episode a blessing," Ela announced as we made our way south through the chaos on the causeway.

Kossal nodded. "The god's ways are strange."

"I'm not talking about the god," Ela replied, then glanced over at me slyly. "I'm talking about Pyrre's fashion sense."

"In that case, leave me out," the priest said, not breaking stride despite the press of human bodies churning around us.

Some people were shoving frantically toward the site of the disaster, shouting the names of loved ones over and over. Others were just as eager to get away, to get off the causeway entirely. Kossal moved through the throng as though he were alone, sliding through the gaps, moving aside troublesome bodies with the occasional well-placed blow to the knee or rib. Faced with one particularly vexing scrum, he toppled a man over the railing, ignored the scream, then moved smoothly through the newly vacated space. We were gone, dissolved into the crowd, before anyone understood what had happened.

"Don't be coy," Ela said, narrowing her eyes at the priest. "You're just as eager for her to find love as I am."

"What I am eager for," Kossal replied, dropping a screaming woman with a quick blow of his wooden flute, then stepping over her body, "is a quiet room and a strong drink. Panic gives me a headache."

Ela shook her head, turned back to me. "He's hopeless," she confided. "Wouldn't know romance if it slipped a warm finger up his ass. But you can trust me when I tell you that *this*"—she gestured the length of my body as though showing me off to the crowd—"is a massive improvement on those baggy trousers you were wearing earlier."

"I'm pantsless," I replied, "and covered in mud."

Not that anyone seemed to have noticed. Half a mile behind us, hundreds of people were dying in the delta. Dying or already dead. On another day, the sight of a mud-smeared woman striding down the causeway in her drawers, knives strapped to her arms and thighs, would have caused people to stop and gawk. Today I was a sideshow at best; one of the disaster's least interesting casualties.

"I'll take muddy and pantsless over soggy and betrousered," Ela replied. "No one was going to look at you twice in what you were wearing earlier."

"I thought we weren't *supposed* to be noticed."

Ela tsked. "You've been listening to Kossal too much. Just because he's old doesn't mean he knows everything."

Three men in chain mail and green tabards shouldered past us, cursing loudly at the crowd to make way as they forced their way north, toward the site of the collapse. Each wore a short sword at his hip, but for the moment they'd left them sheathed, using heavy truncheons to bull a path through the throng.

"Greenshirts," I murmured. "Arriving too late, as usual."

Ela narrowed her eyes. "The city constables?"

I nodded.

"I thought the uniforms looked familiar," she said. "I gave two of them to the god the last time I was here."

A dozen more soldiers trailed behind the vanguard, sweating and cursing in the noonday heat—the Greenshirts maintained way stations every ten miles along the causeway and patrolled the entire length. They were hardly a formidable force—the order had been all but gutted after the Annurian invasion two hundred years earlier—but the sight of them made my stomach clench all the same. We tell children they will grow into adults one day, but that's not quite true. The child never goes away, not fully. The girl I had been, the filthy-faced Weir-rat who grew up prowling Dombâng's more stagnant channels, cringed at the sight of these grown men, men I could now have given to the god in a hundred different ways. I found myself walking faster, averting my eyes, feeling acutely my almost-nakedness as they passed.

"Perhaps I should have a word with them," Ela mused. "I don't like to be critical, but someone really ought to check on the causeway from time to time. Make sure it's not going to fall over."

"They do," I said. "There's a whole division of Greenshirts tasked with checking the pilings."

Kossal glanced over. "Not very good at it."

"They don't have enough men to patrol the full length."

"How many men do you need to watch wood rot?"

I shook my head. "Not rot. Sabotage."

Ela raised an eyebrow. "Sabotage? How delightful! I was having trouble getting excited about rot."

"How do you feel about sedition?"

She shrugged. "More interested."

"They're still at it?" Kossal asked, frowning. "Annur conquered the city, what, two hundred years ago?"

"A little more."

"Seems like enough time for the local religious zealots to realize they've lost."

I glanced over at the old priest. "How much time would it take you?"

"To what?"

"Give up on your god?"

He met my gaze. "I'll give up on Ananshael when creatures stop dying."

Before I could respond, a cry sliced through the noise behind us. We'd finally managed to break free from the densest part of the press, and when I looked over my shoulder, I could see that half a dozen Greenshirts had doubled back, sweaty faces grim as they scanned the crowd. They'd put away their truncheons and drawn swords instead, which didn't seem like a promising development. A pace ahead of them, fingers leveled directly at me, strode the man and woman whom I'd helped climb up onto the broken causeway, the friends of Bin and Vo.

"Her!" they screamed in unison. Through some musical fluke, their voices were a perfect octave apart. The man broke into a run. "She's the murderer."

"Murderer," Ela said, shaking her head. "Such a distasteful word."

Kossal blew out an irritated breath. "Should have tossed them to the crocs along with their friends."

"I didn't think they noticed," I replied, my stomach turning over inside of me.

It sounded ludicrous when I put the thought into words, but the two of them hadn't been looking at me when I threw the knives. They'd been panicked, screaming. The scene below was a maelstrom of blood, and mud, and violence. The open jaws of a croc are a lot more obvious than the hilt of a knife tucked discreetly against a chest, and neither of the two survivors had so much as glanced over at me as their friends fell. They had seemed thoroughly lost in their own grief and disbelief.

Kossal, Ela, and I had left them to their unquiet vigil. We'd managed to follow the railing the length of the downed span, leaping the smashed-open gaps, balancing carefully where there was only one rail, mindful that a misstep would drop us back into the mud and rushes below, where people were still fighting for their lives. Fighting and losing, mostly. When we reached the point where our section had torn away, we found hundreds clustered at the jagged lip of the causeway above. Most were just shouting and gesturing uselessly, but a few had contrived to lower a rope. Kossal went up first, then me, then Ela, folded parasol swinging gaily from the strap of her pack. Of the man and woman we'd left on the fallen causeway, there was no sign.

Evidently, they'd caught up.

The man's face was twisted with rage and grief, but something about the sight of us made him pause, shrink back into the knot of Greenshirts that surged up around him. I couldn't believe that we appeared all that intimidating. I had a lot of knives, sure, but I looked like I'd just escaped from a whorehouse through the privy. Ela was twirling her folded parasol around one finger while Kossal grimaced, tapping his flute against his palm.

"The god is greedy today," he muttered.

I shook my head, smoothed my sweating palms down the front of my filthy shirt. "We can't kill them."

"Six constables and two traumatized idiots?" the priest asked, raising a bushy eyebrow. "Even Ela ought to be able to manage that."

"What about six constables, two traumatized idiots, and a worn-out old priest?" she asked, stabbing at his side with the point of her parasol. He parried the attack casually without taking his eyes from the Greenshirts, who were advancing down the causeway more slowly now, twenty paces distant. The leader, a short, square man, was eyeing us warily. His hand flexed on the grip of his sword.

"I've already begun my Trial," I reminded him. "I can't kill anyone not described in the song."

"You've had a busy morning," Kossal replied. "We'll take care of it."

"There are a hundred people on this bridge," I hissed, "watching us right now. If you give them to the god, the Green-shirts will be hunting us the whole time we're in Dombâng. We'll spend the entire time hiding in attics."

Kossal shrugged. "Attics are quiet."

"No," I said, shaking my head furiously. "I *need* the Green-shirts."

I'd spent well over a month with Kossal and Ela since leaving Rassambur. We'd talked about everything from blackberry jam to garrotes, but I had avoided any mention of my plans for Dombâng or the Trial. Partly, that was because I was still working through the details. More importantly, though, I was afraid to say the words aloud, afraid that translating thought into speech would destroy it, that my hopes, buoyed up like jellyfish in my mind's depths, would wither and collapse if I dragged them out into the air. Which meant I'd never mentioned the fact that the Greenshirts were crucial to all my plans.

Kossal raised a questioning eyebrow, but there was no time to explain. Fortunately, Ela came to my rescue.

"No attics," she said, shaking her head. "I came for the wine and the dancing."

"You're welcome to start dancing," Kossal said, gesturing toward the approaching men.

"Just let me handle it," I said, shoving more confidence into my voice than I felt.

It was a strange and unsettling feeling, not to be able to rely on my knives. Since leaving Dombâng as a child, I had moved through the world comforted by the knowledge that my god was always behind me, silent and invisible, but infinitely patient, always just over my shoulder, waiting to unmake anyone I marked with one of my knives. The day's slaughter on the causeway provided ample proof that he had not disappeared—he was all around us, going about his inscrutable work—but suddenly, due to the strictures of my Trial, he was utterly beyond my call. Despite the crowd, despite Kossal and Ela at my back, I felt alone.

As I moved down the causeway toward the Greenshirts, I tried to emulate Ela's nonchalant grace. It didn't come easily. For as long as I could remember, I'd found a confidence in fighting, in the feel of my knives in my hands, in the knowledge of my own mastery. Denied those knives, I felt lumbering and awkward. It didn't help that instead of a silk *ki-pan,* I was wearing a pair of muddy drawers and a torn shirt.

You're a victim, I told myself, *just like everyone else. You're terrified and confused.*

That role, too, was something I thought I'd left behind when I quit Dombâng. I did not relish stepping into it once more.

"Stop there," said the leader of the Greenshirts, leveling his sword at me when I was still two paces away. "No closer."

I ignored him, turning to my accusers instead, opening my arms as I stepped closer. "You *survived*!"

The mud-covered man was ready for a fight or a chase; he had no idea what to do with my sudden embrace.

"Thank Intarra!" I exclaimed, burying my face in his shoulder. I could feel his hands on me, trying to push me away as I pulled him closer. "You survived," I murmured again, surprised to find tears in my eyes.

"Get *off* of me," he insisted, finally managing to shove me away.

The Greenshirts stood in a loose cordon around us. They held their swords as though unsure whether to swing or sheathe them.

"What the fuck's going on?" their leader demanded, stepping forward, lowering his weapon at last.

"It was horrible," I said, turning to him, trying to pitch my voice somewhere between harried and imploring. "*Horrible*. We tried to fight, but the crocs, they were too *strong*."

"She killed them," the man said, staring at me.

"I tried," I moaned, turning back to him. "I had one of those beasts by the jaws. I left two knives in his back, but it didn't matter. . . ."

"Not the *croc*," he spat. "Bin and Vo! You fucking murdered them."

I tested out a baffled stare. "What? Why . . ."

"What's with the knives?" the Greenshirt demanded, studying the sheaths warily.

"We are traveling performers," Ela said, stepping brightly into the conversation, laying a placating hand on the Greenshirt's wrist. She was wearing doeskin gloves, I realized, although in the moment I didn't understand why.

The soldier yanked away, and Ela let him go, shaking her head sadly, turning to the next man. "We were walking just a few paces behind these two when the causeway collapsed." She managed a shudder that looked entirely real, began to faint, and crumpled into the arms of one of the other Greenshirts, who caught her awkwardly, dropping his sword in the process. A second soldier came to his aid. I glanced down the causeway to find Kossal sitting on the railing a dozen paces distant, looking half bored, half irritated.

I turned back to the leader of the Greenshirts.

"They saved us," I said. "The two who died. The woman—I think her name was Bin—she held off the crocs with a stick. They saved us. . . ."

"Then why did you *kill* them?" the woman wailed. She looked even worse than I did, her flimsy clothes soaked, shredded. Blood washed half her face, carving runnels through the drying mud.

I shook my head, spread my hands. "I don't know why you keep saying that."

Ela draped a comforting arm around the woman's shoulders. "Sometimes there is no one to blame," she murmured, stroking her hair. "Sometimes people just die. Sanni," she said, nodding toward me, "did everything she could. We all did."

The woman stared, eyes blank as the sky.

The man stepped toward me, lips drawn back in a rictus.

"I know what I saw."

The Greenshirt looked from the man to me, then back again. "What did you see?"

"She threw her knives! She murdered Bin and Vo."

I turned to confront the soldier myself. "I *did* throw the knives, but not at his friends. I was in the mud, fighting for my life. Why would I kill the woman who was helping to hold back the crocs?"

"She threw her knives at the croc," Ela confirmed.

The Greenshirt grimaced, obviously searching for a way out of the situation. "Maybe you missed? Hit his friends by accident?"

I shook my head. "I've been throwing knives since I was five. The croc was the size of a boat and three paces away. I didn't miss."

The mud-smeared man leveled a finger at my face. "You're a murderer."

He kept saying that, as though all other thoughts had escaped him.

Ela interposed herself, laid a comforting hand on his chest. He knocked it away, but suddenly I understood.

I turned back to the Greenshirt. "Look. It's madness out here. There are still people stuck in the delta who need help."

"She's trying to get away," the woman insisted.

I shook my head again. "We'll wait right here. Leave someone to watch us, but for the love of Intarra, send the rest of your men north. This tragedy isn't finished."

The soldier studied me for a moment, jaw tight, then nodded abruptly. "Von, Thun, Quon. Keep them here. I don't want anyone moving until I'm back. If they move, kill them. When I get back, we'll bring them to the Shipwreck and figure it out there."

"What did *we* do?" demanded the mud-spattered man. "*They're* the fucking killers!"

"And if they are," the Greenshirt snapped, "then they'll face Annur's justice when this is all finished."

Ela raised a conciliatory hand. "I, for one, am happy to wait." She settled on the railing, oblivious to the drop at her back. "Kossal," she said, motioning toward him imperiously. "Get over here." As the old priest stomped down the causeway toward us, she stripped the gloves from her hands, laid them carefully on the railing. "So much death," she said, shaking her head regretfully. "So much senseless death."

The sun had barely budged in the sky before Thun collapsed. The soldier, who had been watching us fastidiously, suddenly lowered his sword, put a hand to his chest, winced, then fell over. Von knelt beside him, gave him a confused shove, then, when the man didn't respond, put down his sword, tried to revive him with increasingly desperate entreaties, then slumped to the boards himself, pained puzzlement traced across his features. The rest were dead within a hundred heartbeats.

"Well," Ela said brightly, getting to her feet. "I guess that settles that."

"Itiriol?" I asked, studying the corpses.

She smiled. "And here everyone in Rassambur told me you were only good with your blades."

I glanced over at the calfskin gloves. "The powder doesn't soak through the leather?"

"Eventually." She shrugged. "It's not a good idea to dawdle."

Kossal straightened up irritably. "There were faster ways to do that."

"More obvious ways," Ela countered. "Ways that would be remembered." She nodded toward the people swarming over the causeway. A few glanced in our direction, but by this point the wooden bridge was packed with the bleeding and terrified, the exhausted and distraught. A few people lying down by the railing were hardly worth noticing. "This way we can still stay in a nice inn," she added, "instead of holed up in an attic with the bats." She looked at me appraisingly for a moment, rummaged in her pack, then tossed me a tightly rolled *ki-pan*. "As much as I appreciate the legs-and-knives look, maybe you should wear something a little less conspicuous, at least until we get into the city."

We reached Mad Trent's Mountain after dark. Like the causeway itself, the massive elevated platform was a legacy of the Annurian invasion. A quarter mile from Dombâng's northwestern edge, the wooden road, which had run spear-straight and dead flat for so many miles, began to climb gradually, the pilings growing longer, the scaffolding more complex as the delta dropped away below. The huge structure is comprehensively misnamed: a wooden scaffold (many times repaired and replaced over the decades) is hardly a mountain, and General Trent hadn't been remotely mad. Two hundred years earlier, Annurian trebuchets had pounded the northern quarter of the city into flaming oblivion from that manufactured height.

Dombâng was still burning, although the flames had been long since contained, tamed, caged in ten thousand stoves, torches, lanterns, the fire a servant once more. From atop the mountain, the whole labyrinthine expanse sprawled before us like a muddier, nearer echo of the stars. I found myself dizzy looking down at it, dizzy in a way I'd never been atop Rassambur's vertiginous cliffs. It felt as though I wasn't just looking down, but also looking *back* across the abyss of years into my own past.

Hidden City, Goc My's Marvel, Labyrinth of Lanterns—the city bore a dozen names, each one true in the right light, each one a lie. The maze of canals, barges, and floating markets had, indeed, remained hidden for centuries, millennia, but it was hidden no longer, the bonds of causeway and channel shackling her to the world. Goc My had, in fact, worked a marvel centuries earlier, starting the transformation of a small fishing hamlet into the greatest city of the south. On the other hand, Goc My was long dead, and his city had fallen to a greater, less miraculous power two hundred years earlier. The truest name was the last: Dombâng was still a labyrinth—a place of canals and causeways, bridges and barges, passing ropes strung between the tops of buildings, ladders everywhere, ten thousand alleys and backwaters where a woman could get lost, where she could lose herself.

"Ahh," Ela purred, pausing to take in the sight, "I could fall in love here." She wrapped an arm around my shoulder. "Truly a city of romance."

Kossal grunted. "If you think a whole town built on an open sewer and peopled by angry political schismatics is romantic."

"Look at those *lanterns*," Ela protested. "There weren't so many the last time I was here."

Red and amber lanterns hung from the bows of ships, candles flickered in open windows, open flames blazed at the base of wooden statues hewn in the postures of the gods—the *Annurian* gods, Intarra foremost among them. Even at this distance, I could hear hints of music, both the bawdy banging of drinking songs and the softer thread of wooden flutes laid across the night's hot breath.

"What've lanterns got to do with anything?" Kossal demanded.

Ela ignored him, turning to me instead and raising a playful eyebrow. "Good choice, Pyrre. How could you *not* fall in love with so many lanterns?"

"They're fish," I said, shaking my head. "All those lanterns are made of fish skin. Red snapper or ploutfish. They gut them, stretch the skin over a frame, then slide the wick and the whale oil inside."

"I take it from your tone," Ela said, cocking her head to the side as she studied me, "that something about the fishiness dims the romance for you."

"The smell, for starters," Kossal replied.

I shook my head slowly. "They don't smell. Not if they're made properly."

The memory filled me, dredged from the silt of my childhood. I was squatting on a narrow dock between piles of snapper. The fish were still, dead, cool in the morning heat, stupid eyes fixed on the sky. It was my job to gut and clean them, to salt, then hang the filets, then to scrape the skins until they were paper thin, ready to be sold to the old lantern-maker down the street. The fish were fresh enough that they never reeked. It was only later, at night, when people started to light those ruddy lanterns, that I smelled the thick stench soaked into my skin, no matter how much I scrubbed.

"Your problem, Kossal," Ela said, turning to face the older priest, "is that you don't understand romance."

"I'll cut a creature open," he replied. "I'll take out what's inside. I'll hang the carcass up to dry. All part of our devotion. Just don't see where the romance comes into it."

Ela shook her head, then turned to me and rolled her eyes.

"Hopeless," she said, lowering her voice, as though in confidence. "He's hopeless. Always has been." Then, turning back to him, extending her arm and unfolding a hand, as though the whole city were a web of jewels and hers to offer up, she said, "Forget the romance. Can't you just admit that it looks beautiful?"

"In the dark. From a distance." He shook his head. "Stand half a mile off and a pile of steaming shit looks pretty in the moonlight."

"Kossal," Ela demanded, "is there any place in this wide world that you actually *like*?"

"Rassambur." He raised a finger as though prepared to enumerate further possibilities, seemed to consider his options, then put the hand down. "Just Rassambur. Quiet. Not so 'Kent-kissing humid."

"If you love Rassambur so much," I asked him, "then why are you here?"

He didn't bother looking at me. Instead he scowled at the marvel of light and water that was Dombâng. "Because I love my god more."

I shook my head. "The god is everywhere. Someone else could have taken your place as my Witness."

"There may be other work than witnessing to be done here."

Ela raised her brows, surprised for the first time. "Let a lady in on the secret."

For a while he didn't respond, glaring down silently at the city. Finally, he looked over at us.

"Something that needs killing."

"And so you had to come all this way?" Ela swatted him. "Whatever it is, I'm sure it would have died on its own."

"Maybe," Kossal replied. "Maybe not."

Well before we reached the city proper, we began to pass clusters of flat-bottomed barges tethered together on either side of the final stretch of causeway, ranks of lean, long delta skiffs tied rail to rail. Each had a small tent thrown up in the center—just a scrap of canvas to keep off the worst of the mosquitoes, really—but no one seemed to be asleep. Red lanterns hung from the stern of each boat, pushing back the night, bloodying the water's black. On each makeshift, tenuously tethered island, the boats' owners tended to congregate on a single deck, where they could spend the hot evening drinking with their neighbors. The thick smell of smoke and grilling fish and reedfruit hung in the air. Despite the hour, even the children were up, clambering between the hulls, laughing and screaming. Every so often one of them tumbled into the water with a splash. The rest would jeer and shout and then haul their companion from the current and the game would resume.

The ease with which those children climbed free of the water reminded me of the woman earlier in the day who hadn't, of the way she'd screamed as she tried to escape the mud, as the *qirna* closed in to feast on her legs. Most of the delta's most dangerous creatures wouldn't venture this close to the city; the water was too filthy, the air too loud. The children were safe enough, as safe as children anywhere. I'd spent countless days in Dombâng's waters myself, and yet it was impossible not to look at that slick, black surface without imagining some unseen menace lurking beneath, razor-toothed and patient.

The music distracted from the water's implacable silence. In Dombâng there was always music. That, too, I remembered from my childhood, flutes and drums, mostly, the former made from the thick-walled spear rushes of the delta. Those flutes were built for slow, haunting melodies, but the measures of Dombâng were anything but—raucous tunes for rowing or dancing, quick, heavy drums always urging the song on and on, louder and larger.

"I plan to dance," Ela said, pausing to listen to one particularly lively tune, tapping her folded parasol against her heel, "until my feet bleed."

For just a moment, I heard the music through her ears, clear and unsullied. For just a moment, and then, all over again, it was impossible not to hear that music as I'd heard it years ago, not the night's carefree focus, but a mask, a racket drowning the quieter, more intimate sounds of violence. More movement, and darker than dancing, had always waited on that music.

For all the laughter and lanterns, Kossal was right. As we moved into the city proper, I remembered the truth: Dombâng was uglier close up. Lanterns and lights hung from the carved teak of the high-peaked roofs, blousy women leaned from the balconies, men in their bright evening finery—vests over bare chests, long sashes at the waist—called out greetings to one another, but below, in the shadows where the light never reached, rot gnawed constantly at the pitch-soaked pilings. The gutted carcasses of fish, flensed of their soft flesh until only the spines, fins, and heads remained, clogged the backwaters. Where the current was strong, the water ran clear and fast and dark, but in the thousands of eddies where the wide weirs trapped the flow, strange shapes rose slow, awful, dreamlike from the dark, revolved lazily a moment in the light, then disappeared. Rassambur had taught me much about death, but this wasn't death. It was dying. Even as a child I had sensed this. Especially as a child.

I was so lost remembering the rhythms of the city that I almost walked directly into Ela when she stopped.

"Lady and gentleman," she announced theatrically, "I give you Anho's Dance."

With a flourish of her arm, she indicated a tall, wide-windowed building to our left. A narrow canal separated it from the causeway itself, and a small but elegantly carved bridge spanned the water, arcing from the causeway to a broad deck fronting the structure, a deck packed with tables and patrons.

Kossal grimaced. "Why am I not surprised?"

"You are not surprised," Ela proclaimed, "because I promised when we left Rassambur to bring us to the liveliest inn in the city, the establishment with the best music, finest wine, and the most shapely patrons. Which I have, in fact, done."

I wasn't in a position to judge Dombâng's finest establishments—I'd passed most of my childhood in the warren of
toppling stilt shacks at the east end of the city, where the water
was foulest—but I'd spent enough time in other cities later to
see that Ela's claim was more than plausible. A six-person
band—two drummers, two flautists, and a pair of singers, the
man in an open vest, the woman in *ki-pan* slit on both sides
all the way to the hip—dominated the center of the deck. Their
music was better than anything we'd heard on the long walk
in: loud and excited, full of overflowing life, but still intricate,
tight. A score of finely attired dancers moved through the quick
steps of one of Dombâng's classics in the open space before
them, while to either side the rest of the patrons kept time by
clapping.

Bare-chested servingmen—hired, obviously, on the twin
strengths of their grace and beauty—threaded their way through
the crowd with wide trays held above their heads. Women in
flowing, low-cut tops worked the bars at either end, spinning
glasses in the torchlight, catching them behind their backs,
pouring glittering liquor in graceful streams from tall bottles.

"When we left Rassambur," Kossal said, "did you not hear
me say that I'd prefer somewhere small, quiet, and dark?"

Ela pursed her lips, looked up into the star-studded night
speculatively, then shook her head. "No. I didn't hear you say
that."

"You understand," Kossal ground out, "that I could give you
to the god at any point. You would make a great offering."

"You won't."

"That kind of certainty gets people killed."

"I won't be as pretty dead."

"Quite the contrary. You will make a gorgeous corpse."

"If you're going to come for me," Ela said, "you'd best do
it soon. You're not getting any faster as you get older."

"I thought you said, just before we left Rassambur, that I was
still young."

Ela slid a hand around his waist, snugging him close for a moment. He didn't resist as she leaned over to purr in his ear. "That was before we left Rassambur."

Kossal glared at her hard, then pulled free. "I'm getting a room, then going to sleep." He turned to me. "I suggest you do the same."

"It's not even midnight," Ela exclaimed.

"You might be here on a whim," he said to the priestess grimly, "but the girl has work to do tomorrow. Her Trial has already begun. It began the moment she put a knife through that miserable woman's neck. Which means she has fourteen days to finish. A little less, now. Doesn't leave many evenings for drinking and dancing."

"I don't know," Ela replied, letting him go, twining her slender arm around my waist instead, "I've always found drinking and dancing have a way of clarifying the mind."

Then, before I could object, she led me over a narrow bridge onto the deck of the inn, then to one of the tables nearest the music.

"So," Ela said, leaning back in her chair, arching her back as she stretched her arms above her head. "Are you *ever* planning to tell me?"

A carafe of blown glass filled with plum wine sat on the table between us, the third of the night, this one still almost full. The priestess reached out, poured a measure into my glass, set it down, then licked the vessel's beaded sweat from her fingers. She reminded me of a cat, deliberate and indifferent all at once.

"Tell you what?"

With a finger, she drew a slow circle in the air around us, as though to indicate the entire city. "Why we are here."

I took a deep breath, started to talk, thought better of it, and took a sip from my wine instead.

"I understand," Ela continued after a pause, "that you grew up here."

I nodded carefully. The wine brimmed bright and hot inside me. The world seemed wide and tight all at the same time.

"And this is where," she went on after a pause, "you made your first offerings to the god."

I took another sip of the wine, felt the pink on my tongue, in my throat, then nodded again. "If you could call them offerings."

"Every death is an offering."

Over Ela's shoulder, in the center of the emptying dance floor, a man and woman twined around each other. Her hands were everywhere, like something flowering from his body.

"It seemed like I'd have a better chance," I said finally, "if I came back to somewhere I knew."

"You mean to some*one* you knew," she said, leaning in over the table as she spoke. Torchlight shifted over her brown skin until it seemed to glow.

"Everyone I knew from Dombâng is dead," I said. "I killed them before I left."

Ela laughed. "Thorough girl. You'll have to tell me the story sometime."

I shook my head, surprised by the sudden iron in my voice when I replied. "No, I won't."

Our gazes snagged for a moment. Then I looked away.

"Maybe we should go to sleep."

"Oh, undoubtedly!" Ela replied. "We should have gone to sleep hours ago, like Kossal." She raised a finger, as though to forestall my response. "But we didn't, and now we have an obligation."

I blinked. "To?"

"To the wine, Pyrre! To the wine!" She laughed as she gestured to the carafe, the pink liquid so bright with refracted torchlight it might have been a lamp itself. I imagined that wine glowing inside me like a tiny moon.

"You keep pouring me wine because you think I'll tell you a secret."

The words came out slow and stupid. Ela smiled.

"Of course I do. I'll confess—I love secrets almost as much as I love dresses."

"What if I told you there was no reason that I chose Dombâng? Or that I just wanted to see it one more time before you slide a knife into me?"

Ela kept her eyes locked on mine as she refilled her own glass. "Then I'd know that you were lying."

"How?"

Her dark eyes were wine bright. "A lady doesn't tell her secrets."

"And yet you want me to tell mine."

"You're too young to be a lady."

I narrowed my eyes. "And what about you? Can you be a lady if you're already a priestess?"

"You wouldn't believe how often I ask myself that very question."

"And what," I replied, "do you answer yourself?"

"Oh, I hardly think it's for me to decide. According to Kossal I'm nothing more than a thorn in his side."

I stared into my glass, trying to shove my thoughts into some kind of shape I might recognize. The singers had fallen silent, and the flautists, while the two drummers hammered out a brutal rhythm against the night.

"Do you really think he'd kill you?" I asked finally.

Ela pursed her lips reflectively. "He wouldn't be much of a priest if he wouldn't."

"But he loves you."

She shrugged. "Maybe. It doesn't change the fact that we worship Ananshael, not Eira."

Directly above us a pair of wooden shutters slammed open. High, wide laughter spilled out into the night. I caught a glimpse of a pair of hands, a pair of bare arms pulling the shutters closed, and the laughter was gone.

"But you don't love him," I said.

Ela studied me for a while, then shook her head. "It's not something you can figure out by watching others, Pyrre. You can't be me, you can't be Kossal, any more than we could be you. I could tell you everything about my life, every kiss, every woman's hips, every laugh, every sob, every stiff cock, and it wouldn't mean anything. Language is a useful tool, but it's only a tool. The truth is too large for it. If you're going to survive this, you need to find your own way."

I took a deep breath, then lifted the wine to my lips again. The glass was shadow-cool against my skin. I tipped it back, closed my eyes, and drank. I kept my eyes closed for what felt like a long time, listened to the insistent thudding of the drums, to the dozens of voices rising and falling around me, to the hushed susurrus of the Shirvian's split waters running under the deck, threading the pilings, surging blindly toward the salt sea. When I finally opened them again, Ela was still there, still watching me with those wide, dark eyes.

"His name," I said finally, "is Ruc Lan Lac."

Ela repeated the name, "Ruc Lan Lac," then ran her tongue delicately over her lips, as though the syllables had left a salty residue. "Tell me about Ruc Lan Lac."

I hesitated. My own history felt like the drop at a cliff's edge; once I stepped clear of the present, there would be no way to stop falling. "He's here," I said finally, teetering. "At least, he should be. He was a year ago."

Ela arched an eyebrow. "And how did you learn that?"

Heat flushed my cheeks. "Tremiel was in Dombâng last year, for a contract. I asked her about Ruc when she returned to Rassambur."

"You've been *stalking* him," Ela exclaimed, clapping her hands together in delight. "And here, the whole dull march to this city you've been lamenting the hard state of your cold, unbeating heart!" She narrowed her eyes. "But there are four hundred thousand people in Dombâng. How did Tremiel know about Ruc Lan Lac?"

I grimaced. "He's not just a person."

"We're all just people, Pyrre. That's one of Ananshael's oldest lessons."

"Fine. What I mean is, he's famous here."

Ela tsked. "Don't love famous people. I loved one of the Vested in Freeport years ago. It didn't work out."

"I'm not in love with him."

"But you're planning to be."

I blew out a long, frustrated breath. "*Planning* might be a bit of a stretch."

Ela swirled her wine, eyeing me speculatively over the top of her glass. "I'll be disappointed if, during this last month of travel, you didn't come up with at least the faintest glimmer of an idea regarding how you might approach him. People use the phrase *falling in love* as though love is a mud puddle that you just tumble into when you're not paying attention. I find the opposite: love requires a deliberate act of attention."

"I know how to get his attention."

Ela sipped her wine, waiting. I glanced behind me, gauging the distance to the next table, then leaned in, wrapped my hand around the carafe beaded with sweat, then pressed my palm on the wooden table. When I pulled my hand away, the print remained, soaked into the thirsty wood. I left it there for just a heartbeat, then scrubbed it out.

"Do you know what that is?"

"A squat, headless, five-legged beast?"

I lowered my voice. "It's a symbol."

I hesitated, uncertain how to go on. Ela waited a while, then rolled her eyes as she dipped her own finger directly into her wine and drew two semicircles, linked in the center. "Here's a symbol," she murmured in a conspiratorial faux-whisper. "I can never decide if it looks more like an ass or a pair of nicely proportioned breasts." She dropped her voice even lower. "Maybe you could send it in a note to Ruc Lan Lac and ask him which he prefers."

"I *know* which he prefers."

Ela made an *O* with her mouth. "Makes the seduction easier."

"I'm not planning to seduce him."

The priestess's excitement crumpled into a false frown. "How disappointing. One of my jobs as your Witness is, after all, to witness . . ." She shook her head. "No seduction. No ass *or* breasts. So?"

I leaned over the table. "Insurrection."

Ela blinked. "Is that a sexual position?"

"It is the cliff on the edge of which Dombâng has been teetering for decades."

"Teetering. How tedious."

"It will be a lot less tedious after we give it a shove."

"We?" Ela cocked her head to the side. "I came for the dresses and the dancing, remember?"

"You can wear a nice dress to the revolution."

"Any excuse for a party." She frowned. "But what does this have to do with . . ." She gave me an exaggerated series of winks, then nodded to the scribble of water left on the table.

"That," I said quietly, "was a bloody hand."

"I've seen blood," Ela replied. "It's redder."

"It will be when I do it for real."

"Are you going to tell me what *it* is, or do I have to guess?"

The nearest other people on the deck were a dozen paces away, and the music was loud enough to talk without being overheard. I kept my voice low, all the same.

"Did you hear the name Chong Mi the last time you were here?"

"Does she run that brothel on the west end of the city? I only spent one night there, but sweet Ananshael's touch, those beauties . . ." She trailed off, closing her eyes to savor the memory.

"Chong Mi was a prophet, not a prostitute."

Ela frowned, opened her eyes. "Significantly less interesting."

"Interesting enough to see you executed, if you're caught reciting one of her prophecies in Dombâng."

"More interesting," Ela conceded, leaning in once more, her eyes bright with the wine and the candlelight. "Recite one."

"Did you not hear the part about the execution?"

She waved away the protest. "You're planning to give seven citizens of this city to the god—five, since you started early—and you're worried about repeating a few lines of some madwoman's poetry?" She lowered her voice. "You can whisper, if you really need to."

I checked over my shoulder once again, then leaned in toward Ela. We might have been two women gossiping about married life or trading surreptitious opinions on the few attractive dancers still left at the center of the deck, just a couple of normal people talking about love, not religious insurrection.

Although, in truth, I hoped I might find my way to one from the other.

"Woe to you, Dombâng," I began, my voice just a murmur, "for I have seen the day of our salvation.

A snake with the face of a man came to me,
A snake red as blood with eyes of fire,
And the snake spoke to me, saying, "Woe to the faithless.
"Woe to the fickle. Woe to those who forsake their gods."
Three times it spoke, saying, "Woe, woe, woe,"
Then sank its poisoned teeth into my arm. And I saw:

I saw hands of blood, ten thousand bloody hands
Reach up from the waters to tear the city down.

I saw those who worshipped fire burned in their own flame,
Their fickle tongues turned, even in their pleading, to flame.

I saw vipers in a nest of vipers, black snakes driving out
*   the green,*
Three thousand coils curling tighter and tighter.

I saw the vipers of the waters rise up to feed,
Saw them gorge on the hearts of foreign soldiers.

I saw a thousand skulls, a thousand eyeless skulls,
Meat of their minds made mud for the delta flowers.

I saw men and women gorging on foreign coin, choking
    on it,
I heard them cry out in horror, gold dripping from their lips.

In the place of priests, I have seen the beasts of the waters,
Their jaws agape, howling, "Woe, woe, woe."

Woe to you, Dombâng, for I have seen the day of our
    salvation,
I have seen the day and the hour of our gods' return.
Woe, woe, woe to you Dombâng, for I have seen it,
And it is blood and fire and storm. And it is soon.

"That's a lot of woe," Ela observed when I'd finished. "Prophecy is so exceedingly dour. Just once, before I go to the god, I'd enjoy hearing a happy prophecy." She dropped her voice to a portentous register: *"And you shall lick honey from honeyed lips. Yea, and it will be very, very delicious."*

"Happy people don't make prophecy."

"People aren't supposed to make prophecy at all. They're speaking for the gods. That's the point of prophecy."

I nodded. "But the gods of Dombâng have been gone a very long time."

"They're coming back," Ela countered cheerfully. "Soon! According to Chong Mi."

"Chong Mi died a hundred and fifty years ago," I observed pointedly.

Ela spread her hands. "Who can say what time means to a

god? Ten thousand years could be the blink of an eye. A whole age could be *soon*."

"I don't have a whole age," I said grimly. "Or ten thousand years. I have fourteen days."

Ela narrowed her eyes. "Surely you can fall in love without the help of Dombâng's missing deities."

I let out a long, weary breath. "Actually, I don't think I can."

"We're back to the teetering insurrection."

I nodded. "Dombâng has never fully accepted Annurian rule. Five years ago, the city was on the edge of open revolution."

"And then what happened?"

"Ruc Lan Lac happened."

Ela pursed her lips. "Your boyfriend singlehandedly put down an insurrection?"

"He and the four Annurian legions placed temporarily under his control."

"A soldier," Ela purred. "I like soldiers."

"Ex-soldier. When things started to heat up here, Annur sent him back to command the Greenshirts."

"Constabulary," Ela said, grimacing. "I like constables less."

"Most people in Dombâng would agree with you, especially after Ruc got done ripping the throat out of the local insurgency."

"He should have ripped more thoroughly. For a creature with no throat, the insurgency did a pretty good job knocking down the causeway."

I nodded. "Annur's been trying to root out the old worship for two hundred years, ever since conquering the city. The best they've managed is to force it underground."

Ela swirled the wine in her glass. "And what," she asked, "does all this have to do with the warming of your calcified heart?"

I hesitated. Suddenly my whole plan seemed insane. "I thought . . . if I helped him fight the insurgency, we might have a chance to . . ." I shook my head, unsure how to go on.

"To snuggle up close," Ela said, smiling. "I understand. So when do you go find him?"

"Not yet. First, I need to drag the insurgency fully into the open."

"Knocking down causeways isn't open enough?"

I shook my head. "I want to help Ruc fight a war. That means there needs to be a war."

After a moment of silence, the priestess exploded in delighted laughter.

"And where are you going to get one of *those*?"

I pressed my hand against the carafe again, made another print on the table.

" 'I saw hands of blood,' " I recited quietly, " 'ten thousand bloody hands reach up from the waters to tear the city down.' "

"You know," Ela murmured, "that it's supposed to be the work of the gods, fulfilling prophecies."

I shook my head. "I told you. I need a way to get close to Ruc, and the gods of Dombâng have been gone for a very long time."

3

I've always thought it strange that so much of the world remains unbroken. Take something as simple as a clay cup. So much time and effort goes into the making—the quarrying of the clay, the spinning on the wheel, the glazing, the firing, the painting—and yet it takes only a moment to destroy. No malign intent required, no violent design, just a moment's inattention, a careless elbow, fingers too slick with wine, and the vessel drops, lands wrong, shatters. Most things are like this. Daily, by imperceptible degrees, a boat's hull warps with the sun, the rain, the heat, comes uncaulked, springs leaks. Rice takes months to grow from seed; left wet, it will begin to rot overnight.

Our human flesh is better than most things at keeping pace with its own decay, and yet it takes so little—a tiny knife dragged across the windpipe, a dropped roof tile, a puddle three inches deep—to unmake a man or woman. It's amazing, given everything's fragility, that we don't live in a smashed world, all order and structure utterly undone, the whole land heaped with bone, charred wood, carelessly shattered glass. It amazes me sometimes that anything is still standing.

It takes work to keep the world whole. A simple thing like a cup needs to be cleaned each day, placed carefully back on the shelf, not dropped. A city, in its own way, is every bit as delicate. People move over the causeways, ply the canals with their oars, go between their markets and their homes, buy and barter, swindle and sell, and all the while, mostly unknowingly, they are holding that city together. Each civil word is a stitch knitting it tight. Every law observed, willingly or grudgingly, helps to bind the whole. Every tradition, every social more, every act of neighborly goodwill is a stay against chaos. So many souls, so much effort, so difficult to create and so simple to shatter.

I left the first bloody print just before midnight on the central pier of Cao's Bridge. The wide wooden span is one of the largest in the city, stretching north to south over Dombâng's central channel. It's not an easy place to do anything unseen; scores of merchant stalls line either side of the bridge, men and women selling everything from fried scorpions to crushed, honeyed ice beneath their swatches of bright canvas. The bridge is never really quiet. The stalls stay open almost all night, catering to pairs of lovers or insomniac loners until the eastern sky brightens and the ranks of revelers start to give way to more prosaically dressed men and women, some headed home, others still waking up, a mug of steaming *ta* in hand, as they cross the city to their waiting jobs.

Cao's Bridge is never empty, but one of the things you learn early in Rassambur is that a woman need not be alone to go unnoticed. A crowd provides just as much cover as a moonless night. It's easier to hide in a group of hundreds than among just half a dozen. I waited at the bridge's apex for a knot of drunken men to pass, let them jostle me into the nearest fish-scale lantern, then knocked it into the river below. It hissed angrily, then went out. It took only moments, in the shallow pool of shadow, to dip my hand into the mug—the prophecy said blood, but I was using paint—then press my palm against the pier and move along.

No one cried out. No one leveled an angry finger. No one raised the alarm. Women and men crossed the bridge as they had been crossing it all night, oblivious to what I had wrought in their midst. Destruction is like that, sometimes. The cracked cup might take days to finally break. You can stab a man so fast that he doesn't realize until moments later, when the blood starts leaking out. A city, of course, is bigger than a cup, more complex than a man. If I was going to break Dombâng, break it thoroughly enough to serve my purposes, I had more work to do.

From Cao's Bridge I went south, then west over the pollen-stained causeways of the Flower Market. Ten thousand dropped petals dappled the still, dark water between the piers. I left the red mark of my palm on the wall of the central guardhouse while the Greenshirts were distracted harassing some poor merchant about his papers. I left it on each end of the Spring Bridge as I crossed onto First Island, and then again at the base of the huge statue of Goc My that presided over the island's central square. He stared down at me with blank stone eyes. I slipped away while the paint was still dripping, across the open cobbles, into the darkness of one of the side streets, then paused, turning back to study the statue, wondering what he'd make of my night's activity.

Goc My had spent his life in the service of Dombâng, leading the Greenshirts when the Greenshirts were still strong, independent. It was Goc My who had the widest channels of the delta dredged, opening up Dombâng to the trade of deep-keeled ocean vessels, and Goc My, at the same time, who built a canny series of traps and fortifications—underwater chains and fake reefs, guardhouses hidden in the reeds ready to lob crocks of liquid flame at would-be invaders—to protect his city even as he worked to reveal it to the world. Goc My had devoted his life to the safeguarding of Dombâng, but Goc My was a thousand years dead, and Dombâng was no longer the city he knew. Would he curse me for cracking his city's tenuous peace? Or would he be grateful that someone was stirring up hatred of the empire that had forced the yoke on that city's shoulders?

As I watched the still, stone form, half a dozen revelers, listing like boats in an invisible squall, stumbled into the square. At first I thought they planned to cross without stopping, but then the tallest, a muscular, unattractive man with his vest hanging open, lost his footing and lurched abruptly sideways into Goc My's plinth. His companions erupted into a chorus of jeers and encouragement, but the youth cut them off with a theatrically raised hand.

"I stand for such treatment," he announced, stabbing an unsteady finger up at the statue, "from no man!"

Then, after a moment fumbling with his belt, he dropped his pants around his ankles and began pissing on the statue's base.

If the night had been a little darker, or the pisser had been a little drunker, things might have turned out differently. He might have finished urinating, hauled up his tangled pants, followed his friends out of the square and into the night, into the rest of his life. The square, however, was hung with lanterns, and the young man had kept just enough wits about him that when he finally raised his eyes from his cock, he saw in front of him the print of my bloody hand, still wet and glistening.

If he'd been sober, he might still have saved himself, might have turned and walked quietly away. Even during my childhood the red hands of prophecy had a way of cropping up in Dombâng, a few here, half a dozen there, futile gestures of defiance, useless attempts to kindle in the people of the city a righteous uprising. Waist-high children knew enough not to be seen by the Greenshirts near one of those bloody prints. Annur hadn't become the world's most powerful empire by chuckling at sedition. It was worth your life, especially if you were an urchin from the east end of the city, to be accused of fomenting rebellion. If you saw a red hand, you made sure no one thought you put it there.

Evidently, this idiot had never learned that particular lesson. Still holding his cock in one hand, he stretched out the other with the inexplicable determination of drunks everywhere, to lay it over the print. The motion was slow, deliberate, almost reverent. It was also exquisitely timed. Just as he took his hand away, staring in perplexity at the red paint staining his palm, a patrol of Greenshirts entered the plaza.

I wondered if Goc My would have recognized the order he once commanded. During the long years of Dombâng's independence, while priests claimed the highest offices, it was the Greenshirts who were the city's true rulers. The Greenshirts saw to the dredging of channels and the building of causeways and bridges; the Greenshirts ran the courts and collected taxes; they decided which nations to favor with trade and which to punish with embargoes; it was the Greenshirts who protected the priests—an imbalance of power that was lost on no one—and so when the priests spoke, it was with the voice of the Greenshirts; and the Greenshirts were able to do all this because it was they who guarded the city with boats and blades.

Then Annur came and killed them all.

They were replaced, of course. The empire is canny enough to understand that it is easier to keep an office and replace the person holding it than it is to change the political structure altogether. Names have power; it can take people a long time to realize they've stopped meaning what they used to mean. In the case of the Greenshirts, the city's invincible defenders became a second-rate constabulary charged with putting down brawls by the harbor and hauling the most obvious dissidents before imperial courts. The former lords of Dombâng became lackeys, but even lackeys can be dangerous if they carry spears and flatbows and have the weight of an empire behind them.

The men who entered the square were a standard patrol—four soldiers, customary green tabards over their shirts of mail. The soldiers had obviously gone to some effort to keep their armor polished, but Dombâng's relentless wet salt heat had left a thin patina of rust over the rings, rust that streaked the faded green cloth of the uniforms until it looked as though each man had been bleeding from a dozen tiny wounds for weeks. Still, they were more composed, more professional than the Greenshirts from my childhood—Ruc's influence, I assumed—and professional or not, it was tough to miss the figure of the pantsless man urinating on the statue of one of the city's founders.

"Citizen!" shouted the patrol leader. He was large, middle-aged, slabs of muscle deteriorating slowly into fat.

The drunk pisser didn't notice. He was still staring at his own red hand.

"Citizen!" the Greenshirt shouted again. His men fell in behind him as he quickened his pace.

The other revelers saw the coming disaster, tried to pull their friend away from the statue, but trapped by his tangled pants and baffled by drunkenness all he did was to raise his slick palm to show them.

"The red hand," he muttered. Then, disastrously, he quoted from Chong Mi: " 'I saw hands of blood, ten thousand bloody hands, reach up from the waters to tear the city down.' "

The leader of the Greenshirts stiffened—the words might have been an arrow lodged in his chest. After a heartbeat's shock, he leveled his spear, barked an order. The two men with flatbows dropped to a knee, taking aim on the hapless fool.

I watched the scene from the shadows, amazed that my night's painting could turn so quickly to violence. The red hands were only the first step in my plan. I'd half expected them to go unnoticed. What were a few smears of paint, after all, dabbed up in the riot of color that was Dombâng? If I had scripted the evening's events, I couldn't have written a more perfect coincidence. It was almost as though the old gods of the delta were watching after all, standing grim-eyed and silent in the darkness behind me, dragging the city that had betrayed them toward chaos.

One of the pisser's friends, more sober than the rest despite having lost his vest earlier in the night, stepped forward, his hands raised. "No," he said. "It's not . . . We're not . . ."

"On the ground," the captain barked, gesturing with his spear. "All of you. *Get on the ground.*"

The bare-chested man took another step forward, evidently propelled by the conviction that if he could just get close enough, just get the words out, the whole misunderstanding could be

avoided. He walked like a man in a dream, slowly but implacably, his hands raised, while behind him the pisser, finally
understanding the danger, struggled to drag his pants up around
his waist. The rest of the group stood still as Goc My himself,
eyes wide, red with the reflected light of the square's lanterns.

"Listen," the bare-chested man said. "Just listen . . ."

When he had almost reached the captain, he stretched out
one tentative hand toward the man's spear, as though to defend
himself. A mistake, as it turned out. When the soldier yanked
his weapon back, one of the soldiers beside him twitched. Such
a small motion: a jerk of the head, stiffening of the shoulders,
sudden spasm of the hands as they tried to close momentarily
into fists and found the flatbow's trigger. The bolt took the
closest man in the gut—an inexplicably bad shot at such close
range. He gaped in horror, stared at his own ruined stomach,
touched the end of the rudely protruding bolt. Ananshael held
him in his hands already—I could see it in the angle of the
wound and the bleak sheen of the man's eyes—but the body is
stubborn. It can take a long time to die. In the space that
remained to him, the dying man lurched forward, arms
outstretched, and then my god descended, invisible and unerring,
come among us once again to unstring his trembling mortal
instruments.

I've watched my share of brawls. Most don't go much further
than a few busted fists and broken noses. Most people don't
want to die, and they seem to know, instinctively, that the best
way to keep from getting dead is to keep a leash on the fight.
Most brawls are governed by an unspoken, universal set of rules:
leave the fallen where they drop, avoid the eyes, fight with chairs
and bottles, not bricks or stones. In the event that someone
draws a knife, there's almost always a pause, a choreographed
moment in which everyone takes stock.

Those rules don't apply after someone takes a flatbow bolt
to the stomach.

It all happened fast, as though the violence had been there

all along, penned and waiting to be released. The dying man seized the spear with his final, awful strength. The other soldier fired his flatbow. Some revelers fled, some charged forward, screaming their rage. Spears met flesh. Fingers closed on throats. Lips drew back. Teeth, bleeding. More screaming. Bodies pressed lover-tight. Steel twisted in viscera. Blood splashed on the stones. Vicious kicking and stabbing over and over and then, like the end of a great musical crescendo, it was over.

"The god's mercy upon you," I murmured quietly.

He was already gone, of course. Ananshael is never one to linger after claiming his due. Only the bodies remained: eleven dead, sprawled on the cobbles beneath Goc My's inscrutable gaze—seven of the men who had spent the evening drinking and singing, and all four Greenshirts. I've always thought there's something beautiful in that final stillness, the way the dead find rest in even the most awful postures.

The remaining revelers—there were four of them, including, improbably, the man who had pissed on the statue in the first place—didn't share that peace. They stared at the scene, chests heaving, mouths agape, as though in just a few moments the world had become an illegible text, all language dissolved into blood and wrecked flesh.

Finally, one of them seized another by the shoulder. Wordlessly, they stumbled away, the soles of their sandals slapping against the stones, echoing through the night. I knew the world was fragile, but I hadn't figured on just *how* fragile. When I finally turned away, Goc My remained, gazing over the plaza with blank, stone eyes.

It wasn't until just before dawn that I realized I was being followed.

I spent hours quartering the city, slapping my handprint wherever I could find a free space. From First Island I made my way past Old Harbor—the anchorage long since silted up and given over to a maze of rotting hulls; then Little Basc, where most inhabitants had coal-dark skin and spoke a complex tongue somewhere between Annurian and the language of their old island; and on to The Heights, whose eight-foot banks were high only in comparison to the rest of Dombâng's low-lying islands. I spent a few extra moments in the markets fronting New Harbor, studying the huge ships swaying at anchor, wondering if I ought to swim out to leave some paint on their hulls, then decided against it. Though I grew up half a fish in the canals of Dombâng, my skills had soured in the dry, desert mountains of Rassambur, and I wasn't sure about my ability to swim and keep the paint clear of the water.

By the time the unrisen sun had smudged the eastern sky pink, I'd refilled my clay crock with paint a dozen times and left hundreds of bloody palms scattered throughout the city. The prophecy said ten thousand, but I figured no one was likely to be counting. Before returning to the inn, however, I decided to go back to First Island, to see what had become of the violence there. Crossing one of the low, hanging bridges, I glanced behind me, caught a glimpse of a shadowy figure just stepping onto the span, then half turned away before I realized I'd seen the person before, several times over the course of the night, always in the middle distance—across a canal, or several aisles away in the market, face hidden beneath a wide-brimmed hat and streaked with shadow.

My heart bucked inside me, but I kept walking, cleaving to the casual, unhurried pace I'd been using all evening.

Kossal, I thought. The figure was tall and lanky, like the priest, and of course it was Kossal's task to follow me wherever I went. The marvel was I hadn't noticed him earlier.

When I reached the next corner, however, and looked back casually over my shoulder, I realized it wasn't Kossal after all. Not Kossal or Ela or anyone I'd ever seen. The person following me was a stranger, and yet, as he moved through the light of a swaying lantern, I realized with a frigid thrill that I recognized the garb—tight snakeskin pants, black scales glittering red in the lamplight, snakeskin jerkin laced across the chest, bracers of croc hide running from wrist to elbow—and I recognized the tattoo slashed across his face. What I had taken for shadow in the night's darkness was ink, long black lines like rushes streaked across the brown skin from neck to hairline. I knew those tattoos. Everyone who grew up in Dombâng knew them. They were the mark of the Vuo Ton.

For most people, Dombâng was the delta's only safe haven. To stray on foot beyond the city's bounds, or the causeway linking it to the rest of the world, was to die. Even the city's fishers refused to ply the channels much more than a few miles outside the safety of Dombâng's domesticated wildness. No one could survive out there. Everyone knew that. No one except the Vuo Ton.

According to the stories, they'd once been citizens of Dombâng itself, descendants of the same few hundred terrified humans who had first taken refuge in the delta. As Dombâng grew, however, from a collection of shacks to a village, from a village to a town, from a town to a city, there were those who claimed that success had made the people of that city soft. The delta had been driven back too far, they insisted; too much security had made people weak. They tried for a while to bring the city back to the old ways, and then, when that failed, they left, several hundred of them slipping into the delta to establish their own settlement, a place where they could live closer to danger, where they could remember the lessons the delta had taught to its first inhabitants. To a place where they could more properly remember their gods.

People from Dombâng had tried to find that settlement over the years. They had failed. Failed so thoroughly, in fact, that it would have been tempting to believe the Vuo Ton had all perished, except for the fact that they showed up in the city occasionally, one or two of them, dressed in the skins of boa and anaconda, faces inked to blend with the reeds. Usually they came to trade, bartering for iron or steel or glass, the few things they needed but couldn't make themselves. They rarely stayed more than a day or two, slipping back into the delta in their snake-thin boats, disappearing among the rushes, despite the occasional effort to follow them. I knew of only one who had chosen to stay.

There had been a woman in my neighborhood when I was growing up—Chua Two-Net. Two-Net was a legend. She'd been raised in the delta by the Vuo Ton, then quit her people to come to Dombâng for love. Not that the love seemed to have softened her any. Her arms and shoulders were steel-strong after half a lifetime paddling and hauling nets. She'd won the small boat race through the city's main canal three years running, despite—she insisted it was *because of*—drinking a full bottle of *quey* before each contest. She'd strangled a ten-foot keel slider with her bare hands once, then stitched the snake's black skin into a vest that glistened like midnight water wherever she walked. She could swim faster than anyone I'd ever seen, woman or man. She was also the only person I knew who had ever capsized in the delta and survived.

We'd thought her lost when her old canoe fetched up in an empty tangle of roots just west of the city, and after a night of low voices hissing their own fear and recriminations, a group of her fellow fishers took up the search. But how do you search a place that won't take a track, where each footprint is instantly swallowed in the mud, where each afternoon a storm's fury washes away any scent? Chua's friends set out looking, not because they hoped to find her, but because the thought of abandoning anyone to the delta was too awful to contemplate, because all of them secretly feared that one day it might be *their* canoe that capsized in a storm, because they could imagine wandering that watery maze alone, and because they hoped that if that happened someone would come looking for *them*.

They didn't find her, but twelve days later she returned, stumbling over the rickety bridge that separated our quarter of rotting pilings and dilapidated docks from the next island over.

Two-Net had always been the toughest woman I knew, but the woman who returned to the city was almost unrecognizable, one arm black and swollen to the elbow with some spider's poison, one calf shredded by *qirna,* the rest of her legs and chest lacerated by spear rushes. Chua was too tough to die, but she never went back into the delta. Even more frightening, she never talked about what she saw out there, just sat in her run-down shack, a building as far from the water as she could get. Sat there and drank. When kids would come to stare at her, she'd chase them off with a fishing spear, then go back to her drinking, staring into the dark current of the past with her dark, unreadable eyes.

The person following me was not Chua.

He was taller than her and, though he moved with something like her serpentine grace, more thickly muscled.

Our eyes met for a moment. He smiled, revealing sharpened teeth, then turned into the shadow of one of the alleys.

I took two steps after him, then stopped. I could have killed him—probably—except for the limitations imposed by the Trial. He didn't look likely to start singing. He didn't look pregnant. Which left me what? The chance to chase him into the alleyway, then confront him with a series of strongly worded questions? I had no idea why one of the Vuo Ton would be following me, but he'd made no effort to impede my work. In fact, if his smile was anything to go by, it was possible that he approved. The Vuo Ton came to Dombâng to trade, but they had no love for the city—that was why they'd abandoned it so long ago. It was possible that the man who'd been following me *wanted* to see civilization's encroachment on the delta pulled down by my bloody hands.

I turned the question over and over in my mind as I made my way back to First Island and the statue of Goc My. Dombâng had seemed the obvious place to perform my Trial. The *only* place, really. I was born in Dombâng. I made my first offerings to the god there, though I didn't know them for offerings at the time. It was my life in Dombâng that led to my life in Rassambur. *I have to go back,* I had thought. And yet, I had arrived in the city only to discover that the whole place felt like a trap, as though the past weren't the past at all, but some kind of deadfall, the weight of the years suspended by the slenderest of baited sticks, ready to crash down, to crush me the moment I touched anything.

I heard the sound before I reached the plaza at the center of First Island, a buzzing that might have been the hum of a million insects at first, but grew as I approached the overlapping gabble of a massive human throng. I'd expected something—almost a dozen hacked-open bodies have a way of drawing attention—but I hadn't anticipated that the entire plaza would be packed so tight that I had to turn sideways every time I wanted to move. It felt as though the whole population of the island had turned out—fishwives in their wide, oiled aprons; shipwrights in *noc* skirts with tools strapped around their waists; merchants pulled from their stores and stalls by the commotion; carters who had abandoned their labor for the moment, partly because it was impossible to move in the press, partly because they, like everyone else, were trying to get closer to the statue of Goc My, to see what had happened there. The adults gathered in tight knots, whispering, muttering, arguing, dark eyes darting over the shoulders of their companions to see who was close, who was watching or listening. The conversations differed, but over and over I heard the same few words: Chong Mi, bloody hands, revolution.

When I finally neared the square's center, the throng thinned abruptly. It wasn't hard to see why. A dozen Greenshirts armed with flatbows and short spears had formed a rough cordon around the statue and the corpses at its base. Though they were the ones carrying the weapons, most of them looked wary, almost frightened.

"Keep back," growled the nearest of them, an ugly young man whose appearance wasn't improved any by the massive wart plastered across the side of his nose. He prodded at the crowd with his spear, shifting edgily from foot to foot. "Keep *back* or get cut."

The front line of the mob, those confronted with the actual steel, shifted back half a step. Those protected by the bodies of their fellows felt more bold.

"Go back to Annur, you fucking Greenshirts!" someone shouted. A woman's voice. I turned, but there was no way to find her in the press.

"Or come out here!" someone else added. "We'll plant that spear up your ass."

Sweat beaded Warty's face. He glanced over his shoulder, obviously wishing that the men behind him would finish their business before things turned truly vicious.

At first, it was hard to say just what that business was. Through the gaps in the crowd, I could see fragments of the scene. The bodies lay exactly where they'd fallen, sprawled in their final postures. Two Greenshirts knelt in the puddled blood, going over the corpses, though what they hoped to find in the pockets of the dead youths I had no idea. I shifted slightly to see the statue's plinth. My mark was still there, red paint obvious in the daylight. It wasn't the symbol that interested me, however, so much as the man who stood before it.

He was studying the bloody hand, his back turned to both me and the mob, but I recognized the set of those broad shoulders, the small, hook-shaped scar—a scar I'd given him myself—glistening in his shaved scalp, just above his ear. Unlike the rest of the Greenshirts, he didn't wear armor. I could almost hear his voice in my ear, warm and wry: *Who needs steel when you have speed?* He wasn't wearing the standard uniform of the order either. Instead of the loose green tabard, he wore a light, slim-fitting coat of gray wool over a cotton shirt, open at the throat. No insignia. No sign of rank. I had to smile; Ruc Lan Lac had always been a reluctant soldier.

One of the Greenshirts approached him warily.

"Sir," the guardsman murmured. I could barely make out the word.

Ruc didn't move. He was almost as still as the statue itself, studying the paint as though he could see something buried beyond, some secret hidden deep inside the stone itself.

"Sir," the guardsman said again, louder. "The mob is getting restive."

This time, he turned. I'd known those green eyes were coming—green like the churned-up sea just before a storm, green like deep forest in a midafternoon downpour—but they made my stomach shift inside me all the same.

Ela would take that for a good sign, I thought studying his face from beneath the hand I'd raised to shade my own eyes.

It looked as though his nose had been broken again, and a new scar puckered the corner of his chin. Not that it mattered. The scar and slightly flattened nose did nothing to diminish the high cheekbones, the smooth, bronze-brown skin, that serious brow. If anything, he would have been too pretty without the remnants of violence stitched into his face. While the rest of the Greenshirts seemed close to open panic, he scanned the crowd as though noticing it for the first time.

"Restive," he said, shaking his head. "I hate that word."

"Sir?" the Greenshirt asked, glancing warily over his shoulder.

"It sounds like *rest,*" Ruc went on, ignoring the turmoil beyond. "Makes me think *resting.*" He paused, frowned at the mob. "Which they are obviously not."

"Sir . . ." the Greenshirt began again. *Restive* aside, his lexical range seemed somewhat limited.

Ruc nodded, stepped past the man, raised his voice—a warm, deep baritone—to be heard over the clamor.

"Who likes rum?"

Most people don't expect rum at a riot, and the question seemed to confuse the portion of the crowd that heard it. Eyes narrowed, lips tightened, people shushed their companions, leaned forward, wondering if they'd heard right. Ruc had always known how to play a crowd.

"I know this seems very exciting," he said, and jerked a thumb over his shoulder. "Dead people. A handprint. I can promise you, however, that it's quite boring. I, for one, am the opposite of excited. We're going to spend the morning hauling these bodies to the crematorium, then we're going to spend some more time scrubbing blood off the flagstones, cleaning up the statue, and then I'm going to go back to the Shipwreck to spend the afternoon writing an extremely tedious report. You all can watch, or you can have free rum."

He raised an eyebrow, waited.

"Ya can't buy us off with your fucking rum," someone bellowed from the crowd.

"How noble," Ruc replied. "I'm glad someone with principles will be here to oversee the scrubbing. As for the rest of you, a ship from Sellas—*Roshin's Rage*—docked in New Harbor this morning. It's loaded with barrels of red rum and olives. Bring a basket and a large crock to the station manned by my men, and they'll fill both."

Ruc turned back to the statue without another word. The other Greenshirts scanned the mob warily, ready for the assault, but even as I watched, people were repeating the message—*Rum. Free rum.*—and those at the fringes were starting to slip away. A basket of olives and crock of red rum weren't extravagant prizes by the lights of any reasonably wealthy merchant, but most of the men and women gathered in the square weren't merchants. No one grew olives within three hundred miles of Dombâng, and red rum was the kind of spirit they might enjoy once a year—at a wedding or a funeral.

The bodies were still there, of course, as was my handprint, the paint dry in the early-morning heat. Anger still simmered in the crowd, but it was cooling quickly; Ruc had given the mob nothing to do with that anger, nowhere to direct it. I could see why the bureaucrats in Annur had begged him to come back to the city, to take charge of the Greenshirts; he'd just sidestepped a riot for the price of a few barrels of rum.

I like the fights, he used to say, *that I can win without too much punching.*

It was a strange claim, coming from a bare-knuckle boxer, and I never really believed him. Ruc had always seemed ready for the violence, eager. Which was lucky for him, because, though he didn't know it yet, this fight was just getting started, and if I had my way it was going to involve a lot more than punching.

4

The sun hung well above the peaked roofs to the east by the time I returned to our inn. A few dozen patrons were scattered in ones and twos around the teak tables, sipping cups of steaming *ta,* plucking dewy fruit from their bowls, moving slowly and talking low to spare their headaches from the night before.

A bare-chested young servingman greeted me as I stepped off the bridge onto the deck.

"Welcome back to the Dance," he murmured, a sly smile twitching at the edge of his lips.

I realized suddenly what I must look like: a young woman, obviously wearing yesterday's rumpled clothes, her hair all disheveled, returning to her own inn in the surreptitious hour after sunrise.

"I hope you had a pleasant evening," he continued blandly.

I shrugged, met his eye. "About average."

"I'm desolated to hear it." His smile did not look remotely desolated. "I hate to think of a woman like you forming an ill opinion of our city. Perhaps tonight you would permit me to be your guide? If you enjoy plum wine, I know an establishment—"

I cut him off. "I prefer *quey.*"

He raised an eyebrow. "A strong drink for a strong woman. There is a place I know—"

"I'm sure it's delightful, but the only place I want right now is a quiet table and the only company I want is a large mug of *ta.*"

If my brusqueness bothered him, he didn't show it. He just winked, gave a practiced half bow, and gestured me to a table at the far end of the deck, right next to the railing. I realized as I sat down that I was tapping a finger against the knife strapped to my thigh. I'd left the statue of Goc My in high spirits, but something about the young man's flirtation had curdled my good humor. It wasn't the mere fact of his advances; I'd heard worse a thousand times over in a dozen different cities. In fact, it was the banality of the scene that rankled, the ease of his invitation, his obvious indifference to my dismissal. The whole tiny episode just served to remind me how casually most people navigated the seas of romance and attraction, how love and all its more sordid derivatives seemed to come so naturally to everyone but me.

"Bad habit."

I looked up to find Kossal lowering himself into the chair across from me. As a single concession to the heat of Dombâng, the old priest had traded his heavy robe for one of much lighter wool.

"Talking to people?" I asked.

"That too. But I meant the knife."

I realized I was still tapping at the hidden blade with one finger. Grimacing, I shifted the hand away, wrapped it around the handle of my mug instead.

"Where's Ela?" I asked.

He shrugged, laid his wooden flute on the table in front of him. "Tangled between one naked body and another, I'd expect."

I studied his lined face as he waved over a mug of *ta* for himself. *Old* wasn't quite the right word for him; it was too tangled up with other words like *feeble* and *unsteady*. The years had done their work on Kossal—moles and liver spots dotted his shaved scalp; knuckles broken long ago stood crooked from his long, elegant fingers—but like good steel or fine leather, he seemed to have aged into a kind of rightness, as though for decades his body had just been waiting for old age. The thought of him with Ela seemed strange, but not grotesque.

"It doesn't bother you?" I asked.

"Used to. For a few years I gave every lover she had to the god."

"How many was that?"

"Forty-seven."

I blinked. "Anyone you knew?"

"Four priests of Ananshael; two priestesses. One was an old friend."

"Is that why you stopped?"

He took a sip of his *ta*, then shook his head. "I stopped because I couldn't keep up. That woman fucks quicker than I can kill."

Before I could think of a response, a shocked exclamation broke out from a table halfway down the deck. I turned to find a tall man in a blue vest leaning over, whispering urgently, while his audience leaned in. I couldn't hear most of it, but I managed to make out the phrases *Goc My* and *bloody hands*.

"So," Kossal said, studying me through the steam rising off his *ta*. "Looks like word of your evening's labors has caught up with you."

He didn't shout it, but he didn't whisper either.

"You were following?"

He nodded. "Unfortunately."

"I thought you might be grateful for a tour of the city's greatest monuments."

"The peaks of the Ancaz are monuments. What you have here is a pile of rotting wood and a superfluity of stagnant water."

"I didn't see you."

"Engrossed, no doubt, with your artistic pursuits."

I hesitated. "Did you see anyone else following? Tall. Tattoos streaked across his face?"

The priest nodded. "Strange choice for someone in the sneaking business."

"Only if you're in a city. Out in the delta those tattoos blend with the rushes."

"Fisher?"

I shook my head. "The city's fishers stay in their boats. He was one of the Vuo Ton."

"I assume that means something."

"First Blood."

"How illuminating."

"The Vuo Ton left Dombâng not long after the city's founding. Set up their own village in the delta."

"To be closer to the crocs?"

"To be closer to their gods."

Kossal sucked at a tooth, took a sip of his *ta,* swirled it around his mouth while he studied me.

"Tell me about these gods," he said finally.

I opened my mouth to reply, and for half a heartbeat the world seemed to tip sideways. A hot-bright fire blazed across my vision, blotting out Kossal, the deck, the canal, the whole city beyond. There was only the light, endless as the sky, then there, surfacing from the brilliance, two slitted pupils. They were midnight dark, featureless, but it seemed as I stared back at them that they watched me with a predatory delight.

No, I tried to say. It was what I always tried to say when those eyes loomed up in my mind, in dreams or waking visions: *No.* As always, the word would not come. I groped for the table in front of me, caught it, steadied myself, and then the vision was gone, replaced by Kossal and the rest of the world fading back into existence around him. He was still sitting across from me, his eyes narrowed, inquisitive, his pupils blessedly round.

"Want to explain what just happened?" he asked.

I shook my head, trying to clear the last remnants of the vision. "Just tired."

Kossal glanced pointedly at my hand, which was locked furiously on the rim of the table. "Don't wear yourself out holding up the furniture."

It took a moment to pry my fingers open. I flexed them gingerly. "Dombâng worshipped different gods before the Annurians came. Local deities. Creatures of the delta."

"Ever seen one?"

I stared at him, forced down the dread flooding my veins. "You ever see a red crow?"

"Don't exist."

"Neither do the old gods of Dombâng."

The blinding vertigo threatened to engulf me again, but I kept my eyes fixed on Kossal's and hauled a long breath into my lungs. By the time I exhaled, the dizziness was gone.

"There's some folks in this city," Kossal replied after a moment, "seem to be working awful hard in the service of something that doesn't exist."

The mood on the deck in front of Anho's Dance had shifted from relaxed to furtive. Women and men hunched over their tables. Hisses and whispers had replaced the low murmur of casual conversation. From where I was sitting, everyone looked like a conspirator.

"Pick any city in Eridroa," I said, turning back to Kossal. "You'll find people telling stories about old gods."

"Folks here seem to go a bit beyond storytelling," Kossal pointed out. "It's one thing to spin a yarn by the fireside, another to start sawing through causeway pilings and feeding people to the crocs."

"The local mythology took deeper root here because the citizens of Dombâng never witnessed the truth."

"Lots of truths floating around. Which one are you talking about?"

"The truth about the gods. Dombâng's first settlers fled here thousands of years ago, during the wars against the Csestriim. They came to the delta because it was a place they could hide, one of the only places the Csestriim couldn't follow them."

Kossal snorted. "If Annur could conquer Dombâng, you can bet your ass the Csestriim could have managed it."

"And maybe they would have, in time. But they didn't *have* time. The young gods came down, took human form, and helped to turn the tide of the war." I shook my head. "But the people of Dombâng didn't know any of that."

"Too busy hiding."

I nodded. "Word of the young gods spread across Vash and Eridroa, but it didn't spread here. Not until much later, when the war was millennia over and the city finally opened to trade. By that point, the local stories were entrenched and the stories that might have replaced them too far back in history to make much of an impression."

Kossal tapped thoughtfully at the side of his mug, then looked back at me. "And yet, you seem to have escaped the local penchant for superstition."

I took a long, steadying breath. The hot morning air smelled of lemongrass, sweet-reed, smoked fish. It smelled like home, like a place I thought I'd never come back to.

"A greater god liberated me."

"Not yet, he hasn't," Kossal replied.

"He will. Ananshael leaves his mark on the world each day. Unlike the so-called gods of the delta."

"Which you think are just stories?"

"If it's between stories and real immortal deities creeping around in the rushes, I'll go with stories."

The priest explored the recesses of his cheek with his tongue while he studied me.

"Not everything immortal is a god."

It took me a moment to make sense of the statement. "You're talking about the Csestriim," I managed finally. "Or the Nevariim."

He waved a dismissive hand. "The Nevariim really *are* a myth."

"So are the Csestriim," I replied, "at least by this point. We destroyed them in the wars."

Kossal frowned, picked up his flute, fingered a few notes without raising it to his lips. "Not all of them."

I stared. "You think that some survived? That they escaped?"

"I know they did." His fingers ran through a quick arpeggio.

"How?"

"I've spent most of my life hunting them."

"Hunting isn't finding," I replied.

"I've found two. I gave both of them to the god."

The delivery of those last words was so indifferent, so offhand, that he might have been talking about slaughtering sheep or gutting fish rather than finding and killing the last remnants of an immortal race. He raised the flute to his lips, played a few notes to a dance tune we'd heard while walking into the city, switched the melody to a minor key, inverted it, slowed it down, and suddenly it was a dirge.

"Why would Csestriim be hiding in the delta?" I asked, not quite believing the words even as they left my lips.

Kossal played a few more bars, then lowered the flute. "They have to hide somewhere. It is the kind of thing they do."

"Sulk in the mud?"

It didn't seem to fit with the descriptions from the histories. The Csestriim in the chronicles were soulless but brilliant, builders and inventors, masters of lost knowledge beyond all human imagining.

"Become gods," the priest replied. "Twist human credulity to their own end. Dombâng could be their project, their experiment."

"The first people came here to *escape* the Csestriim," I insisted.

Kossal raised an eyebrow. "What if they failed?"

It was almost too much to imagine: Dombâng, thousands of years of history, a city of hundreds of thousands—the toy of a few immortals.

"You think they're here?"

The priest shrugged. "Maybe. Maybe not. I've stopped making guesses."

"And if they are?"

"Then they are long overdue for a meeting with our lord."

He tapped the flute against his palm as though testing the heft of the instrument or trying to dislodge any sound left stuck inside, then raised it to his lips once more.

5

I woke to find early evening smeared across the sky. Though I hadn't used my knives since the causeway, I slid them from their sheaths, ran an oiled cloth over the blades, then strapped them to my thighs once more. After fifteen years, I felt more naked without those knives than I did without my clothes, which I slipped into next: loose-fitting delta pants and a dry vest. When I emerged onto the main deck, I found Ela seated at a small table close to the bar, a carafe of chilled plum wine before her.

"Pyrre!" she exclaimed brightly, waving me over, then gesturing to one of the bare-chested servingmen to bring another glass. She studied the sculpted muscle of his shoulders and torso with open admiration as he poured for me, then slipped him a silver coin. He raised an eyebrow at the extravagance, then nodded his thanks. Ela cocked her head to the side and smiled.

"You could have bought another bottle for that," I observed after he left the table.

Ela laughed gaily. "It's not the bottle I'm after." She pursed her lips, sipped her wine, then shrugged. "Or, not *just* the bottle. How was your night? I've been listening to the talk here on the deck," she purred, leaning closer. "You got up to some mischief, didn't you?"

I forced myself to sit normally, not to glance over my shoulder. Ela just smiled wider. "How clandestine. Tell me everything."

I lowered my voice.

"I did a little painting. . . ."

The priestess waved an impatient hand. "Skip all the tedious preamble about inciting revolution."

I stared at her. "You're not interested in eleven men dead in the middle of a city square?"

"People die all the time, Pyrre. I've seen enough corpses to last a lifetime. Get to the good stuff."

"The good stuff?"

"This delicious man," she replied, brown eyes flashing, "to incite whose favor you've been . . . redecorating the entire city."

I sucked breath nervously between my teeth. Everyone on the deck seemed to be holding a whispered conversation. Everyone had a wary eye for the other tables. *We don't look any different,* I told myself, though that wasn't exactly right. Of all the people gathered on the deck, only Ela seemed entirely at ease. She leaned on one elbow, fingering the rim of her wineglass as she studied me. And, of course, of all the people gathered on the deck, *I* was the only one who had spent the previous night fulfilling prophecy all over the 'Kent-kissing city.

"You saw him, didn't you?" Ela demanded, eyes narrowed.

"I saw him," I admitted, then paused, uncertain how to continue.

"Pyrre," Ela said finally, "I have given women to the god for less frustration than you are causing me right now." She upended the carafe of wine into my glass, gestured impatiently, then waited for me to drink. "Did you talk to him?"

I shook my head.

"Did he see you?"

"No."

Ela frowned. "This story is getting less interesting by the moment. You'll just have to tell me the other one."

I stared at her. "What other one?"

"How you met."

I looked away, out over the narrow canal. "How do you know there's a story?"

"Oh, my sweet girl. There is *always* a story."

I was nineteen when I first laid eyes on Ruc Lan Lac. This was in Sia, the Flooded Quarter of the old city, hundreds of miles from Dombâng. I wasn't looking for him that night, wasn't looking for *anyone*. I'd left my tiny, lakeside room in search of music. I'd been in Sia almost eight months, and though the city, like any city, has music—rough-voiced men belting out shanties from upturned barrels in taverns down by the docks, elegant trios in fine mansions, playing close enough to the open windows that I could stop in the street outside to catch a few bars—I missed the music of Rassambur.

Ananshael's faithful are taught to sing long before we learn to hold a bow or blade. Children of ten, sitting on the mesa's edge, tossing stones into the emptiness below, will make their way merrily through polyphonic pieces beyond the range of most professional bards. I liked Sia, liked the spicy food and the sunrise over the lake, but I missed Rassambur's music. When I heard that Lady Aslim's Singers—a legendary choir sustained by the old woman at great personal expense—would be singing outside the cloistered walls of the lady's piazza, I had to go. When I learned they would be performing Antreem's *Hymn for the Forgotten,* nothing could have kept me away.

That's what I thought, anyway, before I encountered Ruc.

I arrived early to the old temple in Sia's Flooded Quarter. The concert was open to all, an act of Lady Aslim's civic devotion to help commemorate the eight hundredth anniversary of Sia's founding. I expected to find the old stone space brimming with people, but an hour before the performance half of the long wooden pews remained empty.

It made a sad kind of sense, I suppose. Due to the anniversary, the streets outside the temple were packed with jugglers and fire-eaters, acrobats and fruit vendors. On the walk over, I'd been unable to make my way through Adib's Square because the Brotherhood of the Steel Flesh was putting on its macabre act, threading hooks through the muscles of their chests and backs, then suspending themselves above the flagstones to the horror and excitement of all. Lady Aslim's Singers may have been famous in certain circles, but Antreem's Mass was a long, reticent, stubborn piece of music, not ideally suited for drunken celebration. Judging from the relative crowds, most of Sia's citizens preferred large-breasted, sword-swallowing women to ancient choral music.

Which was fine with me.

Though I'd come to Sia as part of my training to serve the god—to do our work, Ananshael's faithful need to move confidently, fluidly through all manner of situation—though I'd spent the better part of a year living and working in the densely packed limestone warrens of the old town, crowds still made me nervous. The press of people reminded me too much of my childhood in Dombâng, not enough of the huge sky of the Ancaz. I was willing to brave a crowd to listen to Antreem, but I was even happier to slide onto an empty bench at the very back of the temple, a dozen feet away from the next person.

And I was less than pleased when someone joined me on that bench, despite the ubiquity of other, better options.

I shifted down a foot or so, until my shoulder touched the stone wall at the pew's end, then glanced over in irritation. My new companion—a young man in his mid-twenties—didn't seem to notice me at all. Which was unsurprising, given that his right eye—haloed with the sick, shiny purple of a new bruise—had swollen entirely shut. The eye, in fact, was the least of it. His nose had been recently broken, then reset, and even as I watched, a drop of blood slid down his upper lip. He wiped it away absently with the back of a sleeve, leaving a smear of red across his teeth. His ear, too, had been viciously ripped near the bottom, as though someone had tried to tear it off with his teeth. Another trickle of blood snaked from the clotting wound down into the collar of his shirt. Part of a uniform, I realized—Annurian legion—though my understanding of the legions suggested he'd have been thrown in the stocks for half a week if he showed up to duty looking like he did.

A drunk, I thought at first, *wandered in off the street looking for a place to sleep it off.*

I considered dragging him outside, tossing him in some alley where he wouldn't interrupt the Mass. On the other hand, he outweighed me and he obviously hadn't come by that busted face avoiding fights. I could give him to the god, cut his throat where he sat, but if anyone noticed blood pooling on the ancient stones, the chaos would get in the way of the singing.

I sat there in irritated silence, shooting him glances while pondering the vexing question long enough that I realized, finally, he wasn't drunk after all. He had closed his other eye, the unswollen one, but he wasn't asleep—not judging from his breath and the set of his head. In fact, with his eyes closed he seemed more attentive, even reverent—the word climbed unbidden into my mind—than most of the concertgoers in the pews closer to the nave. While they whispered and gossiped, buzzing their impatience, he just waited, hands folded in his lap. Those hands, too, were bleeding, half the knuckles split open.

He made no move to applaud when the thirteen men and women of Aslim's choir, all robed in black, finally filed through a low stone door to take their places at the temple's nave. He didn't twitch or open his eyes, but something in his posture shifted marginally, almost imperceptibly, as though he were an iron filing and somewhere on the far side of the city someone had nudged a magnet.

Irritation sizzled inside me. I had come to lose myself in Antreem's *Hymn.* I had been waiting weeks. I had imagined a warm Si'ite evening brimming with lamplight, the whole night trembling with a piece of music dating back to the Atmani, and me lost in it. Instead, I found myself sharing a pew with this bruised, bleeding idiot, and worse than that, for some reason, even as the song began, I found my mind kept wandering back to him, wondering.

Should have killed him when he first walked in, I thought. There were other ways than opening his throat, more subtle ways, things I could have done quickly without jeopardizing the performance. Now that the music had begun, however, I was loath to slide over and wrap my scarf around his neck.

I tried to forget him, closing my own eyes as the singers began, abandoning myself to the music. The first moments of the *Hymn* sketch the central motif, a dissonant figure in a minor key wound tightly on itself, the structure incomplete, as though certain notes are missing, forgotten or torn away. When the second voice threads in beside the first, the ear aches for those lost tones. The counterpoint promises wholeness, then denies it. Finally, with eyes closed, I was able to wander the music's broken ways. I forgot the bleeding man at my side.

When the first movement came to an agonizing close, however, when I opened my eyes, he was still there. He'd stopped bleeding, but started silently crying, which was worse. His fists trembled in his lap, the skin drawn tight over the scabbed, bloody knuckles. My own hands were still—they teach you that in Rassambur—but I recognized that trembling as something done to him by the music. Sometimes it seems the only way to survive Antreem's *Hymn* is to make it to the end, but the man beside me didn't wait. As the singers gathered themselves for the second movement, he opened his eyes, stared at nothing, shook his head as though to clear it, and then, to my absolute amazement, stood up. He met my gaze for just a moment, then turned away toward the temple door and the night beyond.

"You followed him," Ela said. It wasn't a question.

I finished my wine, then nodded wearily. The sun had long since dropped into the western haze. Red-scale lanterns illuminated the deck, swaying in the warm breeze as the flames danced inside. The servingman Ela had been flirting with all night brought over another carafe of wine. This time he lingered, a hand on her bare shoulder.

"Can I get you anything else?"

Ela shooed him away with a playful hand. "Later, Triem. Later."

I eyed the brimming carafe dubiously. "I think I've had enough."

"Nonsense," Ela said, suddenly businesslike as she filled my glass. "I can't get a good story out of you unless I pour you full of wine first. That's becoming obvious." She filled her own glass, then set the carafe to the side. "So. You followed him."

"I followed him," I agreed warily.

Ela studied me. "Why?"

It was a question I had already asked myself a hundred times. One that had no good answer.

"His eyes," I replied.

"I thought you could only see the one. The other was swollen."

"Fine. His eye."

"Care to describe it?"

I hesitated. I'd left that part out, evidently, in relating the morning's events around the statue.

"Moss green," I admitted finally.

Ela smiled. "I like green eyes."

I was just sliding free of my pew when the second movement of the Mass began, all thirteen voices at once, half song, half scream, a single blurred note slammed between the mind and all other thought. I'd known it was coming, and even still, it almost left my legs unstrung. For a moment I hovered there, my hand on the back of the pew. The music almost dragged me back. I almost subsided onto the bench to hear the rest, but something in the young man's bloody face proved equal to the Mass; something in that one green eye had reflected back the music's strength, and grace, and rage, and so instead of letting him go, I followed him into the warm, Si'ite night.

When the heavy doors swung shut behind me, the music cut off abruptly. I imagined pillows slipped over the mouths of the singers, held there while they fought and struggled in silence, breath and sound alike lost in that unyielding softness. It becomes a habit, among those raised in Rassambur, to think of all endings as absolute. The song went on, of course, pouring from those thirteen throats, but for me, on that night, it was finished. I was angry suddenly, and surprised at my anger.

"It's not for everyone."

I turned at the sound of the words to find the young man standing in the middle of the cobbled street, his back to me. He hadn't looked over when he spoke, just stared straight ahead, as though he were studying the torches lining the street. For a heartbeat, I thought he wasn't talking to me at all, that he'd run into some acquaintance, but the truth was there in his posture, legible to anyone who'd spent her life learning to read the human body. He knew I was there, he expected me to come after him, and more than that: he was ready.

For all that coiled violence, however, his voice was quiet; deep, but quiet. Not the voice I'd expected from a man with sunken knuckles and a broken face. He might have been a singer himself—he had the timbre, although the way he spoke seemed to eschew all music.

He shook his head. "Expected something a little more lively out of Antreem? Something better to dance to?"

I considered killing him all over again. I still wasn't sure why I'd left the temple, but it wasn't to trade that perfect music for his derision. I could feel the twin knives strapped against my thighs, their hard weight reassuring as a prayer or a promise. I traced the outline of one of the handles with a fingernail through the cloth of my pants. My god, however, is very clear on the nature of his preferred devotion: Ananshael's priests may kill for justice, or mercy, or even pure, incarnate joy, but our offerings are not to be made in anger. Anger cheapens the gift, profanes it.

"You're the one who walked out," I observed.

"Tough to focus on the music, considering."

"And what is it that we're considering?"

He turned finally. He didn't snarl or glare. His hands hung loose at his sides. Still, there is a way a person moves when readying for a fight—a gauging of distance, a loosening of the neck and shoulders, a settling of the body's weight into the strength of the legs. It had been clear, back in the temple, that this was a man who had fought. Standing half a dozen paces from him now, I could see more: this was a fighter.

"The throat or the gut," he replied, studying me.

"Is this a riddle?"

He shook his head. "Riddles are fun. More fun, at least, than a woman planning to stick a knife in your gut." He pursed his lips. "Or your throat."

I hesitated, suddenly off-balance. His good eye flicked down my body. I had the feeling he could see the slim shape of my knives beneath my clothes.

"Who sent you?" he asked. "Qudis? Shahood?"

The names meant nothing to me. I'd been in Sia since the spring, but Sia was a city of a several hundred thousand souls. I'd met maybe two dozen people, and of those, I'd already given four to the god.

"No one sent me."

He shook his head. "Horseshit. I've still got one eye that works. You didn't just wander in off the street to hear a piece of music by a man a thousand years dead. You were there to find me. You found me. Then you followed me out. The only question is what you're planning to do now." He cocked his head to the side. The cut on his lip had broken open again, and he tested it with his tongue, then spat blood onto the cobbles. "I assume even Shahood isn't stupid enough to want me completely dead."

"I don't know Shahood," I replied. "Or Qudis. And if I wanted you dead, you would be dead."

"Spoken," Ela purred contentedly, "like a woman in love."

I studied her face. If the three carafes of wine had affected her at all, I couldn't see it. Even sitting still, she looked fast.

"I wasn't in love with him. I was furious."

She twirled her wineglass by the delicate stem. There were almost no glasses in Rassambur—a pointless luxury where clay cups served the purpose just as well—and yet Ela seemed utterly at ease holding the implausible vessel.

"Fury might not be love, but it's a road that goes there."

I stared at her. "Next thing, you're going to be telling me you've thrown in with the monotheists, that it's all the same: pleasure and pain, love and hate."

Ela sipped from her glass, then set it down neatly in the ring of its own moisture. "In the end, of course, our god obviates all such questions."

Her certainty galled me, as did the lazy way she waved her hand when answering, like she was swooshing away a fly.

"Of course," I replied, unable to keep the edge from my voice, "we're not quite *at* the end, are we? If I were eager for the god's unmaking, I wouldn't be here, trying to create a reason to run into Ruc Lan Lac."

For half a heartbeat, she narrowed her eyes, as though some dimness had become momentarily, surprisingly bright. Then she smiled.

"You're right, and I apologize. For the death to matter, for it to *mean* anything, there must first be a life."

"I've *had* a life," I snapped, aware that I'd shifted abruptly to the other side of the debate and furious at the awareness.

Ela's smile just widened. "Tell me more about the boy."

"He was twenty-four. A man."

She lifted the wine to her lips again, sipped, then closed her eyes contentedly. "A man. Even better. Tell me more."

It was idiocy, obviously.

Ananshael's faithful are trained to practice a ministry of silence and shadows. We are taught to slide through unlatched windows, to open throats, then to slip away again like ghosts. A little poison smeared on the bottom of a drunkard's crock, a black-fletched arrow through the neck—these are the ways of Rassambur. And yet, here I was, standing in the middle of the street, boasting about killing.

It wasn't love. Ela was wrong about that. She might manage to fall in love during the first movement of a mass, but that degree of abandon lay far beyond the ambit of my heart. It wasn't love, and yet *something* blazed just under my skin; some emotion had goaded me from my seat, some eagerness I couldn't name made me fling my idiotic taunts at him as though they were kisses or knives.

I hadn't noticed when he first sat down, but he was handsome under all the blood and bruises, even beautiful. The swelling could only partially obscure the high, bold bones of his cheeks. Even discolored, even broken, his brown skin looked warm in the torchlight. And there was more: he wasn't just a moss-eyed beauty, but a fighter, too, broad-shouldered and wiry, and not just a fighter, but a fighter who wept at Antreem's Mass. I'd never encountered someone quite like him, not even at Rassambur.

The feeling seemed not to be mutual.

" 'If I wanted you dead, you would be dead'?" He sucked some blood from between his teeth, then spat it onto the cobbles. "What is that? A line from some mid-century melodrama? You hear that onstage a few nights ago?"

He didn't look intrigued. He looked disgusted.

Again my fingers itched for my knives. Rather than reach for them, I sang in my mind the chorus to one of Ananshael's oldest hymns:

> *Death is an embrace,*
> *Not an escape.*

The tune is simple. It is taught early to the children of Rassambur, and with good reason. Most people raised outside our faith must face their problems without recourse to killing. The average woman has only the vaguest idea where to place a knife in a human body to end its operation, which means, when she is angry, that the knife is not the first thought in her mind. People raised outside Rassambur learn early to argue, to barter, to protest, to apologize, and only in the most dire cases do the blades come out. To Ananshael's faithful, however, the knife holds no mystery. To so many questions, it seems the easy, obvious answer, and yet our problems are not the god's; his ways are meant to be more than the means of our petty escapes. Hence the hymn. Hence the fact that I kept talking to Ruc Lan Lac— though even then I didn't know his name—instead of cutting out his liver for making me feel foolish.

"If you're going to pull that blade on me," he said, staring pointedly at my thigh, "go ahead and pull the 'Kent-kissing blade. If I had time to waste, I'd still be in there," he stabbed a finger past me, toward the faceless statues standing vigil at the temple's door, "listening to Antreem, not out here enduring your babble."

Shame blazed in my cheeks. It was a strange sensation.

He spread his arms as though inviting my attack. "Well?"

For the first time, the people crowding the street seemed to notice him. They saw the dried blood on his face, followed his one-eyed gaze, glanced over their shoulders to find me, and then shied away, leaving us standing like two stones, motionless in the larger current.

"I followed you . . ." I began, lowering my voice.

He shook his head. "I don't care. I have a fight to get to. If you're supposed to keep me from getting there, by all means, have at it."

He didn't sound scared. He sounded, if anything, almost bored. Intrigue and irritation warred inside me. I wanted him to know the truth of me, of what I could do. I wanted to show him, to see that beautiful green eye widen in surprise.

By the age of nineteen, I had grown accustomed to feeling stronger, smarter, faster than anyone outside Rassambur. Ananshael's elder priestesses and priests could take me apart joint by joint, of course, but I'd started to think of everyone beyond our white sandstone walls as slow, almost bovine. The muscle-bound men boasting in wharf-side taverns, the crook-nosed merchants' guards, the hard-eyed harlots on the street corner with their bright-pleated dresses and half-hidden knives, the angry drunks and the huge, slow bodyguards of the rich, who carried their own wide shoulders as oxen carried their yokes—they all seemed weak, ignorant, irrelevant. This is a danger, for those of us who follow the god of death. When you can unmake a woman as easily as breathing, it becomes easy to believe that you are somehow greater than that woman, more.

Ananshael loathes this type of hubris. It runs counter to all that he holds dear. In the grave's slender space, there is no room for pride. The final truth of our inevitable ending erases all line between the weak and strong, the great and small, between the priestess with her knives and her pride, and the carter on the street, bent double beneath his load. I used to imagine my god as an avenging force wide as the sky, his hundred hands wielding a hundred weapons. Now, I see him as an old man, patient and slow. He holds spring's wet dirt in his hands, lifts it up to the light so that we can see, repeats the same words over and over, endlessly patient—*You are this. You are this. You are this.*—until we understand.

Back then I didn't understand; not really, not fully. And so the scorn in the beautiful young fighter's voice scalded. I could have borne his rage, but I could not bear this weary dismissal. I could not kill him, not while my mind was disarranged by my own pride and anger, but neither could I let him go.

"What fight?" I asked.

"Pyrre, you minx," Ela cut in, shaking her head in good-natured amazement. "The whole way from Rassambur you've been pissing and moaning about love, and all this time you've been hiding this delicious little story under your skirts."

"I haven't been hiding—"

"Of *course* you have. You've been treating it like one of those jade cocks we saw back in Mo'ir, getting all sloppy and bothered on it when you thought Kossal and I weren't looking, then tucking it away in your pack and playing the stone-hearted, loveless, unlovable killer all the long day long."

I stared at her. "What are you talking about?"

"Don't tell me that you didn't see the cocks. That huge woman with the headscarf and knives was selling them in the morning market. They were thick as my wrist!" She circled her wrist with her fingers by way of demonstration, then narrowed her eyes, suddenly sly. "You bought one, didn't you?"

"What would I want with a wrist-thick jade cock?"

"I'll go ahead and assume that the question is rhetorical."

"I'll go ahead and assume you understand that a polished stone phallus has nothing to do with love."

Ela frowned speculatively. "Let's not say *nothing*."

"I'd imagine falling in love with a rock would be a stretch, even for you."

"Nothing wrong with stretching." She winked.

I bit back a retort, took a long swig of my wine instead, waited until the draught had snaked all the way down into my stomach before responding. "Do you want to hear the end of the story, or not?"

The musicians had packed up early, but a few determined revelers remained on the deck, sprawled around tables in groups of two or three. Two tables over, a young couple was bickering— he kept taking her hand, and she kept pulling it away angrily, holding it close, then laying it on the table all over again, as though it were bait. Past them, a very fat, very drunk man was singing listlessly, transforming a lively dance tune into a dirge. Most of the servingmen had started stacking chairs and mopping the deck, although no one had bothered us yet.

"No," Ela replied finally. "Not tonight."

The words took me by surprise. "Half a heartbeat ago, you complained that I was hiding the whole thing."

"Oh, I like hiding." She drained her glass of wine, locking eyes with me over the rim the whole time. "If no one's hiding anything, then what is there to find?"

I shook my head, suddenly baffled. "I need to go to bed."

Ela rolled her eyes. "You slept all day." She glanced over at the bare-chested young man who had been taking care of us. "And Triem won't be done working for ages."

"I have to go to bed," I said again, standing up unsteadily. "I need to be ready tomorrow."

"Oh?" The priestess raised an eyebrow. "Ready for what, may I ask?"

"Ready to kill someone."

6

Hitting things and drinking things seemed to be the Neck's central activities.

I knew that the enormous soldier was called the Neck because every time he slammed another wooden tankard down on the table, the other men seated around him—soldiers under his command—would chant, *"The. Neck. The. Neck. THE! NECK!"*

It wasn't hard to see how he came by the name; the Neck's neck was a column of flesh dropping straight from his ears onto the foundation of his massive shoulders. Tattoos climbed from the open collar of his legionary uniform, thorny vines and twisted barbs mostly, although an unsteadily inked woman sprawled across his jugular, naked, legs spread as though she were trying—very implausibly—to derive some pleasure from that bulging artery. The rest of the bastard was every bit as big as that neck, as though someone had cobbled him together out of huge slabs of flesh without much regard for the skeletal anatomy beneath.

The Neck didn't chant. Instead, whenever the chorus of cheers around him rose to a pitch, he would pound on whatever was nearby: the table, his knee, the shoulder of a companion, as though insisting on both his drunkenness and his levity.

I didn't believe in either.

Certainly, he'd consumed an impressive amount of beer in the time I'd been watching him, but though he swayed in his chair, the sway wasn't quite right. It looked like something rehearsed, performed. And his eyes—instead of stuttering in the way of the truly drunk, they remained steady. He seemed to be paying attention to nothing beyond the beer and the other men at his table, but his gaze never stopped moving, panning quickly and calmly over the room. Whenever the door opened, the Neck glanced over, the movement so quick that I wouldn't have noticed if I hadn't been watching.

There's a common misconception that big men are stupid. I've heard dozens of explanations: all that muscle steals blood from the brain; their heads are broken from getting into so many fights; they've just never *needed* to be shrewd. In plays, they're usually depicted as comic brutes, in literature as willing idiots of slighter, brighter human beings. It's as though our basic sense of fairness is offended by the idea that the same person could be both intellectually and physically formidable. There should, we think, be some sort of trade: the poor in wealth should be rich in spirit, the homely more noble than the beautiful. It doesn't work that way. Fairness and justice have never interested the goddess of birth. Bedisa bestows her blessings arbitrarily, showering one person with health, strength, wisdom, denying the next the basic comfort of an unbent spine. It is not until death that we are finally made equal.

Of course, the Neck wasn't dead yet—that was *my* job—and to my great inconvenience, he was starting to look like one of those upon whom Bedisa had lavished her most expansive gifts. I glanced at the other men around him—soldiers from his legion, judging from the insignia on the Annurian uniforms. It would have been easier to kill one of *them*. In fact, it might well have been easier to kill *all* of them. They were young, obviously strong from years marching and fighting down in the Waist, but unlike the Neck they were built on a human scale. Their necks looked like bundles of spine and esophagus, windpipe and nerve, rather than architectural features. They also looked nervous.

They did their best to hide it, of course, laughing too loud and clapping one another on the shoulder, pointedly ignoring the other patrons, local folks who sat in loose knots around the tavern's circular tables, their faces barely illuminated by the low light of the red-scale lanterns above. A few of the soldiers were trying to go tankard to tankard with the Neck, although, judging from the slur in their song and the stagger in their step, they lacked their commander's stomach for ale. Even half a barrel of that ale, however, couldn't hide the wary glances, the way their hands kept reaching, as though of their own accord, to the swords and knives belted at their waists. When someone dropped a clay mug over by the bar, even the drunkest of the soldiers lurched halfway to his feet, as though expecting to fight.

I had set the stage for that skittishness, of course, at least partially. In the centuries since conquering Dombâng, Annur had insisted that the city was part of a peaceful and unified whole, as though it were all as easy as signing a few treaties and lifting old tariffs. The world tends to be more stubborn than that.

I used to spend idle hours poring over Rassambur's vast collection of old maps. I still do, actually, and one fact about those yellowing sheets of vellum always strikes me: while the names of the kingdoms and empires shift—smaller polities combining or fracturing off, giving the illusion of change—the most fundamental borders remain the same, century after century. No empire has ever united the lands east and west of the Ancaz. No potentate has brought the cities north of the Romsdals into any greater state. And none of Eridroa's central powers had ever leashed the wild territory north of the Waist—territory including Dombâng and the Shirvian delta—not until Annur.

The empire of the midday sun won a great battle in Dombâng, and suddenly, the world over, a legion of cartographers lurched into work making new maps, as though millennia of loyalties and pride could be elided through a single fight and the shifting of a few inked lines. The old priesthood was still in the city, although hidden, forced underground. Women and men still remembered the old songs. The figures whose statues still stood in the plazas and atop the bridges were those who had ruled Dombâng when the city was fierce and independent. For the better part of two centuries, Annur had forced everyone to pretend that the city had no history, but history is ubiquitous as water, as rot. All it took was a little red paint and my handprint to remind everyone: for all that those legions bearing the blazing sun claimed to be a defending force, they were an occupying army.

It was obvious, watching the soldiers at the other end of the tavern, that they understood that fact. In addition to the too-loud laughter and forced jollity, they all carried their short swords despite the heat and inconvenience, as though they half expected to need to cut their way free. All of which was massively inconvenient, given that I'd come to kill their commanding officer.

In a simpler world, I could have just given the lot of them to the god. My Trial, however, forbid such indiscriminate largesse. Anyone can kill, after all. A Wing of imperial Kettral could have destroyed the entire tavern and everyone in it with a single well-timed explosion. Something more is required of Ananshael's faithful. A priestess of Rassambur must prove her restraint even in the moment of her most perfect devotion.

I'd already confirmed with Ela and Kossal that the Neck could fit the rhyme; what is a soldier, after all, if not a "dealer of death"? I might have killed one of the others for singing, but they were *all* singing, and the song only gave me one. Which meant I needed to somehow separate the Neck, who was already wary, from the rest of his legion.

Across the dimly lit room, the legionaries struck up another raucous song. They had good voices, for soldiers. Three of them carried the melody while the Neck bellowed out the bass refrain: *For a soldier's a soldier no matter how old.*

As he sang, the massive man met my eyes, then smiled. I gave him half a smile of my own, holding his gaze as I raised the cup of *quey* to my lips. The liquor looked like water. It smelled like hate. It tasted like velvet fire on the tongue.

The legionaries kept singing:

> *When he's dead, dig him up!*
> *Bring him in from the cold.*
> *Though his hands are all bones*
> *They still know how to hold:*
> *His cock or his tankard, his sword or his spear . . .*

Then the Neck, still watching me, still grinning, still pounding the table half to splinters, finished the chorus: *For a soldier's a soldier, no matter how old!*

He sang as though performing the verse just for my enjoyment. When the song was over, he slammed his tankard into those of his companions, smiled wide, then raised it to me. To my chagrin, I found myself liking him. Fishing gets tricky if you start worrying about the worm.

Bait, I reminded myself. *He is bait.*

Even if I left him alive, someday something would kill him. Disease, dagger, drowning—or one of Ananshael's other subtle, unnumbered tools. The death that I planned to offer him ranked among the kindest: fast and painless. I would cut him free from the world in his undiminished prime. Presumably there were other ways to fall in love, ways that didn't involve wading through a pile of dead bodies, but in all the long trek from Rassambur, I hadn't managed to think of one. Call it a failure of imagination.

He kept his tankard raised, but instead of meeting the toast, I glanced down at my open palm, dragged a finger across it, then pressed it to the table. The gesture was quick, subtle. To most people it would have looked like no more than a young woman fidgeting, but I counted on the Neck to be more observant than most people. Which he was. His gaze hardened. After a moment, he set down his own mug and pushed back from the table, as though getting ready to stand. I gave an incremental shake of my head, nodded toward the door at the rear of the tavern, laid a quick finger across my lips, then rose from my seat.

The rear door of the tavern opened into a narrow hallway that fronted a series of stalls, privies that dropped directly into the canal below: there was a reason that the slums of Dombâng were all to the east, downstream. I entered the farthest of the five—a tiny room barely large enough to sit down, a wooden bench along the back wall worn smooth from generations of asses, the hole in the middle just large enough for me to squeeze my body through; if the Neck brought the rest of his legion, I wanted a way out that didn't involve a hallway filled with soldiers and swords. I was, however, counting on him not bringing the others.

Enormous men might not be any stupider than their smaller brethren, but they are, as a rule, less careful. The Neck outweighed the tavern's average patron by as much as a small pig; he wasn't used to feeling vulnerable. If the notion of the whole city rising up in rebellion had done little to slow his drinking, it seemed unlikely that one lone woman—relatively small, seemingly unarmed—would give him pause. In all Annur, there might have been a few dozen women—Kettral, probably, or other priestesses of Ananshael—who could kill him in a hand-to-hand fight. Following me into the privy wasn't a stupid bet.

Unfortunately for the Neck, even the smartest bet can lose. That's why they call it a bet.

The soldier bellowed his way through one more song before coming after me. While I waited, I slid both of my knives from their sheaths. I sank one into the wood of the privy wall just behind the door, the other I plunged into a rafter overhead, so that the handle hung down within reach. It was one of the strangest things I learned in my first years at Rassambur, this kind of willing disarmament, but I'd had plenty of chances since to see the wisdom: people, especially soldiers, are trained to watch for someone pulling a knife, trained to see the motion and counter it. Reaching *past* a man, however, or above him, sparks none of that training. Most people will turn instinctively to see what you're reaching for, will only notice the knife after you've pulled it from the wall and started parting their flesh. I could have waited for the Neck with the knife already in my hand, but I figured he'd have a good look at me before actually entering the privy. He seemed more likely to come in and close the door behind him if I wasn't brandishing a pair of naked blades. It took me only a moment to strip the sheaths from my thighs and tuck them into the thatch above.

Water sloshed and chuckled around the piers below; I could hear oarsmen farther out in the current, the slap of their broad blades as loud as their curses. Waves of shouting and laughter washed out of the tavern itself, gathering, cresting, crashing, then gathering once more. I could make out no sign, however, of the dull clomp of the Neck's heavy boots. Only when the latch to the hallway door clinked shut did I realize he was coming after all, moving far more quietly over the squeaking boards than I'd expected from someone his size. His knock on the door to my stall was likewise soft, as though he had tapped with a single knuckle.

I pulled the door open.

He made no move to enter, scanning the inside of the privy with a careful eye before turning his attention to me. Close up, he looked even bigger, at least two heads taller than me and so broad I wondered if he would fit through the door without turning sideways. A pair of small scars creased his shaved scalp—too rough and jagged to have been made by blades. A jaguar, maybe. Or crocodile. Depended how long he'd been down here. His short sword looked more like a long knife hanging from his belt, and though he'd left the weapon in its sheath, one massive hand rested on the handle. He was pale, obviously not from Dombâng, and his cheeks were ruddy with ale. He remained steady on his feet, however, and his gaze didn't waver.

"What?"

I beckoned him in. "A message."

"Tell me."

"Ruc Lan Lac sent me."

He sucked at something between his teeth. "Never seen you before."

"That's the point. Get the fuck in here before someone walks through that door, notices us both, and gets killed just for wanting to take a piss."

"Killed?" He raised a brow. "Who's going to do the killing?"

I bared my teeth. "You will, once you hear what I have to say."

I held his stare while my pounding heart marked out its quick, silent tempo. This wasn't training anymore, this was my Trial. I had little doubt I could survive the encounter, little doubt I could kill him, but I needed to do more than just kill. I needed time with the body after, time I wouldn't have if I botched the cut, or if the big bastard managed to shout, or if it took so long to get him in the 'Kent-kissing privy that one of his friends came looking to see what was wrong.

I stepped halfway out the door, reaching for his tunic, as though to pull him in. It was the move of an idiot or an amateur, the kind of thing that left me off-balance and open to attack. That was the point. The less professional I seemed, the more likely he might be to drop his guard. He seized my wrist, then dragged me into the hall. I gave a small cry, loud enough for him to appreciate, quiet enough that no one outside the hallway would hear, then put up a vague and ineffectual struggle as he ran his hands down my sides, up my back, down each leg, then up over my ass.

"Ruc didn't tell me I'd be molested for my trouble," I hissed.

He rolled his eyes, shoved me back through the door into the privy, then followed a step behind.

"Save the outrage. I've been in this city long enough to know that even kids like you carry knives."

The privy felt suddenly tiny with both of us inside. I held up my bare palms. "No knives, asshole. Now, if we can close the fucking door . . ."

I reached past him. As he turned to follow the motion, I plucked the knife from the post, then drew it back across his neck, opening his throat.

Even huge men die surprisingly easily. Chop off a cock's head, and it will run circles, blood gouting fountains from the wound. The Neck, by contrast, just gave a rough, quiet cough, took me by the shoulder, his massive hand strangely gentle, leaned forward, as though to murmur a secret in my ear, then collapsed onto the privy bench.

"The god's mercy upon you," I whispered.

It was harder than I'd expected to shift him onto his back, but once I'd managed it, it took only moments to unbutton his leather vest. I found two wide pockets stitched inside. The first held half a dozen Annurian silver moons—enough to cover an evening drinking with his men, and then some. I left the coins where they were. The second pocket was empty. I fished inside my trousers, then slid free the note I'd composed earlier in the day. The paper was damp with my own sweat, and the ink had bled slightly, but the writing was still legible—two simple lines, no name or date. I glanced over it once more, hoping it was enough, then tucked it inside the Neck's empty pocket.

I'd just finished buttoning his vest when the door from the tavern into the privy hall slammed open.

"Neck, you thick bastard, don't think you can hide in here all night." Boots thudding on the floor, a heavy fist hammering on the first of the stalls. "A bet's a bet, and there's no way in 'Shael's darkest pit I'm letting you sober up before you face it."

I retrieved my second knife from the rafters above, tucked the sheaths into my belt, glanced down through the hole in the bench, and grimaced. I'd been hoping to walk out the way I went in instead of bobbing out toward the distant sea with the shit. The Neck gazed up at me somberly, as though he understood. I patted him on the cheek; like me, he'd been hoping to walk out.

I sighed, checked over the tiny stall once more, then lowered myself through the hole. The water was a dozen feet below; I hit with a small splash, but managed to keep my head above the surface. Almost directly overhead, the soldier was pounding on the door to the final stall. It would be obvious soon enough how I'd escaped, but I wasn't concerned. The night was dark and the current swift. By the time the Neck's men got over the shock and thought to come after me, I'd be gone.

A few strong strokes took me out toward the middle of the canal. Fish-scale lanterns hung all around me—from decks, from fishing weirs, from the sterns of narrow, silent boats—lacquering the water's black with a slick, red light. When I was well clear of the docks and wooden pilings, I rolled over and floated on my back, letting the current take me. After years swimming in the chilly mountain streams around Rassambur, the delta water felt blood-warm, at once welcoming and strange. From the balconies and windows above, from the gently rolling decks of the boats, I could hear voices, dozens of them, hundreds, testing the whole range of human emotion—a man growling the name of his lover over and over, children bickering over their bed, an old woman singing the same few notes of an ancient Dombâng rowing song. I floated unseen, unknown between all those lives. After a while, I let my ears slip below the surface, where the only sound was the water's bass thrum.

"Three," I murmured to myself.

I'd been back in Dombâng less than a week, and I was almost halfway through my Trial. The easy half. I had ten days left to make four more offerings—fine. Ten days to fall in love. My limbs felt heavy, suddenly reluctant. The water lifted me, carried me lazily eastward. There was a peace in being so still in the midst of so much motion. I imagined the Neck beside me, also floating, caught in the soft grip of Ananshael's warm and unrelenting hand, both of us carried all the long, silent miles to the waiting sea.

"Someday," I said.

He didn't reply.

Slowly, I opened my eyes, rolled onto my side, and started swimming for the bank. There's no point setting a trap, after all, if you don't plan on being there when it springs shut.

7

The Purple Baths comprised a steaming labyrinth of pools—public and private; cold, hot, warm, perfumed; some intimate, some large enough to float a small oceangoing ship—all beneath a soaring wooden roof held aloft on massive pillars of mahogany and dripping with red-scale lanterns. Almost as amazing as the bathhouse itself was the sheer acreage of naked human flesh. I was used to seeing women and men in all states of undress—Rassambur is no place for the prudish—but I had forgotten the scope of Dombâng's bathhouses. There might have been five thousand people in the vast hall on the evening when I stepped inside—the night after I'd killed the Neck—some submerged to their necks, others floating lazily on their backs, still others plucking towels from massive stacks, rubbing palm oil into their skin before getting dressed, turning to the nearest companion—male or female, stranger or friend—for help reaching shoulders and backs.

A good number of those ministrations ranged well beyond the purely practical. Sex in the bathhouses was frowned upon, but no one looked twice at the two men kneading a woman's naked buttocks, or the lovers in one of the hot pools, the length of their bodies pressed tight together. I wondered suddenly at the wisdom of choosing this place, of all the spots in Dombâng, for my reunion with Ruc, then glanced down at my body, aware in a way I had not been for years of my own nakedness. I was a shade paler than most of the city's inhabitants—a legacy of my foreign-born father—and slightly taller than most of the women. I certainly had more scars. Eyes lingered on me as I passed. I wondered what Ruc would see. Did I look like the woman who had accosted him outside the Si'ite temple years earlier, or had I changed?

It was a relief to sink into the massive pool running down the center of the hall. Warm, lemon-scented water closed over me, steam wreathed my face, and as I floated out toward the middle, people lost interest, shifted their gazes to the naked bodies closer at hand. Just what I'd hoped for. Although the main pool was open to all eyes, no one paid it much mind—the city's richest and most beautiful preferred the smaller, more secluded baths tucked behind carved screens along the walls. Anyone looking for gossip was looking there, hoping to catch a glimpse of something exciting.

When I reached the perfect center of the pool, I sank down until just my nose and eyes were above the water, then waited, wondering if my plan was insane. I had little doubt that Ruc would come—he was thorough enough to search the Neck's jerkin, and there was no way he would ignore the note I'd hidden there. Meeting him, however, was just the first step. It was possible that *he* had changed, possible he hated me for the way I'd disappeared six years earlier, possible he'd arrive in the bathhouse with a dozen Greenshirts at his back. And my own unknowable emotions were even more worrisome.

Back at the statue of Goc My, Ruc had seemed like the man I remembered: casual, confident, just a little dismissive. On the other hand, I'd only seen him for a few moments, and from some distance. Hardly enough time to guess if I could fall in love, to know if whatever ember had smoldered in my breast all these years could be coaxed into an open flame.

I'd half convinced myself that the whole thing was a fool's errand, that I'd be better off hurling myself at one of the other innumerable naked beauties in the pool, when I saw him. Most men and women tend to sink slowly into the bath, luxuriating in the clean water, letting it wash them, wash over them.

Not Ruc.

He waded in as though the pool were an impediment beneath his attention. He had none of the awkwardness of men trying to walk through water. Instead of just charging ahead, churning up a bow wave, holding his arms awkwardly clear, he moved like a knife slicing the surface, slow but inevitable. I'd missed the way he moved. That smoothness alone was worth watching, never mind the fact that he was naked.

I remembered those shoulders, broad but lean and well muscled. I remembered running my hands over those ribs, trailing my nails over the brown skin, and I remembered slamming my fists into him, trying to find the liver or the kidney beneath that solid flesh. I remembered his fists, too, and though he was too far away for me to make out the detail, I could see, in my mind's eye, the scarred knuckles, the crook in his middle fingers where he'd broken them over and over. Dark stubble covered his face—he hadn't shaved in a couple of days. And then there were those green eyes, unmistakable even through the steam.

He was still ten paces off when he spoke, his voice low and level. "You owe me a bottle of *quey*."

Six years. Six years since I'd walked out on him in the middle of the night, slipping away from the room we shared without warning or explanation—six years in which, for all I knew, he could have thought I was dead—and instead of any shock, any expression of surprise or disbelief, *this* was what he had to say.

"I suppose," he went on, drawing closer to me, "you didn't bring it with you."

"As I recall," I replied, matching his lazy drawl, "the bottle was already half empty when I finished it. We split the first half before you unchivalrously fell asleep."

"Half a bottle of *quey* then."

I smiled. "I'd be happy to. Name the place and time."

"Here," he replied. "Now."

"You just got here."

"And I already found what I'm looking for. How exceptionally fortunate."

This was the tricky part. Ruc had come to the baths because of the note he found on the Neck, a note indicating a rendezvous with an unknown contact. It was *my* note, obviously. I wrote it; I was the contact. According to the rules of my own fiction, however, I was supposed to be expecting the Neck. Which meant I *ought* to look confused. Confused, but not baffled. I needed to exude an air of competent improvisation, to let him see that I was improvising without letting him see that I was letting him see it. And it wouldn't hurt if I looked a little bit glamorous into the bargain.

I pulled my shoulders back a fraction, brushed my wet hair from my eyes, tried to look lush and languorous. Rassambur hadn't afforded much practice when it came to looking lush and languorous.

"Someone break your nose again?" I asked.

He shrugged.

"You ought to quit letting people hit you. Your face is nice, but it gets a little uglier each time someone breaks it."

That last wasn't exactly true. I liked that slightly crooked nose, those faint smooth scars marring his skin.

"If I remember right," he replied, "you're responsible for some of the breaking."

I shook my head, took a couple strokes toward him, paused when I was an arm's span away, then raised a hand to his face, touched the scars on his chin, his right cheekbone. My stupid heart was thudding away in my chest, far faster and more violently than it had been in the moments before I killed the Neck. I supposed that seemed promising, in a very uncomfortable way. Thudding hearts and stupidity seemed to be hallmarks of love. On the other hand, the incessant hammering made it difficult to concentrate. I'd forgotten what it was like to be close to him. The hot steam folded around us, blotting out the rest of the pool, the rest of the world.

Ruc made no move to block my hand. He stood chest deep in the water, still but ready—he always looked ready, even when he slept—watching me the way a boxer watches an opponent's first moves in the opening moments of a match. I dropped my hand, took a step back.

"If you'd been faster," I said, "I might have hit you less."

He snorted. "How are your ribs?"

My hand searched out the spot under the surface of the water. I could still feel the ridge where they'd mended.

"Better than Bedisa made them."

"How long did that take?"

"A couple months. Well worth the lesson."

He raised an eyebrow. "Which was?"

"Keep the elbow tucked until the hook's already in motion."

"Kid's mistake."

"I was a kid."

"You were pretty fucking vicious for a kid."

"Emphasis on *pretty, fucking,* or *vicious?*"

"High marks on all three."

I winked at him. "I love getting high marks."

My breathing was hot and fast, the way it always was before a fight, and my heart kept hammering away, as though it were a bell hung above some outpost town, and a sentry were pounding the alarm. He ran his eyes over my shoulders, down the front of my body.

"Some new scars."

I nodded toward a patch of puckered skin on his shoulder, the remnant of a nasty puncture wound, one he hadn't had in Sia. "I'm not the only one."

He shrugged. "I keep telling myself I'm going to stop fighting. Take up pottery or something. Somehow I never get around to it."

"We're made how we're made."

"Not a philosophy," he observed, "that leaves a lot of room for personal growth."

"Pythons don't mature into lily roses."

Ruc studied me for a while, then shook his head. Coming from someone else, the motion might have indicated some sort of capitulation. Ruc, however, was not one to capitulate. "What are you doing here, Pyrre?"

I glanced over my shoulder, as though looking for the Neck, then turned back to him. If anything, he was more muscular than I remembered, not just stronger, but harder, like a statue dropped in the middle of the baths and abandoned.

"The same thing as you, would be my guess."

"Then your guess is wrong, unless you pulled a note out of a dead man's vest."

I raised an eyebrow. "I try to stay out of the clothing of dead men."

"An admirable trait, but not always practical in my line of work."

"So it's true. Annur gave you command of the Greenshirts."

He nodded. "I should have kept boxing in Sia. More honest."

I glanced around the bathhouse again. "City seems to be thriving under your watch."

"How long have you been here?"

"Long enough to see that it's not on fire."

"Don't read too much into that. It's tough to burn down a city built in the middle of a fucking river."

"I'll keep that in mind."

Far overhead, lost in the gloom and steam, the bathhouse gong began tolling the evening hour, the hour indicated on the note I'd left inside the Neck's vest. The deep bass trembled inside my chest. Ruc waited until it was over, then shook his head.

"He's not coming."

I cocked my head to the side. "Who's not?"

"The man you're hoping to meet."

"How do you know it's a *man*?" I asked, pursing my lips. "Have you been keeping tabs on my bathhouse assignations?"

"I know it's a man," Ruc replied, "because he was found in the privy of The Bronze Croc with his throat slit, bleeding through the shitter into the canal. He had a letter," Ruc tapped his bare chest, just where I'd tucked the note, "details for a meeting. That meeting is here." He patted the water in front of him gently. "Now."

"Ah." I gave the syllable time to breathe. "And you think it has something to do with me."

"Here you are."

I cast an eye around the huge open space.

"Lots of people here."

"Not with your history."

"You don't know my history."

He nodded. "Exactly."

"Meaning?"

"Meaning I tried to find you, six years ago. I'm good at finding people. It's what I did in the legions, when I wasn't killing people. It's the reason the Annurian *kenarang* put me in charge of the Greenshirts. When you disappeared, I looked for you, and do you know what I found?"

I tapped a finger against my lips. "Nothing?"

"A truly remarkable amount of nothing. A woman who fights as well as I do, probably *better* than I do, if you give her a knife, appears out of nowhere, dominates, alongside me of course, the bare-knuckle boxing scene in one of Annur's largest cities for months, then disappears. No one knows her. No one trained her or trained with her. No one saw her before she appeared, evidently out of thin air, and no one saw her after." He moved closer to me as he spoke, slowly but inevitably as the rising tide, until he stood just inches away. "And now, after six years in occultation, she appears here, at the precise point where a murdered Annurian legionary—not just a legionary, but the *commander* of an entire legion—was supposed to arrive for a secret meeting, and at the precise time."

I wet my lips. "Imagine your surprise."

He shook his head. "Quite the contrary: I feel an old wound finally beginning to mend, the rent of a long-standing mystery starting to stitch itself whole."

"Well, you don't need me if the mystery is stitching itself."

I took a step back, silently praying that he would follow.

He raised his brows. "Retreating? Not like the Pyrre I remember."

"Just giving you some space."

"You gave me six years' worth."

"So another few days won't hurt."

"No."

"No," I said, testing out the syllable. "Hard to know what that means without a little more context."

"It means that until this is finished, you're not going to disappear again."

I tried to look cool despite the sweat beading on my face. The meeting had gone just as I hoped: Ruc knew I was in the city, was curious about why, and intended to keep me close, at least for a while longer. He had taken the bait; all that was left was to set the hook.

So why, I asked myself as I watched him watching me, *do I feel like the one caught?*

8

"I figure there are two possibilities," Ruc said.

I'd followed him out of the pool, into the warren of benches and cubbyholes, wooden trunks, hooks hung with robes, and ranks of narrow closets running the length of the long northern wall. He'd been studying me silently as we toweled ourselves dry. My skin was still flushed with the water's heat, a fact for which I was both irritated and grateful. I didn't want him to think I was blushing; on the other hand, I wasn't sure I wasn't.

It's amazing how easy it is to be naked around someone who doesn't interest you; bodies are simple, straightforward, no more worth noticing than the walls. Add attraction, however, and all that cool composure goes to shit. As Ruc twisted and stretched to dry the difficult spots, I couldn't figure out where to put my eyes. Whenever I looked away, I felt like a cloistered milkmaid, but whenever I let my gaze linger—on his ass, on that perfect joint where his leg met his hip—I felt the blush burning up through my cheeks.

He didn't seem to share my dilemma. His skin was darker than mine, which gave him an advantage in the blushing game, but I suspected that even if he'd been pale as the moon my nakedness wouldn't have fazed him. He'd been watching me with such frank curiosity as we dried then dressed that when he finally spoke, the words were a relief.

"You were working with the Neck," he went on, pausing with his pants half buttoned to gauge my response. "Working with him or about to start. The note I found on his body was from you. That's why you're here."

"That's one possibility," I conceded.

"The question is what *kind* of work you hoped to accomplish. That's where we get to the possibilities."

I glanced casually over my shoulder. A knot of women occupied the far end of the bench, laughing, chatting, and getting dressed, but they were a few paces away and paid us no mind.

"Either," Ruc said, raising a finger, "you're working for Annur, which puts us on the same side. Or you're working with Dombâng's seditious priests, in which case things start looking a lot less rosy for the two of us."

"I'd tell you the answer," I said, "but I can see you're having so much fun figuring it out all on your own."

Ruc flashed me a smile. "Why don't I tell you a story," he suggested. "There was a woman, born in Dombâng, who wanted nothing more than to drive Annur from her city—"

"Lousy start."

"I thought," he said, raising an eyebrow, "you were going to let me work it out on my own."

"It's the storytelling I'm objecting to. Don't tell the listener everything in the first sentence. You'll spoil the mystery."

He picked up his sheathed belt knife, slapped it contemplatively against his palm a few times, then threaded it through his belt. "I find you can skip the mystery as long as there's enough screaming and blood."

"Nothing like playing to a crowd's finer sensibilities."

"And sex," Ruc added, winking at me without cracking a smile. "Let's not leave out the sex."

"Wouldn't dream of it. If we can't have decent storytelling, at least we can enjoy the violence and fornication."

Ruc pursed his lips. "A pretty sound approach, I'd say."

"So . . ." I bent to strap my own knives to my thighs. "According to this tawdry tale of concupiscence and blood . . ."

"Our protagonist," he said, nodding to me, "this daughter of Dombâng, tailed me six years ago."

"For the sex," I asked, straightening up, "or the blood?"

"The one was a means to the other. She tried to enlist me in the city's uprising, plying me with all her feminine wiles. When she failed, she vanished. Now here she is again, reappearing just days after someone has begun spanking my city bloody with red-painted palms."

I felt less exposed with the weight of my blades strapped to my thighs. Less exposed but still naked. I started to pick up my pants, then left them where they lay. This whole thing—the story, the indifferent pace at which he was getting dressed, the tapping of his knife against his palm—it was all the circling and feinting before a fight, and I'd be fucked if I let him see me flinch. Instead, I stepped closer, put a hand on his bare chest, traced a line down his stomach to his belt, then tucked a finger in behind the leather and the cloth beneath. He was still warm from the water. Not just warm—hot.

"I'm waiting to hear why this woman, one of Dombâng's chief conspirators, was planning to meet with the Neck, the Annurian legionary responsible for dismantling her carefully planned revolution."

Ruc glanced down at my hand, made no effort to move it, then met my gaze. "For the same reason she found *me* six years earlier: she hoped to seduce the Neck into some kind of collusion."

"Your grasp of female characters leaves something to be desired."

"Oh?"

"For starters, the woman in question, this revolutionary genius, seems to rely somewhat single-mindedly on her vagina."

"I shouldn't have made her sound so simple," Ruc conceded. "She also excels at punching."

I smiled. "Let me tell *you* a story. I call it *Betrayal of a Native Son*."

"Lighthearted."

"You'll die laughing."

"The title seems to give away the mystery."

"Not if you don't know who's going to be betrayed." I ran my finger back up his stomach and chest, up to his neck, lifting his chin. "The fun is in seeing it play out."

"Sure that *fun* is the right word?"

"Oh, the most vicious stories can be the best—provided you're not the one living them. Are you going to listen or keep interrupting?"

Ruc put a hand on my bare hip. "I'm listening."

It was hard to concentrate with him so close. It was all just part of the sparring, each of us trying to knock the other off guard, but I could still feel the heat in his hands, his breath tangling in my hair, his smooth chest brushing for just half a moment against my own. Memory's delicious ministrations slid over me: those warm Si'ite nights, the breeze through the open window tangling my hair, his hands on my hips, the small of my back, gliding up in the insides of my thighs, his eyes deep as the jungle and every bit as easy to get lost in. My heart bucked like a paddocked horse eager to be free. With an effort, I shackled all that recollected passion, forced myself to focus on the story.

"There was a young man," I began, "a scion of his city, heir to a proud but dilapidated legacy. He might have been expected to lead his people—these centuries enslaved—to a long-awaited freedom."

Ruc chuckled. "Expected by whom?"

"Those who know the truth—that he is descended from Goc My, the greatest of the Greenshirts—"

He raised an eyebrow. "The same Greenshirts that quit mattering two centuries ago, when Annur conquered the city?"

I shook my head. "The past never quits mattering. Dombâng's silent priesthood was only waiting for the right moment, the right man—"

"This legionary?" Ruc asked. "Someone who served the empire for eight years rooting savages out of the Waist? Doesn't seem as though you've thought through your characters, their motivations."

"Haven't I? Who better than this legionary, one trusted by the decadent minds of the empire, one well versed in their ways and wiles, to bring Annur to its knees? Who better than the son of Goc My—"

"All Goc My's sons are centuries dead."

"The *spiritual* son of Goc My, then. Who better, as I was saying, than this prince of Dombâng to see the Greenshirts *and* the priesthood returned to their former glory?"

"Someone should have told him he was a prince. He would have quit boxing, saved himself some bruises and broken bones."

I met his eyes, traced the scar running up the edge of his jaw. "No, he wouldn't have."

"Not everyone needs to fight."

"*He* does," I murmured.

"Let me see if I can guess how it ends. At long last, this prince heeds the call of his downtrodden people. He begins murdering the very Annurians charged with helping him keep order in the city, starting with a legionary known—quite color-fully, I might add—as the Neck."

"We knew the betrayal was coming. . . ."

"Then he goes to the baths to find the legionary's secret ally and murder her as well."

I nodded, never taking my eyes from his. "An audience likes betrayal. They like a story that ends with everyone drenched in blood."

Ruc slid his hand up from my waist, brushing my breast, coming to rest gently against my throat. "It's an exciting story," he said. "Compelling. The trouble with it is—and I'm sure you've noticed this—you're still alive."

"As are you."

"Which means," he said, "that either we're slow when it comes to killing, or we're on the same side."

I nodded. "That could prove useful, what with a revolution brewing."

He narrowed his eyes. "What do you know about that?"

I shrugged. "The same as everyone else. Paintings dashed up on the statues and bridges. The kind of painting that has a way of getting people killed and whole huge chunks of the city burned down." I smiled. "I'm here to stop it."

"I thought that was my job."

"It ought to be. There are those, however, who have developed the opinion that you don't seem to be *doing* that job."

Ruc snorted. "Back-room second-guessers. A bunch of clean-fingered bureaucrats who've never set foot outside Annur."

"I can't comment on the cleanliness of their fingers, but some of the second-guessers rise well above the level of 'bureaucrat.' The Kettral don't take orders from bureaucrats."

I winked, stepped back, took my pants from the bench, and slid into them, forcing myself to patience as I waited for his response to the lie.

I'd thought hard, during the long slog to Dombâng, about what kind of life to invent for myself. Finding Ruc Lan Lac was, after all, only the first step. Once I found him, he would have questions, and while I'd managed to side-step most of those six years earlier, I had a nagging worry that he would prove less trusting the second time around. My new identity needed to be unassailable, utterly unfalsifiable, even by someone as smart and tenacious as Ruc. Just as important, the tale I told needed to be *relevant*. If I was going to fall in love with him, I had to give Ruc a reason to talk to me, to work with me, to keep me close.

It took me weeks to come up with the Kettral cover—strange, given that it wasn't just the perfect story, it was about the *only* one to fit the bill. For starters, Ruc could never check on my lies. The Kettral, elite warrior-assassins of the Annurian empire, were notoriously secretive. They lived, according to rumor, on an archipelago of hidden islands—the Qirins—the location of which was known only to themselves, a handful of merchant captains with military clearance, and the ocean's bolder and more desperate pirates. Ruc had no way to reach the Kettral, no way to follow up on a story about a young woman, such-and-such a height, so many years of age. . . .

Even better, the Kettral backstory gave me a reason to work with the Greenshirts. Ruc himself, of course, had been tasked with crushing any rebellion inside Dombâng. The legions provided the muscle. It seemed only natural, however, that Annur would have a contingency plan, another set of eyes and knives keeping watch, not just on the city, but on the city watchmen. For all I knew, the story was actually true. Somewhere in Dombâng there could have been one or two Wings of Kettral, the empire's greatest soldiers posing as fishermen or barkeeps. It was *plausible,* at the very least, and even better—it explained my unlikely abilities. Servants of Ananshael are trained to be discreet, and I'd certainly managed to hide the bulk of my training from Ruc the last time we crossed paths. Even the little he'd seen, however, was enough to raise eyebrows, a level of martial ability completely unbelievable from most of the world's professions.

The Kettral provided me with the perfect lie, one he couldn't *not* believe. . . .

"I don't believe it," he said, voice flat.

I raised an eyebrow, sucked a slow breath in between my lips, tried to find a way to strike back. "How many other people do you know who could go toe-to-toe with you in a bare-knuckle fight?"

He drummed a thumb absently over his ribs, just the spot where I used to hammer him in the ring.

"Of those," I went on before he could respond, "how many weigh forty pounds less than you? How many are nineteen-year-old women?"

"If you're Kettral," he asked slowly, "then what in 'Shael's name were you doing in Sia?"

I shrugged. "Work."

"Where was the rest of your Wing?"

"We don't always work in Wings."

I had no idea if that was true or not, but I was betting he didn't either.

"What was the mission?"

"Everyone off the Qirins who knew the answer to that is dead. I wouldn't suggest joining them."

"And your mission here, in Dombâng?"

"Meeting the Neck, for starters."

"Not off to a great start."

"Just means we have to do things the hard way."

He studied me a moment. "We?"

I nodded. "The rest of my Wing."

"You just said you didn't work with a Wing."

"That was last time. Different mission. Different parameters."

"And this mission, beyond chatting with a dead man?"

"Under normal circumstances," I said slowly, "I wouldn't tell you."

"When are the circumstances ever normal?"

"A valid point," I conceded.

"Let me see if I can guess the rest," he said, appraising me with that unfairly green gaze.

"I'd be disappointed if you didn't."

"You're Kettral, or so you claim. You're here in Dombâng because the city's sedition seems to be rolling to a boil all over again. Annur put me in charge of the Greenshirts, loaned me a few legions to keep the peace, but something happened back in the capital, and someone there doesn't trust me as much as they used to. So they sent you to watch me." He raised an eyebrow. "How's my narrative sense now?"

"Improving." I patted him on the cheek. "We're here to watch you. If your loyalties haven't shifted, we stay in the shadows, let you do your work, then we clean up whatever mess you leave behind."

"So, I'm either a traitor or an idiot."

"I assured them you weren't either."

He eyed me. "And yet, here you are."

I shrugged. "I go where I'm told."

"Why *you*?"

I pursed my lips. "Maybe you are an idiot after all."

"Fine," he snorted. "You're from Dombâng. You know the city. . . ."

". . . And I know you."

He tapped absently at the handle of his belt knife. "Is that it? You're supposed to drag me to bed, fuck the suspicion out of me, get at all my secrets?"

I frowned, put my hands on my hips. "Did we not just discuss some of the ways in which my skills extend beyond the spreading of my legs?"

Ruc ran his eyes the length of my body, but I couldn't read his gaze. Was that a sliver of lust? Or just the steel glint of a fighter sizing up another fighter?

I tried to imagine I was Ela, a woman well versed in the ways of the world, as comfortable moving from one man to the next as she was changing her dresses. I pictured her brown eyes as she raised her wineglass, the way they brimmed with lamplight, seeming to laugh even when she didn't move. I leaned back against the wooden wall, trying to find something like her languid pose, that way her limbs fell that whispered readiness and relaxation at the same time.

Maybe I managed it. It was impossible to tell from Ruc's face. In truth, my palms were damp, my mouth dry.

"Of course," I went on, reaching for Ela's easy, throaty voice, "Kettral need to be prepared for *all* contingencies. I'm certain, if it becomes absolutely necessary, that I could find the willingness to bed you for the sake of our great empire."

The line was supposed to be coy, enticing. Ruc didn't look

enticed. In fact, he looked as though he hadn't heard me at all. Instead, he was gazing past my shoulder, down the length of the narrow room. He'd barely moved, just a small shift of his weight, a slight dropping and angling of the shoulders, but I recognized the posture at once. I'd seen it dozens of times in Sia, and each time it meant the same thing—he was about to hurt someone, probably quite badly.

"The woman in the gray is the Asp," he murmured as we stepped out of the bathhouse into the hot Dombâng night.

It took me a moment to find her again—a short, middle-aged woman with a pockmarked face and a slight limp. No one I would have looked at twice. She made her way slowly through the dozens of people crowding the wide bathhouse steps, moving aside for knots of revelers, bowing almost reflexively when someone jostled her, eyes downcast the entire time.

"Doesn't look like the kind of person to name herself after a venomous snake," I said.

"She didn't. It's the name we've been using for her."

"Her own wasn't exciting enough?"

Ruc shook his head grimly. "I haven't been able to learn it."

He started down the steps, slicing fluidly through the crowd as I followed half a step behind.

"Why are we so excited to see her?"

"Not just her," Ruc said, "but the person she's with."

I squinted. Dozens of red-scale lanterns flanked the steps, but they cast shifting, inconsistent shadows as they swayed with the night breeze.

"I don't see anyone."

"Not there," Ruc muttered, increasing the pace. "Down at the canal. Third boat back, the one with the black awning. The man approaching it."

It took me a moment to find him, a tall, slender figure in a calf-length *noc* and black vest. He glanced over his shoulder before stepping into the vessel; I was able to catch a glimpse of a long face, high forehead, hatchet nose.

"They don't seem to be together," I observed.

Ruc nodded. "That's the point. There's a reason I haven't been able to dig out the roots of this priesthood, even after five years."

"So they're priests."

"The one in black is. The Asp works for Lady Quen, although we didn't know that until a few months ago."

"Is Quen a name that should have been in my briefing?"

"Depends on how good your briefing was. She's one of the richest people in the city, an outspoken critic of Annurian policy, but so far I haven't been able to tie her to anything that might survive a trial."

I raised an eyebrow. "You've got hundreds of Greenshirts and I don't know how many legions under your command. Who needs a trial?"

"You don't understand Dombâng," Ruc replied. "This city's balanced on a blade. Most of the citizens appreciate Annur—the empire's laws, her trade, her prosperity—but the quarter that don't could turn the place upside down in half a day. Whenever I take a person down I need proof, I need bodies, I need piles of stolen loot, and even then there's a risk that the whole thing turns into a riot."

"Maybe you should have stuck with the boxing after all."

"You have no idea how often I think that."

The man in black—the priest—had disappeared beneath the boat's canopy. The Asp paused at one of the stalls lining the bottom of the bathhouse steps, spent a few copper flames on a leaf filled with crushed ice and honey, then crossed to the edge of the canal where she picked at the dessert with a bamboo spoon while looking out over the water.

"If they're trying to keep secret," I asked, "what are they doing meeting here, in the largest bathhouse in Dombâng?"

"It's harder to keep track of them that way. We watch Lady

Quen's mansion day and night, but she knows that. She'd gut any priest who came within a hundred paces of her doors or docks. So they do it this way: surrogates, discreet signs, public places. Could be here, any of the markets, the harbors, the taverns. Different priests have different circuits. It's always changing."

"What is the *it*?" I asked, although a sick dread churning in my stomach suggested I already knew.

Ruc looked over, met my eyes. "Sacrifice," he replied quietly. He nodded toward the Asp. "Come on."

The woman finished the last of her honeyed ice, tossed the leaf into the canal, watched it bob away, a diminutive little ship, then strolled the length of the dock to the same boat the priest had boarded earlier. The bathhouse docks were a hive of activity: slim swallowtail boats, opulent pleasure barges, snub-nosed wearies shouldering through the press of hulls to deliver passengers or pick them up. There was nothing remarkable about the vessel with the black canopy. I wouldn't even have noticed it, if Ruc hadn't pointed it out. The Asp stepped lightly from the dock onto the rocking hull without even a glance back, just one of the thousands of people who would pass over the same decking each day. She murmured something to the oarsman, then ducked under the canopy and disappeared.

I glanced over at Ruc. "Should we kill them?"

He shook his head. "If I wanted the priest, I could have taken him months ago. I want Lady Quen."

"I suppose it would be too simple to assume she's waiting quietly in that boat."

"The good lady is anything but simple. It's the Asp's job to make contact, to bring the priest to Quen, and to make sure she's not followed."

"So we need to be sneaky."

"I hope you've stayed fit," Ruc said, running his eyes over me once more.

"How fit do I need to be to lie in the bottom of a boat while we trail them?"

"We're not going in a boat. They'd spot us."

"Please tell me we're not swimming."

"We're not swimming."

I studied him. "We're swimming."

He nodded. "Of course we're swimming."

"Sweet Intarra's light."

"I thought Kettral were good swimmers."

"We are," I replied. "But I prefer water that isn't an open sewer."

"Lucky for you, we're at the clean end of town."

"How lucky."

The Asp's oarsman had shoved off from the docks, was poling his way through the press of vessels, bellowing abuse at the owners of the other boats.

"Let's get messy," Ruc said, striding into the crowd.

I took a deep breath, checked my knives, and followed him.

Dombâng is a city unlike any other I've seen. Most of the streets aren't streets at all, but canals, winding waterways that thread between blocks built up out of the mud on thick, tarry stilts. Causeways and wide promenades front some of those canals, running for miles alongside the slow-moving current. We started out along one of those, keeping to the densest part of the crowd, following the black-canopied boat at a safe distance. If we'd been able to do that all night, the job would have been easy. Unfortunately, the Asp knew her work well enough not to make things easy.

After the quarter mile, the boat turned from the main channel into a narrow canal branching off to the north, leaving us on the wrong side. As the boat slipped out of sight, I glanced over to find Ruc stripping his vest, shucking his boots, then his pants. Passersby slowed to look him up and down with obvious amusement. A few, seeing me watching, made lewd suggestions that Ruc ignored.

"Swim in your shirt if you want," he said, "but if you fall behind, I'm not waiting."

As I watched, he vaulted the railing. His splash bloomed like a flower in the dark water. With a muttered curse, I tugged my shirt over my head, dropped my own pants and sandals, and followed him into the water. The last waves of the boat's low wake were already fading.

"Far dock," Ruc said, pointing to a private landing directly across the channel, then fell into a strong, steady stroke. After all the lying and verbal sparring in the bathhouse, it felt good to swim, to throw my body into a simple, physical task requiring no finesse or second-guessing. It had been a long time since I'd swum hard for more than a few dozen paces—the largest pools in the Ancaz are little bigger than bathtubs—but the motions of my childhood came back to me in moments, carrying me forward though my arms and shoulders burned.

I reached the dock a few paces behind Ruc, who had already hauled himself out of the water.

He reached down to pull me out, and my wet body slid over his as he straightened. When I looked up, his face was inches from mine. For a moment he didn't let go of my wrist.

"Weren't we chasing some evil-doers?" I asked, pursing my lips.

I could feel his chest shake with his chuckle. "Just giving you a breather."

"Oh, I'm just getting warmed up."

The side canal into which the boat had disappeared stretched away into the darkness. It was obvious why we'd climbed clear—two swimmers splashing their way up the narrow waterway would be even more noticeable than a boat. Unfortunately, there was no other way to follow. This was a residential canal—no walkways or promenades, just a handful of docks, some illuminated by lanterns, protruding at regular intervals into the current.

"How long do you want to wait?" I asked.

Ruc shook his head. "I don't."

Before I could respond, he crossed the narrow dock to the door, tested it, found it locked, then kicked it in with his bare foot.

I raised my eyebrows.

"They go around the blocks," he said. "We go through them."

"And if the owners of the houses object?"

"We go through them, too."

That first block couldn't have stretched more than two hundred paces from one end to the other. In that space we broke down fourteen doors and two windows, climbed two brick walls—one to get into a gorgeous flowering courtyard, one to get out—threatened one angry man with a knife, knocked out another with the bottle from which he'd been drinking, burst through a white-curtained bedchamber—the massive wrought-iron bed at the center of which held at least four naked bodies—knocked out a screamer with a candlestick, told the others to shut up, rammed through a wooden gate into yet another garden, then found ourselves peering over a low wall onto the moon-lapped water beyond, where the narrow canal we had been flanking drained into a small basin. The Asp's boat was halfway across, angling toward the gap beneath a low, delicate bridge.

I glanced over at Ruc. He was soaked with sweat, and his chest heaved with the effort, but his eyes, when he met mine, were bright.

"That was easier than I expected," he said.

I was doubled over, hands on my knees, trying to catch my breath. "I thought you were the one in charge of keeping the city's peace."

"I'm also in charge of protecting the innocent. Sometimes the two don't mix."

When I'd gulped enough air into my lungs to stand up straight, the bow of the boat was just slipping beneath the bridge.

"You know," I managed finally, "Kettral usually go a little heavier on the planning."

"I have a plan."

"Want to share it?"

"Keep going."

He leapt up onto the low wall, then dove into the water below.

We must have traversed several miles that way, busting down doors, swimming across channels, sprinting through narrow alleys. Four or five times I thought we'd lost the boat, but in each case Ruc was able to come up with a shortcut, a leap of faith, an educated guess that led us back to our quarry, sometimes a few paces ahead, looking down from a window or balcony, often quite a bit behind. The Asp was both fantastically careful and staggeringly paranoid, her watery path wandering in great loops, doubling back on itself three times to shadowy alcoves where she could watch unseen for pursuit. As Ruc predicted, however, she was watching the water, not the insides of the houses. Not the fucking roofs.

In the end, evidently satisfied, she charted a more direct path southeast, finally arriving in Old Harbor. Centuries earlier, the harbor had been the city's heart, the one basin deep enough to accommodate the draft of the oceangoing vessels that brought trade from as far away as the Bend and Anthera. As Dombâng grew, however, as more and more ships came to dock and trade, the harbor became overburdened. When Anho the Bald completed the massive dredging project that became New Harbor, the old port fell into disuse. Warehouses began to rot, then crumble. Ships damaged by storm and abandoned at the dock by destitute owners slowly settled into the mud as the river silted up the neglected basin. It made a surreal sight. What had once been an open body of water five hundred paces across had become a wide mud flat divided by a few narrow channels and punctuated by the hulks of stranded ships.

The boat we'd been trailing and another of similar make and coloring were tied up alongside the shadowy hull of one of the largest wrecks, a huge schooner, three of the four masts snapped off or chopped down, the one remaining stabbed up into the belly of the night sky, shreds of rotten rope that hadn't been scavenged twisting idly in the breeze. I could just make out the name in faded gilt up near the prow: *Heqet's Roar*. A ladder of much newer rope hung from the rail of the listing vessel thirty feet above, where two guards stood watch. I could make out the outlines of flatbows in the moonlight, the bulky shape of armor, the swords strapped to their hips, but nothing of their faces.

"Quen's men," Ruc murmured, laying a hand on my shoulder, then pointing.

The two of us had fetched up a few dozen paces away, behind a pile of waterlogged roots and branches, detritus washed down the Shirvian from the north, dragged out of the canals by the maintenance crews, and dumped here to be burned later. My legs ached from the chase, and my shoulders screamed, ready to rip from their sockets after so much swimming. At the same time, I felt bright in the darkness, warmed by the chase, alive. I couldn't tell if my heart's hammering came from Ruc's momentary touch or my own exhaustion. Maybe both. Whatever the case, it felt good to be close to him, to be hunting. Amazing how fast an old intimacy can come back. When I first set out from Rassambur, I hadn't dared to hope for so much.

But is it love? I wondered, sliding my gaze along his moonlit skin.

"What are you looking at?" he asked, narrowing his eyes.

I hauled my mind back to the work at hand, wiped a smear of blood from his shoulder—we were both covered with a dozen minor grazes and cuts.

"Just making sure you're not about to collapse on me. You hit some of those doors pretty hard."

"The doors didn't have flatbows," he said, then gestured to the ship once more. "They do."

"Where's Lady Quen?"

"Down below, I'd guess. Somewhere in the hold." He shook his head. "It's a son of a bitch to sneak up on."

I nodded slowly, studying the scene. The only approaches were over the open mud or up the canal. The gibbous moon gleamed like silver on the wet flats. Anyone trying to cross might as well carry a lantern and bang a drum. There was no subtle way to do it.

"The far side?" I asked.

"She's not an idiot. She'll have someone posted there, too."

"We'll have to float in." I gestured to the logs in front of us. "There's more of this back around the last bend, out of sight. If we drag a few branches into the water, we can drift in behind them."

"It's going to be ugly," Ruc said, "but if we come in on this side, we could cut free the boats, hope to create some commotion. Maybe lure them down the ladder. We'll be in the shadows, and the bastards won't have much of an angle."

The bastards in question hadn't moved since we first arrived. They weren't talking, or pacing, or sitting down.

"They're vexingly disciplined," I pointed out. "Not exactly the type to go chasing off after the nearest distraction."

"If you've got another way inside that hull, I'm listening."

I tapped the knives strapped to my thighs as I contemplated the situation. Then, I smiled.

"Let's get floating."

It was all a question of angles and rot.

If the planking of the ship was too steep or too sound, I wouldn't be able to drive the knives in far enough. If, on the other hand, the boards were too rotten, they wouldn't hold my weight, let alone Ruc's. The curve of the ship's hull shielded us from the guards above, but I moved slowly all the same, testing a few different places before driving my blade into the chink where the planking had sprung loose. It flexed when I pulled on it, but held. Slowly, I slipped another knife from its sheath, pulled myself up on the first, so that only the lower half of my body remained in the water, reached up as high as I could with my free hand, and slid the second blade into the wood. From there, it was easy enough to get a foot on the first knife, stand up, slip a third from the sheath at my waist, and place it half my body height higher than the last.

Back at Rassambur some of my brothers and sisters had teased me about carrying so many blades—*Giving people to the god is a great devotion, Pyrre, but you don't need to give them all at once.* Four knives, however, had always struck me as a reasonable number: one on my belt where everyone could see it, one on each thigh, and one strapped high on my arm.

I vowed, after that night scaling the ship's hull with Ruc, to carry more, as soon as I could return to Rassambur and have them made.

We climbed the hull, angling for the ship's prow, on a shifting ladder of four knives. As soon as Ruc's weight was off of the lowest, he would stretch down into the darkness, yank it from between the planks, straighten, then hand it up to me. It was slow work, especially as we were trying to be quiet. In one way, at least, the guards' vigilance was working for us. They assumed any attack would come up the ladder, which meant they didn't budge from that spot. They couldn't have expected to find us inching up the glistening hull.

None of which made our job any easier. If I drove the knives in all the way to the hilt, Ruc had trouble pulling them out again. On the other hand, he was heavier than me. Whenever he would reach up to grab the handle of the blade on which I was standing, I could feel it flex beneath my bare feet, threatening to tear free of the soggy wood altogether. I had no doubt that we could survive the fall, but Quen's guards weren't likely to ignore the loud smack of bare skin against wet mud, mud that would hold us motionless while they filled us with crossbow bolts. I had no objection to dying in Ruc's arms, but

I wanted to survive long enough to fall in love with him, to pass my Trial.

When I was finally able to toss a hand over the ship's top rail, I let out a long, quiet breath, then pulled myself up slowly. The deck was a wreckage of smashed crates, downed spars, the remnants of what might have been long-abandoned tents, canvas rotted and shredded by the wind. Lady Quen's guards were well out of sight behind the piled trash. I pulled myself over the rail carefully, then reached back down for Ruc.

He was bent double, prying the lowest knife out of the wood. When he had it in hand, he passed it to me, stepped up onto the next knife, caught my hand, then tried to hurl me headfirst over the ship's rail and into the mud below.

That was what it felt like, anyway.

It took me half a heartbeat to realize that the knife beneath his foot had torn free, that he was dangling in the darkness, one hand wrapped around the handle of the last remaining blade, the other caught in my grip. The fallen knife landed with a quiet *thunk* in the muck below. For a few moments I didn't move. I was bent halfway over the rail, the wood grinding into my ribs, my breath searing my lungs. Sweat dripped the length of my arm, weakening my grip on Ruc's hand. I reached down with the other arm, caught his wrist, and tried to haul him in.

He grimaced, then gave a tiny shake of his head.

Somewhere off to my right, I could hear the guards talking to each other, grumbling in the way men with a boring post are wont to grumble. I tried to breathe even more quietly.

"Just hold," Ruc mouthed.

I nodded, redoubled my grip.

His eyes locked on mine, he let go of the last blade, caught my wrist, and for a moment all his weight was on me. To my shock, he smiled. Then he tossed his foot up onto the handle of the remaining knife, shifted his weight over it, and he was up. I didn't let go of him until he'd stepped over the rail.

"It's a good thing," I whispered, "that I brought a lot of knives on this mission."

He leaned in so close I could feel his lips as he murmured in my ear. "And how does this compare to your other missions?"

I squelched a wild urge to laugh, turned my head, slid my lips over his cheek's stubble to his ear. "Sort of boring, actually."

He pulled back just enough to look in my eyes. "I'll have to find some other way to keep you entertained."

A delicious ache opened inside me.

Yes, I thought, meeting his shadowed eyes. *Yes, you will.*

Whatever thrill had come over me on the ship's deck evaporated inside the hold.

We'd managed to drop down to the first level through a dilapidated hatch near the bow. I'd expected near-perfect darkness, but a bloody light seeped up through the cracks in the boards beneath our feet. It was easy enough to follow it half the length of the hold—moving slowly to avoid tripping over the shattered lathes of broken barrels, the dusty remnants of various nests, all the rest of the garbage littering the inside of the ship—to another hatch, this one with a ladder sticking up from below.

I put an eye to a gap in the decking and peered down.

The narrow chamber beneath was illuminated by candles, dozens of them, far more than necessary to light the small space, some standing on the floor, others perched on the wooden stays running between the ship's ribs. Blinking against the sudden light, it took me a few moments to understand what I was seeing.

Six bodies lay across the wooden floor, each bound at the wrists and ankles. Black hoods obscured their faces, but it was obvious enough from the sizes that two were children, maybe eight or ten years old, while the others were adults. Regardless of age, the clothes they wore bordered on rags—scraps of cast-off cloth tied at the waist and shoulders mostly, bits of sail canvas repurposed into pants or vests. Only one of the six wore shoes, and those were little more than decomposing sandals.

Beside me Ruc made a low sound in his throat, almost a growl.

At the far end of that low-ceilinged compartment stood the Asp, two guards, the priest we'd followed from the bathhouse, and a graceful swirl of a woman who could only have been Lady Quen. Like her servants, the lady had made some effort to be nondescript. Unlike them, she had failed. Her gray silk cloak might have blended into the night's shadows well enough, but by the light of the candles it was obviously cut from cloth that only Dombâng's richest could afford, tailored to her form in such a way as to draw the eye rather than avoid it. She was striking, even regal, and stood like a woman enduring the supplication of a suitor she knew to be beneath her, dark eyes sharp, hawklike; black hair streaked with gray, drawn back from her temples, and held with a silver clasp; her lips pressed together in silent disapproval.

"Lady," the priest said, bowing low. "It is a great offering you make."

"I did not expect to be making it so *late,*" she snapped. "The sun will be up by the time this is done."

"Apologies, lady," the Asp murmured, staring deferentially at the floor. "Annurian eyes are everywhere. I wanted to be certain we were not followed."

Quen bared her teeth, gave a quiet hiss of vexation. "A day will come when they will no longer dare."

"Indeed, lady," the priest said, nodding his head sagely. "Indeed. But it is *we* who must hasten that day through our struggle and our sacrifice."

"I've been hastening it my entire life. For all the good that's done."

"Have faith," the man replied, his eyes aflame with reflected light. "Red hands have risen to pull the city down. The day of the prophecy is at hand."

One of the figures on the floor, one of the children, twitched, then began to thrash.

Quen shook her head, rounded on the guards. "They were supposed to be sedated."

The man bowed almost to the ground. "Apologies, lady. Deepest apologies. The child is small. I did not want her to die before her time."

Memory lashed me: memory of a rope binding my hands, of my face pressed against the hull of a boat, of mud, blood, terror. A memory of eyes slitted like a cat's, but belonging to no cat, of a woman stronger than any woman.

"Your man is right, Lady Quen," the priest murmured, crossing to the child. "She is no good to our gods already dead."

Slowly, almost lovingly, he peeled back the hood to reveal a girl's filthy face, mud-streaked and smudged with tears, green eyes wide, horrified. She opened her mouth to cry out, but the priest produced a rag from somewhere in his *noc,* stuffed it in her mouth, then turned to Lady Quen, smiling beneficently. "The child is strong. The Three will be pleased."

"And *I* would be pleased," Quen responded, "if we could complete this ceremony before we all grow old."

"Of course," the priest said, ignoring the thrashing child as he rose. From a shelf beside one of the candles, he lifted a wide, short, double-bladed knife, its handle the yellow of old ivory, the blade of cast bronze. Crossing the room, he stepped carefully over the bodies, then passed the weapon to Lady Quen.

For the first time, the distaste faded from her eyes. Veneration replaced vexation as she closed her hand around the knife, then turned it back and forth, admiring it in the light. When she turned back to the priest, I could hear a new fever in her voice.

"They will rise soon," she murmured. "They must."

The priest nodded eagerly. "It is we who forsook the Three. They have been *waiting* to return, waiting all this time for us to prove our worth. Your sacrifice," he said, indicating the prisoners, "will show the gods we have not forgotten, that we are still willing, in our faith and our obedience, to give up that which is most precious to us."

The captives tied on the floor didn't look precious to anyone. Unless things had changed in Dombâng, Lady Quen had ordered her henchmen to round up a few drunks and orphan children too weak or stupid to run. According to the stories, when Dombâng was founded, only the greatest warriors went into the delta to face their gods, to offer their own bodies as sacrifice. We had fallen a long way, however, from the stories.

"My lady," the Asp murmured. "As you say, it is late. . . ."

For a moment, Quen seemed not to have heard her. She was gazing, rapt, at the knife in her hand, deaf to the whimpering of the girl who had awoken. Then, as though jolted from some beautiful vision by the rude hand of an ugly world, she turned to the nearest body—a man, judging by his size and shape—pulled down the front of his filthy shirt, and dragged the tip of the blade across his chest, deep enough to cut, to bleed, but not so deep as to give a serious wound. It was all part of the theater. The priest would bring the prisoners into the delta. The priest would abandon them to die. To reap the favor of the gods, however, Lady Quen needed to draw the first blood.

The man groaned slightly in his stupor, rolled onto his side, then fell still.

Ruc touched me gently on the shoulder, put his lips to my ear.

"She'll cut them," he whispered, "and then she'll go. She'll leave the others to get the bodies out. We'll take her at the top of the ladder. You kill the guards."

I'd known, of course, that it would come to this. We hadn't tracked the Asp and the priest halfway across the city just to sit down together over a bottle of *quey*. The trouble was, I couldn't kill them, not without violating the rules of my Trial. If one of them fit the song, of course, I could give them to the god, but the odds didn't look good. No one in the room below looked pregnant. None of them seemed to be singing. Of course, there are ways to incapacitate a man without killing him. Silently, I slid one of my knives back into its sheath, switched my grip on the other, then shifted into the shadows just above the hatch.

I waited to strike until the second guard had stepped off the ladder, brought the heavy pommel of my blade down across the crown of his head, then pivoted, slammed the second man in the stomach with my fist, caught him by the throat, squeezed the arteries along the side of his neck as he flailed for his sword and then went slack, collapsing onto the deck in a clatter of steel.

"What's going on?" Lady Quen demanded from below.

I ignored her, focusing instead on the two guardsmen. My attacks wouldn't leave them unconscious for long—I couldn't risk killing them—which meant I needed them incapacitated before they woke. It was grim work slitting the tendons of their wrists and ankles, the sort of thing I'd never thought to do as a priestess of Ananshael, and I felt filthy when it was over. There is a beauty, a terrible nobility to a fast, clean death. What I'd just done felt more like torture, like a version of what was happening in that hot, cramped room below.

"Three more above," Ruc murmured, then dropped straight down through the hatch, ignoring the ladder.

Just under my feet, I heard Lady Quen's strangled curse, the priest's screaming, but before I could glance down, the guards from the deck above were leaping through the hatch. The first of them almost landed on my head, but these—their eyes useless in the dimness—were even easier to dispatch than the first two. I reminded myself, as I went about hamstringing them and snipping the tendons in their wrists, that they were here as part of the sacrifice. They were complicit in the bodies lying bound in the hold below.

It may seem strange that a worshipper of Ananshael would object to such a sacrifice. What was I doing in Dombâng, after all, but offering women and men into the nimble hands of my god? People have such a fear of death that they tend to conflate the two, to see fear and death as two sides of the same coin. It's hard for most to imagine the annihilation offered by Ananshael without that attendant fear.

In truth, however, my god abjures terror almost as much as he does pain. Both are antithetical to the peace he offers. The most perfect offering is one in which the sacrifice is dead before they feel the blade. It is, in other words, the opposite of the sacrifice that happens in Dombâng. In Dombâng, the terror of the victims is all part of the act. They're *supposed* to struggle, to fight, to plumb the depths of dread—for days if possible— before they die. Under other circumstances it would have felt good to put a stop to such suffering, but bound by the rules of my Trial, I could only trade the misery of the victims below for that of the guards.

The five of them thrashed on the deck, bellowing like mad bulls, unable to stand. One reached out to seize my ankle, but I had wrecked their hands as well, and his fingers slipped uselessly from my skin. He stared at his own hand, aghast, a ruined moan draining from his lips. I turned away from the carnage, sick to my stomach, and leapt through the hatch to join Ruc in the hold below.

He had killed the Asp, shattered her neck with one curt blow, then backed both the priest and Lady Quen into the far corner.

Quen stared at him, contempt resplendent in her eyes.

"Ah," she said. "The traitor, come to betray his own people once again."

Ruc gestured with his sword to the bodies lined up across the floor. "Why don't we ask them who they think has betrayed them?"

Quen snorted. "Backwater trash. Three drunks who wouldn't have survived the year, the other three so starved they're halfway dead already."

"Truly," Ruc said, "a great sacrifice for your mythical gods."

The priest drew himself up. "The Three are *real,* and they

will *consume* you. We will feed you to the serpent and storm. We will give your blood to the river."

"Actually," Ruc cut in, "we're going to do something different. We're going to have a nice trial. Plenty of people to testify very publicly." He nodded toward the captives still trussed on the floor. "Then, once we've squeezed out all your secrets, all the names in your seditious little cabal . . ." He shrugged. "I don't know if Intarra is real or not, but I know you'll feel the fire."

"Blasphemers," hissed the priest, his voice a high, pinched whine. "The goddess will swallow you. She rises. She *rises,* her executioners at her side."

"This," Ruc replied, "is the same song I heard the last time your ilk started splashing paint on the buildings. Maybe you remember how that turned out."

The priest sneered. "It is as it was in the first days. The waters seem to recede. The enemy, emboldened, enters, only to find himself swallowed at last by the righteous flood."

"Too bad for you, you won't be here to see it." Ruc turned to me, eyes hard as shards of jade. "Kill him."

I tensed. "What about squeezing the secrets, giving him to Intarra, all that?"

"It's her secrets I want," Ruc said, nodding to Quen. "We've been following this idiot for months. I know everything I need to know about him."

"So why kill him now?"

"Because I don't know everything I need to know about you." He cocked his head to the side. "Let's just say killing him would provide further evidence that we're actually on the same side."

"I'm not sure it would," I replied, scrambling for some way out, some way around it. "He's more dangerous to any insurrection as your prisoner than as a corpse. There's always another secret he might reveal as long as he's not dead."

"You're right, obviously," Ruc said, then narrowed his eyes. "But you're also stalling."

My chest felt tight, my breathing pinched.

He gestured to my blades, dripping blood in the candlelight.

The priest, too, was staring at them, rapt. Suddenly, however, he ripped his gaze away.

"Whatever you do to me," he snarled, "they will come for you. The Three will come for you."

Then I saw the way.

"Who the fuck are these *Three* everyone keeps yammering on about?"

Quen was watching me in the way a raptor studies a piece of meat.

"Kettral," she said quietly. "So the empire's most rabid dogs are finally here."

"It's birds, actually," I replied, glancing over at her. "The founder of our order briefly considered riding dogs, but decided on monstrous, man-slaughtering hawks instead."

The priest, lost in his own fervor or terror, didn't seem to hear the exchange. He was nodding vigorously, almost rabidly, as though working himself up to something.

"Sinn," he hissed finally, the word halfway between a curse and an invocation. "Hang Loc. Kem Anh. They will avenge me. They will avenge all Dombâng's fallen and oppressed. You can open my throat now but—"

The names still wet on his tongue, there was no need to let him finish. I cut his throat with a backhand flick, wiped the knife against my leg as he collapsed, my mind carried back down the dark current of memory.

Sinn, Hang Loc, Kem Anh.

They were names I had not heard since my childhood, and even then, only in whispers. One of my young companions had shown me the forbidden icons of his family once, climbing into the reed-thatched rafters of his house to draw out three statues of crudely modeled clay, two men and a woman, hand-high, naked, muscular, cocks half as long as the arms, buttocks high and taut, shoulders wide, legs spread in readiness. I can't remember the name of the young boy, but I remember the names he recited, voice and hand trembling as he touched each statue in turn. Sinn, bloodred, whip-thin; Hang Loc, larger and darker; Kem Anh, the goddess, the largest of the trio, her arms outstretched, eyes the product of some violence, jagged, as though someone had gouged them into the wet clay with the tip of a knife.

It is the nature of names to come unmoored from the world. Down the centuries, the syllables grow remote, then incomprehensible, the language that birthed them lost, their only right to concrete things a right that we bestow. It is easy to forget that names, too, were words once, no more august than any other words. So, too, were these, in the ancient language of Dombâng: *serpent, dark storm, river death.*

The ancient gods of my city were crueler, closer, hungrier than the bright, inscrutable goddess of Annur.

Even so, the empire might have tolerated them. A part of the Annur's brilliance was the willingness of its emperors to tolerate other faiths. The royal Malkeenian family worshipped Intarra, of course, but the capital hosted hundreds of temples, thousands, to deities beyond the Lady of Light, old gods and young rubbing shoulders in the same streets and plazas. A merchant might murmur a prayer of thanks to Intarra on the sun's rising, leave an offering to Heqet—a bowl of rice, a strip of meat—on her household shrine, then stop midafternoon in the temple of Bedisa to pray for a pregnant daughter. Even the more obscure cults, discredited by the mouths of the gods themselves millennia before, persisted unmolested in the empire's quieter corners. The Malkeenians had no desire to see newly conquered people rise up over some irrelevant theological grievance. Only in Dombâng had the empire set its shining boot on the throat of the old beliefs.

The conflict lay in the nature of Dombâng's gods. While the stone spirits of the Romsdals or the mythical fish-men of the Broken Bay posed no barrier to Annurian rule, our gods were both bloody and jealous. They were creatures, not of some celestial sphere, but of the delta itself. Their blood was the water, their flesh the mud, their screams the thunder of the summer storms. Their arrangement with the people of the city was both simple and cruel: sacrifice, and you will be protected. Make offering of your young, strong, and beautiful, and we will crush all those who come against you.

A fine deal, until it collapsed straight into the shitter.

When the Annurian legions attacked Dombâng, no deities erupted from the waters to stop them. The army took the city, put the leaders of the Greenshirts to the sword, tore down the main temples, all without the slightest divine opposition. A man proclaiming himself Hang Loc slathered his naked body with mud, then hurled himself bare-handed at an Annurian garrison. He was taken by the soldiers, castrated and decapitated beneath Goc My's statue, then tossed into the canal. A week later, a woman claiming to be Kem Anh took to North Point in the midst of a great storm, exhorting the waters of the delta to rise and smother the Annurians. The waters rose, as they always did during a storm, then fell. The Annurians, in their methodical, unimaginative, brutal way, decapitated her as well, then tossed her into the canal. No further aspiring divinities came forth.

The Annurian triumph was evidence to many that the gods of Dombâng had never existed at all. There was no place for them among the great pantheon laid down during the long wars with the Csestriim, when the young gods had walked the earth in human form. For centuries, traders from far-off lands had mocked our local superstition. That our gods did not, in the end, save us, was proof to many that they were no gods at all, just a set of dolls painted to remind us of the dangers— flood, serpent, storm—of the home chosen for us by our ancestors.

Proof, I say, for many. Not for all. In the eyes of some, it was not the gods who had failed Dombâng, but the people of Dombâng who had failed the gods. To these, the presence of

Annur was a call to a greater piety, a more severe observance
of the old forms, a committed resistance to the foreign plague.
That resistance failed. Annur was rich, ruthless, tireless. The
legions rooted out the underground priests, beheaded them,
threw still more bodies into the canal. For good measure, the
tiny statues of our trinity, still balanced impotently on shrines
outside each home, or carved into the tillers of boats, were
smashed or sanded out, banned from the city they were supposed
to protect. People were thrown in stocks for whistling the wrong
tunes, and executed for singing the wrong words. The old holy
books were burned, priests tortured. Like all occupations, it was
ugly. Some thought the newfound peace and prosperity worth
the price. Some did not. I might have hated the Annurians with
the same fervor as Lady Quen were it not for my own experi-
ences with our outlawed religion. Annur kept the old festivals,
but changed the names. Kem Anh became Intarra; Sinn and
Hang Loc, her servants, Heat and Fire. Even at this desecration,
our gods did not rise up. The two centuries following proved
enough time for many to forget them.

Many. Not all.

The priest dead at my feet, the bodies tied behind me, the
haughty woman back against the wall were proof enough of
that.

"Kem Anh rises," she sneered. "You will choke on her waters."

Ruc shook his head. "Do you know that you are the one
hundred and forty-first prisoner to tell me that? Those exact
words?"

"Her truth," Quen replied, baring her teeth, "will not be
denied."

"Maybe not, but it's been five years since I came back to this
city." He tapped at his throat with a finger. "No choking yet. I
keep killing you, and yet the waters . . ." He paused, put a hand
behind his ear as though listening, then shook his head again.
"Nope. Not rising."

When he turned to me, his eyes were wary, searching.

It was a triumph of sorts, and yet the bright hope with which
I'd started the night, the thrill I'd had chasing with Ruc through
the buildings of Dombâng, had drained away. I didn't know
what I felt in that moment, but it wasn't love.

"Dead," I said, pointing to the priest.

"Dead," Ruc agreed.

A giver of names, I told myself, my mind tracing the melody
of Ananshael's sacred song as I glanced down at the priest's
body one final time. I had given my god a giver of names, and
ancient names at that.

9

Despite the late hour at which I finally returned to the inn, my sleep that night was fitful, stalked by a woman with a mane of black hair, her teeth dripping blood, pupils slitted like a cat's.

I woke with my heart pounding, half reached for my blades, then subsided onto the bed. Outside the window, in the predawn dark, the canals were already alive. Flame-fishers were rowing back in their narrow sculls, oars creaking at each stroke, the night's catch piled in their bows. Men and women called greetings, taunts, and curses from the decks of the larger, flatter, ocean-bound vessels, while carts jolted over the ramps and walkways. In the room next to my own, someone with a limp was moving ponderously around. I heard the shutters clatter open, then a splash as the contents of the chamber pot hit the water. The thick, ever-present reek of the city rose up with the smoke of the morning fires: charred fish and sweet rice, mud, stagnant water, rotten wood, and, scraped over it all, the faintest lick of salt on the hot wind blowing in from the east: a promise of the unseen sea.

My whole body ached from the previous night's race through the city, and for a long time I lay still, reviewing everything from the meeting in the bathhouse to that final spasm of violence. We'd loaded Lady Quen on her own boat, along with her six prisoners, and rowed slowly back to the Shipwreck—the local name for the sprawling wooden fortress of the Greenshirts. I hadn't talked to Ruc the entire way back. Partly that was because of the other ears in the boat, but mostly it was because I could think of nothing to say. My plan had moved faster than I dared expect. I'd managed to inveigle my way into Ruc's confidence, had made myself a partner in his fight against the city's insurgents. And yet that early success only reminded me of an uncomfortable truth: it might well prove easier to foment a full-scale revolution than to fall in love.

I studied Ruc's eyes in my mind, rehearsed our banter, felt all over again the various jolts of excitement as we charged through Dombâng, covering each other.

What does it mean? I wondered, staring at the ceiling. *What did I feel?*

Excitement, certainly. The double-flutter of lust and uncertainty. Giddiness. Elation. Almost all of love's diminutive, trivial cousins—but love itself? I closed my eyes, delved down into myself, explored each organ, each part of my body in turn— heart, lungs, loins. My ribs ached. My chest was raw from so much running. I'd scraped the skin off the knuckles of both hands climbing the hull of the wrecked ship. They burned when I flexed them. All familiar sensations. Nothing I could identify, cut out, hold up to the light and say, *This is love*.

Finally, driven partly by the twin needs to drink and piss, I rolled myself out of the bed, crossed to the window, and tossed open the shutters. The sun had risen high enough to peer blearily from beneath a low lid of cloud. Mornings in Dombâng are haze—cook-fire smoke mingling with river fog. It was already hot. After using the chamber pot and guzzling half the water from the clay ewer standing beside the bed, I strapped on my knives, slid into my light cotton pants and silk shirt, and went looking for food.

I found Kossal seated at a table by the very edge of the inn's deck. A cup of *ta* steamed into the morning mist on the table before him, but he ignored it, focusing instead on the wooden flute he held to his lips. Despite the fact that we'd both lived most of our lives in Rassambur, I'd only heard the priest play half a dozen times. He tended to explore his music alone, in the mountains, staying away from the fortress for days sometimes, his only companions that flute and a large crock filled with water. Coming across him here, on the deck of an inn in the middle of a city, men and women seated at the tables just a few paces distant, was a little like finding a wild crag cat perched on one of the benches, lapping milk from a wineglass.

The other patrons of the inn up early enough to take their breakfast at the dawn hour seemed to feel the same way. They couldn't know that Kossal was a priest, of course, but their eyes kept flicking to him, then nervously away, then back again, as though they understood that this old man was a creature unlike anyone they knew, something strange and perhaps dangerous, despite the beauty of his music. Kossal himself seemed not to notice the attention at all. He played with his eyes closed, coaxing the smoke-thin notes from his flute as though he were alone atop a sandstone cliff in the high Ancaz. At first I didn't recognize the song, then realized it was an old, local dance tune, but played at a far slower tempo, until the silences between the notes seemed as much a part of the music as the notes themselves.

When he finished, he laid down the flute, but kept his eyes closed. A few tables away, a man and a woman started to clap. The old priest's face tightened.

"I will confess that I am tempted," he murmured, barely loudly enough for me to hear, "whenever someone claps, to give them to the god."

I studied him, the lines inscribed into his face, then glanced over his shoulder to the applauding couple. I gave them a smile that I hope intimated something other than the possibility of their immediate slaughter at the hands of a priest of Ananshael.

"They appreciate the music," I suggested quietly.

"If they appreciated it, they'd stop making that racket."

"But the song is over."

Oars slapped the water below us. A dozen paces upstream,

at the inn's docks, hawsers creaked. Seabirds screamed their tiny furies.

Kossal opened his eyes. "How do you know?"

"You played the last note. You put the flute down."

He raised his bushy brows. "And if I picked it up again?" He lifted the instrument, flicked a tongue between his lips, then began playing once more, pouring his breath into the polished wooden tube, listening to it emerge as music. It was the same dance figure as before, but inverted this time, as though the original song had been a cry flung into the world, and this newer, transmuted music the long-delayed response.

"Be careful," he said, when he finally laid the flute down again, "about saying something is over."

Whatever that meant.

The nearby couple started clapping again. Kossal ground his teeth, lifted his steaming cup to his lips, and drank.

"I made my fourth offering last night," I said.

"The Giver of Names. Ela told me."

I stared. "How did she know?"

"She is your Witness. Said it was quite a night."

I tried to imagine it. We'd been so focused on trailing the slender boat that I hadn't spent much time looking behind me. It was just possible that we'd been followed.

"Where is she now?" I asked.

"Sleeping, I would assume. That woman sleeps like a drunk pig. Have you heard—"

A new voice, Ela's, cut him off. "I take issue with that characterization." I turned to find the priestess sauntering toward the table. She wore a new *ki-pan*—jade green slashed with black, fine silk slit even higher up the side than the one I'd last seen her wearing. She seemed to have an inexhaustible supply, despite the fact that she'd carried only a small pack on the trek from Rassambur. If she was buying them here, she'd already spent what would have been a year's wages for one of the local fishermen. "I'm quite certain," she went on, sliding into one of the seats, waving over one of the servingmen with a manicured hand, "that *when* I sleep, it is as a graceful dove tucked quietly among gossamer." She ignored Kossal's dismissive snort, turning to me instead. "I say *when* I sleep, because lately I haven't had the chance, busy as I've been following our impetuous young charge all around this lovely city." She flicked open a filigreed paper fan, began to fan herself with it. "Quite exhausting, really."

I studied her. She didn't look exhausted. She looked like she'd spent the still hours before dawn bathing, then applying makeup, then oiling her skin until it glowed a warm, smooth brown. Her tight, cascading curls were still wet. She smelled of lilac and lavender.

"How did you follow us?" I asked, regretting the stupidity of the question even as it left my lips.

Ela glanced at Kossal, lowered her voice, as though feigning concern. "The poor thing is pretty, but I'm afraid she's not very bright, is she?"

Kossal didn't bother with a reply, and a moment later one of the young men approached the table, a steaming copper pot of *ta* in one hand. Like the rest of them, he had evidently been chosen for the perfection of his shoulders and chest, and Ela appraised him frankly as he poured, running her tongue over her lips, making a sound, half growl, half purr, deep inside her throat. He met her eyes, found, to his obvious surprise, that he couldn't hold that gaze, and looked away, flustered.

Ela leaned over to me when he had gone, her voice a delicious whisper. "I like making them flinch."

I opened my mouth, found no words inside, and closed it again.

"Of course," she went on, as though she hadn't noticed my awkwardness, "it's easy with these. That man of yours, though—Ruc Lan Lac . . ." She lingered over the syllables of his name. "He's not so easy to spook, is he?"

I shook my head, finding my language finally. "No. No, he is not."

Ela leaned in. "Tell me more," she murmured. "As I recall, you left off recounting the story just at the point where you'd chased a beautiful, bleeding, green-eyed man out of a concert and into the street. There was something about a fight he needed to get to. . . ."

Rishinira's Rage was so packed with human bodies that there didn't seem room for a pair of arm-wrestlers, let alone for two bare-knuckle fighters and the ring to put them in. People packed the main floor—men, mostly, lake sailors and canal boat hands, judging from their bare feet—bellowing to be heard by companions standing half a pace away. The sound was a wall, and the hot, sweet reek of sweat and spilled plum wine almost choked me. After the dry, open air of the Ancaz Mountains, even a crowded city square could feel tight. Walking into Rishinira's Rage was like shoving my way down the gullet of some house-huge, fetid beast. I felt as though the place were digesting me.

My companion didn't seem to be having the same problem. Despite the fact that he'd been ready to beat me bloody outside the temple just a little earlier, he seemed to have forgotten all about me as we made our way through Sia's winding streets. He didn't appear to have much regard for anyone else either, walking straight past the four cudgel-bearing louts at the tavern door. When we hit the press of bodies inside, he didn't bother to raise his hands, didn't bother to slide past or push people out of the way. He just walked straight ahead, leading with his chest. He wasn't a very big man, but when he bumped into people he just kept walking, like someone striding through a dense field of wheat, deaf or indifferent to the curses that he kept jolting free. Sailors would round on him, sloshed wine forgotten, fists half raised until they saw his face. Then, eyes wide with sudden recognition, they'd take a step back, hands falling to their sides. The young man ignored them all. He might have been alone.

My passage through the room wasn't quite as effortless. I was smaller, for one thing, and I was a woman moving through a room of loud, drunken men. I broke the hand of the first idiot who reached for me, then stepped past him as he howled. As I slid on into the crowd, the sounds of other conversation closed over his bellows. By the time I caught up with my bruised, music-loving fighter, I'd shattered two ankles and twisted one idiot's scrotum so tight he couldn't stand. If there had been fewer people, the scene could have turned ugly for me; even Ananshael's most studied priestesses can't stand against dozens of men at once. The crush and press actually protected me. Each time I tended to a would-be suitor, I had only to move away, move forward, to lose myself in the crowd.

Despite the unwanted attentions, I was almost enjoying things. Ever since arriving in Sia, I'd been trying to be circumspect. Ministers of my god aren't generally encouraged to embark on campaigns of indiscriminate slaughter. Those of us still in training leave Rassambur mostly to learn the ways of the world, to start to understand the minds and manners of the uninitiate. Certainly, I was required to make a number of offerings during my year-long sojourn in the city, but for the most part I was there to study, to learn. It felt good to use my body again as I'd been trained. I'd even managed to slide a cup of wine from the hand of one man as he fell, and I was sipping happily from the chipped rim when I almost ran into my own young fighter, who had stopped abruptly in front of me.

It took me a moment to understand what was happening. The press of human bodies gave way to a large open space at the center of the room, a square cordoned off with a waist-high rope. When I stood on my toes to look over my companion's shoulder, I realized that the floor fell away, marching down in graduated benches to a dirt ring several paces below. Most of those seats were already filled, and, judging from the clothes and comportment of the men and women sitting there, filled by people who had more money than the ripe-smelling sailors

crammed into the room above. A dozen brutes with cudgels—
hired muscle, evidently—kept back the throng.

At first, no one seemed to notice the young man standing at
the rope. Then one or two people glanced up, pointed, exclaimed.
A moment later, a massive woman who had been sitting in the
lowest rank of benches rose from her seat, turned to face us,
then smiled a wide, gap-toothed grin. When she spoke, her voice
was a gong, crashing through the surrounding tumult.

"Ruc Lan Lac!" she declared, staring at my battered fighter.
"I was starting to think you had gone soft at last."

That was the first time I heard his name. *Ruc Lan Lac.*

I'd suspected from the moment I saw him that he wasn't from
Sia. Not many people in the city had his shade of skin, that
glossy black hair, the same tilt of the eyes. Either his parents
were foreign, or he'd come from somewhere to the south, Chan-
nary, probably, maybe even Dombâng. His name all but
confirmed it. *Lan Lac* was an old name in the city of my birth,
a noble one once, though long fallen from grace.

The crowd behind had pressed me almost up against him,
but I shifted to the side, putting space between the two of us,
lifted the cup of plum wine and drank deep. The joy of moments
ago had evaporated, though what it was I felt in its place, I
couldn't say; something brighter, but barbed.

At the sound of Ruc's name, the clamor inside the tavern
ground slowly to quiet. Shouted arguments settled into heated
debates, cooled to murmurs, then faded, finally, into silence. It
took a little time—Rishinira's Rage was a large place—and I
used that time to turn my attention forcibly from Ruc to study
the woman who had spoken his name. She stood at the center
of that pit now, a giant, half again as tall as me, her chest like
a barrel. She must have been nearly forty, but there was no
softness to her. The muscles in her arms and shoulders rolled
lazily over one another when she moved. When she smiled that
jagged smile, the tendons in her neck stood out like ropes.
Someone had torn away half of one ear years earlier, and her

crooked nose had obviously been broken and reset half a dozen times. No one would have declared her a beautiful woman, but there was an irresistible vitality to her, a joyous strength in the way she moved, a humor in that broken smile, that almost erased her body's many breakages. I found myself wanting to know her, but she wasn't looking at me. Her gray eyes were fixed on Ruc Lan Lac.

"You look like you've been kicked by an ox," she exclaimed.

Her voice was a bronze bell; his the ring of good steel hammered on an anvil.

"Hello, Nayat," he replied. "I was starting to suspect that bastard you had me fight last night wasn't fully human."

The crack brought laughs from the crowd. The huge woman, Nayat, smiled wider, but there was something keen and calculating in those gray eyes.

"And yet here you are again, one night later."

Ruc spread his hands, that same empty invitation to embrace that he'd given me in the street earlier.

"What can I say? I missed your smile."

Nayat raised her bushy brows. "There are people calling you a fool. Most men would rest a week or two. Spend some of that money you just won. Have a few drinks. Find someone to fuck."

"Sadly, I don't get paid to fuck."

"Oh, I don't know. Body like yours? I think there'd be some crossover."

Ruc cocked his head to the side. "So cross on over, Nayat. You're the one paying. For ten golden suns, I'll do whatever you want."

That brought a chorus of hoots and bawdy cheers from the crowd. Nayat's eyes narrowed. She waited until the clamor died down to respond.

"Tempting, but my patrons came for a show."

Ruc just shrugged. "For ten golden suns, you can fuck me right here in the ring. Easier way to make the coin than letting those oxen you call men hammer me in the gut." He shrugged out of his light cotton shirt, tossed it aside. The muscles of his back and shoulders shifted with the motion. He was lean, obviously strong, but bruises purpled his ribs, and his lower back trickled blood where something sharp had gouged out a fingernail-sized scrap of skin. "Honestly," he went on, turning so the crowd could see him even as he spoke, "I'd welcome the change of pace." He put a hand to his leather belt, as though to unbuckle it. The hooting from the crowd rose even higher. "I promise I'll be gentle as a lamb with you, Nayat. I get my coin, you have your fun, and these assholes get their show. Just give the word."

Nayat smiled that broken-toothed smile and shook her head slowly, almost regretfully, as she waited for the noise from the crowd to subside. I edged backward, putting even more space between Ruc and me. I was still hoping, at that point at least, to remain unnoticed.

"I appreciate your offer," Nayat said finally, "and I hope you won't take this the wrong way, but I prefer . . ." She looked down at her own body, raised her brows as though surprised by the size of it, the obvious strength, then nodded approvingly. "I prefer a lover with a little more heft."

No one would call Ruc small, but Nayat was at least a hand taller, and obviously outweighed him. The man put his shrug to use once again. "Then I guess I'll be fighting after all."

Nayat studied him. "You could wait. Heal up. Come back in a week. People came here to see you punch, not to watch you bleed, stumble around, and fall down."

Ruc smiled genially.

"The thing about fighting," he said, "is that there's usually a little bit of both."

As it turned out, there was almost none of either.

Nayat had found a man even larger than she was to go up against Ruc, a scarred, broken-nosed, hump-shouldered giant with the pale skin of a Nishan or Breatan. He roared when he entered the pit, spread his arms, flexed in quick succession the muscles of his shoulders, arms, and chest, then began punching the air, running through half a dozen basic combinations. He was huge, and he was fast, but he was sloppy. He didn't bother tucking his chin when he jabbed, and his cross—which looked vicious enough to knock a barn door off its hinges—left him badly off-balance. Men that big tend to ignore the little things. They're used to fighting people who are too short to get inside their reach, or too weak to do much damage if they do sneak past.

Ruc was neither.

Instead of raising his own fists, he stepped forward, hands loose at his sides. He cocked his head as though gauging the distance, then stepped inside the giant's reach. The blond beast took the bait, roared as he swung, carved an arc through empty air with his meaty fist, stumbled slightly when he didn't hit what he expected to hit, then met Ruc's fist, which was coming up in a quick, efficient uppercut, driven by the full force of his legs and uncoiling torso. The big man took half a step backward, extended a hand as though searching for a friend or a railing. Whatever he was looking for, he failed to find it, stood stupefied a moment, then tumbled backward to the dirt.

Ruc studied him a moment, shrugged once more, then turned his attention to his knuckles, opening and closing his fist as though testing to see that it still worked. The crowd inside Rishinira's Rage, which had started heckling and hollering as soon as the fight began, went sickeningly silent as the blond man fell, then, when it realized the fight was over, that there would be no more entertainment, erupted. Half of them seemed to be cursing the giant for his idiocy, while half vented their fury on Ruc, who ignored them entirely. A man beside me had hurled his tankard of ale down toward the pit, and was shouting, "Rigged! Rigged!" over and over.

The blond fighter's friends had vaulted into the ring. One was trying to help the huge man sit up, while the other stalked back and forth, alternating between glaring at Ruc and hurling insults back at the crowd. A moment later, Nayat stepped into the ring. She looked less than pleased as she raised a hand for quiet.

Slowly, reluctantly, the huge room began to fall still. The most strident voices kept on for a while, demanding a rematch, or a reckoning, or their own coin back in their hands, but Nayat just stood there waiting until they, too, gave up, if only momentarily.

"It seems," she said, turning to Ruc, "that I was wasting my time worrying about you."

He smiled. "You have no idea how your concern warms my heart."

She frowned. "Maybe I should have paid you to fuck after all. We would've had a longer show, at least. You've left me with a room of deeply unsatisfied customers."

"You pay me to fight, not to satisfy."

"I had hoped that the two might go hand in hand."

"I hope for a lot of things."

Nayat raised her brows. "Do you?"

The fighter seemed to consider the question, then shook his head. "No, I guess not." He glanced around the packed room. "You want me to fight someone else?"

"You'd do that?" Nayat asked, wrapping a thick arm around his shoulders. Standing side by side with her, he really did look small. "For me?"

Ruc shook his head, but made no move to extricate himself. "No. I'd do it for another ten suns."

The offer detonated a round of wild cheers from the crowd. Behind me, some of those patrons not fortunate enough to enjoy a seat in the stepped benches had climbed up onto the tables instead, partly to see the action, partly to bellow their own encouragement. The crowd stiffened at my back, pressed forward, and I had an unusual moment of panic.

Rassambur is a fortress of air and light and open space; a woman might go to the god there, but she will do so on the broad stone beneath the wide sky. The memories of my child-hood, on the other hand, were all of hot, cramped spaces. Our teak shack stood packed so tightly against those on either side that it seemed the only thing keeping it from tumbling forward on its rotten stilts was the weight of those other sorry dwellings pressing in. When my father came home from the docks, when he slammed the door behind him, there was nowhere inside that tiny cube to go, nowhere to hide. Even those times when I escaped, slipping beneath his clumsy, drunken grasp, there was only the warren of Dombâng's tight, twisting canals, the pre-carious planks and walkways laid between piers and makeshift houses, the cramped, reeking hulls of the spear-fish boats.

Rishinira's Rage was a long way from Dombâng, but the irresistible press of bodies, the smell of too many people packed in too small a place, the way the heat and anger had nowhere to escape—it all reminded me of home, my first home, before I found my way to Rassambur. It made me want to shove back, to turn and fight my way free, but the loose mass of men through which we had moved on the way in had hardened into a wall. Sweating, suddenly, gritting my teeth, I turned back to the scene playing out below.

It was clear at a glance that, without even moving, Ruc had backed Nayat into a corner. The men and women sitting on those seats around the pit hadn't paid good coin to watch a fight that lasted barely four heartbeats. Even those who had won money betting on Ruc seemed vaguely disappointed, and those who lost were howling for the opportunity to double down. The scene hadn't quite turned ugly, not yet, but it was clear from the tension in Nayat's neck and shoulders that she felt the menace just the same as I did, the coming violence like a sound pitched just on the edge of human hearing.

Nayat raised her hands for quiet. The quiet was longer in arriving this time, and when it came it was frayed at the edges with mutters and murmurs.

"I would pay you," she said, turning back to Ruc, "but I

don't have anyone for you to fight." She jerked a thumb over her shoulder, toward where the blond man's friends had carried him away. "I didn't plan on you shattering Fion's jaw quite so quickly. Maybe tomorrow night. . . ."

And then, while she was still speaking, while the mass of men and women in the room were still leaning forward, angry and eager to hear what would happen next, I did something that I still can't quite explain.

I think that partly it was the crowd pressing in behind me. The only open space was in that pit, where Nayat stood with her arm around Ruc's shoulders, and something, some old voice inside me that had been silent almost since childhood, whispered in my ear: *It's safer there.* This, obviously, was madness.

Or maybe it wasn't actually that voice at all, but the same girlish impulse that had driven me to follow Ruc out of the temple in the first place, some visceral thrill at the simple sight of him, the cut of his chest, the way he moved, the beauty of his skin beneath all those bruises. Or, maybe I just wanted to test myself. Rassambur is filled with tests, opportunities to pit the mind, or body, or spirit against something greater. Life outside those walls can feel blanched and attenuated, a series of motions leached of their meaning. Maybe it was as simple as that: I wanted to see what I could do.

"I'll fight him," I said.

The words landed in the pit, bright and unmistakable as coins, though what I hoped to buy with them, I had no idea.

Nayat heard the challenge, but when she raised her eyes to find the source, she looked right past me, presumably scanning the throng for some more obvious pugilist. I stepped down into the topmost rank of benches.

"I'll fight him," I said again.

Nayat saw me finally, frowned, then shook her head.

"Who in Hull's name are you?"

"Does it matter?"

"As a matter of fact," the woman replied, "it does. People

come here to see a fight. I know every fighter in this city. I do not know you."

Ruc, who before had seemed almost indifferent to the entire proceeding, looked up at me sharply when I spoke, narrowing that one unswollen eye to the barest slit, as though he were trying to see me through a blaze of a blinding light. As he studied me, he slipped out from beneath Nayat's broad arm. It didn't look like much—just a casual step to the side—but he shrugged as he moved, loosening his neck and back. He flexed the hand that he'd used to knock down the blond giant, testing it.

"I'll fight her," he said quietly. He'd never stopped looking at me.

It wasn't until he smiled that I realized just how stupid I'd been. Since arriving in Sia, I'd given three people to the god— one every two months—and though I was certain no one had seen me, it was ludicrous to flaunt my presence. Not just my presence, but my skills. Which brought me to another part of the stupidity—for all I knew, Ruc Lan Lac would take me apart down in that pit. I might leave Rishinira's Rage with a broken leg or a missing eye. Judging from the way Ruc punched, I might not leave at all.

It wasn't the thought of death that bothered me; even then, I trusted in Ananshael's justice and his mercy. A *purposeless* death, however, one that I'd thrown myself into for no other reason than a stranger's green eyes—eye, I corrected myself—it would be an indignity to the history of my order, to the women and men who had labored so hard and patiently to train me. Worse and more probably, I might leave the pit alive, but with an injury that would leave me unfit to serve my god.

Those, of course, were the risks and possibilities I should have considered *before* opening my mouth. By the time Ruc had agreed to the fight, every glazed, drunken eye in the place was on me. In moments, the underlying chord of all those voices shifted from the thrumming bass note of building rage to the quicker counterpoint of argument and negotiation. I could only catch scraps of the conversation:

. . . She's inches shorter. . . .

. . . A woman . . .

. . . All beat up. If she just . . .

. . . Four to one. Eight . . .

Though Nayat hadn't yet agreed, her bookmakers were already moving through the rows of men and women, trying to drum up the next round of betting.

Ruc ignored it all. He seemed to have a knack for ignoring things. His gaze stayed fixed on me even as Nayat turned to him.

"Want to introduce your paramour?"

"I wish I could," he replied. "I only just met her myself."

Nayat frowned. "Doesn't seem like you."

To my surprise, Ruc grinned. "What? Meeting a woman?"

"Fighting someone who can't fight back."

"Oh, she can fight."

Nayat turned back to me, her eyes sharp, appraising. "How do you know?"

"You remember how it is," Ruc replied. "Sometimes you just know."

The huge woman nodded as she considered me a moment longer, ran her eyes over the crowd, nodded to herself, as though she'd come to a decision, then turned back to me.

"You got a name?"

I nodded. "Perra."

"All right, then, Perra. What's your price?"

I hadn't considered this. Violence, for the priestess of Anan-shael, is a form of devotion. Our order accepts contracts, of course, sums of thousands to kill important people quietly, thoroughly. Whatever I'd been thinking of, however, when I first stepped toward that pit, it hadn't been money. Still, it would look strange—even stranger than it already looked—if I didn't ask for anything.

"Ten suns," I said. "If I win, they're mine."

"And just on the vanishingly small chance that you don't win?" Ruc asked. His face was still, sober, but I could hear the smirk in his voice.

"Where I was raised, a woman doesn't get paid for losing."

Looking back, sometimes I think the difference between being a woman of fifty and a girl of nineteen is half a heartbeat. Or, to be more precise, thousands of half heartbeats, millions of them, inserted between each hot impulse and the action that follows, just a sliver of calm consideration. It is an entirely reasonable amount of time, although for me, for quite a few years, that moment for reflection and reevaluation proved stubbornly elusive. And so here again, standing in front of hundreds of people, I'd said something very, very stupid.

Nayat snorted. "And where, exactly, were you raised?"

Ruc just lifted his eyebrows, patiently waiting for the response.

I shook my head, though half the damage was already done. Hot blood flushed my cheeks.

"I'm not going to win any coin if we spend the whole night talking."

"I'd wager," Nayat replied, "that you're not going to win any coin either way, but you want to fight, he wants to fight. They," she went on, gesturing toward the restive crowd, "want you to fight. I'm not gonna get in the way."

I don't remember actually descending the steps through the ranked benches. One moment, it seemed, I was standing on the warped boards of the first floor of Nayat's tavern, the next I'd reached the damp dirt at the bottom of the pit. It was like standing at the center of some huge, thousand-petaled flower, each of those petals a leering human face. A score of broad lanterns hung on chains from the beams directly overhead; the light was almost sun-bright, but shifting, unreliable, so that those faces in the crowd seemed animated by something beyond their own emotion, as though their own shadows writhed unseen just below the skin.

Ruc's face, by contrast, was still.

"So," he said, when I reached the center of the pit. "You were following me after all."

I started to shake my head, to try to explain the whole strange situation all over again, then stopped myself. The truth—that I'd met him by chance at Antreem's Mass, then followed him here, then offered to fight him based on an inexplicable urge—was too strange to believe. Instead of arguing, I smiled.

"Can you blame me?"

"Not sure it's really a question of blame."

I cocked my head to the side. "What *is* the question?"

"What you're trying to do, and how bad I need to hurt you to stop you from doing it."

"How do you know you don't want me to do it?"

I was aiming for coquettish, ended up hitting a little wide of petulant.

Ruc just snorted. "Call it a hunch."

"While I enjoy," Nayat cut in, "a pre-beating courtship dance as much as the next woman, I wonder if we might move toward the main event."

I glanced up at the crowd once more. The bookmakers were still working in pairs taking bets, one man collecting the coin, the other jotting down names, odds, and amounts in some kind of shorthand. Those who had already made their wagers settled into the typical taunts of the bombast of bettors everywhere. From what I could hear, no one seemed to think much of my chances, which was understandable. Ruc Lan Lac had to outweigh me by forty pounds, his reach was at least a full hand longer than my own, and he was clearly no stranger to the ring.

On the other hand, he hadn't been trained by the priestesses and priests of death.

I turned away from the crowd to meet his level stare. "I'm ready."

"No," Nayat said, stepping forward, "you're not." She waggled a finger at my legs. "You move like you've got some steel tucked away under those pants. I don't mind a little death in my pit, but if you plan to kill a man—especially a good-looking fighter like Ruc—you're going to have to do it with your fists."

By this point, I'd waded so deep into my own idiocy that it didn't take much to slip the twin knives from their sheaths and toss them to the dirt. That brought an angry hiss from the crowd, and a renewed round of taunts. Ruc glanced at the blades, then back at me. He shook his head.

"Why are all the interesting people the ones who are trying to kill me?"

"If I were trying to kill you," I replied, "I would have held on to the knives."

"It's easy enough to kill a man without knives."

"I'm not trying to kill you."

"Well," he said, shrugging, "I guess we'll find out."

Nayat picked up the knives, tucked them into the back of her wide leather belt, then turned to us.

"I have to say," she began, using her show voice, "that I, for one, am very interested to see what happens next." She gestured us forward, took me by one wrist and Ruc by the other. Her grip was even stronger than I'd expected. She looked at me, frowned, then shook her head. "Try to stay on your feet a little longer than the last asshole."

Before I could reply, she dropped our wrists, stepped back, and Ruc was attacking.

It wasn't what I'd expected, wasn't at all the way he'd fought the last fight, and the surprise almost undid me. Instead of waiting, gauging the distance, looking for the counter-strike, he came at me with a snake-quick right cross. Only my thousands of hours sparring in the wide sandstone squares of Rassambur saved me. I slipped to my left, felt the punch slide by my face, fell into a roll that gave me a tiny bit of space, then came up with my hands in front of me.

Ruc grunted. "Yep, you're a fighter. Sometimes I hate being right."

It will sound like an excuse, but it's nothing more than the simple truth when I say the crowd won the fight for him that night. Or, to be more precise, the crowd is why I lost. Ruc was fast and smart. Lots of people know how to hit; some fighters even know how to move. Only a very few, however, have the experience and presence of mind to see the pattern beneath all the skin and speed, to work inside that pattern, to twist it to their own purposes. Ruc was one of the latter.

It was almost immediately obvious that in a stand-up fight he was better than me. On the other hand, aside from taking my knives, Nayat had said nothing about forbidden moves, and I knew a lot more moves than Ruc. He was good, but he was used to bruisers like the one he'd brought down earlier in the night, big men who would come at him with blows to the face and body. I discarded that approach before the fight even started. Instead, I spent most of my time ducking and rolling, attacking him with stiffened fingers rather than fists, striking for the more obscure targets that were actually within my reach: the nerve at the elbow, the tendon at the side of the leading knee. He was quick and adaptable, but his instincts were all wrong, and instincts take years to change.

What I hadn't counted on was the noise of the crowd. It's not uncommon, back in Rassambur, to spar in front of the other priestesses and priests. I'd fought hundreds of times in front of a large group, but not all groups are the same. Ananshael's faithful tend to watch fights, even fights to the death, with a combination of bright interest and cool, intellectual detachment. In fact, most of my sisters and brothers approach a fight the same way they approach a piece of music: as something to be studied, critiqued, and, in the case of the true masters, revered. That night in Rishinira's Rage there wasn't much study, critique, or reverence. In their place, I found an almost incandescent wall of noise.

In the first few moments, I was too involved deciphering the language of Ruc's movements to even hear the roar. As we settled into our stances, however, into our dance of probing and retreat, that roar started to weigh on me. Sometimes I could make out individual voices hurling insults. One particular idiot, whom I would have found and killed later if I'd known what he looked like, kept screaming at Ruc to *"Punch the cunt in the cunt."* I needed all my mind on the fight, on my opponent and my own body. Instead, I found my focus wobbling like a candle flame caught in a midwinter draft.

It was a good lesson. Later, after returning to Rassambur, and in future journeys out in the world, I trained to fight in just such chaos. I even spent one particularly chilly winter brawling in the Stone Pens of Erensa, and eventually I learned the skill, mastered the practice of closing off the portion of my mind that heard the noise, or that cared about it. It was not, however, a lesson that I could learn in a single night. As the fight drew on, I found myself caught in the grip of that vast fist of sound, compressed by it, until it felt as though I was battling two foes: Ruc, with his vicious punches, and the whole of Rishinira's Rage.

It was almost inevitable, in retrospect, that he'd notice my lapses, those tiny lags between movement and response, inevitable that he would twist them to his advantage. The surprising thing was that it took so long. It wasn't until partway through the seventh round that I misread his feint, ducked to the side, found his fist there, and felt my cheekbone break. He could have stopped there—I was already falling—but falling is not finished, and he knew enough about his business to end the job properly.

I woke to the smell of peaches, an old Ghannan melody drifting in the warm air, and a burning spike straight through my side. I forced my eyes open, but the world's dim blur refused to resolve. I could make out the shifting glow of a lantern, a rectangular break in the darkness that might have been a window, and a shadow crossing through the greater gloom a few paces away. The singing came from the shadow. I almost recognized the voice, turned toward the figure, and then the pain in my side flared, blotting out all other thought.

When I came to again, the singing was gone, and the figure bent over me. This time I could make out his face, which bled from a cut just above the eye. His nose was a bruised mess, broken recently, then carelessly reset. And those eyes—sea green in the lamplight. I remembered the eyes, but couldn't drag a name into my memory, or any recollection of where I was.

"Drink this," the man said.

"Who . . ." I croaked, the word rusty on my tongue.

"Drink this," he said again.

I took the chipped cup. It was cool against my lips. When I'd managed three or four painful swallows, I tried again.

"Where am I?"

He smiled. It was a strangely gentle smile in that battered face. "Well, you're not dead, despite invoking Ananshael forty or fifty times."

Fear blazed beneath my skin. If I had revealed who I was, if I'd said anything about Rassambur, or my brothers and sisters, I'd have to kill the young man with those green eyes. I shifted on the low cot, tested a fist. The knuckles burned as I tightened them, and the bones in my hand ached, but there were other ways than punching to give a man to the god. The crockery cup was heavy enough. . . .

"I know how it feels to want another go at a thing," he said, closing his hand around my wrist. "But maybe we could keep the fighting in the ring."

And like a slap across the face, it all came back to me: Antreem's Mass, Ruc Lan Lac, the pit, my idiotic decision to go down into that pit, the crowd's screams, thinking I was winning, realizing I was losing, Ruc's fist like a hammer burying itself in my side over and over. . . .

I studied his face in the lamplight. Some of the cuts were

old, but one of his eyes still leaked blood, and there was that bruised, broken nose.

"So I hit you the one time, at least."

Ruc raised an eyebrow. "You hit me a lot more than once." He let go of my wrist to probe at his elbow, then his shoulder, wincing as he found the bruises. "I thought you had a knife up your sleeve after all."

I shook my head, immediately regretted it, closed my eyes, and lay back. "Pain points," I muttered.

"No shit," he snorted. "I had no idea being poked in the elbow could hurt so bad."

"I would have hit your head more, but you were taking care of it. Hardly sporting."

"You're one to talk. I had to hit you in the ribs a few hundred times before you finally dropped your guard."

I found myself smiling at something in his tone. "Glad I didn't make it too easy."

"I've led year-long campaigns that were easier."

I tested the flesh over my ribs gingerly.

"I think you broke one or two."

He nodded, flashed a smile that bordered on the apologetic. "I wanted to be thorough."

"That wasn't very nice," I managed to murmur between my teeth.

He studied me with those green eyes, then leaned in slowly to kiss me on the forehead. I winced as my body shifted toward him, as though of its own accord. With one weak hand, I wiped away the blood at his hairline. When he finally straightened, he shook his head regretfully. "If you wanted someone nice, you shouldn't have been looking for men at the Rage."

"I found you at the temple," I reminded him.

He grimaced. "They probably won't perform Antreem's Mass again for another decade." Then he tilted his head to one side. "You want to go?"

I stared at him through the haze of pain. "What? In ten years?"

He used that shrug again. "Only if you want to."

I started to smile, winced, then settled for a nod. "Of course I want to."

10

"Busted knuckles and nose, those shoulders, and green eyes that don't look away, that just keep on going." Ela closed her own eyes, reviewing some private image. "I can see why you like him."

I found myself, to my great surprise, suddenly jealous. I couldn't say I loved Ruc, not yet, but I still hoped to. I'd come to Dombâng to *try* to love him, at least, not so that some other priestess could spend her evenings skulking in the shadows and licking her lips. Even if that priestess was quickly growing into one of Rassambur's legends.

Ela raised her *ta,* seemingly oblivious to the turbulence churning inside me. Only when she'd taken a small sip, savored it, then set the cup down once more did she go on. "A good choice—arranging your first meeting at the baths. If you're going to see a man, you want to see *all* of him. Then again—"

I cut her off. "I didn't see *you.*"

"The Witness does the witnessing. Not the other way around."

"Where were you?"

"Close enough to hear what I needed to hear. To see what I wanted to see." She luxuriated a moment in her own lazy smile. "Did you know about that scar on his thigh?" She tipped back in her chair, drew a line up the inside of her own thigh with a painted fingernail. "Right here?"

"Yes," I snapped. "I did know. It's from one of those jungle spears."

Ela nodded approvingly. "I like a man with scars." She waved a hand toward the serving staff. "These are pretty enough, but too smooth, like little figurines. They feel like porcelain whenever I run my hands over them." She frowned. "Warm porcelain."

I stared. "I thought you were spending all your time following me."

"*All* my time?" Ela's laugh was bright and rich, a chime ringing in the hot morning wind. "How exhausting. You've been running all over the city since we got here, painting little symbols, killing people, visiting the *baths*. . . ." She made no effort to lower her voice, even at the mention of my murders and sedition. "If I spent all my time following you, when would I enjoy Dombâng's more leisurely charms?" She nodded toward the bar, where two of the servingmen were conferring. "Kam and Keo aren't going to pleasure themselves." She pursed her lips, then reformulated. "Well, I'm sure they *do,* but I like to think I bring a little something extra to the experience."

"What about watching me?"

Ela reached across the table to pat my hand. "Don't be jealous, Pyrre. I'm not neglecting you. It's true that Kossal takes half of the shifts, but when it's my turn to keep my eye on you, I promise—my gaze is yours alone."

"When you're not watching Ruc."

"All a part of my piety," she replied, then winked.

"Piety?" I managed, almost choking on the word. "Where's the piety in studying Ruc's scars, his shoulders? You're a priestess of Ananshael."

"Which means that I need to know, when you finally give him to the god, whether you love him."

I stared at her.

"And that knowledge requires you to skulk around the baths studying his naked thighs?"

"Skulking." Ela made a face, as though she'd bitten into an unripe firefruit. "Such an ugly word. Mostly, I was floating on my back."

"The position is irrelevant."

Ela pursed her lips. "I've found that the position—the *right* position—can make all the difference." She put down her clay mug, then cocked her head, studying me. "Yours, for instance, leaves something to be desired."

As so often with Ela, I felt like I was falling. The ease with which she moved from Ruc's thighs to her own piety then back again to sex left me dizzy, disoriented, as though the ground had tilted beneath me. Even her tone escaped me. One moment, it would seem as though she was laughing at me from behind those brown eyes; the next, her smile—perfect white teeth flashing between her upturned lips—seemed like an offering, a secret invitation to some private confidence, one offered to me alone in all the world. I could never quite decide whether to fight or to smile back.

I felt like a little girl when I finally managed my reply, one who knew nothing of the world or its people. "I don't know what you're talking about."

"Obviously," she replied, rising smoothly from her seat. She stretched her neck to one side then the other, quirked an eyebrow at me, then gestured. "Get up."

"Where are we going?"

"To the private deck behind my room."

I narrowed my eyes. "Why?"

Ela smiled. "Education."

I tried to look normal as I stood on the wide deck, casual. Faced with the bright amusement of Ela's gaze, however, everything about my body felt suddenly strange. I couldn't seem to find a normal stance, couldn't remember how my arms were supposed to hang at my sides. I tried crossing them over my chest, felt ridiculous—like a blustery soldier from the stage—then let them drop. Ela raised her brows.

"Ananshael's sweetest kiss, Pyrre, you're even more awkward

around me than you were around him. Are you *trying* to look like one of those long-legged birds from the delta?"

"They're called sticklegs," I ground out.

"You have beautiful legs, but the way you're posed there . . ." Ela took a step back. "You don't need to use the privy, do you?"

Shame splashed my cheeks. "I didn't know mockery was a part of the Trial."

"Normally, it's not, but these are desperate times. You've got a perfectly gorgeous green-eyed, broken-nosed brawler out there just waiting to lap you up, but if you can't even stand the right way, you're never going to fall in love."

I ground my teeth. "What does how I stand have to do with falling in love?"

Ela blinked. "Surely you don't mean that."

"Assume I am stupider than you realized."

"Much stupider?"

"You might as well start at the beginning."

The priestess let out a low whistle, wetted her lips with the tip of the tongue, then waved me toward her. I took a step forward. "Closer," she said. "Stand just outside your striking range."

This, at last, was language I understood. My years in Rassambur had been short on discussions of love, but I knew my striking range—with each of half a hundred weapons—down to a finger's breadth. Ela watched me, then shrugged. "You may as well get out a knife, while you're at it—anything to make you feel a little more at ease." I hesitated, then slid a knife from the sheath at my thigh. The weight of the weapon in my hand made the whole world seem more stable.

Ela made a little flourish with one hand, as though she were introducing me to a crowd. "So, posture matters, obviously."

"When you're trying to kill someone."

"Love is like killing, but without all the blood." She frowned, as though reconsidering. "Usually. The point is, you know more than you think you know."

"What I know," I growled, "is how to put this knife in your

eye, or your chest, or your throat, or any of a dozen other places—"

"Actually," Ela said, raising an elegant finger in objection, "you know how to put that knife in the eye, or the chest, or the throat, or any of a dozen places belonging to someone a good deal slower than me, but never mind that. The point is, love is like this. It matters how you hold your body."

She was smiling, but it seemed to be her normal smile, warm with the joy of a woman at one with herself and at home in the world. I studied that smile for a hint of mockery. "If this is some joke about sex . . ."

She waved away the objection lazily. "Any fool can fuck—perhaps not well, but that's beside the point. We're discussing love, here, Pyrre." Sunlight sparkled in her eyes, tiny stars bright enough to survive the daylight. "Please try to elevate your mind above such carnal pursuits."

I realized I was glaring at the priestess. "This is what I look like when I'm elevated."

Something about the fighting pose had righted me, returned my equilibrium. Things felt familiar again. Somewhere out of sight, the gong began to sound in Intarra's Temple, massive, sun-bright bronze trembling out the noon hour beneath the priest's hammer. I spared a glance for that sun—furious, hot, lodged for just a moment at the day's apex. Sweat slicked my back, matted my hair to my scalp, but poised as I was in one of Ananshael's oldest forms, none of that mattered. Instead of an idiot who didn't know what to do with her body, I was a vessel for the god, the never-ending possibility of death made flesh.

Ela stretched her arms languorously above her head, graceful as an unfolding flower. Her eyes were closed, face uplifted to the sun. "Now," she murmured. "Kill me."

I stared. "Excuse me?"

A tiny frown creased her expression, but she didn't open her eyes. "Do you say that every time you kill a woman?"

"I don't understand."

"That's why we're doing this." She took a deep breath, chest filling against the silk of her *ki-pan,* as though she were savoring the warm air in her lungs. "It's time to kill me, Pyrre. And please, try your hardest."

I hesitated only half a heartbeat. Someone is always fighting in Rassambur, sparring with broad blades on the sun-baked clay, going knuckle-to-knuckle in the blocked-out squares inside the training barns, hammering through spear forms on top of one of the neighboring mesas. You learn early on how to pull punches, how to twist a blade at the last moment to avoid a killing stroke. It's not that killing is forbidden—we would make strange servants of Ananshael if it were—so much that each killing should be deliberate, an act of true devotion, not just a mistake made in training. I debated, in my half heartbeat of hesitation, whether to go at Ela with a curtal Manjari thrust, an attack that would draw blood without killing. Back in Rassambur, it would have been a reasonable assumption, but we had left Rassambur behind months earlier. She'd told me to kill her. If I succeeded, Kossal would still be alive to Witness the end of my Trial.

The smooth skin of her throat was exposed. I went after it.

Ela didn't parry. She didn't even really dodge. As my knife came at her, she took a step back, quick and smooth as a dancer caught up in the music, dropped her arms to her side, and bent away from me. My motion ended with hers. I was at the full extent of my lunge, the tip of my knife bright against her neck, touching, but not quite close enough to cut. Ela winked at me.

"You see?"

The question seemed to suggest an end to the fight—if it could even be called a fight—but the priestess hadn't told me to stop trying to kill her, so I didn't. My next attack was awkward, a clumsy stumble forward out of the full lunge, but my knife was already against her neck. I had to close with her only a finger's breadth to nick the smooth artery beneath her skin. Ela anticipated the attack, moved with the knife, keeping the blade against her skin without allowing it to cut.

It was the most ostentatious display of competence I'd ever seen. Priestesses and priests of Ananshael are encouraged to be discreet. It is easier to give people to the god if those people believe you to be a wheelwright or a gardener or a haberdasher— anything but a member of the dreaded Skullsworn. As a result, the training at Rassambur emphasizes speed and efficiency. If you can kill a woman in one heartbeat, it's sloppy to use two. There's almost no place for the kind of dangerous, showy game Ela was playing with my knife and her neck, but then, Ela had never quite fit with the rest of the priests in the first place. There weren't a lot of silk *ki-pans* in Rassambur.

She smiled at me over the length of gleaming steel. "You're thinking about love all wrong."

I almost hurled myself forward into yet another lunge, but my lunges hadn't done much good. I wasn't sure just how I was giving myself away, but Ela obviously knew the signal. I took a step back, letting my arm drop into a low guard, ready to feint left with the knife, then level the true attack with a stiffened fist. Instead of taking the offered space, however, Ela matched her advance to my retreat, moving forward with the knife, so close the blade sliced down the front of her *ki-pan* as I shifted to the low guard. She was close enough that I could smell the jasmine on her, close enough that I could have leaned forward to kiss her. She smiled, and for a moment I was too shocked to move.

"You think love is something that happens in here," she tapped me once between the eyes, "or here," in the center of my chest. Then she frowned, her brow wrinkling. "Don't stop killing, Pyrre, just because I'm talking."

I slammed the blade into her stomach, ripping upward through her diaphragm into the lung. I would have, anyway, if she hadn't pivoted with the attack, letting it slide by her. My knife parted the silk along her waist, then sailed off into empty space. Hauled forward by the violence of the attack, I tripped over Ela's outstretched foot, falling clumsily to the wooden deck.

"See?" she said again.

That word was starting to wear on my nerves.

"Killing is not something you do privately, in the space of your own head. It happens here." She opened her arms, as though to embrace the whole world. "In the relationship between bodies."

I pushed myself slowly to my feet, turned to face the priestess once more. I'd managed to hack away a neat section of her *ki-pan,* but the smooth skin beneath seemed untouched. I flipped the knife, catching it in the old Antheran grip, then drew its companion from its sheath. I might have been holding a pair of potatoes for all Ela seemed to notice.

"It's the same with love," she went on. "You're going at the whole thing as though it's a problem with you, *inside* of you, sealed off from the rest of the world. It's not. Love isn't a part of you or your lover. It's not something you can have, like a pile of gold or a pet pig. Love is this," she said, gesturing to the emptiness between us. "The space between."

I took half a step forward, testing that space, searching for the right distance, close enough to kill without being killed.

"There's space everywhere," I growled, "between everyone."

"Don't be obtuse, Pyrre. It's the *nature* of the space that matters."

Then, abruptly, she turned her back on me. This time, I didn't hesitate. I went high with one blade, low with the other, raking the air in opposite directions even as I closed. Ela, without turning, caught both of my wrists in the moment before the steel drove home. It was impossible; even a priestess of Ananshael couldn't block an attack without *seeing* it. Then I saw her brown eyes reflected in the glass of the window, her amused smile.

"This configuration, for instance"—there was no strain in her voice, despite the fact that I was putting my full weight behind those blades—"is wrong. There is a shape to a kill without which it is not a kill, just as there is a shape to love, without which it is just flirting, or fawning, or fucking." She shrugged, twisted, shifted my blades, and was free.

My breath chafed in my throat, hot and ragged. Barely a pace away, Ela glanced down at the fabric of her *ki-pan,* ran a finger along the rent, then shook her head regretfully. "You know, Pyrre," she said, looking back up at me, "there are other ways to get a woman out of a dress." She picked up her cup of *ta* from the railing where she'd left it, then took a long sip.

"That's all it is to you, isn't it?" I demanded. Back in Rassambur, I would never have spoken to a priestess that way, but then, back in Rassambur no one had ever taunted me. I'd been defeated certainly, hundreds of times over in training and sparring matches, beaten or bloodied with just about every conceivable weapon. Priestesses and priests had mercilessly revealed the flaws in my technique, and yet it had all felt like a part of our greater devotion. There was no shame in straining to better serve our god.

What Ela was doing now, however, didn't feel like devotion; it felt like a game she was playing. She wasn't trying to make me a better killer or a better priest. We were fighting—sort of—but she wasn't teaching me anything new about my knife work. Instead, she just kept smiling and taunting me about my own failure. I found, standing there panting, that I really did want to put a knife inside her. Not a sentiment worthy of a servant of Ananshael, but I didn't feel like Ananshael's servant. I felt like a stupid little girl, a girl so broken she couldn't even fall in love, not with anyone, not even once. I ached to drive a knife into Ela's eye, but failing that, I lashed out with my words, pouring as much scorn as I could into my voice.

"That's your great lesson? That love is just a matter of bodies? Of the way they line up next to each other? Stick a knife in a neck or a chest or a gut, and it's killing; get a tongue in your cunt or a cock in your ear, and it's love, is that it?"

"Sometimes," Ela agreed mildly. "I'd try, personally, to discourage the ear scenario, but we all have our peccadilloes."

My words seemed to have found no more blood than my knives. "There's a reason," she went on, "that lovers tend to speak with their bodies. It can be easier to see the space between two people when you're dealing with flesh, to apprehend the shape of it, to believe." She tapped a finger against her lips, as though caught by a momentary thought or a memory. "A warm tongue tracing the right circles has a way of . . . confirming one's faith."

"Meaning you can't be in love unless you're fucking."

Ela laughed, a long, breathy sound. "You would have liked Thurian," she said, then narrowed her eyes. "I hope you haven't quit trying to kill me. I didn't take you for a quitter."

I took a long breath, shifted right, trying to box her into a corner of the small deck. She moved with me, smooth as a dancer, sliding around until she stood just at the railing, back to the canal, the whole city to the east spread out behind her. A hot, thick wind was blowing in off the ocean, scraping green-black clouds over the delta, blotting the sun.

"Who was Thurian?" I asked, only half listening for the answer.

"A priestess," Ela replied. "Very serious." She waggled a finger. "Like you."

This time I threw the knife, a quick, underhand flick that sent the steel spinning toward her gut. Ela barely moved. She'd been holding her clay cup in front of her, two fingers slipped through the handle. As I threw, she let the vessel slip, pivot around her fingers, so that where the blade should have plunged into her stomach, it met the inside of the cup instead, steel grinding against the hardened clay, then clattering to the deck in a splash of spilled *ta*. It had been so slight, that movement that saved her life, an afterthought, an accident.

She righted the cup, peered inside, then shook her head. "I was enjoying that."

The rain dropped around us like a cage, drumming its furious cadence on all the surfaces of Dombâng, ten million silver fingers testing the roof tiles, the deck, stippling the water, staining the silk of Ela's dress, running in streams down her face. She licked it off her lips as though it weren't just a summer squall, but the wine that had spilled so recently from her cup. I glanced at my fallen knife where it lay between us. Ela had moved effortlessly enough so far, but she wore high wooden clogs, while I was still in my bare feet. I'd be faster on the newly slick deck, more nimble.

I dove for the blade, caught it in my left hand, rolled to my feet, used the momentum to bring both knives down in a sweeping, overhand attack. Ela turned sideways, narrowing the target, but I felt the knives bite home hard all the same, the shock of impact shuddering up through my arms and shoulders. The priestess smiled. It took my mind a quarter moment to realize that both blades had swept past her, missing her flesh, plunging into the railing instead, the front one so close that it caught the torn flap of her *ki-pan,* pinning it to the wood. It was a strange almost-embrace, my fists still wrapped tight around the knives to either side of her, and Ela stepped into it, kissing me lightly on the forehead as she slammed a fist into my stomach.

I sprawled backward across the deck, blades torn from my grip.

"Of course, Thurian was a heretic," she continued amiably.

I managed a noise somewhere between a cough and a groan, wondered if the other woman had crushed anything crucial inside of me.

"She believed that we are something other than this. . . ." As the priestess stepped away from the railing, a long swath of her dress tore away. She touched her bare stomach, the skin soaked with rain. "Thurian believed that a woman—or a man, for that matter—is something other than her body. Separate from it."

I tried to stand, felt one of my ribs grind unsteadily inside me, then subsided back onto the deck. The rain had dissolved the world. I couldn't see the buildings across the canal anymore, or any of the river craft in the canal itself. The outlines of our own inn were barely visible above me, looming through the sheeting rain. Ela and I might have come untethered from the mortal world. The wood beneath our feet might have been the deck of a ship suspended in the storm, caught between something too dark to be day, too green-gray-bright for night.

"I had to kill her, of course," Ela went on.

I tried once more to shove myself upright, managing, this time around, to sit.

"You killed another priestess because she wasn't obsessed with her own body?"

Ela watched me a while through the rain's sodden veil, then let out a long, ostentatious sigh.

"I had hoped to spend more time buying dresses and less time lecturing."

"No one's stopping you."

"I suppose not," she mused. "Just my overdeveloped sense of duty." The word should have seemed ludicrous on her lips, but she managed to say it without cracking a smile. She shrugged, then continued. "Poor little Thurian thought there was something inside her, something that was *more her* than all the parts she could see and feel."

Ela crossed the deck, extended a hand to me. I took it warily. She was stronger than she looked, and hauled me to my feet easily, then set a hand on my shoulder as I steadied myself. I tried to ignore the pain lancing through my side while planning the next attack.

"She wanted to be more than her heart," Ela said, touching my chest with a finger. "More than her face. More than all those adorable organs hidden beneath her skin." She shook her head. "I don't know why. She had a beautiful face—wide brown eyes, delicious lips. I took her heart out of her body to look at it; you've never seen such a sweet little heart."

"Maybe . . ." I managed, twisting slightly in the priestess's grip, "you should have left it inside her a while longer."

I shifted my hips as I said the last word, seized the hand she had set on my shoulder, twisted at the waist, then hurled her across the deck. She landed on her back, and then I was on her.

My side felt like someone had buried a knife in it, but for just a moment I seemed to have the advantage, and I didn't intend to let it go. I made hammers of my fists, then went for her face. Ela caught me by the wrists.

"She was a heretic," she said, as though we were sitting casually across from each other in some bureaucrat's office rather than fighting in the middle of the driving rain.

"Because she believed there was more to her than bone and blood?"

"Exactly. What would you be, Pyrre, without your blood?" She lifted her head incrementally from the deck to nod toward my neck. "I can see it beating in your veins right now. What would this fight be without blood and bone? What would it mean? If you deny all this," by which she seemed to mean everything—the blood-warm rain, the purple-gray bruise of the sky, our two bodies straining against each other, "then you deny life itself."

"We're not priestesses of life."

"You are not a priestess at all," Ela pointed out. "If, however, you manage to pass your Trial, you will come away knowing one thing: there is no death without life."

"I thought you were supposed to be teaching me about love."

Soaked through by the rain, Ela's grip was loosening on my wrist. I took a deep breath, rolled to the side, twisted, felt free for half a moment, then realized my mistake: if my hand was free, that meant that Ela, too, had an extra hand, one she used to seize my hair, then, as she rolled aside, to slam my face into the wood. I managed to twist away, but eel-quick she was on top of me, legs scissored around my waist, a tiny knife she had pulled from somewhere in her shredded dress pressed against my throat. All I could see was the slick wood inches from my face.

"What I am teaching you is this," she purred in my ear. "We are our bodies. What we do with them is what we are. This position . . ." she tapped the blade against my neck, "is almost killing. . . ."

Then, in a heartbeat, the knife was gone. She slid a hand along the side of my chin, pressed her soaking cheek against mine. "This is almost loving. . . ." Her hand shifted, taking my chin in a grip I knew all too well, one quick twist away from breaking my neck, "Almost killing again. . . ." I went slack against her grip, ready for the last, absolute blackness. She let me go, rose fluidly to her feet, crossed to the railing to stare out into the rain. I managed to prop myself halfway up to stare at her back. When she spoke again she hadn't really shed her lazy, playful voice, but there was another voice beneath it now, or inside it, something normally hidden or drowned out, a note almost beyond all hearing, felt mostly in the bones.

"Love is like killing," she said. "You do it with every part of you, or not at all."

11

Night's last mud-dark weight still sat hot and quiet on the city when someone began hammering furiously on my door. I went for my knives first, shoving aside the light sheet, snatching the blades off the bedside table, then rolling to the floor. The floor isn't generally a coveted position from which to enter a fight, but I wasn't in the fight yet, and I'd spent too much time studying the "Knock, Wait, Stab" approach to killing to go near the door with my head held high for the convenience of my adversary.

Be where you shouldn't—an old Rassambur aphorism.

The frantic hammering paused for a moment, replaced by a man's voice: "Pyrre!"

I was still bleary-eyed from sleep and aching from Ela's drubbing, but I wasn't about to give away my position. After a moment, the drumming started up again, so violently it seemed he wasn't knocking so much as trying to beat down the door. With the tip of one knife, I silently lifted the hooked steel lock.

"Pyrre," he growled again. "The commander sent me."

This time, just as the pounding resumed, I lifted the latch, then yanked the door inward. Carried forward by the force of his own urgency, a young man stumbled into the room. I tripped him with an outstretched ankle, then leapt on top, setting the tip of my knife against his throat. The position reminded me uncomfortably of Ela's lecture the night before. I could hear her voice murmuring in my ear: *It's the space between the bodies that matters.* I glanced down at the man's mud-spattered tunic, the short sword belted at his side, at my own bare legs pinning his shoulders to the floor, then grimaced. Somehow, in trying to create the *About to Kill* space, I'd stumbled into something . . . else.

The young Greenshirt—he was wearing one of the standard uniforms—didn't seem to notice my nakedness. Instead, his gaze was fixed on the hilt of the blade I'd laid against his throat, eyes nearly crossed with the effort, as though he could keep the length of steel from plunging through his neck with the power of his stare. He seemed an unlikely assassin.

"I'm going to get up," I said, trying to speak in a voice slow and calm enough not to panic him, "and I am going to put on some clothes. Please don't try to kill me."

His lips moved in some silent prayer, but he seemed unable to respond. I shifted the tip of my knife from his neck, but his stricken gaze followed the blade.

"Hey," I said, slapping him on the cheek until he met my eyes. "Are you going to kill me?"

He shook his head stupidly, slowly. "No. The commander sent me. I'm here with a message. . . ."

"Save the message," I said, rising to my feet, "until I'm wearing pants."

When I went to close the door, I found Ela leaning against the casement. *She'd* had time, I noted irritably, to slip into a loose silk bed shirt. Or maybe she'd been sleeping in it. Or maybe she hadn't been sleeping at all. Whatever the case, the priestess looked relaxed and amused.

"When I suggested you pay more attention to your body, I didn't mean you had to go at it hammer and tongs right *away.*"

"He's a messenger," I growled.

Ela just shrugged. "That's what I like about you, Pyrre. You never pass up a chance to learn."

The Greenshirt was getting unsteadily to his feet behind me. "Who is she?" he managed.

"No one," I said, slamming the door with my foot. "Who the fuck are you?"

"Anho," he managed.

I suppressed a frown. It had always seemed a unique form of cruelty, naming children after famous women and men. As though the burden of one's own proper name, one's own unlived life, were not weight enough already to crush a person. I'd almost forgotten that about Dombâng, how so many people were named for the city's founders and protectors: Goc My, Anho, Chua, Thum, Voc. It was, I suppose, one of the only ways left for the parents of the city to hold on to some of the history that the Annurians had denied them.

He stared at me, momentarily wordless, as I snatched my pants off the back of the chair, slammed my legs into them, then pulled a loose, sleeveless tunic over my head. I flicked aside the curtain to the room's single window. Off to the east, night's indigo dye was fading into dawn. "What does Ruc want so bad he can't wait till the sun's up, Anho?"

I couldn't hear Ela's footsteps retreating down the hallway, but that didn't mean anything. I hadn't heard her approach, either. Not that it mattered. It was my conversations with Ela that I needed to hide from Ruc and the Greenshirts, not the other way around.

"You have to come," he said, reaching for my wrist, intending, evidently, to drag me out of the room. Not too bright, this one. By this time, though, I'd woken up thoroughly enough not to kill him. I knocked his hand away, took him by the throat, and pulled him close. His artery throbbed in my grip, and his warm eyes went wide, but he made no move to pull away. He couldn't have been far into his twenties, just one more kid in Ruc's dilapidated army. I let up on the pressure slightly, tried to make my voice friendly, even cheerful.

"Anho," I said, speaking slowly. "Stop pounding on things and shouting and trying to drag me out the door. Just tell me Ruc's message."

His brown face was purpling toward plum. When I let him go, his words splashed out all in a single gasp.

"They hit a transport."

I frowned. "*They,* I assume, being the local insurgency, and the transport being a ship carrying more legionaries from Annur?"

His head yanked up and down in a puppet's nod.

I tried to imagine the scene. Any transport would have been carrying at least a full legion, maybe two, over a hundred armed soldiers, almost certainly veterans, if they'd been sent to Dombâng. This, against a rabble of idolatrous zealots. Hardly seemed like a fair fight.

"How many prisoners did you take?"

The young soldier gaped at me. I slapped him gently on the cheek. "How many?"

He shook his head in a mute, bovine denial, wandered his own mind a while before finding the words. "None. They're all dead."

I whistled. "No prisoners? Ruc must be less than pleased. I wouldn't want to be the legionary commander when Ruc catches up with him."

Anho stared at me. "He's dead."

I frowned. "The commander?"

"All of them. The legionaries, the insurgents. Everyone. They're all dead. Someone massacred them all."

I spent most of the morning sulking, standing at the rail of the ship, staring down into the murky water as it slid past.

The sudden, unexpected arrival of Ruc's messenger had filled me with excitement. Whatever was happening, Ruc had sent for *me.* It meant my plan was working. He wanted my perspective, my advice, and maybe he wanted me around for something more. The thrill of the night's chase through the canals of Dombâng came back to me as I followed the messenger over the causeways, then in through the iron gates of the Shipwreck—the huge, haphazard wooden fortress of the Greenshirts.

I'd given Ruc his space when we loaded up—his men didn't know me, and I didn't want to get in the way of his command. I'd stayed well out of the way as the sun rose grudgingly above the rushes and the ship fell into the creaking rhythm of oars and grumbled orders. Since casting off the hawsers, however, he'd barely glanced at me. His indifference, in fact, was so absolute that I might have stumbled onto the boat entirely by accident, an irrelevant, extra passenger fetched up on the deck.

Sick and prickly with my own disappointment, I retreated to the rail, tried on a look that seemed appropriately military and aloof, and remained there most of the morning, watching the deadly creatures of the delta slide silently past.

I'd been surprised to discover, when I first set foot outside Dombâng, that everyone else on the continent seemed to view the Shirvian River with a kind of complacent indifference. For the majority of its great arc across Eridroa, the current is easily navigable—sinuous and swift above Lake Baku, wide and strong below, broken by only two cataracts. To the people of Sia or Ghan, the river is little more than a benign, undying mule, one that can be relied on, season after season, to patiently bear the people and property of half a dozen atrepies on its broad, glistening back. Everywhere above the delta, the river is a servant.

In the delta itself, however, in the thousand braided channels that constantly threaten to strangle Dombâng, the river is a god, and not a gentle one.

Maps are almost useless. The delta is always changing and growing in unpredictable ways. Deep channels will silt up in months, become suddenly impassible. Islands that might have made reliable points of reference sink into the murk almost overnight, swallowed in mud and reeds, leaving no sign of their passage. New mounds of clotted earth are constantly cropping up where there had been nothing more than silently swirling water. Only the city's fishers, who ply the waters with their nets every single day, can stay ahead of the constantly shifting labyrinth, and even they fall prey to the delta.

Of course, Dombâng would never have grown to its current size if no one had done anything to drive the watery labyrinth back. Among Goc My's many achievements was the establishment of a corps of engineers charged with building and maintaining a reliable channel, deep enough for heavy seagoing vessels, linking the upper course of the Shirvian to the sea. The city doubled in size in a single generation, then doubled again, and again. Even as gold and silver flooded in, however, borne in the hands and hulls of foreigners from a dozen nations, there were those who whispered that Goc My had betrayed his city and her gods. *In all these years, it is the delta that has kept us safe,* they whispered, *and he has profaned the delta. He has had the hubris to try to tame it.*

From the deck of the double-hulled boat where I stood, the delta looked anything but tamed. We were following Goc My's central channel eastward, the oarsmen working with the sluggish current. From the relative safety of the deck, I could make out the slick-bellied eels twisting in our wake, the long snakes basking in the riverbank mud, the crocodiles floating silently, patiently along the river's edges, waiting for some unwary prey. Boulders broke the current's surface in some places; in others, the jagged rocks lurked just beneath, stone teeth ready to tear the bottom out of our hull. The boat's navigator perched in the bow, shouting directions back to the helmsman—*Avoid the bank there! Hard port! Slip wide of that eddy!*—who handled the tiller with one steady hand, his face lost in the focus of the moment.

Ruc didn't seem to notice any of it, not the sandbars or the crocodiles, not the deck rocking softly beneath our feet. He'd had his eyes fixed on the horizon for most of the morning, as though staring at something past the limit of mortal vision. As the sun climbed higher, however, baking the deck, glittering like a million coins on the ruffled water, I began to hear Ela's voice—smooth and sly as the priestess herself—murmuring inside my mind:

If you can't even stand the right way, you're never going to fall in love.

I took a deep breath, then turned my attention to the arrangement of the space between us. Ruc stood up in the bow, just a few paces behind the navigator, back straight as the boat's mast, scarred hands clasped behind him. In my irritation, I'd taken myself almost as far away from him as I could get, all the way into the stern, where I could lean on the rail while resting an arm over the transom.

Once I'd drummed up the courage to consider the situation, to really look at what was going on inside my own fool head, it became clear what I was doing. I had retired to the stern of the boat in the hope that Ruc would notice my absence and *follow* me. It was, I had to admit, a strange vision of intimacy, one based on retreat and pursuit, one in which the proof of his interest would lie in his willingness to hunt me down regardless of how far I fled. I could almost hear Ela laughing in my ear: *Are you a woman, Pyrre, or a little girl?* I sidestepped that question, raising my eyes to study Ruc instead.

Vexingly, he had not hunted me down, if *hunt* was even the word for a stroll of a dozen paces down an open deck. He hadn't even turned since I left him in the bow, didn't even have the good grace to seem *wary* of me. With his back turned like that, I could have driven a knife between his shoulder blades, bursting his heart before he had a chance to cry out. I'd gone to great lengths, of course, to convince him that we were on the same side. I *wanted* him to believe I was Kettral, to believe we both served the same empire, but I didn't want him to be so 'Kent-kissing *relaxed*.

How much could a man love a woman, after all, if he wasn't a little worried she might kill him?

I realized I was tapping my knife. I stopped, gritted my teeth, pushed myself clear of the rail, found my balance as the boat rolled gently beneath me. If Ela was right, then I was all wrong. There were no hot edges in the space I'd built between us, no hooks. I'd come to the far end of the boat hoping he would join me, but he hadn't joined me. I could wait, hope, pine, or I could try something different. I spared a silent curse for Eira, whose canny ways were so unlike those of the god I'd chosen, then strode forward.

I tried to feel the emptiness between us as it closed, tried to find the shape of it, the angles and edges. The first few paces made no difference, but by the time I stood an arm's length from Ruc's back, something had changed. I could feel it inside me, as though someone had tied a hair-fine invisible cord to my softest organs and was using it to pull me, gently but insistently, toward Ruc. It irritated me that Ela was right, but I didn't have time for irritation, because Ruc was turning, finally taking his eyes off the maze of the delta for the first time. Whether he, too, felt that silken tether as he met my gaze, it was impossible to say.

"We'd be there already if we had your bird," he said.

I shook my head. "There's no place to hide a Kettral in Dombâng. If we'd tried, half the city would know we were here."

For a while, he didn't respond, just looked at me, eyes warm and dangerous as the delta itself, and slightly narrowed, as though he were trying to make out the shape of some dangerous sandbar through a heavy morning fog. Unlike the rest of the Greenshirts on the boat, Ruc wore no armor, just a loose pair of cotton pants cinched tight at the waist with a rope belt, and the customary vest favored by everyone in Dombâng. He'd unbuttoned the top buttons—Ruc had never been one for starched uniforms or martial bedazzlement—and I could see an old scar carved across the muscle of his chest, one he'd acquired down in the Waist years earlier, the healed flesh smoother and a shade paler than the rest of his skin. Like everyone else on the boat, he was sweating, but unlike the Greenshirts, who looked hot and miserable in their helmets and mail, Ruc looked ready, like a fighter warm and limber for the contest to come.

I could hit him.

The thought bloomed inside me, quick and unbidden. A part of me knew it was ridiculous, but then again, it had worked when we were in Sia. I had yet to find Love's undiscovered country, but I felt certain it shared a border with a darker realm, one that I knew all too well, a land of constant struggle governed by Violence and Fury. Breaking my fist against the stone-hard muscles of his ribs might not be love, but it was some kind of intimacy, at least, the touch of skin against skin.

I shoved the thought aside.

For one thing, attacking the commander of the Greenshirts on the deck of his own vessel in front of a score of his own men wasn't likely to further my claim that we were allies. There was more to my reluctance than that, however. I could remember all too well Ela's arm locked around my throat, her whispered insistence on the tiny distinctions and degrees of all human intimacy. *Almost loving,* she murmured, her brown eyes so violently close to my own. I felt her lithe body shift. *Almost killing.*

I had already tried hitting Ruc. We'd fought each other half a dozen times, and though the violence led to several months sharing the same bed, we hadn't, either one of us, fallen in love. I could tread that path again, and easily enough, but I needed something better this time, something more. I tried to imagine how the other women of the world—women raised outside Rassambur, women trained in other arts than the cutting of throats and the ending of lives—potters, maybe, or princesses— might approach a young man standing on the deck of the ship.

I could hug him.

I couldn't imagine a more irritating vision: leaning in, pulling him close, resting my grateful head against his chest like some sort of supplicant or idiot. The thought redoubled my desire to hit him, and to resist that, I shifted half a foot away.

"If it wasn't the local insurgents," I asked finally, stepping up to the rail beside him, "then who?"

The Greenshirts had been eyeing me warily all morning, obviously unsure who I was or why I was there. A couple of the oarsmen muttered under their breath as I approached their commander, but they were too far down the boat to hear us.

"It's the insurgents," Ruc replied.

"Not what your man told me when he tried to kick in my door. Said they were all dead—both the legionaries and whoever attacked them."

"My 'man' is a terrified twenty-year-old telling you a story he heard from another twenty-year-old who heard it from a pair of fishers who were so drunk when they finally got to the Shipwreck that they couldn't stand up."

"You think they're wrong?"

"I think," Ruc said, flexing his hand, testing out the fist, "that the only people you tend to find after an ambush are the dead ones."

"When's the last time the insurgency hit an Annurian transport?"

He shook his head grimly. "Never."

"Historical moment," I said, smiling brightly.

"I'd have thought Kettral would be a little more vexed by assassination and open rebellion."

"When vexation starts making the bad guys dead, I'll look into it." I glanced down the channel, which was overhung by rushes on both sides. Tiny birds in the rushes cried their feathered fury at our passage, then fell silent. "Have you considered that this whole thing might be a trap?"

Ruc's stare was flat as the ocean before a storm.

"Let me rephrase," I said. "What are you planning to do if it *is* a trap?"

"We have ten boats," he said, gesturing to the vessels behind us. "Two hundred Greenshirts."

"There were a hundred legionaries on the transport," I

pointed out, "and according to your man, they were all slaughtered."

"That boat was vulnerable, alone, taken by surprise. When the trap slammed shut, there were no other vessels to back it up."

"Meaning, if there is a trap, you intend to row straight into it."

"Only the first boat. The others will hang back."

I glanced over my shoulder at the vessels creasing the dark water behind us.

"I can't help noticing that we're the first boat."

I wondered what degree of concern to feign. The truth was, I didn't much care if it was a trap. I'd spent most of the trip thinking about Ruc, about love, about whatever was wrong with me that meant I needed to think so hard about the first two things. I knew, obviously, that a ship full of slaughtered soldiers waited at the end of our foray, but that was nothing new: Ananshael waits, finally, at the end of all voyages, bottomless and patient as the sea. I had had a lifetime to get used to that truth, and yet it seemed that I ought to try to look . . . what?

Frightened? That couldn't be right. I'd never met any of the Kettral, but as a fighting force they were legendary, equal to my sisters and brothers. Kettral weren't likely to be scared by the thought of a little violence. On the other hand, the Kettral weren't priests of Ananshael. Death, to them, was failure. I tried to find my way into the character I'd created—a strong, fierce young woman who had trained all her life to fight for the glory of her empire, who had come back to the city of her birth to see it pacified, to make sure the job was done right. I shifted my face into a new expression, one that I hoped might approximate a resolute and unflinching civic devotion.

Ruc narrowed his eyes. "If you're going to be sick, do it over the rail."

That was the last time in my life that I aimed for an expression of civic devotion.

I turned away to hide my irritation. Our boat's navigator had taken a side channel, one far narrower than the river's main course. The current ran more sluggishly here, and the banks were closer, as though threatening to choke off the flow altogether. The small man was sweating, leaning halfway out over the boat's stem, desperate to spot the rocks or sandbars before we ran aground.

"None of the soldiers noticed they left the main passage?" I asked. "Or that the banks were getting uncomfortably close?"

"Would you?" Ruc asked.

I turned to face him once again. Despite the mounting tension, Ruc didn't scowl, didn't snarl or shout. His hands remained clasped behind his back, his face still. I knew that stillness, though. When Ruc stopped moving, it meant he was holding something back, some violence that couldn't be safely unleashed.

I liked that violence.

I moved closer to him, my mind only half on the conversation. "Of course I would. Goc My's channel is a hundred paces wide. It runs straight east-west. This . . ." I waved a vague hand at the encroaching weeds, "doesn't look anything like it."

Ruc shook his head. "You grew up here. The soldiers on that transport, most of them wouldn't know a reed snake from a rock. They trusted their pilot and helmsman."

"Good lesson, I guess, in trusting fewer people."

"This from the woman insisting I trust her."

"I said fewer people, not none."

"And you, I suppose, are one of the few?"

"I figure I've earned a spot."

It felt good to be sparring again. The verbal jabs tossed back and forth offered something like the intensity of a physical fight, but without all the fists and blood. I shifted my footing, as though we were actually back in the ring together, using the rolling of the deck as an excuse to step closer. Ruc didn't move back, but I could see the change in his posture, the way he turned at the waist to match my movement, how he unclasped his hands behind his back, let his arms fall to his side. It seemed, for just a moment, that we were dancers exploring a set of undiscovered steps. But of course we were not dancers.

Dancing was something for other people, for women who knew better the clandestine measures of their own beating hearts, who understood what it was to love or be loved. Fishers or farmers could dance. People who could barely keep time with a stick on the bottom of a barrel could, inexplicably, dance. Women whose bodies were entirely untrained, who stumbled through the most basic movements, still found a way to animate their own clumsy motion with something even I could see was true feeling.

I, on the other hand, could move through the steps of a complicated piece with relative ease—the training of Rassambur is good for more than killing—but I never liked dancing. I never *understood* it. I felt wooden when I danced, slack-limbed and pointless in a way I never did while hunting or fighting. Not that dancing was love, but it seemed the same breakage in me was responsible for my failures at both. Love, Ela claimed, was a matter of bodies, and I didn't understand my own if I wasn't doing something dangerous with it.

"Hold water," the pilot cut in, raising his hand to signal the oarsmen.

A hundred paces on, the channel twisted sharply, winding out of sight. The delta seemed unnaturally quiet when the oars finally fell still. A blue-throat croaked out its pained, discordant music somewhere in the bank off to the right, then fell silent. The sky, fat and bright with hot afternoon light, crouched low overhead. The Greenshirts behind us shifted uneasily, muttering, checking weapons. I glanced over my shoulder. The other boats were nowhere to be seen, hidden behind the last bend, holding back as Ruc had ordered, waiting to see if we would spring a trap.

I tapped gently at the knives strapped against my thighs, an old familiar eagerness rising inside me. I might not know how to dance, but this was no time for dancing. When a sluggish gust kicked up out of the north, I caught the thick, too-sweet, meaty scent of rot. There were bodies not far off, already putre-fying in the equatorial heat. I could feel the quiet, implacable grandeur of my god swelling through the air, could feel my own heart swelling to meet him, the quick, even beat of my devotion.

For just that moment, love stopped mattering. I could stop agonizing over my own romantic inadequacy. Death waited around the bend in the canal, and if the men behind me were terrified, I felt relief, a clean red eagerness to be reminded of his clarity.

12

Maybe you've stood inside a hall or private home the morning after a great festival. The guests are gone, the revelry finished, the music silent, but signs of the evening's delight remain—half-full glasses of wine, burned-out lanterns, that one scarf tossed over the back of a chair as though whoever had forgotten it might return at any moment. There's a particular feeling to an empty room that hours earlier was brimming with human life, a taste to the quiet, a melancholy. The transport ship reminded me of that.

The broad-beamed, shallow vessel was no hall, of course, and instead of glasses and scarves, we had swords, bloody organs, piles of the festering dead, but the feeling was the same: the party was over. We had stepped into a space where something singular had happened, where people had poured themselves utterly into the moment and then departed, never to return. The great celebration of Ananshael's glory was finished. All that was left was the detritus.

One of the Greenshirts vomited over the side of the transport. Another was crying quietly, staring at the scene, not even bothering to wipe the tears from his eyes. Unlike my sisters and brothers, these men were not accustomed to the aftermath of my god's passage. I tried to put on an appropriately Kettralish expression of stern regret mixed with just a touch of fury. It was hard to say if I was succeeding, but it hardly mattered; Ruc had turned away from me once more to shake his soldiers from their horror.

"Truc," he growled. "I want a dozen men on each rail, eyes on the banks. Hu, find me the pilot and helmsman, but *do not* move their bodies. Mah, divide the rest into teams of four. Search for survivors first. Check every pulse, I don't care how dead the poor bastard looks. Anyone left alive might tell us ... *VOC TAN!*" He hacked that last name through the rest of what he'd been saying like an ax.

One of the Greenshirts—he looked almost as green as his shirt—spun around, eyes wide and glazed. He'd half drawn his sword.

"Sheathe that blade," Ruc said quietly. "The next man I see with bared steel is swimming back."

"But the ..." The young soldier trailed off, gesturing to the carnage on the deck.

Ruc crossed to the soldier, put a hand on his arm. "They're gone. Whoever did this is gone. Put your blade away and get to work."

Only when the Greenshirts had scattered over the deck did he turn back to me.

"All this talk of traps," I said. "I'm surprised you're not *demanding* they have their weapons out."

Ruc shook his head, lowered his voice. "They're not Kettral."

"More reason to be ready."

"A weapon doesn't make a man ready. They're strung so tight right now they're more likely to put those blades into their friends than any of the nonexistent enemy."

"Speaking of whom," I said, turning to study the deck once more. "Still think it was your insurgents who did this?"

Even by the forgiving measures of Rassambur, the deck was a mess. The transport was a good-sized vessel, wide and double-decked, almost a barge, with just enough oars to make progress against the delta currents. A single Annurian legion comprised a hundred men, at least two-thirds of whom lay scattered across the wide planks of the upper deck, their flesh already festering in the heat. And the Annurians were not alone. As many or more of their attackers sprawled dead in the chaos, natives of Dombâng, judging by their hair and skin, by the light delta spears some still clutched in their hands. Thousands of dusk beetles crawled over the corpses, the iridescent shimmering of their folded wings bright with the late sun, furiously alive against the dull brown of the dead.

I knelt by the nearest of those corpses. The beetles buzzed angrily when I flicked them away, hovered above the body in a glittering cloud, then dispersed. The soldier had been young, barely into his third decade from the look of it. He had the pale skin and flame-red hair of Breata, more than a thousand miles away. I wondered how long Ananshael had been following him, how many miles, how many years, before choosing this moment to do his quick, inimitable work. The young man had managed to draw his sword—his fingers were still clenched around the handle—but the blade was unbloodied, while his own throat had been hacked open; the windpipe and esophagus dangled obscenely from the ruin, both of them snapped.

"Whatever he was swinging at," Ruc observed, "he didn't hit it."

"Strange," I replied, leaning closer to scrub away the blood. "He can't be what . . . twenty? Someone better with a blade—"

"He wasn't killed with a blade." I pointed to the four punctures at the edge of the wound, laid the tips of my own fingers into those gouges. "Someone tore out his throat by hand."

Ruc squatted down beside me, ran a finger along the ragged end of the windpipe, then whistled slowly. "Not cut."

"You see a lot of that kind of thing in the city?"

He studied the wound a moment longer, as though it were a mathematical problem, or a vexing phrase in a language he'd never learned to read, met my eyes, then shook his head. "No."

He glanced back at the dead soldier appraisingly. "I didn't even realize that was possible."

"For most people, it's not." I straightened up, unsure how much to explain. Some of my brothers and sisters were fast and strong enough to tear out a throat. As a child, I'd watched old blind Rong Lap plunge his gnarled, stiffened hand into the body of a sheep and come out holding the creature's still-beating heart. I'd never seen anyone else do that though, not in the rest of my years at Rassambur, and Rong Lap was a decade dead and more.

"Here!" One of Ruc's men was scrubbing vomit from his chin while waving us toward the stern. "The helmsman."

As we threaded our way through the litter of corpses, a flock of winebeaks passed overhead, dark wings spread wide, casting quick, fleeting shadows over the deck below. When they'd passed out of sight, the sky seemed suddenly still, like a great, leaden weight pressing down on the delta.

"He still has a neck," Ruc observed, when we reached the helmsman.

"Not doing him much good," I replied.

Unlike the bodies strewn everywhere else on the transport— bodies torn apart in dozens of different ways, bodies missing throats or arms, bodies with the slick ropes of the intestines ripped free of their guts—the helmsman didn't even look hurt. He lay on his back, head propped up slightly against the inside of the hull, glazed eyes staring at the sky. For some reason, the glittering dusk beetles had not alighted on the corpse, though they swarmed everywhere else on the transport.

"Maybe he's not dead," one of the Greenshirts murmured.

"He's dead," Ruc said flatly, then narrowed his eyes. "What is that?"

He squatted beside the body, took the man's jaw in his hands, and forced open the mouth. Something slick and black dangled between the teeth. I took it for the helmsman's tongue, at first. Strangulation can have that effect, but there was no sign that the man had been strangled, no bruising on his throat or purpling of his lips. Then, too, that black bit of flesh was too narrow, too pointed for a human tongue.

It twitched.

The soldier beside me jerked back, blurted out something halfway between a scream and a shout. Ruc, however, just dropped a hand to his belt knife, growled at his man to lean closer, studied that strange, black not-tongue for a moment, then drew his blade. When he prodded the thing with the steel's shining tip, it moved again.

"Soul snake," he said grimly.

I blinked. The Greenshirt beside me gasped. Ruc considered the situation a moment longer. Then, with a single deft movement, drove his knife through the snake's tail, skewering it. The helmsman's throat spasmed, as though he were still alive, were trying to swallow over and over. Of course, he was finished swallowing. The motion came from the snake trying to writhe deeper into the lungs of its host.

Ruc had it, however, and slowly, pulling with the back of his blade against that rigid tail, inch by glistening inch, he drew the creature out. It was longer than I expected, almost two feet long. Most of it must have been coiled inside the helmsman's chest, feeding. When the snake's head finally came free, the creature whirled on Ruc, yellow eyes blazing in that scaled midnight face, fanged jaws agape.

The soldier stumbled back, crying out in dismay, but Ruc just waited for the creature to strike, then caught it neatly beneath the head with his free hand. He examined the snake, as though trying to read something in that ravenous, alien gaze, then pulled his knife free of the tail and cut the head from the body.

The deck of the transport was silent for a moment, the only sound the splash of water against the hull, the twittering of blue throats in the rushes. Then one of the Greenshirts dropped to his knees, face gone gray.

"*'I saw the vipers of the waters rise up to feed.'*" He murmured the words as though caught in a trance. *"'Saw them gorge on the hearts of foreign soldiers.'"*

Ruc turned to face the soldier. People had been hanged for reciting Chong Mi's prophecy, but though it was Ruc's job to do the hanging, he didn't threaten the soldier, didn't even chastise him. Instead, he reached down, helped the man to his feet, then held out the snake's severed head. The soldier tried to draw back, but Ruc held him in place.

"Look," he said, rolling the grisly trophy around his palm. "It's just a snake."

"It's a soul snake," the man protested.

Ruc nodded. "The delta is filled with them. Do you know what they do when people aren't around?"

The man shook his head, mute.

"They crawl down the gullets of sick or dying animals, creatures too close to death to move."

"They are the delta's vengeance," the soldier managed.

Ruc shook his head. "They're trying to stay alive, just like every other beast out here. Just like us. The corpse provides food and hiding until it rots."

The Greenshirt stared at him unsteadily. Ruc held the stare.

"They're not some kind of divine scourge," he said quietly. "They're just snakes."

To punctuate the point, he tossed the head overboard. Ripples spread outward from the spot where it struck. A moment later, I caught a flash of silver-white just under the surface—some fish braving the razor-beaks of the delta birds to seize its prize.

"If the gods were here," Ruc went on, gesturing toward the lazily spreading ripples, "do you think they would choose such puny messengers?"

The Greenshirt shook his head hesitantly, his eyes still fixed on the water.

"Go," Ruc said, pointing. "Help Truc's team."

The soldier trembled, as though shaking himself awake, then finally turned to make his way down the deck.

"Just a snake?" I asked when Ruc and I had the stern to ourselves.

"Scales, triangular head, no legs—fits the description."

I sighed. "I understand that you don't want your men to panic. I understand you don't want rumors started in the city." I patted him gently on the shoulder. "But I'm not one of your men. I'm not going to start any rumors. You brought me out here to help, but I can't help if you won't talk to me as though I'm a grown woman with her own two eyes and a working brain sitting right behind them."

Ruc glanced down at the hand I'd left on his shoulder. My gesture had felt natural at first, casual, but faced with those bottomless green eyes, lost in the stretching silence, I began to feel awkward, then foolish, a girl who once again didn't know what to do with her body. I let the hand drop.

"Someone put that snake down the helmsman's throat," I said, tossing the words into the silence between us as though they might plug the gap. "You know it and so do I."

"Soul snakes crawl down throats all the time. It's what they do."

"They crawl down the throats of creatures that are *sleeping*. I doubt the helmsman slept through a pitched battle in the middle of his deck."

"He could have been dead."

I shook my head. "Soul snakes are called soul snakes because they feed on the living."

Ruc grimaced, looked past me down the deck to where the Greenshirts were still poring over the carnage. "If you want to see Dombâng burn," he growled, "keep talking."

"I don't really think I'm the problem here."

"As long as you keep talking, you are."

I raised an eyebrow. "You think if I keep my mouth shut your men will take this for a simple ambush?"

"Nothing simple about an ambush."

"Especially not an ambush with three different sides."

Ruc put a hand on my shoulder, turned me away from the deck to look out over the transom. Half of me wanted to knock that hand away, or to break his wrist. The other half hoped he would leave it there. I liked the weight of it, the strength, even as I loathed being led. To even the score, I leaned in, so close I could feel his breath on my cheek as I murmured into his ear.

"Are we being sneaky now?"

He dropped his hand, pulled back. "My men are watching."

"Your men are puking all over their uniforms."

"That won't stop them noticing your tongue in my ear."

"If they notice that, I think they'll notice there was a third faction that came to this party. A faction that killed a lot of people, then departed."

"My men aren't Kettral. They don't have your training reading a battle."

"They don't *need* to be Kettral," I exclaimed. "The Annurians are carrying swords. The men who attacked them are carrying knives and spears. But half the men on this deck were killed with someone's bare hands."

"If a soldier loses his weapon, he'll fight with his hands."

I gave him a flat stare. "Save the shit for your men. You know as well as I do that there was someone else here, someone fighting *both* sides."

Ruc studied my face, then nodded fractionally. "You think you can avoid announcing that to my entire crew?"

"Strange strategy—relying on the dimwittedness of your own troops."

"They're not dimwitted; they're young. This"—he gestured to the deck—"is a language no one taught them to read."

"Fortunately," I replied, "you and I are literate. The question is: What story are we reading?"

Ruc started to reply when a shout from one of his men cut him off. A group of them had gathered at the starboard rail, pointing toward the shore. It took a moment after joining them to see what had kicked up all the fuss. Over on the bank, just a few paces away, someone had arranged fifteen or twenty severed heads, pressing them into the mud so that they stared into the sky. They would have stared, that is, if someone hadn't scooped out their eyes. Instead of the lifeless gaze one tends to expect from severed heads, the sockets had been emptied out, then packed with dirt, faces turned into makeshift planters, from each of which grew the graceful stalk of a swamp violet, slender purple flowers dipping and nodding with the breeze.

I was alone, evidently, in finding the sight strangely beautiful.

Half the Greenshirts were cursing, vowing revenge—implausibly, it seemed to me, given how little we knew about whoever had attacked the transport—spluttering their impotent outrage. The other half seemed more frightened than angry. Hands drifted toward the hilts of swords once more, despite Ruc's orders, and several of the men were muttering prayers, old wards against the ancient anger of the delta, prayers begging the mercy of old gods, gods that, according to Annur, had never existed in the first place.

Ruc rounded on the soldier nearest him, a middle-aged man, his face marred, probably in childhood, by the ravages of the whispering sickness. He was muttering a refrain I half remembered from my life before I left Dombâng:

> Spare us, O lord of serpents,
> Spare us, O lord of storm,
> Lady of flood and fury,
> Spare us your—

"Enough." Ruc's voice was a knife of pitted iron sliced across the prayer.

The soldier stopped, stared at Ruc as though baffled, then turned to point in mute appeal at the eyeless, flowering skulls, as though the simple fact of their presence there changed everything. The rest of the men grew silent, too, scanning the banks as though they expected their own deaths to leap screaming from the reeds.

The delta met our sudden silence with a silence of its own. The wind fell still. The reeds unbowed, straightening their razor-sharp spines. The bright-winged birds that had been darting through the thickets disappeared between one instant and the next, ducked into their hidden nests or winged off somewhere else. Only the water moved, patient, silent, laving the transport's hull, as though trying to persuade it of some secret. Without the breeze the day was unbearably hot, the air thick and heavy, the sky like a damp pillow pressed down over our mouths. It seemed impossible that an entire city waited somewhere to our west, that people had managed somehow to defy the delta, to carve their own channels, to hold back the death that gathered on every side. It seemed, standing on the deck of the transport, that we had come to some alien, inhuman place, a sky-vaulted temple purged by flood and storm, sanctified with blood. I suddenly understood the desire of Ruc's baffled soldier to pray, to beg the mercy of some unseen powers.

Ruc was having none of it.

"Those are skulls," he said, pointing. "Just like the skulls inside your own heads."

By way of illustration, he rapped one of his men on the brow with his knuckles, then turned to the deck. "Those are bodies. That's blood. This is a ship. That, right there, is the bank of mud where the ship got stuck. That's the sky. Those are some reeds."

He hammered down on those blunt monosyllables as though each one were an iron nail, as though he intended, through the force of language alone, to affix this strange, silent, inhuman world back onto something we all knew.

"We're here," he went on, "because some cowardly bastards lured the transport out here and attacked it."

"But the soul snakes," one of the Greenshirts protested. "The skulls. The dead men . . ."

Ruc turned to face the man. "What about them?"

The soldier shook his head, baffled and aghast. "Something *tore out their throats.*"

I knew how fast Ruc could move, and even I was surprised when he lashed out, seizing the man by the neck. The muscles in his shoulder knotted as he half lifted his own soldier from the deck. The soldier's face darkened, his eyes bulged, but he made no move to fight back. Ruc looked past him to the rest of the Greenshirts, meeting their horrified stares with the trackless jungle of his own.

"Anyone," he said, the surfaces of the word planed perfectly smooth, "can tear out a throat."

The soldier managed a sort of strangled gargle.

"It is a matter of squeezing, then pulling." He turned his attention back to the man who had started to twitch in his grasp, shook his head, then let him drop. As the Greenshirt gasped on the deck, Ruc waved a hand at the skulls. "A child can scrape away skin, gouge an eye from a socket. A grandmother can plant flowers."

"But *why?*" someone managed.

"Because this is how they win," Ruc replied grimly. "The attack is the least of it. The murder of a hundred Annurians, good men, just like you, just coming to do a job—that is the least of it. This is a trap, but these poor fools weren't the prey." He swept his stare across the assembled men as though it were a scythe. "They were the bait."

A few of the Greenshirts glanced nervously over their shoulders, as though they expected something horrible to burst blood-toothed and howling from the leaves.

"No," Ruc went on, addressing the unasked question. "They don't want to attack us. The men—and they were men, not monsters, not the sneaking gods from the stories your parents whispered to you when you were kids—the *men* who did this don't want a single one of you hurt. They want you alive and terrified. What they want is for you to go back to the city and spread this ridiculous story. They want you to tell your friends, your brothers, your mothers that some *thing* was here, that the delta itself rose up against these soldiers."

He shook his head, disgusted, gesturing to the deck.

"All of this is fake. It is posed."

"Except the dead part," I couldn't help interjecting. "They are actually quite dead."

"But the violets," protested one of the men. His uniform was damp with his own vomit. "The soul snakes. In all stories, those are the marks of the gods. In the myths—"

Ruc silenced the man with a glance.

"Anyone who grew up in Dombâng knows the myths," he growled. "We've all heard them. Half of your parents probably still have the old idols hidden away somewhere. Your grand-parents probably still mutter the old prayers. And do you know *why*?"

He raised a brow, studying one man after another.

"Because they're scared. You'll notice the gods of our delta aren't gentle. Our myths are filled with storm and blood, poison and flood. We don't have any stories of the gods walking among us curing disease or bringing food in a time of famine. In Dombâng, people worship the old gods because they're terrified of what will happen if they *stop*."

"The gods protected the city," murmured one of the men. "When we forgot them, the Annurians came, conquered us."

"And when Annur conquered the city," Ruc asked quietly, "what happened then?"

He spread his hands, waiting. He hadn't even glanced at me, but I couldn't pull my eyes away from him. I'd never seen him like this before. Back in Sia, he'd been a bare-knuckle fighter with a love for music. I knew he could hold the attention of a room, knew he could trade barbs as quick as anyone, both in the ring and out of it, but this . . .

Standing astride the deck of that bloody transport, I realized for the first time just why Annur had made him a commander, and his speed with his fists was the least of it. He was—and I realize the word sounds slightly ridiculous when applied to a sweating soldier with his vest hanging open, his irritation scribbled across his face—but he was *regal*. Another leader would have coddled his men or belittled them.

Ruc, however, just met their eyes and set his will against the rising flood of their fear. And they believed him. I could see that clearly enough in the dozens of gazes. They were willing to forget everything they'd been told as children, all the myths they'd heard whispered of Kem Anh and her might, at least as long as Ruc kept talking. There was something thrilling about the sight.

"I'll tell you what happened," he went on, "after Annur conquered the city: it became larger, richer, and safer." He paused a moment, waiting for someone to object. No one did. "You can walk through one of Dombâng's markets and find goods from two dozen cities. If you're robbed while you're there, you can appeal to one of the Annurian courts for redress. If a block of the city burns, it's rebuilt faster than it would have been two hundred years ago. So why do people keep whispering myths of the old gods?

"Fear.

"That's what those myths are *for*, to scare people. And who benefits from that fear?" He shook his head. "Not you or me, obviously. Not the fishers or the merchants. Not the kids swimming in the canals. I'll tell you who benefits: the priests, the men and women who used to offer sacrifice to those imaginary gods, who lived in the finest temples, took first catch from the nets, who were able to seize our very children from our homes . . . all in the name of those myths. Annur defeated them, but they never forgot what they lost.

"This," he went on, indicating the carnage on the deck, the skulls with the violets planted in the empty sockets, "is their work, their attempt to take it all back. They don't have argument or policy or military might on their side. All that they have is the old stories, stories of snakes in throats and violets in eyes—those stories are their only weapon, and stories are only weapons if you *repeat* them."

He studied his men one at a time. Late-afternoon gusts tugged at his vest, his clothes. He met my eyes for a moment, then looked away.

"What happened here," he said quietly, "was treason and it was murder. It was not the work of some invisible gods."

Which all sounded reasonable, of course. The world is wide and filled with competing pantheons of gods. Every backwater town and mountain village has its own tales, its own stories, some of them even older than those of the Annurians. Not all of them can be true. If Kem Anh and her consorts really *did* rule the delta, where were they? Where had they been when Annur conquered the city two hundred years earlier? Were we really supposed to believe that they were still out there, lurking in the mud and reeds, enduring this centuries-long occultation simply because the people of Dombâng had failed in their worship? The whole tale, seen through Ruc's eyes, looked ridiculous, almost childish.

But then, there were those bodies on the deck to consider. I ran an eye over the slaughter once more, the arms torn free of their sockets, the heads wrested from the necks as if by sheer brute force. I didn't know much about the gods of the city of my birth, but I knew something of death, and whatever had made those men dead, it was something faster, stronger, altogether *better* than a group of greedy, dissatisfied priests.

We burned the transport. Ruc's men slopped the deck with pitch, then, when we were safe on our own boat, set the entire vessel alight. Hot, sluggish gusts smeared the smoke low and thick across the sky. Ash fell on our deck like snow. The Green-shirts brushed it away as though it could still burn them; covered their mouths as though they expected to choke.

"Seems like a waste," I pointed out. "The men are dead, but the transport was still good."

Ruc shook his head. "The other choice was tossing the bodies overboard, giving them to the crocs and the *qirna*."

I shrugged. "So give them to the crocs and *qirna*. The beasts have to eat, too."

I've never understood the human fascination with burial practices. Death itself is a great mystery, of course, the moment when my god's finger touches the world. But after Ananshael's work is done, the person is gone, replaced by a heap of bone, gristle, and meat. I understand, of course, the impulse to respect the dead, but I can't quite follow the argument when people start associating so much carrion with the vanished person. In Sia, for instance, they dress the slabs of decomposing meat in the absent person's finest clothes, then bury the whole ridiculous puppet under ten feet of dirt. You can see the mourners at the grave's edge, staring down into that dark well, as though they might still catch a glimpse of the person they'd loved, as though it makes sense to call that skin bag filled with bone and puddled blood *father, mother, brother*. In Rassambur, when someone goes to the god, we heave the leftovers off the edge of the mesa and have done with it.

"Is that how the Kettral honor their dead?" Ruc asked, studying me narrowly through the smoke.

I felt the old, familiar thrill blaze through me at the question, the sudden, absolute focus that comes in the moment you realize an opponent has slipped inside your guard.

"We tend to put more emphasis on staying alive," I replied blandly, trying to sound bored by the whole conversation while scouring my memory for any scrap on the Kettral view of death.

"Even Kettral die," Ruc pressed.

"If we can get them back to the Islands," I replied, "we burn them."

He shook his head. "I heard there was a burial ground. Something about a huge, black tree filled with bats."

Which was more than I'd ever heard about the Kettral or their dead, and with an alarming degree of specificity. Backpedaling, however, had never worked against Ruc. He could taste hesitation.

"You heard wrong," I said, turning away.

In the end, the crocs and the *qirna* had their feast after all. The transport burned unevenly, listed hard to port as the starboard side went up in flame, then tipped, dumping its mortal cargo into the channel. Bloated with the sun, the bodies stayed up, bobbing on the surface, some charred, some miraculously unburned, looking almost placid. The crocs, for all their ungainly weight on shore, moved through the water fast as spilled shadow, great jaws opening silently, closing around an arm, a leg, then dragging the unstruggling body down. They managed to take three or four before the *qirna* arrived, a riot of iridescent scales and teeth churning the river so violently that it seemed to boil, rendering the corpses to their constituent parts, illustrating with absolute clarity the final, undeniable point: what had once been men were men no more, just blood to stain the water red, gobbets of wet flesh, the occasional bright flash of bone.

"Sweet Intarra's light," murmured one of the Greenshirts, transfixed by the scene.

A little farther on, one of his companions shook his head grimly. "Whatever happened here, Intarra's got nothing to do with it."

13

The lanterns were already lit by the time we returned to Dombâng. Our vessel slid silently past Rat Island, through the Water Gate, beneath Bald Bridge, then up Cao's Channel toward the Shipwreck. I felt like a stranger in the city all over again as the tall teak buildings loomed above us. Threads of song twisted out from the windows and alleys to tangle in the wind, then fall apart. We'd been gone barely a day, hadn't left the delta, and yet the channel where we burned the Annurian transport might have been in a different time or a different world altogether. The hot, bright silence of that lost backwater shared nothing with the human shapes and rhythms of the city. It seemed a miracle, suddenly, that we had gone there and returned.

As our pilot leapt onto the dock, Ruc turned from the rail to face the Greenshirts on the deck. The men looked exhausted, even those who hadn't been rowing, as though the horror at what they'd witnessed were a weight they'd been carrying all day, the hot heft of it bowing their shoulders, weakening their knees. They studied their commander warily in the light of the dock lanterns.

"Anyone who speaks of what we saw today," Ruc said quietly, "will be executed. If that seems extreme, consider this: our city is on the brink of civil war. An Annurian commander was found murdered in an outhouse, and someone has been slapping bloody hands on every building in sight. The legion charged with helping to keep the peace is the same legion we just found massacred in the delta.

"At this point, most commanders would try to reassure you. They would tell you that everything is under control, that we have nothing to fear. I am not going to tell you that. Dombâng is in danger. Everyone you love is in danger. *Not* from some mythical triad of gods. The gods, if they exist at all, don't trouble themselves with our affairs. We are in danger from the very citizens we've sworn to protect. If there are riots, people will die. If there are fires, people will burn."

He slid his gaze over the assembled soldiers.

"It is your job to see that there are no riots or fires. You will do what you swore to do, which is to protect this city, and you will keep your mouths shut while you're doing it. If you're tempted to whisper something to your wives about what you saw today, to your friends, remember this: that whisper could kill them as surely as a knife in the eye. Continue the normal schedule of patrols. Continue to guard Dombâng as you have done since you joined this order. Uphold your oaths. I know you'll do this, because you are Greenshirts." He paused. "Are there any questions?"

After a moment, one soldier raised an unsteady hand. "What are we going to do? About what happened out there. About what we saw."

Ruc smiled. "Leave that to me."

I waited until all the men had filed off the boat to approach him. I couldn't quite make out his eyes in the darkness, but I could see the planes of his face reflected in the light of the dock's swaying lanterns.

"And just what are *you* going to do?" I asked.

"Talk to some people."

"Which people?"

He shook his head, then started to turn away. When I took him by the arm, I could feel his body shift, dropping toward a crouch, getting ready to throw me or to strike out. Then he caught himself, and it was over. Anticipation drained out of me, leaving behind a dry, dull disappointment.

"What do you want, Pyrre?" he asked quietly.

"I want to do the job I came here to do," I replied. His skin was warm beneath my hand. "I want to help you."

"Why do you think I brought you out to the transport?"

"The transport was the start of this, not the end."

Ruc shook his head slowly. "This started a long time before the transport. Whoever hit that boat, they might have been acting out scenes from the bloody delta ballads no one's allowed to sing anymore. The soul snakes, the fucking violets in the eyes . . ." He trailed off, shaking his head.

"So who are you going to talk to?"

He scrubbed his face with a weary hand. "We have prisoners. Men and women instrumental to the insurgency."

"The insurgency," I pointed out, "was one of the two teams that got slaughtered out there."

Ruc turned away from the dock and the lanterns, away from me, back toward the black water running silently past. The corded muscle of his forearms flexed as he gripped the rail of the vessel.

"Obviously, it is more complex than I realized. Multiple factions."

The vision of a woman with serpent's eyes blazed across my mind, then vanished, leaving me blinking in the darkness.

"You think it's just people," I murmured quietly.

"Of *course* it's fucking people," Ruc growled. "Don't tell me the Kettral sent you here to dig up a handful of missing gods."

I stared at the back of the man I had come to Dombâng to love, to kill. The reason Ruc made a good military commander was that he didn't succumb to the shibboleths and superstitions of most soldiers. If someone hit him in the face, it wasn't because the day was unlucky or he ate the wrong thing or forgot to bathe the right way; it was because he made a mistake, and once he identified that mistake, he never made it again. A fight, a battle, a city on the verge of chaos—to Ruc, they were all the same: problems to be solved, problems that sprang ultimately from people. If he could see the person, find the weakness, he could win.

I wasn't sure, however, that whatever killed the legionaries was a person.

I'd spent so much of my life in Rassambur, where men and women talked to a god daily, where they gave themselves willingly, happily into his infinite embrace. I didn't believe the old gods stalked the delta beyond Dombâng, but the thought that there might be *something* out there, something I didn't understand, something beyond the ken of mortal women and men—the notion, at least, was something I'd been raised to entertain.

Kossal had come all this way for the same reason. The old priest could be gruff and elusive, but if he believed there were Csestriim hiding in the delta, maybe he was right.

"The Vuo Ton," Ruc said finally.

I looked over at him, yanking my mind from my own thoughts.

"What about them?"

"They could have done it."

"The Vuo Ton haven't meddled with Dombâng since they abandoned it."

"Ask a pig, sometime, about the trouble predicting the future from the past."

I stared at him, trying to decide if he was joking. "I've been short on prognosticating pigs."

"Life is perfect for a pig," Ruc said. "Plenty of slops. A shed to keep off the rain. A good wallow. Every day for months a pig wakes up to the same perfect life. Sometimes for years. Then someone ties his hind legs together and cuts his throat while he squeals."

"And in this vivid analogy," I concluded, "Dombâng is the pig."

"The fact that my head's still attached at my neck doesn't mean no one's sharpening a knife."

I watched the bloody light of the lanterns play off the water as I tried to think through the idea. The thought that after more than a millennium out of sight the Vuo Ton would suddenly attack Dombâng seemed implausible. But then, *everything* about the Vuo Ton was implausible. *Someone* had murdered the soldiers and the priests scattered over the transport deck, someone fast and dangerous, someone capable of melting back into the delta without leaving a trace. I thought again of the man who had followed me through the city, the black slashes inked across his face, the way he'd smiled when I finally noticed him.

"We need to find Chua Two-Net," I said finally.

Ruc turned. "Who is Chua Two-Net?"

"A fisher, although she quit fishing before I left Dombâng. She must be fifty years old by now."

"Why do we need an elderly fisher?"

"She knows the delta."

"A thousand people know the delta," Ruc replied, shaking his head. He gestured across the canal to where a flotilla of boats were tied up for the night, bobbing quietly with the small waves, creaking against each other. "There are fishers right over there."

I shook my head. "Not like Chua. She was raised by the Vuo Ton."

"Chua Two-Net." Ruc narrowed his eyes. "I think I *have* heard of her, actually."

"She spent two weeks alone in the delta without a boat. Came out alive."

"Happened while I was down in the Waist with the legions," Ruc said. "Sounded made up."

"It wasn't."

"How do you know?"

"Because I was there when she came back."

Ruc studied me, then nodded. "I can't leave the Shipwreck

now. I'm going to be up half the night trying to contain this mess."

I wanted to grab him, to drag him with me into the night in search of Chua, but Ruc had never been one to be dragged.

"Tomorrow," I said. "I'll come here midmorning."

He nodded again. "Tomorrow."

All rivers flow toward an ocean. Which means that everything people toss in a river—all the piss and shit and rotten slop—also flows toward an ocean. If you look closely, you can see the channels of Dombâng grow fouler and murkier as you move east, but there's no need to look at the water. If you want to know what direction you're going, it's easier to take note of the buildings. All the sprawling teak palaces and bathhouses stand on Dombâng's far western end, where the channels run quick and clear. East of New Harbor the dwellings crowd together, stacked into three-story tenements that overhang the canals. Still farther east, at the city's last fringe, the tenements give way to warrens of shacks tacked up on rickety stilts, rotting docks bobbing on the water, a patchwork of permanently tethered barges. Instead of causeways, narrow planks span the gaps between platforms.

On maps, this end of the city is called Sunrise. Everyone who lives there thinks the name is a joke. You can never see the sunrise. There's too much smoke from the cook fires and not enough wind to blow it away. Clearly, the idiot responsible for the maps never visited. The people who live there call it the Weir, which sounds almost picturesque until you realize that *weir* is just another word for *trap*.

"You're going to see things here," I said, turning to Ruc as we crossed one of the wobbly bridges into the quarter, "that offend your notions of order and law."

He snorted. "I grew up in Dombâng. I've been commanding the Greenshirts for years. We send patrols into the Weir all the time."

"We're not a patrol," I pointed out. "We're not here to bring the bright light of Annurian justice. We're here to find one particular woman, ask her some questions, then get out without killing anyone."

I took a deep breath, then immediately regretted it. The Weir reeked of sewage and offal, smoldering cook-fire smoke, thick fish soup, and the hot delta peppers people mixed in with everything to disguise the taste. That smell was my childhood, and I realized, standing on the swaying wooden span of the bridge, that I was not eager to go back.

"I won't kill anyone if you don't," Ruc said.

"No promises," I replied. It was in the Weir, after all, that I'd first discovered the might and silent mercy of my god.

He shrugged. "How do we find her?"

From the top of the bridge's arc, the Weir seemed to stretch away forever, all crooked wooden roofs, dogleg canals, and shoulder-wide alleys hazy with smoke. A woman could spend a day wandering around down there and not find her way out—and that was if no one put a knife between her ribs for something she said, for something she had.

"Chua used to live on the water," I said. "She and her husband slept on their boat down in the Pot."

"I know where it is. Let's go."

I shook my head. "After she came back, she didn't have the boat anymore. Or the husband. She went as far from the water as she could get."

Ruc considered the web of brown canals stretched out below us. "Which is just how far, in the Weir? About a dozen feet?"

"A dozen feet can mean the difference between watching the crocs and feeding them."

"I thought she was too fast for the crocs."

"Everyone gets slow, if they live long enough."

"That an argument for dying young?"

"Argue all you want; death comes when it comes."

"How philosophical."

I glanced over at him, then nodded toward the warren ahead. "You grow up down there, you either become a philosopher, a corpse, or a madwoman."

"I'm glad you didn't decide on corpse."

"Who says I got to decide?"

The Weir closed around us like a net. After twenty paces, it was impossible to look back and find the bridge we'd crossed. The stained walls of the shacks threatened to shove us from the narrow walkways into the sluggish water below, and though I'd grown up swimming in those same channels, almost oblivious to all but the worst filth, my standards had changed. I'd forgotten just how vile everything was. There were no bathhouses in the Weir, no real ways to get clean. Fishers washed in the river outside the city; everyone else just lived with the stench until their noses went dead.

Almost worse than the smell was the chaos, the racket. People lived right on top of one another. Voices and bodies, entire lives spilled out of perpetually open doorways. Cook fires burned in wide clay bowls in the center of the walks. If you wanted to get anywhere, you had to step over people, around them, had to elbow garrulous mothers with children on their hips out of the path and skirt the small circles of gamblers squatting in the alleys. It was the opposite of Rassambur. Where the mountain fastness of my god was all emptiness, stone cliff, knife-edged shadow, and the stark sun, carving its perfect arc across the sky, the Weir was sweat and rot and life, ten thousand voices, ten thousand hands, all so close they seemed to press against your flesh.

By the time we reached Rat Island, I was ready to stab someone in the eye just to make a little space. The island, fortunately—the only true island in the whole quarter—was less crowded than the canals surrounding it, and for obvious reason.

There are no burials in Dombâng—there isn't enough dirt to bury anyone. According to the stories, the city's earliest inhabitants laid their dead in slender canoes, set them alight, then

shoved them out in the current. It sounds like a beautiful practice. As Dombâng grew, however, the tradition became
impractical. There would have been an armada of burning canoes
blazing through the channels every night, getting hung up on
docks, setting the wooden homes alight. The city wouldn't have
lasted a week. Instead, the dead are cremated, the very rich in
broad plazas inside their homes, everyone else on Rat Island.

Unlike literally every other structure in the Weir, the crematorium sat all by itself, ringed by a firebreak of ten paces on
every side. Four stone walls—some of the only stone walls in
Dombâng—delimited a wide courtyard. The walls were high
enough to block the sight of what happened inside, but not so
high that we couldn't see the flickering tips of the fires. I'd
climbed those walls once as a child—part of a dare—and I could
still remember the sight: five long troughs carved in the dirt,
each one filled with dozens of bodies, bundles of rushes piled
under and over the corpses. I'd watched, horrified, mesmerized,
as workers doused the pits with oil, then set them alight. *Not
so different from cooking,* I'd thought, my stomach twisting. Ash
settled over the whole island, white and silent. You could see
your footsteps in it each morning. When I first saw snow, years
later, my first thought was that it looked like the ashes of my
city's dead.

"She lives here?" Ruc asked.

I pointed to a small shack just at the edge of the firebreak.
"Like I said, she doesn't like the water."

"There are places to get farther from the water. Even in
Dombâng."

"Not if you're a fisher who's quit fishing."

Unlike most of the structures in the Weir, the door to the
shack was closed and latched from the inside. Maybe to keep
out the ash.

I knocked. No reply.

"How long ago did you leave the city?" Ruc asked after a
moment.

I grimaced. "Fifteen years."

"She could be dead by now, gone somewhere else."

"She said she meant never to go near the water again."

"People change their minds."

I knocked again, louder this time, then tried the door once more. The stench of the crematorium clogged my nostrils, coated the back of my throat, but I caught a whiff of fish congee from inside the hut. A moment later, through the crack between the door and the frame, I glimpsed someone moving.

"Chua Two-Net," I called out. "We need to talk to you. It's worth a full Annurian sun if you open the door."

Ruc shot me a glance. "Who's supplying the gold?"

"You are."

"Not the Kettral?"

"You're the one in charge of keeping the city from going up in flames. I'm just here to help." I turned back to the door, "Chua—"

The spear slid through a chink in the wall fast as a striking viper. I saw it at the last minute, knocked it aside, caught the shaft with one hand just below the head—a fishing spear, I realized, with a barbed fork rather than a leaf blade—then twisted. Usually, that would have been enough to get the person on the other end to drop the weapon, but in this case the person on the other end was strong as an ox; I managed to yank the spear a few inches out through the gap and then it was being hauled back. I wrapped my other hand around the shaft—I didn't intend to give the weapon back until I knew no one was going to stab me with it—and after a momentary struggle we settled into a stalemate.

"Well, you may be stupid," a woman's voice drawled through the wall, low and ragged, "but you're fast. I'll give you that."

"Chua," I replied. Even after sixteen years, I remembered that voice. "You want the gold, or you want to keep trying to stab me?"

"I was planning to do both."

"Time for another plan. Can we come in?"

"Let go of my spear."

"So you can stick me with it when I walk through the door?"

"Don't be an idiot. Spear's no good in here. If I'm going to come after you, I'll use the gutting knife."

I found myself smiling. "You've got a strange notion of hospitality."

"You've got a strange notion of the Weir," she spat back, "if you think pounding on strangers' doors bragging about all the money you got is a good way to stay alive."

"I don't have the money," I said, then nodded toward Ruc. "He does."

"Who the fuck's he?"

"Ruc Lan Lac. The commander of the Greenshirts."

Ruc had taken a step back when the spear snaked through the wall, but aside from that he remained still, those inscrutable green eyes of his wary, ready.

"Long way from home, Greenshirt," Chua said after a pause.

Ruc shrugged. "The Weir was part of Dombâng last time I checked."

"When was that? Don't see too many green shirts this far east."

"I imagine you don't see much of anything," Ruc replied evenly, "if you insist on talking to everyone through the wall."

"I like to know a person before I invite them into my home."

Ruc spread his arms. "Now you know me."

The spear twitched in my hands. "And you? You got the delta accent, but it's strange."

"I've been away."

"Away. Lucky for you. Why'd you come back?"

I glanced over at Ruc. "Dombâng is in trouble."

"Dombâng," Chua replied, "is a rotting cesspool sinking slowly into the delta, and one dumb girl isn't going to change that. I don't care how quick you are."

"The rotting and the sinking aren't really my concern," I said. "I'm more interested in the slaughter."

"Slaughter *is* a mite more interesting than rot," Chua conceded.

"Especially for people in my line of work."

"Which is what? Grilled meat?"

"Fighting."

"You don't look like a soldier."

"Kettral," I said quietly.

It was getting easier, each time I said it, as though simple repetition could transmute the most basic lie into truth. I wondered briefly if the same thing could work with love. I glanced at Ruc. If I just said it over and over—*I love him, I love him, I love him*—would the bare words flower into actual emotion? It might have been easier to imagine if we'd been somewhere else, *anywhere* else. Outside the ramshackle door, however, a spear shaft clutched in my hands, ash from burning bodies falling softly on my hair, love seemed as distant as the sky.

"Kettral and Greenshirts," Chua said after a long pause. "It might be fish shit, but it's not boring—I'll give you that." I felt her let go of the spear. There was a clattering and scratching, as of multiple latches being undone, and then the door swung open.

When I'd left Dombâng, Chua Two-Net had been somewhere in her middle thirties, which put her around fifty now. The woman I remembered had been black-haired, brown-skinned, brown-eyed, like most people native to the delta. The resemblance to her fellows ended there. Where most citizens of Dombâng wore their hair long and glossy, Chua kept hers shaved to a dark stubble. She'd caught me once watching her as she dragged a long knife again and again over her oiled scalp. *You want to stay alive out there,* she'd said, *you don't want hair. Just another place for the spiders to hide, another thing to tangle in the net.*

Coiled around her shoulders and arms—her body was muscled like the ropes used to tether ships in New Harbor—someone had inked dozens of serpents, red and green and black, all writhing upward, ringing her throat with a necklace of slit eyes and bared fangs, each tattooed viper arrested in the attempt to reach her face. According to the stories, she inked another every time she killed a snake, a claim that, judging from the species, meant she should have been dead a dozen times over. Chua, however, had always been defiantly alive, a character too large for the narrow alleys of the Weir, like one of the heroes who stepped straight out of the songs the old folks sang nightly around the embers of cook fires, someone as fierce and terrifying and glorious as the gods we had forsaken.

She looked like a god no longer. I recognized the snakes, of course, still hissing silently at her neck, but she'd grown her hair halfway down her back and her wide shoulders were slumped, the muscle cording her arms half melted away. The old scars from when she fought her way free of the delta raked her skin into puckered welts. Half of her face was badly discolored, a red stain spreading beneath the brown—the reminder of a fang spider bite that would have killed someone weaker. Aside from her eyes, she looked like an old woman who might have trouble on the city's more rickety walkways. Those eyes, however—bright, defiant—were the eyes I remembered.

"Never them," I said, nodding to her.

She blinked. Until that moment, until seeing her standing there before me, I'd forgotten Chua's unique salutation. In any situation, greeting or farewell, she would say those two words: *Never them.*

"*Evening, Two-Net.*"

"*Never them.*"

"*Luck out there in the rushes today.*"

An incremental nod. "*Never them.*"

No one seemed to know if it was a promise, or a warning, or a curse. No one I knew was ever brave enough to ask. I'd forgotten all about it in my years at Rassambur, but it came back to me now, as so many things had come back since returning to Dombâng.

"I don't know you," she said, studying me.

"I grew up here."

"Said that once already."

"I saw you win the New Year boat race three times."

"Eight times."

I nodded. "I was too young to remember the first five."

Chua glanced over at Ruc, chewed at her lip for a moment, looked past me, over my shoulder, then back at me and nodded. "Come in and close the door. The dead will choke you, if you breathe them long enough."

The small shack was comprised of a single room. A rush mattress lay in the corner. A woven mat, thinner, but of the same rushes, covered the rest of the floor. There was a clay bowl, half filled with the congee I'd smelled, a pitcher of water, also clay, an empty basin, half a dozen salted fish hanging from a low rafter, along with a bundle of dried sweet-reed tubers. A fire pit sat at the center of the room, but when I glanced up, I saw the smoke hole above it was closed.

The older woman followed my eyes. "I get my fires finished before they start theirs." She nodded through the wall toward the crematorium.

The space was cramped, grimy, unkempt, save for the wall immediately behind the mattress. Two fishing nets hung neatly from a series of pegs. Above them, horizontally on a wooden rack, lay a series of spears—forked, barbed fishing spears like the one I was holding. In Dombâng, fishing spears are as common as fish. Every child has one. You can see women and men on the bridges and docks any time of day, chatting idly while they wait, arms cocked, for the right moment. The spears on Chua's wall were not like those. I wasn't a fisher, but it was obvious from the smooth, clean grain, from the *qirna* teeth laid into the head as barbs, from the patterns painstakingly burned into the shafts, that these were, in the way of tools passed down from generation to generation, sacred. In a small rack below them, sheathed in snake-skin, hung three gutting knives, bone handles carved for the best grip.

The rush mats hadn't been changed in weeks, maybe months. The fire pit needed digging out. The fish stew was starting to congeal in the bowl. Those spears and knives, however, were meticulously oiled. None of the ash that had settled around the rest of the room had touched them.

"The bottom two belonged to Tem," Chua said, settling herself cross-legged on the mat by the burned-out fire.

"Who is Tem?" Ruc asked.

"My husband. He died."

And that, of course, was the part of the story I'd forgotten. Everyone had been so shocked to see Chua Two-Net come in from the delta after twelve days missing that it was easy to forget that her husband, Tem, had not come back. Part of the problem was that he had never fit easily into Chua's legend. Everyone knew that she'd been born outside the city, raised and trained in the hidden village of the Vuo Ton, that that was where she'd learned to row, to fish, to survive in the delta. It made sense.

What did not make sense was the next part. According to the story, she'd crossed prows with Tem one day, fallen in love, forsaken her home and her people, and come to Dombâng. We might have believed it if Tem had been something other than what he was . . . a reed-slender fisher with a pronounced limp and no particular renown. He could sing, he could tell a tale that would make children squeal in horror or delight, but he seemed a small person beside Chua—he was even known around the Weir as Small Tem—and so when he died, it seemed only right. Of course Small Tem couldn't survive in the delta. Of course Chua Two-Net came back. When people told the story, they forgot him.

Chua, evidently, had not forgotten.

"My condolences," Ruc said.

"Are worth less than a holed canoe," Chua replied. "Where is the gold?"

Ruc glanced at me. "My friend gets ahead of herself sometimes." He rummaged in a vest pocket. "I have a handful of silver. The gold is at the Shipwreck."

"And the fish are in the river," Chua replied, face souring.

"He's good for it," I said.

Ruc's jaw tightened, but he didn't say anything. I passed the spear across to Chua, then sat down. After a moment, Ruc joined me.

"So," the woman said, studying us. "Doom comes for Dombâng."

"You don't sound concerned," Ruc observed.

Chua croaked a laugh. "I'm not!"

"No love for your adopted city?"

"Your city's a pisspot."

"I notice," Ruc replied, voice perfectly level, "that you're still here."

"Lot of people in this world end up places they didn't mean to, places they never should have went in the first place."

Chua shifted her gaze to me as she said the words. My guts roiled. Memories choked me, as though I had breathed them in with the ashen reek of the crematorium.

"Someone slaughtered a transport filled with Annurian legionaries," I said, my voice a good deal steadier than I was.

Chua laughed. "No shortage of hatred for the legionaries in this city." She looked pointedly at Ruc. "Or for the Greenshirts. That'll happen, if you kill enough people just for believing what they believe."

"This didn't happen in the city," Ruc replied quietly. "It happened in the delta. Southeast of here."

"So the priests managed an ambush."

I shook my head. "The priests were there. Whatever killed the legionaries killed them, too."

The woman went suddenly, perfectly still. Her stare slammed into me.

"Killed how?"

"Throats torn out. Soul snakes in stomachs. Delta violets planted in the sockets of skulls. Between the legionaries and the priests who planned to ambush them, there were over a hundred people. Well over."

"All dead," Chua murmured, half to herself.

Ruc leaned forward, eyes narrowed. "How do you know?"

She turned to stare at him. "Because the Three don't leave people alive."

Low sunlight lanced through the cracks in the hut, turning the flecks of fine floating ash to flame.

"No," Ruc said after a moment. "There are no gods haunting the delta."

"How much time you spent in the delta?"

Ruc shook his head. "I don't believe that three creatures, three *anything* could slaughter over a hundred armed men."

"Oh, they don't need you to believe," Chua replied. "They just need you to bleed."

Ruc rose fluidly to his feet. "I'm done. I can hear this same shit on any bridge in the city."

"*Something* hit the transport," I pointed out quietly.

"Some*one*," Ruc insisted. He turned back to Chua. "The Lost."

She shook her head slowly, almost hypnotically, eyes fixed on something beyond us. "The Vuo Ton want nothing to do with your city. They care nothing for your politics."

"Politics," Ruc said grimly, "is just a word for people trying to get what they want. The Lost are people—I've seen them in the harbor, in the markets—and all people want things. Maybe they resent the city's spread. Annurian incursions into the delta . . ."

Chua laughed a long, mirthless laugh. "There are no incursions into the delta."

"The spread of the northern quarters?" Ruc demanded. "The causeway?"

"The causeway is a ribbon looped around the neck of a tiger. The delta could swallow your northern quarter in a single flood. If you have not lived in the rushes, it is impossible to believe how small this city is, how insignificant."

"You came here," Ruc observed. "You quit the Lost to come to Dombâng."

Chua's grip tightened momentarily around the fishing spear, as though she planned to plunge it through his throat.

"I did not come for the city. I came for a man. Now he is gone."

"Then why don't you go back?"

"Because I have no desire to pay homage to the gods who took him."

"What gods?" I demanded.

She looked at me. "If you grew up here, you know their names."

"Sinn," I said quietly. "Hang Loc. Kem Anh."

"Myths," Ruc growled. "Kept alive because they're politically useful."

Chua looked at him. "Does a myth rip out throats? Do politics pull heads from bodies, then plant flowers in the sockets of the eyes?"

"Men do, when they want something bad enough. If the Lost want the city, they'll want it weakened, divided. . . ."

"You are not listening," the woman said. "The Vuo Ton are not Lost. They know exactly where your city is. They do not come here because they do not *care*. Their lives, every day of their lives, are bent to the struggle."

"What struggle?" I asked.

"Against the Three."

"You just said they *worshipped* their gods," Ruc cut in. "That they pay homage."

Chua shook her head, as though baffled by his stupidity. "The struggle *is* the worship. The fight is the devotion."

"So these gods of yours can be fought."

The woman cocked her head to the side. "A hundred heartbeats ago you insisted the Three were a myth. Now you want to fight them?"

"What I want," Ruc said, "is to find whoever hit the transport and killed the legionaries. I think it was the Lost. You think it was these mythical gods. Either way, I'm not going to find the truth here in Dombâng. I need to go to the village of the Vuo Ton."

"You can take us," I said quietly.

Chua stared into the blackened ashes of her fire pit for a long time, then shook her head. "I escaped the delta enough times. I do not intend to go back."

Ruc's jaw flexed. "The Greenshirts will pay you five Annurian suns," he said at last. "In addition to the one already promised for this meeting."

I shook my head, cutting in before Chua could respond. "Five hundred golden suns."

Chua's eyes narrowed. Ruc blinked, then began to shake his head. "No guide is worth a fraction—"

"There *is* no guide," I said, riding over him, "who can take us to the Vuo Ton. You know that as well as I do."

"I will not go into the delta again," Chua said. "Not for any pile of gold."

I turned away from Ruc to meet her eyes. "The gold is not just gold."

She studied me. "The coins . . ."

"Are miles," I concluded. "They are the distance you can put between yourself and this delta. With five hundred suns, you can take a ship to Annur, or Badrikas-Rama, or Freeport. In Freeport, there are no snakes, there are no venomous spiders. Snow falls every day of the year; men and women live underground, warmed by the fires of the earth. People there have never *heard* of the Three."

When Chua finally responded, her voice was dry as a husk. "And what would I do in Freeport?"

"You would *live*. Instead of hiding inside the furthest shack from the water, suffocating beneath the ashes of the dead. You could be free."

"The only work I know," she said, hands closing and unclosing around the spear, "is the work of the delta."

"You're not *in* the delta," I said. "And with five hundred suns, you won't *need* to work."

Chua looked down at the spear in her hands, began tracing the markings, as though she were a child learning her letters, as though an answer was written there somewhere, if only she could read it.

"If the money's not enough," I said, "there is the other thing."

She glanced up at me. "What is the other thing?"

"I believe in your gods," I said quietly, ignoring the irritation pouring off of Ruc. "I grew up here, in the Weir, and so they are my gods, too."

"Your belief changes nothing."

"It might when I kill them."

Chua shook her head wearily. "They cannot be killed. The Vuo Ton train their entire lives to fight against them."

"The Vuo Ton are an inbred population of several thousand with no access to modern weapons, no access to explosives, no access to birds of prey large enough to devour a croc in a few bites. The Kettral are the best fighting force in the world."

"The delta is not the world," the woman said. Still, there was a brightness in her eyes that had not been there before.

I shrugged. "Maybe you're right. If so, I'll be rotting on the river bottom while you're sitting on the deck of a small mansion on the Breatan coast a thousand miles from here. If *I'm* right, whatever killed your husband, whatever ripped out the throats of all those legionaries, will finally learn what it feels like to die. I'm not alone. There are other Kettral with me, Kettral bent on finding your gods and destroying them. You just have to go back out there one more time."

The woman closed her eyes. "The Vuo Ton might kill you. They might offer you to the gods."

"Not your problem."

"We might not even reach the village."

"A thorn spider might bite you in your sleep. You want to die in here, hiding, or out there, trying, at least, to get free?"

She opened her eyes. "Five hundred Annurian suns."

I nodded.

"You will wish you never went out into the delta."

"I have a lot of wishes," I replied, glancing over at Ruc. He sat motionless as an idol skewered by the low bars of sunlight. "I'm getting used to not having them come true."

14

There were tracks in the fine, white ash outside Chua's shack—bare feet approaching the southern wall, then departing the way they had come. As promised, Kossal had been trailing me, watching. I scanned the ramshackle buildings ringing the crematorium, but he knew his work well enough to stay out of sight. I wondered if he'd been on the boat somehow, when we'd found the transport. It seemed unlikely, but he wouldn't have made a very good priest if he'd restricted himself to the realm of the likely.

Ruc didn't notice the tracks. He didn't seem to notice me, either, as he stalked away from Chua's hut, then through the alleys of the Weir, eyes fixed straight ahead as he threaded his way between drunks, fishers, and orphans. One grubby kid of maybe ten or eleven tried to lift the knife Ruc wore at his belt. Ruc caught his wrist and tossed him into the canal without breaking stride. He only stopped when we emerged from beneath the overhanging roofs into the open space of the Weir's harbor.

The sun had sagged beneath the peaked roofs to the west. Cramped shacks stretched their shadows across the darkening water. Unlike New Harbor, which was deep enough for the proud-masted, oceangoing merchant vessels, the Pot—the local name for the harbor, really just a collection of docks around the fattened backwater of one of the canals—was a mess of canoes and hide coracles, half-sunk rafts, permanently tethered craft that no sane person would trust out in the delta. People had begun lighting their lanterns, hanging them from long poles. The red of the lanterns was the sunset's red, as though someone had stolen that horizon-wide light and sealed it inside the carcasses of dead fish.

Ruc had his back to the nearest lanterns, and a shadow fell like a mask across his face. Red limned the hard line of his jaw, the muscles of his neck, but I could barely see his eyes.

"Five hundred suns?" he asked.

I shrugged. "Cheaper than seeing the whole city burn."

People jostled us, but Ruc's face kept away the beggars and thieves. Since the transport, something had changed inside him. He'd always been a fighter, a soldier, but there had been music in his violence, a sly wit in his voice, even when he wasn't smiling. Another man, one with less curiosity and more anger, wouldn't have spent the last few days bantering and sparring with me. I'd been counting on Ruc's love of adventure when I decided to return to the city. The man I'd known from Sia liked taking chances; he thrived on it. I was starting to worry, however, that after what we'd seen on the transport, Ruc was done taking chances.

"You think she can find them?" he demanded.

"The Vuo Ton?" I cocked my head to the side, trying to get a better look at his face. "Or the gods?"

He turned to me. "There are no gods, Pyrre. Or if there are, they don't give a shit about us."

I fought down the urge to reach out, seize one of the anonymous bodies that kept passing, offer the person to the god, and *show* him Ananshael's might. My Trial, however, didn't allow killing for the sake of theological argument, and Kossal was still out there, watching. Besides, Ruc wasn't talking about Ananshael.

"How do you know?" I asked, keeping my voice mild.

"Wrong question."

"Seems to me the woman asking gets to decide what she asks."

He shook his head. "Ask all you want. Still the wrong question. Might as well ask me how I knew you were gone."

"I'm right here."

He shook his head. "That morning back in Sia, all those days after."

I took a slow breath, steadying myself. "Just because you don't see a thing, doesn't mean it's not there."

"Is that right?"

"I might have been."

"Might have been *what*? Hiding just out of sight? Following me around?"

"Good Kettral practice." I'd meant it as a joke, but the line landed like a dead eel on the deck.

"I *could* have thought you were coming back," Ruc continued after a moment. "I *could* have believed you just stepped away unexpectedly for a day or two, forgot to leave a note, that you were going to climb back any night through my window and into my bed. I could have believed that just the same way that everyone in this 'Kent-kissing city thinks their gods are going to come back and save them.

"But that wouldn't have been reasonable, would it? I wasn't asking myself why I should believe you were gone—that would have been an insane question. The sane question was why I should believe you were coming *back*.

"I did ask myself that one. Asked it more than once. And do you know what I told myself?" He drove the last two words like nails into my silence. "She's *not*."

His hands hung slack at his side, but he was ready to fight, eager. I could feel my own pulse pressing at the vessels of my neck, the eagerness woven through my own flesh. *Eagerness for what?* I wondered. To feel him pressed against me, fucking or fighting, his elbow locked around my neck, my fingers binding his wrists. It had been like that in the ring and in his bed; hot and cold all at once, dizzying, euphoric.

But not love, I reminded myself, then wondered if I was right.

Maybe love was just this: the fury, the delicious anticipation, the release. I wanted to scream, clenched my teeth hard around the sound tangled on my tongue, pouring up through my throat. When I finally spoke, it was only two words, two quiet syllables to set against his own.

"I *did*."

"On a mission."

"A mission I requested."

His green eyes were black in the shadow. When he moved, they glinted red. "Why?"

The bold answer was obvious, laid out before me naked for the taking: *Because I wanted to see you. Because I needed you. Because I love you.*

I couldn't say it.

The problem wasn't the lie; I'd lied to Ruc about a dozen things since returning to the city. I couldn't say the words because I was afraid of them, afraid that once I'd shaped them on my tongue, laid them on the air between us, that I wouldn't be able to live up to them. As long as they remained unspoken, they could be denied, disowned, but saying a thing gives it strength. What if the story I told about myself proved more vibrant than the life I'd lived? What does it mean, when the lies one tells about oneself are brighter than the truth?

"I was curious," I said finally, loathing the word—its vagueness, its smallness—even as I spoke.

"Curious?"

"About you. To see if you'd changed."

He turned away, back toward the Pot. "Everyone changes."

I shook my head, put a hand on his arm. It was a dangerous position, overextended. If he tried to break my elbow, it would be hard to stop him. I left it there anyway. "You seem the same."

"The same as what?" He didn't even glance at my hand. "You didn't know me then, and you don't now."

The words hurt. I wondered if that was a good sign, if the

pain and shame were handmaidens to something more. It seemed possible. Or maybe the pain was just pain.

"So tell me," I said, "what I don't know."

"There's a list."

"Tell me what you want. What you believe."

I hoped he would say something about me, but that door, open momentarily, had swung silently shut while I groped hopelessly for the right words. When he spoke, it was with his customary calm, that perfect reserve, the wry glance that was his best defense.

"What I want is justice.

"What I believe is that *people* killed those legionaries and priests. Not gods. Not monsters from the delta. People. I want to find them and I want to stop them before they do more and worse."

The words left me hollow, cold. They were noble enough, sure, but I would have preferred his rage, would have preferred him to roar at me, to try to break my hand, which was still perched like a brainless bird on his arm, than that impossibly distant civic devotion. Of course, preferring a thing doesn't make it so. I exhaled slowly, silently, feeling my excitement drain out with the air, turned my attention back to the dull business of massacres and lost gods.

"If you believe that," I said finally, "if you believe the Vuo Ton are really behind the attack on the transport, then going to find them is like laying your arm in the croc's mouth. If they're the enemy, they'll kill us the moment we arrive."

"Maybe."

"Maybe?" I shook my head. "You're not a fucking idiot, Ruc. There's something you're not telling me."

"And because I'm not an idiot, I'm going to continue not telling you."

"You still don't trust me," I said wearily.

He shrugged. "You haven't tried to kill me yet. And I've given you chances."

I shook my head. "But it doesn't matter. You don't trust me."

"Would you?"

It was a vexingly good question.

I *was* lying, of course, doing everything I could to see his city burn just for the excuse to be close to him. He was smart to distrust me, but surely love, whatever it was, transcended being smart. In all the songs and plays, lovers were forever ignoring the sensible, pragmatic course, spurning the advice of friends and family, ignoring a thousand signs and signals that whispered *stop, go back*. Most of the time it seemed that love was inextricable from bad judgment. Any love that left the rational mind intact seemed a weak, watery thing, not really love at all. And Ruc's rational mind was still very much intact. Of course, so was my own, and I was the one who needed to feel the emotion.

I let him go, spread my hands, as though inviting an attack. "If I'm lying, if I'm not Kettral, then what do you think I'm doing here?"

"I don't know," he replied after a pause. From someone else, in another situation, the words might have been an admission, even a capitulation. From Ruc, standing on that dock beneath those lanterns, they were a wall, a fucking fortress.

Out in the harbor, hulls rocked on the small swells. A polyphony of discordant voices filled the night: a woman screaming over and over, demanding that someone—a lover, a child—just leave her alone; the rumble of old men grumbling into their clay cups; shrieks that might have been fear or delight; so many lives crammed so close together. Down below us, on a long, narrow barge, a group of children were playing a game involving dice and a knife, chanting the same refrain between rolls:

> *One for your heart,*
> *Two for your eyes,*
> *Three for the ones*
> *Who will weep when you die.*

Four for your limbs,
Five for your lies,
Six for the ones
Who will laugh when you die.

Dead Man's Dice, we called it when I was a kid, or sometimes just Bloody Cuts. I remembered playing in the alleyway a few streets over from my shack, the quick, eager thudding of my heart as the dice flew, the scramble to grab the knife, the hot, warm wash of the blade slicing my fingers when I failed. I never really liked Dead Man's Dice, but every night I could I snuck away to play.

Caught up in the chant, seized by some impulse I couldn't quite explain, I turned to Ruc.

"Come with me."

He didn't move. "Where?"

"Not far. Just the other end of the Pot."

I thought he was going to refuse, but after a moment he nodded, sliding away from the wooden railing smooth as a shadow. We didn't talk. The night was crammed enough with voices without us adding our own. The wooden walkway swayed and creaked beneath us. I wondered if I was making a mistake as I led the way out onto an empty rotting dock.

I could make out a man's voice on a gill-netter across the way, singing the refrain to one of Dombâng's love songs, a simple, antique piece. The fisher didn't seem to know the verses, only the refrain, and he worked through the same handful of notes again and again, rising above the tonic, falling below it, then returning to that base note over and over. The music reminded me, for some reason, of a bear cub I'd found years earlier in the Ancaz. His mother had been killed by rockfall, her hindquarters utterly crushed. The poor, baffled cub kept wandering a few feet away, then coming back to nuzzle at his mother's fur, wandering away, then coming back, as though in the whole vast world he could think of nowhere else to go.

I pointed across the Pot to a line of dilapidated shacks canted precariously toward the water.

"That's where I grew up."

I didn't look at Ruc. After a moment, I stopped looking at the shacks, too. I had not intended to come back.

"Why are you showing me this?" Ruc asked after a while.

I shook my head. "I don't know."

"Why did you leave?"

"I was finished."

"Your parents?" Ruc asked.

"Dead."

"I'm sorry."

"Don't be." I hesitated. "I was the one who killed them."

Lanterns swayed, as they had swayed all evening, from the poles at the sterns of the boats. The current tugged at the vessels with slender, undeniable fingers, the same tonight as on every other night. You say a thing, sometimes, that you expect to change the world. When the world doesn't change, it's hard to know what to do next. Ruc didn't respond, so I plunged ahead, my own story closing over me like the river, warm and welcoming and rotten.

"My father came here from the north, from Nish—I inherited some of the lightness of his skin, his eyes. He was rich when he arrived, a merchant. He met my mother, married, they had a child, lost him. I don't know my brother's name; they never spoke it. My father blamed himself, blamed my mother, blamed the entire world, started drinking *quey*. By the time I was born, he'd lost his fortune. Their house at the western end of the city was gone. The only home I knew was here.

"He'd come home at nights, hit me if he could find me. Hit my mother. He kept the knife for himself, though. After he'd bloodied my lip or blackened her eye, he'd go out on the dock and drag that knife over his skin again and again. I never knew if he was doing penance for hurting us, or for losing my brother, or for ruining his own life. Probably for all of it."

I fell silent, gazed out over the harbor into the hot, cramped chambers of my past. When Ruc put a hand on my shoulder, I almost hit him. I felt like that child again: lost, terrified, broken-hearted.

"My mother tried to save him," I went on, finally. "I came home one day from scavenging in the canals to find my father gone and a strange man in our shack.

" 'Who's this?' I remember asking.

"At first my mother didn't meet my eyes. 'He is a priest.'

"That word, *priest,* sent a thrill through me. Priests were secret and powerful. It was like learning we had a stash of gold hidden somewhere in the house. Only we didn't have gold. The only thing we had was me."

Ruc made a sound in his throat that might have been a growl. His fingers tightened on my shoulder.

"The priest smiled, gave me something to drink, told me I was going to save my family. When I woke up, I was alone in the delta, a sacrifice to the gods."

"How did you survive?" Ruc asked.

"Luck," I replied. It was partly true. I left out the golden eyes, the woman with the scale-black hair. For all I knew, she was no more than a nightmare.

"I realized something about life then: it's not always good. People hold on to it because they don't know anything else, like Chua refusing to leave the city even though she loathes it. She just needs a little help, a little nudge, something to show her another way. So did my mother and father. They were just worshipping the wrong gods." I shook my head. "They didn't need Kem Anh and her consorts. They needed Ananshael."

Away over the water, the fisher was still singing the same handful of notes over and over, as though there were no other in the world.

"When I got back to the city, I killed them both. It was so easy. They were asleep. His arm was wrapped around her. They looked peaceful, in love. I couldn't understand why I hadn't done it years earlier."

It was strange, I thought when I finally fell silent, that so many days—an entire childhood—could fit in so few words.

"And then what?" Ruc asked quietly.

"I found the Kettral," I replied. After so much truth, the lie caught in my throat like a broken bone.

"Why are you telling me this?"

"I'm not sure," I said. Then, after a moment, I shook my head. "No. I'm telling you because I want you to know."

"Most people would try to hide a story like that."

"I've been hiding it for a long time."

I stepped closer to him, close enough that I could finally see the planes of his face beneath the shadow, the movement of his eyes. He didn't pull back when I put a hand on his chest, didn't even tense. His skin was warm in the warm night air. I could feel the strength waiting in the muscles beneath.

"I want you to kiss me," I said, the words barely breaking into breath.

He didn't move. Didn't flinch or lean in. Across the canal, the fisherman followed the sad notes of his song out and back, out and back. Ela's voice whispered in my ear: *It matters how you hold your body.* I shifted just slightly, following some instinct older than my own perseverating thoughts, moved marginally closer to Ruc, faced him more directly, and this time he moved with me, one hand slipping behind, sliding up my spine, closing firmly on the back of my neck, and drawing me slowly, inexorably forward.

I was shocked at how much I remembered, details I'd thought I'd forgotten flooding back: how he kissed the way he fought, patient and implacable both; the tiny chip in his tooth that my tongue always seemed to find; the vibration of his chest beneath my hands as he half growled, pulling me closer; the way his skin smelled of salt and smoke and something else I'd never quite been able to place; how he didn't ever close his eyes. I could feel my own body responding, loosening and coiling at once, something that might have been hunger uncurling from my stomach up through my throat, through my tongue, and down into my legs.

When we finally broke apart, I felt like a marionette with half its strings cut.

"Does that mean you trust me after all?" I managed.

We'd shifted as we kissed, turned toward the lanterns, so I could see his eyes when he replied, green and alien as the delta we'd just survived. "No," he said quietly. "It does not."

Across the canal, the fisherman had finally fallen silent. Maybe his nets were furled and tucked away, or maybe he was still over there, working in the darkness, but had grown tired of the song.

15

I took the long way back to the inn.

Ruc split off from me just west of the Weir, returning to the Shipwreck to begin preparation for our second foray into the delta. I could have carried on, following the series of islands and bridges that flanked the northern side of Goc My's great canal, but instead I wandered south, reluctant to return to my bed, to the dreams that so often came with sleep. After being so close to Ruc, after feeling his body pressed against me, his lips on my own, I needed time to be alone, to try to understand what had happened, what it meant.

Not that I was truly alone.

I didn't see anyone behind me when I glanced over my shoulder, but those had been Kossal's footprints in the ash outside Chua's shack. If there is one thing the priests of Rassambur do as well as killing, it is stalking. Which meant Kossal had been watching me and Ruc down by the Pot. He had witnessed our kiss. Maybe he'd even been listening as I poured the story of my childhood out into the hot night. Ela had told me, that first night back in Rassambur, that the two of them would decide in concert whether I passed the Trial, which would mean deciding whether or not I was in love. I wondered what Ruc and I had looked like in the ruddy lamplight, his hands tangled in my hair, mine on his chest. From inside my head, the whole thing was baffling.

I turned deliberately in place to study my back trail. I'd been strolling alongside one of the smaller canals—I couldn't remember its name—following the wooden walkway that hung out over the water on posts cantilevered from the walls of the buildings. It was only a few feet wide and I could see back twenty or thirty paces, to where it doglegged, following the canal out of sight. There were only a few people behind me, all of them in loose pants and vests, none even vaguely disguised, none that could be Kossal. I wondered whether he'd gone home early. It seemed unlikely.

Down in the canal itself, a few thin-waisted minnow boats parted the dark water. A rower stood in the stern of each, propelling the vessels forward with a long oar set in the transom. They were far enough away from the walkway and the red hanging lanterns that I couldn't make out faces, could barely even see the shapes. One of them might have been Kossal; there was no way to tell.

Not that I had anything to hide from my Witnesses. Still, if you're being followed it's nice to catch a glimpse of the pursuit every so often. I thought of the crag cats that made their home high in the Ancaz, lithe, fast predators that moved over the stone like the shadows of clouds. Being followed, when you can't see what's following, starts to feel a lot like being hunted. I tapped my knives through the fabric of my pants, shrugged the tension out of my shoulders, and kept moving. What had I learned, after all, in my years at Rassambur if not that simple fact: we are all hunted, always. No one hides from Ananshael.

A quarter mile farther on, I reached a wide span bridging the canal, the graceful arch hung with fish-scale lanterns and crowded with merchants' booths, all of them bustling with traffic. Bridges, in Dombâng, serve the same purpose as market squares in most other cities; they're places to meet, to trade, to gossip. Given the delta heat, most of that trade and gossip happens after dark. I slowed as the crowd clotted, let the human current nudge me this way or that. It felt good to be around people who didn't know me, whom I didn't know. People I had no need to love.

The hum of a hundred conversations washed over me, loud but indistinct, the way sound is underwater. I passed a woman selling flat-fin heads from wide rush baskets. The eyes of the fish bulged wide and accusing. Their jaws gaped, revealing twin rows of needle-sharp teeth. I imagined Ruc's severed head set among them on the rushes. His green eyes locked on me, glazed and serious. I could read nothing in the gaze.

A few stalls down from the fishmonger, a blind man was hawking squeezed rambutan juice. I gave him a copper for a cleverly folded leaf filled with the stuff. It slid down my throat, warm and sweet, but somehow it seemed like cheating to have the juice without shucking the fruit, without working around the hard, unyielding seed at the center.

I had just tossed the leaf into the canal when a conversation resolved out of the general hum, a few women muttering to one another a few paces behind me.

"The goddess," one hissed, her voice low enough I knew she wasn't talking about Intarra, "was never *gone*. She was only *waiting*."

"All these years? For what was she waiting?"

"For *us*."

"We've been here all along," a new voice cut in, tired but caustic. "Our mothers before us and their mothers before them, and where was Kem Anh *then*?"

A chorus of hisses and hushes half smothered the end of the goddess's name, but the speaker remained undeterred.

"Speaking her name's no crime. Never has been."

"Close enough," the first woman growled.

"Fish shit. I'll talk all I want. It's *worship* the Greenshirts won't stand."

I turned fractionally, just enough to catch sight of the women. They were older than I'd expected, probably into their seventh decade, backs stooped, hands twisted into claws—the reward for years tossing and hauling nets. They weren't part of any organized insurgency; their loose, foolish talk out here at the

base of the bridge for everyone to hear was proof enough of
that. They might have seemed harmless—a few old women
gossiping in the way of old folks everywhere—and yet, if rumor
of revolution simmering in Dombâng had reached even these
utterly unconspiratorial women, if they were invoking the name
of Kem Anh here in the open, then Ruc's hands were about to
be very full indeed.

I smiled, nodded to them, then winked.

They stared at me, gap-toothed and mystified.

"She rises, sisters," I whispered, stepping closer. "Just
yesterday, deep in the delta, the goddess and her consorts slaughtered a full Annurian legion."

The shortest of the three—a woman with a sagging face but
shrewd eyes—proved to be the boldest. Finding her voice first,
she hissed at me, "How do you know? Who *are* you?"

"A friend," I replied. "A loyal daughter of Dombâng." I
pressed her hand between mine, let my fingers linger around
the cool, papery skin, then winked again and melted back into
the crowd.

I lost sight of the women almost immediately, but found that
I couldn't stop thinking about them. Their conversation should
have been reassuring. It meant that my graffiti was working.
Rumor was spreading. The insurgency was starting to reach out
past its secret councils and cabals into the very streets. Ruc
needed me now, or thought he did, which was just as good. It
was all happening fast, faster than I'd dared to hope, and yet
that speed gave me pause.

The bloody hands were mine, of course, as were the corpses
beneath Goc My's statue, at least in a way. I'd set out to remind
people of Chong Mi's prophecy, and I'd succeeded. I expected
the city to rise slowly to a boil, but I had not expected someone
else to pick up my work reenacting the prophecy, certainly not
someone so viciously efficient. The vision of those severed heads
of the delta violets swaying lazily in the breeze, filled my mind
once more.

I saw a thousand skulls, a thousand eyeless skulls,
The meat of their minds made mud for the delta flowers.

It had been barely five days since I spent the night painting the city with my palms. Who could have arranged a hit on the transport in five days? My sisters and brothers in Rassambur would have been hard-pressed to manage such a strike.

I glanced over my shoulder, half expecting to catch a glimpse of the tattooed Vuo Ton. Of all the people in Dombâng, only Kossal, Ela, and that unnamed man from the delta knew what I had done that night. If Ruc was right, if he had returned to his hidden village and told them what he'd seen, it was just possible that they might have managed to ambush the transport.

Except there had been no corpses of the Vuo Ton on the deck. However deadly they were, however ruthless, however capable in the delta, I couldn't believe they could tear apart over a hundred foes and disappear with no casualties. They might have carried their dead away with them, of course, but there was still the matter of the wounds I'd witnessed on the ship. Could the Vuo Ton have ripped out so many throats with their bare hands? It didn't seem likely.

Events had outpaced my expectations, dramatically outpaced them. In other circumstances I might have tried to slow things down, to stop scheming long enough to understand what was happening. There was no time, however, to stop scheming. I was eight days into my Trial—over halfway—and I had yet to fall in love.

The kiss on the dock had been hot with promise, but I needed more than promises. If the murder of a hundred Annurian legionaries and local priests could lead to a kiss, what kind of emotion might come from a riot? I imagined me and Ruc tangled in each other's arms, the sheets soaked with our sweat while somewhere below the insurrection surged to open battle in the streets. I imagined pinning his arms above his head while the

Greenshirts and legionaries faced off against Dombâng's secret priests and their faithful. I imagined him inside me while the city crumbled. It was ludicrous, obviously. If the Greenshirts were fighting, Ruc would be there with them, and yet somehow, in some way I still can't quite put into words, I felt as though the city had become a part of me, had *always* been a part of me, one I had forgotten in my long, sky-blue years at Rassambur.

Dombâng's dark, sinuous canals had run silent, somnolent, unnoticed in my blood. Her songs trembled in my tongue. Like the city of my birth, I had been busy, but complacent. When I closed my eyes, I could see the truth: for my own heart to catch fire, Dombâng would need to burn.

Goddesses and gods are less practical than haberdashers and fishmongers; they don't tend to hang signs over the doors to their establishments, for one thing. The devout, it is assumed, will find their way. They will recognize the lineaments of their religion in the angle of a roof or the fluting of a wooden column. They will recognize the scent of the burned sacrifice, the incense or meat turning slowly to ash.

I didn't recognize the temple that I stumbled upon sometime well past the midnight gong. I certainly hadn't searched it out. I hadn't been searching for anything during my long, meandering walk back toward the inn. I wanted to be alone, to taste the air, to interrogate the details of what had happened with Ruc, to try to make sense of Ela's inscrutable lessons. I might well have kept on walking half the night—roaming over bridges, following the creaking wooden walkways suspended above the canals, threading my way through crooked alleys—had it not been for the singing washing out from between the open teak doors.

The single female voice wasn't particularly good—rough and threadbare, tired, ever so slightly off key—but it was unique. In the way a face can be striking without approaching beauty, that voice was striking. The woman wasn't singing a complicated piece, more chant than melody, a low, plangent drone, the kind of music that doesn't dance but leans against the ear, against the chest, the long notes coming like winter waves against the shore, patient, laving away the sand in slow, inexorable degrees. It was only after listening for a while that I noticed the wooden trellis arching over the tall open doors, oiled wood spilling over in a cascade of night-flowering ghostblossom. Carved into the door itself, almost obscured by the tendrils and blooms of the plants, was a low relief, a wooden heart held in a wooden hand. I had come—following some long-forgotten memory or stumbling along in the footsteps of blind chance—to the temple of the goddess who so steadfastly denied me: Eira, the Lady of Love.

Like a moth wandering mindlessly toward the candle's flame, I stepped inside.

I saw the swords first, twin blades flanking an aisle just within the open doors. The hilts were sunk into marble pedestals, and the points—waist high—stabbed straight up toward the vaulted ceiling above. White light from the scores of glass lanterns hanging above turned the steel of the naked blades to ice. Beside each weapon stood an acolyte in a red robe, each holding a white silk cloth slashed with dark lines. I took those lines for ink at first, some kind of pattern. Then, as my eyes adjusted, I realized it was blood.

"Be welcome, sister," murmured the nearer of the two figures, a young, gawkish woman who reminded me of one of the skittish delta birds. Without raising her eyes, she gestured to the sword at her side. "The goddess harries. . . ."

She paused, obviously waiting for me. It wasn't hard to figure out what was required, and after a hesitation of my own, I ran my finger along the blade. It was sharp, so sharp I almost didn't feel my skin part. The blood welled a moment afterward, a neat red line, jewel-bright in the light of the lanterns. The woman stepped forward, took my hand in hers, and wiped the blood away. Then the other acolyte—rounder and sturdier than his companion—approached, dipped his own muslin cloth into a small bowl of ointment, took my hand from the woman, and wiped it clean. The salve's cold soaked into my skin, erasing the pain.

"The goddess harries," the man intoned, his head bowed, "and she heals."

The woman wiped my blood from the gleaming blade, both of them returned to their original posts, and that was that. For the price of a few drops of blood, I had entered the sanctuary of the goddess of love. I glanced over my shoulder, studying the sword. I don't know what I expected of Eira. Maybe a huge room filled with pillows. Different behavior from the people at the door. Hugging? A chaste kiss? Less blood, probably; fewer swords. Of course, Rassambur's tidy gardens and whitewashed walls, the espaliered fruit trees and deep wells, the utter absence of bloody corpses or fountains of blood should have taught me long ago the ways in which we misunderstand the faith and devotion of others.

I turned back to the hall, a high, graceful nave supported by carved pillars. The altar at the end stood empty—it was almost midnight, after all. The singing I'd heard came from one of the small chapels flanking the nave. The singer knelt in prayer before a single candle, long black hair flowing water-smooth down her back. I watched her for a moment, then took a seat in one of the pews facing the altar. I tried for a while to imagine the type of service that might be held here during the day, the shape and nature of this worship, then gave up. In a full day of speculation I never would have guessed the sword at the door. Instead, I knelt, closed my eyes, and while the singer traced the lines of her melody across the passing night, one note at a time, I offered up a prayer to Eira.

It began unpromisingly.

Goddess, I said silently, *I've always thought you were a bitch. You're a picker, a chooser, a player of favorites. Ananshael comes for us all, eventually, but you? Some people go their whole lives barely catching sight of you. While you're busy lavishing love* on one woman, surrounding her with family and friends, filling her heart to the brim, you're neglecting her neighbor. While your chosen ones are falling asleep, safe and warm in the arms of their mothers, fathers, lovers, the rest of us, the ones from whom you've turned your face, are left with no more blanket than the night's dark.

How do you decide? It doesn't have anything to do with deserving, obviously. It's not something we earn or fail to earn. Some children have love the moment they slide into the world bloody and bawling, they inherit it as though it were a birthright. Everyone else makes do with the scraps.

Well, I'll tell you what: I was fine with the scraps. I never wanted to be a fish on your hook anyway. I've seen what you do to people, how you make them weak in the knees, the way you turn reasonable women into fools. I've always preferred my legs to stay steady under me. The madness you're selling? I don't need it.

Um.

I didn't need it, that is.

Now I do.

I have no idea why my god—an older, stronger, more merciful god than you'll ever be—insists on muddying his ritual with love, but it's not my place to question. We've been strangers my whole life—you and I—but the song says I need to love, and so I'm here. I left my blood on that sword by the door. I'm praying to you.

Probably I should be more polite, apologize for calling you a bitch, but if you can hear this prayer, you can probably hear the rest of what's going on in my head, so what's the point? You know what I think, which means you know I think you're a bitch, but you also know that I need you now. You know this is a true prayer.

I need you.

I don't know how you choose which hearts to fill with love and which to leave empty, but please, pick mine.

Pick mine, Eira. Goddess, I beg you.

I shook my head silently.

Fuck you, also, for making me beg.

I opened my eyes. Nothing inside the temple had changed. The lanterns still cast their warm, white light across the wooden floor, the wooden pews. The altar remained empty. Not that I'd expected Eira herself to come down to answer my prayer. A few silent accusations followed by a little begging weren't likely to change her lifelong absence from my life. I thought of Ruc, imagined his green eyes staring back at me, remembered the kiss we'd shared on the dock, his hand on the back of my neck, pulling me close. My heart beat faster at the memory, but what did that mean?

How fucking long does it take?

That seemed, somehow, like the wrong question.

I rose from the pew, suddenly tired from the long day out in the sun. It was time to quit wandering around, to go back to the inn and get some sleep. Ruc would be up early, and I wanted to be up with him. I wanted another kiss; I wanted *more* than a kiss. I was failing—that was obvious enough—but I intended to fight the whole way. When Ela came for me with her knives, I intended her to find me naked in Ruc's arms, in his bed, my legs locked around his hips, his lips at my throat. Sex wasn't love, obviously, but I didn't know what else to try.

I glanced over at the singer as I passed. She was still kneeling before that candle, still pouring her song into the warm night. I continued on toward the door, then paused, turned back.

Her hair was silk soft in my hand. It smelled like jasmine when I tipped her head back. She didn't stop singing, even as she met my eyes. Music can do that to a person—it's a labyrinth in which you lose yourself. She smiled at me around the note, her dark eyes gazing up as though I were a friend or a long-lost lover—maybe Eira's devout feel love for everyone all the time. How would I know? As I cut her throat, I tried to imagine what that might be like.

One who sings, lost in the song.

That song faltered as the god took her, but I'd been listening to it since before I stepped into the temple, and I picked it up easily enough, singing as I wiped my knife on her robe, slid it back into the sheath, then made my way toward the door.

I could pray to the goddess all night long, I could beg for her favor, but Ananshael was my one true god, and I had neglected his worship too long.

16

I returned to the inn to find all the intricate architecture of my lies in shambles.

Despite the preposterously late hour, Ruc was sitting on the deck, all alone at one of the Dance's round tables. My pulse quickened at the sight of him. My mind churned through the possibilities. Had he learned something else about the transport, something about the insurgency or the Vuo Ton? Or had he come here for me, for another kiss, for something more? Just as I started to call out, I saw Ela approaching him, a fresh carafe of wine in her hand, that delicious, throaty laugh spilling out of her throat.

"I notice you still haven't touched your *quey,*" she said, pausing to elbow him in the shoulder. "It's enough to make a woman think you don't enjoy her company."

Ruc didn't even glance at the clay cup in front of him. "I'm still on duty."

"That's what you've been saying for the past hour. When is the duty *over?*"

"Soldiers have been grappling with that question as long as there've been soldiers."

Ela made a face. "I like a man in uniform, but all this talk about duty is getting tedious."

She leaned across in front of him, so close he could have kissed her on the neck, took his mug of *quey,* straightened, then tossed it back in a single gulp. She was wearing a blue *ki-pan,* the cut even more revealing than normal. It was impossible not to notice the way she brushed up against the man I was supposed to learn to love as she slid the cup back into place on the table. She took the seat right next to him, not across the table, where I would have sat.

I watched them from the wooden walkway beyond the deck. I felt as though there were one or two small mice trapped inside me, right below my diaphragm, nibbling at something important. The bites weren't large enough to hurt, not really, but I could feel that something was wrong.

The scene was a study in contrasts: Ela drinking bright plum wine from a long-stemmed glass, Ruc ignoring the empty cup before him. She was all languid motion, all crossing and uncrossing of legs, all stretching out to touch his hand; Ruc remained still as a baited snare. Ela had lowered her voice when she sat down. I couldn't quite make out her words, but she was talking, evidently recounting a story, words spilling out like water in a brook. Ruc remained silent. Ela laughed over and over, brown eyes aglitter. Ruc did not laugh.

I felt guilty watching them, though I couldn't say why. I interrogated that guilt, tried to stare it down, to see the true shape of it, but it flitted away like a bat darting through lamp-light. I almost felt like a bat myself, a creature unseen in the darkness, looking in on the light with wide, glassy, imperfect eyes. It seemed, suddenly, like I wasn't supposed to be there. Ruc had come because of me, obviously, but my absence hadn't hampered whatever was taking place between them. He didn't look excited, didn't look happy, but he hadn't looked happy since the transport. Not even when we kissed. He was sitting there silently, listening to Ela's laugh, watching her smooth limbs as she mimed a series of inscrutable gestures. Whatever he'd come for, he wasn't looking for me anymore. That much was clear.

"*Now* do you see why I constantly consider giving her to the god?"

The voice was right at my ear, and I'd slipped my knife from the sheath before my mind processed the familiar dry drawl: Kossal.

"Sneaking up on people is a good way to get killed," I muttered, not turning to face him. For some reason, I didn't want him to see my eyes.

He grunted. "The god will take me when he takes me."

"Don't you want your last sacrifice to be more than a stupid mistake?" I demanded, channeling my inexplicable anger.

"Mistake or martyrdom—dead's dead."

I was only half listening to his answer, my eyes fixed on Ela. "What is she *doing*?" I hissed.

"Looks to me like she's seducing the man you were kissing by the river a few hours earlier."

"Why?"

He shrugged. "Presumably because she likes the look of him. And because you moved too slowly."

"And *that*," Ela was saying as we drew closer, "was the last time we tried dressing Kossal up as a concubine."

She shook her head at the invented memory. "Let's just say there wasn't anywhere to hide a dagger, let alone a decent sword. Ah!" She clapped her hands together, as though she'd just at that moment noticed my approach. "Here they are now. Pyrre! Kossal! Sit down and pull up a glass."

Kossal stumped past me, dropped into a chair, then waved over one of the servingmen.

"*Quey*," he said.

"One cup?" the sculpted young man asked.

"Bring the bottle," Kossal replied.

I made no move to approach. My eyes were locked on Ela. She smiled, her perfect white teeth flashing red in the shifting light of the lanterns. She might have just bitten through someone's throat, except for the fact that throat biters weren't supposed to look so lovely, so composed.

"What are you doing?" I asked her.

Ela gestured expansively to Ruc. "Entertaining the commander of Dombâng's Greenshirts. Did you know that he's descended from Goc My himself?"

"I did."

Ruc turned his gaze from Ela to me. "Your Wingmate has been regaling me with your Kettral exploits."

"Has she." I glanced at Ela. I hadn't explained my cover to her or Kossal, but if she'd really been following me all around Dombâng, she'd probably heard at least a few of my conversations with Ruc.

"And you," Ruc said, turning to consider Kossal. "I understand you're the Wing's demolitions expert."

"Nope," Kossal said, glancing over his shoulder as the young man returned with his bottle of *quey*.

"May I pour, sir?"

Kossal shook his head. "Just put it there."

"No?" Ruc asked, raising an eyebrow.

My heart kicked restlessly. My palms had begun to sweat. The Kettral cover was solid enough. I could keep it up, even against Ruc's constant pressure. Kossal and Ela, however, were another matter entirely.

"Don't mind that old goat," Ela said, waving a negligent hand toward Kossal.

"Actually," Ruc said, cutting through her objection, "I'm curious about the old goat. What do you mean, 'no'?"

Kossal put his flute on the table before him, took a long swig from the bottle, winced as it went down, then wiped his mouth with the back of his hand.

"I mean I'm not Kettral," he said blandly.

Ruc shifted just slightly, putting a little more space between his body and the table, making sure the sword at his left hip was free.

"How interesting," he said, looking over at Ela, then up at me. "And yet, your Wingmates tell such vivid stories. . . ."

I could feel all my work unraveling, my plans torn apart like rotten nets, everything I'd hoped to catch sliding silently through and away. If Ruc discovered the truth, our tenuous partnership was over. There would be no more boat trips out to the remote delta to look at bodies, no more kisses, no more opportunities to try to shape the space between us into something that resembled love. At best, he'd stop trusting me; at worst—if Kossal actually convinced him we were servants of Ananshael—he'd try to have us captured and executed. At which point I could either flee or fight, neither of which would get me any closer to completing my Trial.

Ela leaned across the table toward Ruc, murmuring from behind a cupped hand. "Kossal takes mission security very seriously." She winked.

I sat down at last, heavy and ungraceful, as though someone had hacked my legs from underneath me.

"Kossal is a horse's itchy, fly-bitten nutsack," I said grimly. I was looking at Ela, not Ruc. "And so are you."

Kossal grunted. I could see him take another pull on the bottle out of the corner of my eye. "Fly-bitten nutsack doesn't sound all wrong," he conceded. "More accurate than Kettral, anyway."

Ela met my eyes, raised her hands helplessly. "He's ungovernable. What can I say?"

"The thing is," Ruc cut in, "we *do* have a government in this city. And it's my job to make sure that government stays right where it is. So when strangers show up claiming to be Kettral, then claiming not to be Kettral, I start to experience what I can only describe as a more than mild concern."

He didn't look concerned. Ruc didn't pick at his fingernails or chew the inside of his cheek. He hadn't raised his voice when he spoke. Well before I met him, he'd filed off all the tics and habits that might broadcast his play before he made it. Anyone else on the deck who happened to glance over would see a man nearing his thirtieth year, serious but relaxed, one bare, well-muscled arm tossed over the back of his chair, the other resting casually on his knee. I saw the violence beneath, boiling like a school of *qirna* just below the river's gorgeous, motionless, sun-spangled surface.

Ela pursed her lips. "Mild concern I can abide, but anything *more* . . ." She fanned her face with a hand. "I get hives," she confided quietly. "Not just on my face, but *everywhere*."

"I don't see any hives," Ruc said.

"Of course not!" Ela laughed. "I'm having a delightful evening."

"It might get less delightful if my men on the roof opposite start firing their flatbows."

"Flatbows," Ela murmured, leaning into the table once more, her eyes fixed on Ruc's, as though the snipers concealed on the rooftops were of less than no concern. "How *exciting*. Who are we hunting?"

"*We* are not hunting anyone."

"We are, in fact," I cut in.

Ruc shook his head. "The men on the roof have their bolts aimed directly at your chest."

"My chest?" Ela raised one hand, laid a languid finger just above her heart. "Here?" She slid the finger down between her breasts. "Or here?"

"Knock it the fuck off," I growled. "Both of you. You know as well as I do, Ela, that even twenty-five years' training on the Islands isn't going to save you from a flatbow bolt."

"Oh, I don't think he'll actually shoot me," Ela protested. "We're just getting to know each other."

"According to your friend," Ruc replied, nodding slightly toward Kossal, "that's not quite right. How much can you know about a woman if she just spent half the night lying to you?"

Ruc studied Ela as he spoke, but that was just a feint. The question's sharpened edge was directed at me.

I shook my head. "When did you get so 'Kent-kissing twitchy?"

"There was a commander I served under years ago," Ruc replied, turning slowly to face me, "down in the Waist. Northern guy, pale skin, strange blue eyes. His name was Collum, but everyone called him Cool Collum. Not because he *looked* cool, I can tell you that. He was a big bastard and sweated by the bucket. We called him Cool Collum because nothing ever rattled him. Nothing spooked him. Nothing made him twitch. Local tribes would be filling our fort with arrows and Collum would stand up on the walls, perfectly exposed, like he didn't even notice. The man absolutely refused to worry about anything."

"Sounds familiar," I said, glancing over at Ela.

She smiled.

"Everyone loved Collum," Ruc went on. "Everyone admired him. He thought he was unbreakable, and so everyone else thought he was unbreakable, which meant that we thought *we* were a little more unbreakable, too, just by being near him."

"I'm starting to suspect from the structure of the narrative," Ela said, "that he wasn't actually unbreakable."

Ruc shook his head. "One hot, foggy morning he was walking the walls, bellowing at us the way he always did, and one of those short little jungle arrows took him through the throat."

Kossal let out a low curse. At first I thought he was dismayed by Collum's death—which seemed strange, all things considered— then realized he'd been ignoring the entire conversation, trying instead to coax the dead snake in his *quey* out through the neck of the bottle. Evidently, he found the lesson of Cool Collum's demise less than fascinating.

"I get it," I said, turning back to Ruc. "We're supposed to be scared of the men you've got hiding in the shadows. We're supposed to be on edge. You've made your point."

"I'm not sure I have," he said, turning to me. "I don't care if you're on edge. I don't care if you're merry, or terrified, or drunk. You asked me when *I* got twitchy: that was when—the moment I saw Cool Collum pitch over the wooden rampart. That was the moment I realized that taking chances might look great, it might make for great stories, but it's a shit way to run a life, let alone a military force. I took over that unit after Collum died, and we quit taking chances. That's why Annur put me in charge here. And I'll tell you something else. Right now, the three of you look like one enormous fucking chance; one I could solve with the wave of a hand."

The words were so steady, the tone so conversational, that if I'd been distracted—by Kossal prodding at the snake with a long splinter of wood, for instance—I might have missed the extent of the menace. Ruc wasn't one to boast. He didn't get in the ring unless he was ready to pound someone to a pulp. If he was showing his hand now, it meant he was absolutely certain he could kill us, but it also meant something else: he didn't want to.

Hope washed through my heart, so hot it almost hurt.

Despite Kossal's absolute refusal to back my play, Ruc hadn't given his snipers the order. It was a measure of my desperation that I took the absence of my execution as a promising romantic development. My mind scrambled for purchase on the tricky, shifting situation. After a moment, I rounded on Kossal.

"Tell him what we are."

The old priest was grimacing. He had the snake impaled on the wooden splinter, but couldn't manage to draw it out through the neck of the bottle. "And for the love of all that's holy, why don't you just drink the rest of the fucking *quey* if you want the snake so bad?"

"Have to stay mostly sober," he said, obviously distracted by his task, "in case I have to kill someone."

Ruc cocked his head to the side. "You have anyone in particular in mind?"

"Plenty of options," Kossal muttered. He jerked his head toward Ela. "I'm always tempted to start with her, but my god disapproves of offerings made in frustration or anger."

"Your god?" Ruc asked quietly.

Kossal grunted. "Your god, too. Everyone's god. Ananshael."

"You're telling me you're Skullsworn," Ruc said, voice flat.

Ela laughed, a long, joyful sound straight from the belly. I wanted to punch her in the throat.

Kossal just shrugged. He had the snake pinned against the wall of the bottle now, and was drawing it up slowly through the neck.

"We're Skullsworn," I said, "who just happen to take a vivid interest in the civic life of Dombâng."

There was no forcing Kossal's words back into his mouth, no pretending they hadn't been spoken. The only hope was to ride them out. If I judged the old priest correctly, he wouldn't have any more interest in convincing Ruc of the truth than he did in convincing him of my lie. He didn't seem to give a pile of slippery shit what Ruc thought at all, actually.

"What do you *want* us to be?" Ela murmured coquettishly, pursing her lips as though tasting the alternatives. "Skullsworn? Or Kettral?"

Ruc looked at the woman a moment, then turned to me.

To my own shock, I found myself laughing, all the tension of the day shaking itself free in great, breathy spasms.

"I'm telling you the truth, Ruc," I said. "So is Ela. Kossal's just a cantankerous old bastard who takes military regs about revealing our identities way too seriously." I shook my head. "But does it matter? There's *something* out in the delta. Maybe it's the Vuo Ton, and maybe it's something else, but either way, you need to find it, and you need to kill it."

Kossal had just bitten off the head of the snake, but he paused in his crunching, interested for the first time.

"That's what *I* want to talk about."

Ela glared at Ruc. "We've been sitting here half the night, and you didn't even tell me about your adventures in the delta?"

"Lower your voice," Ruc growled.

Ela ignored the warning—all the other patrons on the deck were several tables away—and leaned toward Ruc instead.

"We're *very* good at killing things," she purred, then glanced at me. "What are we killing?"

"Something capable of ripping the throat out of half a hundred armed legionaries," I replied. "Something planting violets in the eye sockets of the dead. Something pretending to be a god."

"It's not a god," Ruc said.

Kossal swallowed the snake head into the side of his cheek. "The woman in the shack seemed to think so."

Ruc turned to study the old priest. "You followed us into the Weir?"

"We follow her *everywhere*," Ela said. "I was there in the bathhouse, for your first reunion."

Ruc was just about the most unflappable person I'd ever met. I'd seen him take a club to the ribs and barely wince, and yet even Ruc wasn't used to dealing with the likes of Ela and Kossal. His composure, normally so absolute, was starting to fray, if only in ways so minor that only I would have noticed them.

"And you didn't even notice me," Ela said, shaking her head regretfully.

"What were you doing in the bathhouse?"

The priestess spread her hands. "Pyrre's more than capable when it comes to putting sharp pieces of steel in the softest parts of the enemies of our shining empire, but sometimes," she winked at him, "you need a woman along who can make your whole world explode."

She lingered on that last word, shaping her lips into an *O* around the vowel.

"You're in demolitions, too," Ruc said.

"I prefer to tell people I'm in conflagrations."

"She's a priestess," Kossal cut in irritably. "I'm a priest. She . . ." he went on, stabbing a finger at me, "is an acolyte of our god. Now," he rounded on Ruc, "can we discuss what we saw on the transport?"

"Why do you care about the transport," Ruc asked warily, "if you don't care about Dombâng?"

"He does care," I said. "He's Kettral. He's been fighting for Annur for the last fifty years, but he inherited the last generation's rigid, idiotic secrecy protocols, which means he's never going to *tell* you he's Kettral, even if you tie him to a table and light him on fire."

"Which I, for one, do not recommend," Ela put in.

"I care what happened on the boat," Kossal said, as though we'd never spoken, "because anyone ripping the throats out of armed men is a servant of my god, an adept servant, and I am always eager to meet my fellows in the faith."

Ruc shook his head. "The people who ripped out the throats on the boat worship the old gods of this city: Kem Anh, Hang Loc, Sinn."

"Ananshael is an old god. These others are imposters."

"On that we agree," Ruc said. "But they're imposters who have proven surprisingly durable. People in this delta have worshipped them for thousands of years, as far back as the records go and further. All the way to Dombâng's founding during the Csestriim wars, if you believe the city's myths. Annur outlawed the worship, but all the legions they send can't seem to kill the old trinity."

Kossal drummed his fingers on the table, noticed the half of the snake he'd set aside, picked it up, and bit into the scaly hide. "We're coming," he announced around the flesh filling his mouth.

"Coming where?" Ruc asked.

"With you into the delta. To see these Vuo Ton."

Ela laughed again. I half hated her, but a woman could get drunk on that laugh.

"You want to help?" Ruc asked. "If you're Skullsworn, then what the fuck do you care about the politics of Dombâng?"

"I don't," Kossal replied, pausing to pick a bone out from between his teeth with that same wooden splinter. "But I take offense when I hear of things that can't be killed. In the name of my god, I'm inclined to find them and kill them."

"A moment ago you wanted to find your fellows in the faith. Now you want to murder immortal imposters. Which is it?"

"Worship," Kossal replied, "is a coin with two sides: killing, and dying. I'm here to make sure everyone takes a turn at each."

Ruc just stared at him a moment, then shook his head. "Sweet Intarra's light," he muttered, then turned to me, that green gaze of his uncharacteristically open. "Why does it seem like my life would have been so much easier if I'd never met you?"

I frowned. "I'm trying to hear that as a compliment."

He coughed up a laugh.

"Let's just say there aren't too many people who surprise me, but the three of you . . ." He trailed off, wordless for the first time.

Surprise. I repeated the word to myself. Could surprise grow into love? It sounded possible, at the very least. Maybe more than possible, if I burned down a little more of the city.

"You can always shoot us later," Ela suggested brightly.

"If I shot you now, I wouldn't have to watch my back."

"If you shot us now," I pointed out, "we wouldn't be there to help."

"When did you get the idea I needed help?"

"When I saw your men puking over the rail of that transport," I replied. "Whatever you're fighting, the Greenshirts aren't up to the job."

"I have the legions."

"The same legions we burned, then fed to the fish?"

Ruc's face tightened. "I don't trust you."

"Then don't trust us," I said. "You already know what you need to know. Skullsworn or Kettral, we're excellent at killing things. . . ."

"*You* are," he cut in. "All I've seen the two of them do is drink and flirt."

"A woman can't be cutting throats every moment of every day," Ela objected.

I met Ruc's gaze. "You've sized up enough fighters."

He sucked air between his teeth, then shook his head. "I feel like Cool fucking Collum strolling along up there on the wall."

"Would you rather be cowering somewhere?" I demanded.

"Yes," he said. "I'd rather be cowering."

The smile bloomed on my face, fierce and certain. "No you wouldn't."

I wanted to kiss him again. My whole body ached to lean toward him, to seize his chin in my hand and pull him close.

"You should kiss her," Ela suggested merrily, nudging Ruc in the shin beneath the table.

"They already spent half the night kissing," Kossal groused.

"Pyrre!" Ela objected, rounding on me. "You canny little ferret. When were you going to *tell* me? This is too delicious. Something ripping out throats *and* a budding romance!" She purred contentedly. "Dombâng really is a city of love."

By the end of the night none of Ruc's hidden crossbowmen had shot us, which I took for a good sign; on the other hand, by the time he finally left the deck of Anho's Dance, Ruc had made no effort to include us in the finer details of his plans.

"Be here," he said, straightening up from his chair. "I'll send someone when it's time."

"Where are you going?" I asked.

"To get things ready."

"Want to tell us what things?"

He shook his head. "No."

"A mission tends to work best," I pointed out, "when everyone on the team understands the objective, the resources, and tactics."

"The objective," Ruc replied, "is to find the Vuo Ton and pry the truth out of them. Chua Two-Net is one resource, and the three of you are the other. Isn't that what you just spent half the night arguing for?"

"I was hoping for a few more specifics," I said. "How is it, exactly, that we're planning to pry the truth out of the Vuo Ton?"

"I love specifics. Unfortunately, since no one aside from Two-Net has ever seen this secret lair of the Vuo Ton, there's going to have to be a lot of improvising when we get there, a lot of making shit up on the fly."

Ela beamed. "I love improvisation."

Ruc ignored her, studying me instead. "That's what the Kettral are for, right? That's what you're good at."

I nodded at the same time that Kossal, weary or irritated, ran a hand over his eyes. "We're not Kettral."

17

For a full day, I watched from the wide deck of Anho's Dance while Dombâng unraveled. The city, like the canals threading it, looked calm enough on the surface: women and men going about their business and their lives, crowding the bridges and walkways, plying the channels in their narrow boats, obedient to the rhythms of work and commerce, revelry and rest. If you sat long enough, however, staring into that current, you could see past the bright, unblemished surface to the perturbations beneath.

People looked over their shoulders too often, even in the middle of the day. When they spoke, they leaned close, lowered voices, husbanded their words. When we first arrived in the city, most people had been going about their days alone; now they seemed to travel in groups of three or four, even when there was no obvious need. Ruc had outlawed the carrying of swords, but everyone seemed to have a knife, some sheathed in plain sight, others inexpertly hidden beneath the fabric of vests or pants. Emotions were raw. I'd watched two women try to claw each other's eyes out over a broken crock, a man shove another into the canal for refusing to step aside on the walkway. Children raced in feral knots through the alleys and over the bridges, mocking the cries of their elders, chanting the words to outlawed songs. They couldn't have understood what was going on, not really, but they could smell the rot in the air.

On the morning of the day after Ruc's abrupt disappearance,

I rose before dawn, bathed, then found my way to the deck, where I sat sipping a mug of bitter *ta*. Down in the canal, white-finned fish rose through the murk to take flies at the surface, then faded back into the depths like thoughts or memories, something lost or forgotten. The sky sat heavy and bright on the teak roofs, as though it had been stacked there. The day was hot, and going to be hotter.

"Would it have killed you to try to fall in love with someone a little more efficient?"

Kossal, as usual, had approached without my noticing, his bare feet silent on the wooden deck. He dropped into the seat opposite mine.

"He's efficient," I replied. "I just wish I knew what he was being efficient *at*."

"Gone into the delta without us?"

I hesitated, then shook my head. "Not his style. If he decided he didn't trust us, he wouldn't leave us where we could burn down his city while he was away."

"Then what is he doing? Doesn't take two days to load a boat with supplies."

"I should have followed him."

The old priest looked at me like I'd just started drooling on the table. "What you should have done is continued your work instead of wasting time pining. There's more to Ananshael's Trial than the last lines."

Before I could respond, one of the young servingmen approached. His name, I remembered vaguely, was Vet. Ela had lured him into her bed days earlier, but Ela wasn't up yet—most days she slept until almost noon—and he gave me a sly smile, one that suggested he could keep a secret if I could. Kossal, predictably, shattered the mood.

"Bring me *ta*," the older priest said, "and something to eat that doesn't smell like fish."

"At once," Vet murmured, then turned to me. "And anything else for the lady?"

That confident smile suggested my list of options extended beyond the offerings of the kitchen.

I shook my head.

"Perhaps later," he said, smiled again, then turned away.

I watched him as he threaded his way between the tables. It wasn't hard to see what Ela liked about him. He was built like a statue, all square jaw and bare shoulders. He wore his vest open, like the rest of the serving staff, to show off a chest and stomach that looked carved out with a chisel. And that smile . . . somehow it managed to be mischievous and reassuring all at once. What would it be like, I wondered, to peel off that vest, to feel his hands roaming over my body? What would his voice sound like, murmured in my ear? Would it be possible to thread the discrete facts of attraction into something that felt like love? *Someone* could love him; I was certain of that, just as I was certain that that someone would never be me. For all that my life depended on it, I could not say why.

I turned back to Kossal.

"It doesn't matter that I haven't given anyone else to the god. None of that matters. If I fail at the last lines," I concluded quietly, "I fail."

"Sometimes the failure is the devotion."

"That doesn't mean anything."

"Our bodies go," he said, gesturing to himself. "Then our minds. Failure is what it means to be mortal."

I shook my head. "No."

Kossal didn't reply. He watched me, both eyes open now, his pupils still, sharp-edged, absolute, as though they'd been cored from his irises with a knife. I shoved forward into his silence.

"You passed your Trial. Ela passed hers. No one told *you* to fail in the name of your devotion."

"You were twenty years unborn when I faced my Trial," the priest said, his voice quiet. "You have no idea what I was told."

"I know you're *here*," I burst out. "I know that you survived."

"Survival," he said. "What does the Lord of the Grave want with our survival?"

I stared at him. "Then why are we *doing* this? Any of it? Why all the songs, the training, the Trials? Why don't we just open our own throats and be done?"

It was a question, I realized suddenly, that had been rising in my chest for years, ever since I first arrived in Rassambur. I had never doubted Ananshael. The god's mercy and justice were as obvious to me as the sky. I wanted nothing more than to serve such a lord, and yet there was something in the service I had always struggled to understand. My brothers and sisters gave thousands of souls to the god each year. More than that, they offered themselves in dozens of ways. Not a month went by without one of the faithful stepping from a precipice or sipping quietly from a poisoned cup. *When the god calls,* we say in Rassambur, *listen.* And yet, the whole process seemed somehow . . . inefficient. If Ananshael wanted us, and we wanted to give of ourselves, the simplest obeisance seemed suicide.

It was a paradox. We were expected to kill, to die with a heartfelt smile, but never to rush. I'd raised the question half a dozen times over the course of my years in Rassambur, without ever receiving a sensible reply. There seemed to be a hundred aphorisms and no actual answers, just inscrutable stuff like *The wheat does not find the scythe.* After a while I stopped asking. Rassambur was a beautiful place to be alive. The sun burned bright, the blue air blazed, I was both young and strong. Someday, I told myself, I would understand.

Suddenly, that looked a lot less likely.

I was going to die. When my time was up, either Ela or Kossal would open my veins and drain my blood out into one of Dombâng's canals, and I still didn't understand the most basic thing about my faith.

"Every year we live," I murmured, "every *day*—it's just a delay, an abdication of faith. You're right. Why am I even *trying* to survive?"

I stared down at the shifting water of the canal. It would be so easy to step over the railing, tumble forward, break the surface with a quick slap, then sink into the depths, let the current carry my body to the sea. I'd seen a drowned woman in Sia once, facedown in the shallows of the lake, white dress unfolding around her like the petals of a flower, arms spread as though she was flying. I'd never seen a body quite so beautiful.

"Survival," Kossal said quietly, "is not life."

I studied the old priest. "I don't know what that means."

"What is it we give to the god?"

"Our selves. Our lives."

"And what kind of life do you want to give him? What kind of self?"

I tried to find some answer that might fit the question, failed.

"Why do you think, at my age, I'm still stomping all over this 'Kent-kissing continent? What do you think I'm doing in this miserable city?" He waved a hand at the canal and everything beyond. "The whole place smells like soup."

I hesitated. "Ela says you're doing it for her. Because you like to be around her."

"For *her*? Because I *enjoy* being around her?"

"That's what she said."

The priest looked like he was going to spit. "That woman," he ground out finally, "is a daily ordeal."

"*She's* the ordeal?" I was too confused to consider my words. "The whole way from Rassambur Ela was kind, cheerful, curious . . . while you've been what? An old bastard with a kidney stone. Every time we sit down, you look like someone pissed in your *quey*. The only time you stop scowling is when you're playing your flute."

"I play my flute," Kossal said, "to keep from killing people I should not kill."

I stared at him. "You mean Ela."

"Yes," he agreed, "Ela. Although you're managing to elbow your way onto my list as well."

"Which list is that?" I demanded. "*Kill?* Or *Do Not Kill?*"

His eyes narrowed beneath his bushy brows. Then, to my shock, he exploded into a long, rich laugh.

"There's just the one list, kid," he said finally.

I shook my head. "And that is?"

"The ones who matter. The ones who aren't just scenery. The ones who turn survival into life."

"Why would you want to kill them?"

He raised his bushy brows. "Because life, Pyrre—it's a lot harder than survival."

"And Ela makes you feel alive."

"To my unspeakable exhaustion."

We fell silent as Vet returned with a steaming kettle, poured Kossal's *ta,* then withdrew, his eyes lingering on me as he went. I tried to imagine what we looked like to him: just an old man and a young woman, not Ananshael's faithful. We might have been talking about anything—the antics of a drunk relative, someone's tumble into one of the canals, the ludicrous price of fire fruit—anything but the silk-thin line dividing the living from the dead. I tried to imagine what it might be like to live that sort of life. What did most people think about when they got up in the morning? Pissing and *ta*, probably. Maybe the job they had to do that day. It seemed a sad way to live—pale, attenuated.

"What do you think we'll find," I asked finally, "out there in the delta?"

Kossal swirled the *ta* in his cup, took a sip, pursed his lips, then looked at me. "I don't know."

"What's your best *guess?*"

"I learned a long time ago that my guesses aren't all that good."

"So you just quit guessing? Quit having expectations?"

The old priest nodded. "Been working well enough this past half century or so."

I studied him, the lines etched into his weather-beaten skin, those calm, strong hands. "You're lying."

He raised an eyebrow. "Quit doing that too. My lies weren't much better than my guesses."

"But you're curious," I pressed. "You think there's *something* out there worth fighting."

"Fighting?" Kossal frowned. "I dislike fighting."

"Killing."

He shrugged. "A heart doesn't tend to find its way out of a ribcage all on its own, and there were an awful lot of naked hearts on that boat."

"You think it's the Vuo Ton?"

He shrugged again. "First time I heard about the Vuo Ton was a few days ago. For all I know, they're a group of tuber-eating pacifists. Only one way to find out."

"But you *are* going to find out." I shook my head. "Which means you think it's not the Vuo Ton. You think it's the gods out there."

Kossal studied me through the veil of steam rising from his wide cup.

"If there *is* something out there other than some idiots with knives and an interesting myth, it's been there a long time."

"You really think there's a chance that the city's gods are real?"

"Doubt it. But there are other things than gods that don't die without a little persuading."

"You mean Csestriim."

It was still hard to believe we were actually talking about it. For all their implausibility, the gods of Dombâng were familiar. I'd grown up with their names on my tongue, the shapes of their forbidden idols rough in my hands. The Csestriim, however, despite the ample historical record, despite Kossal's claims to have found them, killed them, seemed like creatures from a storybook, immortal foes of the human race vanquished from every corner of the world so long ago that they might never have lived at all.

"Csestriim," I went on, "hiding in the Shirvian delta, impersonating gods."

"Not really, no. But if there are, they've been cheating Ananshael for a very long time."

"And if not?"

He took another sip of his *ta*. "Then I'll see if any of these Vuo Ton need to be given to our lord."

He discussed it all so casually, both the question of the Csestriim, and the more quotidian issue of his own devotion.

"How do you decide?" I asked, thinking back to the priestess of Eira, to the few drops of her warm blood that had spattered my hand as I lowered her to the temple floor.

"I assume there is a second half to that question."

"What offerings to make. The world is filled with people. Even Dombâng . . ." I trailed off, imagining the canals crowded with boats, the oarsmen shouting at one another, women and men jostling on the wooden walkways, leaning from the windows of teak houses, shouting at children who forced their way through the scrum. "You can't kill them all," I concluded finally.

"There have been priests who tried."

I blinked. "Really? What happened?"

"Didn't work."

"I gathered that."

"People notice what you're doing when you start going building by building, block by block, cutting throats. They start to take exception."

"But if you don't do that, how do you decide?" I pressed. "We see thousands of people pass by each day from where we're sitting right now. There are two dozen people right on this deck. You haven't killed any of them."

"Two," Kossal said.

"Excuse me?"

"I killed two."

I glanced around the deck. People sipped their juice or *ta*, alone or in groups of two or three. No one was dead. No one seemed to be dying. I turned back to Kossal, wondering if he was joking. "I don't see any corpses."

He waved away the objection. "The poison takes a while."

Not joking, I concluded. That seemed like the end of the conversation, but after a moment Kossal went on in that low, rumbling voice of his.

"Devotion isn't a system, Pyrre. You pass a hundred people, a thousand, and nothing. Then, when you pass the thousand-and-first, you feel the god seeing with your eyes, you feel him stirring in your limbs. The way you know the will of a god is not the way you know the area of a square or the distance to Annur. It is not a matter of facts or equations. Our devotion is not a list of chores."

I shook my head. "Sounds like the way Ela describes love."

To my surprise, Kossal nodded. "I suppose. Death, love— they're both the work of a god framed in mortal flesh."

"How are you supposed to know one from the other?"

Kossal swirled the *ta* in his cup, then stared down into the miniature whirlpool. "I'm not sure you do."

18

Ruc's messenger knocked furtively on my door, waking me from an unsteady sleep sometime in the hot, foggy hours between midnight and dawn. I had been dreaming of Ruc and Ela, of the two of them naked, tangled in each other's limbs, eyes closed with the bliss of their tight-pressed bodies. I called out to them, but they didn't hear me, or they heard me, but refused to respond.

I tried to move closer, but I was tied to something, rope wrapped around and around me. When I looked back up, Ruc was on his back, Ela on top of him, astride him, riding him, smiling as she reached down to pull him to her . . . no. She was reaching down to strangle him. Her fingers closed around his throat even as her back arched with pleasure. I couldn't tell if Ruc was struggling to be free or just fucking her harder.

He doesn't know, I thought. *He doesn't know what she is, what she'll do to him.* I screamed into my gag. Silence.

I wished for a knife, and a knife was in my hand. As quickly as I could, I sliced my way free of the ropes, sawing desperately through the thick, bristling strands, focused on nothing but getting loose, stopping the priestess before she finished her strangling. When the last coils fell away, I lunged forward, hurling myself across the undefined space. When I reached the bodies, they were still, bloody, dead. Ela's head lay on Ruc's muscled chest, the haze of her dark hair matted with blood. Someone had stabbed them, stabbed them both over and over. When I looked down, the knife in my hand dripped dark blood. The drops hit the floor—*drip, drip, drip*—the measure of a music that didn't yet exist, or had already stopped.

By the time we reached the docks of the Greenshirt fortress, the vision had faded, but sweat still slicked my hands, my chest; and my heart, normally so steady, leapt into my throat when Chua stepped from behind a stack of barrels piled on the dock. Not an auspicious start to the day that wasn't likely to get any easier.

The woman carried a folded net and two fishing spears, both as long as she was tall. She wore a slender filleting knife strapped to one thigh and a longer, heavier blade for hacking sheathed on the other. It was standard kit for a fisher headed into the delta. Her vest and trousers were not. Most of the fishers working the channels around Dombâng wore cotton or, if they could afford it, silk—light cloth that wasn't too hot in the wet afternoon heat. Chua's clothes seemed to glisten in the dock's fickle lamplight, to shift and writhe each time she moved. It took me a moment to realize her tight vest and trousers were stitched from some kind of skin: snake or maybe crocodile, something with dark, glittering scales.

She ran a hand over the hide when she noticed me studying her. "Blocks spear rushes," she said, "and most things with fangs."

"Must be hot."

"If you are hot," she replied, dark eyes glittering, "then you are alive."

"I, for one, *despise* being too hot," Ela said. The priestess, unlike the fisher, had dressed less than practically for an expedition into the delta, although she *had* traded her customary *ki-pan* for a light silk *noc* and sleeveless top. Both seemed unlikely to block either spear rushes or things with fangs. "You must be Chua," she said, smiling as she stepped forward. "Pyrre tells me you're quite resourceful."

The older woman examined her, as though she were some exotic fish hauled up onto the deck, then glanced over at me.

"This one is Kettral?" She looked wary. "Where are the weapons?"

"Weapons?" Ela shot me a wide-eyed, panicked look. "Pyrre! Did you forget the *weapons*?"

"She might not look like it," I said, ignoring the priestess's theatrics, "but she's Kettral."

"But what is a Kettral without *weapons*?" Ela went on. "I forgot my broadswords at the inn."

"Less noise," Ruc growled. "We're leaving before dawn because I don't want the whole city to notice our departure."

"It is not the city you should be worrying about," Chua said.

"Luckily," Ruc replied, voice flat, "I've gotten good at worrying about more than one thing at a time."

He made up for Ela's lack of weapons: a short sword on one hip, a dagger on the other, and a crossbow strapped across his back. He gestured to the slim swallow-tail boat tethered up at the dock. Two Greenshirts sat at the oars, half-shrouded in shadow.

"Who are they?" Kossal asked.

"Dem Lun and Hin," Ruc replied. "They'll be doing the rowing."

Chua eyed the two skeptically. "They are soldiers, not fishers."

The nearer of the two men turned. He was older than I'd realized, almost as old as Chua. "Your pardon, ma'am, but we grew up fishing the west channel, both me and Hin."

"We're not going to the west channel."

Dem Lun nodded. "Understood, ma'am. But water's water. We both remember how to pull an oar."

"I'm grateful for the help," Ela announced. "I've never pulled an oar in my life, and I was up half the night entertaining." She leapt lightly into the stern of the boat and, while the rest of us found our places on the wooden benches, settled herself between the thwarts.

As we were loading up, a soldier I didn't recognize rolled two small wooden barrels over a gangplank and into the boat, lashing them in the stern just ahead of the tiller.

"What are those?" I asked.

"Supplies," Ruc replied.

"Want to be a little more specific?"

He shook his head as he untied the painter. "Nope."

Without another word, he set a foot on the transom, shoved off from the dock, then stepped nimbly into the boat.

Night's hot, salty fog had settled over the city, shrouding bridges and causeways, making vague the red lights of the hanging lanterns. Dem Lun and Hin rowed in silence, oars slicing soundlessly into the water, pulling free at the end of each stroke with a slick, whispering sound. We passed a few dozen craft as we worked our way south, flame fishers returning from their work, low cargo scows loaded past the rails with barrels and crates, a single wide pleasure boat, lanterns blazing at prow and stern, the revelers doggedly finishing off the last of the wine, belting their drunken songs into the night.

The sun had just blistered the eastern sky when we left behind Dombâng's buildings. In moments, the house-high rushes closed around us. Aside from the smoke smudging the sky behind, the city might have been swallowed up, hundreds of thousands of souls, all their hopes and hatreds sinking into the mud in the space between one stroke of the oars and the next. The sky sat on the delta, heavy, gray, bright as steel. The day was hot, and going to be hotter.

Ela laid her head back against the hull of the boat, crossed her legs over the far rail, and closed her eyes.

"Wake me up," she murmured, "when it's time to kill something."

Chua shook her head. "More likely, something will try to kill us."

Ela smiled without opening her eyes. "I'll wake up for that, too, I suppose, but only if it's very, very exciting."

Without the sun overhead, I would have lost track of west, south, and every other direction almost instantly. The delta was a web of green-brown streams and backwaters threaded between tiny islands, mud bars, stands of spear rushes, a thousand branching channels that all looked the same: reeds and mud, sluggish water tugging imperceptibly toward the sea. Crocs lazed on the flats, but they left us alone. Aside from the occasional scream of some hapless creature struggling, then dying out of sight, the day was calm, almost soporific. For long stretches there was no sound but the steady rhythm of the dripping oars, water chuckling under the hull, the light breeze feathering the rushes.

Since leaving the city, Chua had pointed the direction at each forking channel with her long fishing spear. She didn't speak aloud until midmorning, as we were passing a wide stand of blood rushes.

"Stop here."

The Greenshirts paused, oars hanging motionless above the water.

"Why?" Ruc asked.

The woman pointed to the rushes. "We need one of those."

I glanced over at the long stalks. The rushes were named for their color—a red the hue of dried blood—and for their edges, which could slice through human skin as readily as a carving knife.

"Why?" Ruc asked again.

Caught in a slight breeze, the boat drifted toward the swaying reeds.

"Not too close," Chua said, ignoring Ruc's question, drawing her blade. "Things live in those shallows."

"What kind of things?"

"Things we do not want on the boat."

When we were still a full pace away, she tucked a foot under the thwart, then leaned backward out over the rail, stretching until her body was parallel with the water. The motion was at once gracefully acrobatic and perfectly natural. As the rowers held water, she sliced one of the rushes just above the waterline, let it fall into the water, then picked it out carefully, pinching the flat of the stem between her thumb and forefinger.

"Shove off," Ruc said, and Dem Lun, who had been eyeing the bank warily, drove the blade of his oar into the mud, forcing us back toward the center of the channel.

Chua ran the back of her knife along the full five-foot length of the reed, first one side, then the other, slicking the water from the fibrous stalk, pausing for a moment when she reached a thumb-sized spider.

"Widow's kiss," she said, pointing with the tip of her knife, then flicked the creature into the water.

The surface tension held it up a moment, legs twitching and jerking, slick, black carapace drinking the light. I remembered the name from my childhood. Fishers bitten by the spider did not come back alive. Ruc ignored it, his eyes on Chua.

"I assume there was a reason for the risk."

She nodded, sighting down the length of the rush, first one side, then the other. When she was satisfied it carried no other passengers, she slid the base down through the small hole in the front decking through which the boat's painter was threaded.

"It is a flag," she said.

"Meaning what?" I asked.

"It says we are searching for them."

"Searching?" Ruc said, narrowing his eyes. "You told me you knew where they were."

"In the delta nothing stays in the same place."

"So how do we find them?" I pressed.

The older woman fixed her eyes over the bow, as though looking through the rushes, past them, into some vision of her childhood.

"There is no one place," she replied finally, "but there is a pattern to their movement. When we get close enough, there will be signs."

"And this thing?" I asked, pointing again at the red, swaying reed.

"They will see it," she said, "and know that one of their own has come back."

The woman didn't turn when she spoke. From my bench in the center of the boat, I watched her back. Since leaving Dombâng, she seemed different; not changed, but changing, as though the scarred skin of the broken woman we'd found in the shack by the crematorium was something she was in the process of molting.

"What if we didn't have it?" I asked. "What if we just went searching without the flag?"

"They would kill us."

Ruc nodded, as though the woman's words had confirmed some long-held belief. "The Greenshirts have sent boats after the Vuo Ton. Not recently, but there are accounts in the records. Most returned exhausted, defeated, having seen nothing. Some did not return."

Chua shrugged. "The delta offers a thousand deaths."

"One of which," Ruc noted drily, "is at the hands of the Vuo Ton."

"How do the Vuo Ton survive?" I asked.

Chua glanced down at the spear in her hand. "The people of Dombâng understand building, and coin, and trade. The Vuo Ton know what lives on the water and underneath, what stalks the reeds and rushes. They learn early to face their gods. To worship and to sacrifice."

"Sacrifice." Ruc shook his head grimly. "I've seen what passes for sacrifice. Kids or idiots too drunk to fight back, tied up and tossed into the delta. All to appease these fucking gods."

Chua shook her head dismissively. "The people of Dombâng are weak. They mean nothing to Kem Anh and her consorts."

"They die all the same. I've seen the bodies."

"The Three have no interest in the dead."

"And just what is it," Kossal asked lazily, "that they're interested in?"

The priest had been sitting on one of the narrow benches,

elbows on his knees, chin in his hands. He'd been silent all morning. Now, however, at the mention of the gods, he straightened up, dark eyes bright with the sun, posture giving the lie to his indolent drawl.

"They are hunters," Chua replied.

"Good place for it." Kossal nodded toward a flock of tufted ducks floating silently past. "Plenty of waterfowl."

Chua's smile was all teeth. "The Three prefer more spirited prey."

"Have you ever seen a duck defending her nest?" Kossal raised one eyebrow. "Very spirited."

"Less so than a woman fighting for her life." The fisher glanced speculatively into the shifting reeds. "Or a man, for that matter."

I shook my head. My wrists ached with the old memory of cord biting into my flesh. I could feel the ribs of the boat pressed against my own ribs, hard and unyielding.

"The people sacrificed to the delta don't *get* to fight."

The words came out as a snarl, and the old fisher looked over at me, her weathered face grave.

"The sacrifices of your city are blasphemy. Worse than the worship of the Annurians."

Ruc hadn't shifted his eyes from the channel. His right hand rested calm and steady on the tiller. His voice was absolutely casual when he spoke, but I could see him testing his left hand, flexing it just slightly.

"Sounds as though your people would be pleased to see the whole city burned," he observed. "Priests and legionaries alike."

Chua snorted. "Your city is nothing to the Vuo Ton. A tiny, reeking privy, meaningless in the vastness of the Given Land."

Ruc frowned. "The Given Land?"

"The delta," the fisher replied, sweeping her spear in a wide arc to indicate the water, the reeds, the hot and shifting sky.

"Given to who?" Kossal asked. "By who?"

"Given to us by the gods," Chua said.

Kossal shook his head. "The Three didn't make the delta."

"No," Chua said. "But they made it safe."

I stared at her. "*Safe?* By hunting people?"

"That was the bargain. We sacrifice; they stand guard."

The old priest's gaze was a naked blade. "Guard against what?"

"Against what chased us here in the beginning."

Hidden in the reeds, an unseen bird scratched out a few strident notes against the stifling silence.

"The Csestriim," Kossal said quietly.

Chua parried his gaze with her own. When she finally spoke, it was in the cadence of words handed down through uncounted generations. "In the beginning, the folk knew only terror and flight. They fled from the deathless across mountain and desert until they came to a land where the gods still lived. The Three turned back the deathless, and in return, we agreed to worship them. . . ."

"So you could be slaughtered by 'gods' instead of Csestriim?" Ruc demanded.

"*Never them,*" the fisher replied quietly. "This was our pledge. We would live in the delta and die here. We would give ourselves to these gods and to their servants, but never to the Csestriim. *Never them.*"

"Shitty fucking bargain," Ruc said, "now that the Csestriim are millennia dead."

"An oath is an oath," Chua replied. "The people of Dombâng forsook this oath."

"So did you," Ruc observed. "A lot of righteousness here from a woman who quit her people to live with the filthy apostates."

Chua tensed. For a heartbeat, I thought she was going to plunge the barbed wooden spear directly into Ruc's chest. Then she shook her head. Her eyes went distant, vague.

"I paid my price."

"I thought it was an honor to your people," Ruc growled. "You made it sound like the Vuo Ton want to die in the delta."

"The Vuo Ton want to be worthy of the hunt."

Ruc nodded, as though that settled everything. "They want to be sacrificed."

"What they want," the fisher replied quietly, her eyes fixed past Ruc's shoulder as though he weren't there at all, as though she were talking to the delta itself, "is the honor of facing their gods."

The strike, when it came, happened so fast that Hin was dead before he finished crying out.

He had stopped rowing a little past noon, and when I glanced over, he looked embarrassed.

"I've got to take a . . . short break," he said vaguely.

Ruc just nodded.

The boat slowed, swayed as Hin stood on the bench. A moment later I could hear his piss splashing into the river. A flock of winebeaks passed silently overhead. I watched them gliding south until they disappeared. Ruc was checking on the twin barrels he'd loaded aboard the boat, testing the seals with his thumbnail. I tried, as I'd been trying all morning, to guess what might be inside. Some sort of bribe for the Vuo Ton, if we ever found them? *Quey* or plum wine? Did he hope to get them drunk, then slit their throats in the night? It seemed like an implausibly shitty plan.

Ruc raised his eyes, found me staring. For a moment we were locked there, linked in our silence. Then he winked at me—the first bit of levity I'd seen from him since we discovered the transport—and I found a grin twitching at the corner of my lips.

Then Hin started screaming.

The Greenshirt's cries were more terror than pain, a wordless animal howl over and over until he collapsed.

I drew my knife as he dropped, but couldn't find anything

to stab. In Rassambur we learn to kill people, not snakes, and at first I didn't even see the black ribbon slithering up the inside of the boat's hull, flowing over the thwarts and benches fast as a shadow. Chua didn't share my blindness. The woman pivoted and thrust all in one fluid motion, driving the forked point of her fishing spear down around the snake's head, pinning it against the planks. The serpent—dull black and twice as long as my arm—hissed furiously, lashed the empty air with its tail.

Hin had tumbled into the boat's bottom, eyes straining from his head, limbs convulsing, swollen tongue—purple and foaming—twitching between swollen lips. Dem Lun abandoned his oars, seized his friend, hauled him up onto the bench. It was a human gesture and futile one—my million-fingered god had the Greenshirt in his grip, and Ananshael, when he closes his fist, does not let go.

Ruc was trapped in the stern of the boat, unable, given the vessel's narrow beam, to move past Ela or Kossal. Another man would have been bellowing useless orders or waving a sword. Ruc kept his hand on the tiller, keeping us clear of the banks. His jaw was clenched so tightly I thought it might break, but he stayed silent, letting the people near the fight do the actual fighting.

In the space of a few heartbeats, the snake had managed to writhe free of Chua's spear. It reared up, looking for another target, and Kossal caught it just below the head, his movement as casual as a man picking up an old, familiar tool before setting to work.

"Kill it," Chua said grimly.

The old monk didn't seem to hear. He lifted the snake until its slit eyes were inches from his own, the jaws unhinged for another bite. The tail lashed him over and over, but Kossal paid it no mind.

"Kill it," Chua said again.

"What is it called?" Kossal asked, never taking his eyes from the snake.

"'Tien tra'," Chua replied. "Four steps."

"A strange name," Kossal observed, "for a creature without feet."

"It is named for the paces of its prey. When it bites you, you walk four steps. Then you die."

Hin hadn't made it that far. On the bench behind me, Dem Lun cradled the dead man's shoulders, stared blankly into those blank, bulging eyes. The surviving Greenshirt seemed not to notice anything else in the boat, or anything beyond it. He was shaking his head slowly, murmuring over and over the same low syllable: "No. No. No."

Kossal wrapped another gnarled hand around the snake, just below his first. The creature whipped furiously as he began to twist, slowly and inexorably.

"It would be easier," Chua said, "to use a knife."

The priest ignored her. The muscles in his forearms corded with the strain, but his face was calm, thoughtful, as he finally tore the head from the body. The tail he tossed overboard, where it thrashed, then sank. He studied the head a moment longer, then carefully closed the mouth, sheathing the fangs, and tucked it into a pocket in his robe.

Chua watched him through slitted eyes. "A dangerous trophy," she observed finally.

"It is not a trophy," Kossal replied, shaking his head. "It is a reminder."

"Of what?"

"That my god is everywhere, and one day he will gather even the ministers of his mercy into his patient hands."

No one spoke. The current flowed on, opening its throat beneath the boat's sharp bow. Half crouched on my bench, I wondered at the snake's perfection, the way it had slipped silently into the boat and killed a man before the rest of us even noticed. It was only a beast, of course. It killed to eat, not to worship, but the thing's humble grace made me feel foolish and ungainly. I straightened finally, slid my knife back into its sheath, then turned to look at the wrecked flesh that had been Hin. While I plotted and fretted and schemed, while I spent days trying to fall in love, to pass my Trial, to become a priestess, Ananshael had a million servants like the snake—patient, unordained—going about the work, unmaking lives and the misery and confusion woven through them. What need did the god have of me, of my clumsy devotion? What did it matter, finally, if I loved Ruc and killed him, or if, when I failed, Ela took my throat in her long, perfect hands and held it until I was gone?

There is an inexplicable hubris in any decision to serve a god.

I turned to look at Ela. During the whole frantic episode, she hadn't stirred. Even as Hin screamed, twitched himself to stillness, she'd remained asleep, bare feet kicked up on the rail, brown legs glowing in the sun, hands folded behind her head. Now, though, as though she felt my gaze upon her, she opened a single, lazy eye. Without moving she glanced over the boat, the small, floating tableau of death, then closed her eye again and sighed.

"Does this mean I have to row?" she asked.

19

We reached the village of the Vuo Ton just before dusk.
At first, I thought Chua had lost her way. The channel
in which we'd been traveling tightened, then tightened further,
spear rushes leaning over our heads until we drifted through a
brown-green tunnel, cut off from the sky and sun. When there
was no more room for Dem Lun to ply the oars, he shipped
them silently, secured them inside the hull, then picked up a
wooden paddle from the boat's bottom. The hot air was heavy
with the sweet smells of mud and rot. Hidden in the stalks to
either side, invisible creatures hissed and chittered. I kept seeing,
out of the corner of my eye, flickers of motion, quick slitherings,
but every time I turned there was only the wall of rushes, the
still green water.

"This," Kossal observed mildly, "reminds me of a chute where
animals are slaughtered."

The prospect didn't seem to bother him. Ruc, however, was
scanning the rushes, one hand on the tiller, the other holding
his loaded flatbow. He shifted to aim the weapon at Chua.

"If you have betrayed us," he said, "the first quarrel goes
through your throat."

The woman glanced at the weapon, then turned away to prod
at the reeds with her fishing spear. "If the Vuo Ton wanted to
kill us, we would be dead."

"What are you looking for?" I asked.

For a while, she didn't respond, just kept testing the rushes, sliding her spear between them down into the muddy bank, then pulling it back. Finally, she found a place where the forked head came back dripping water instead of covered with mud.

"We go through here."

I eyed the rushes. "Looks like a perfect place for more widow's kiss. Or snakes."

Chua shook her head. "The Vuo Ton scatter ash and salt on the water. The spiders and snakes stay away from it."

Salt and ash seemed like meager shields against the predators of the delta, but we had come this far under Chua's protection. Ruc studied the reeds for a while, then nodded to Dem Lun. The Greenshirt—his eyes still wide and blank with the horror of Hin's death—began paddling once more, and the boat nosed into the rushes, parting them, gliding up the hidden channel until we were surrounded by the swaying stalks, the open water behind us lost. No one spoke. Bright-winged birds—red, flame-orange, blue—flitted back and forth, vexed at the encroachment on their nests, but no snakes slipped into the boat. No spiders dropped from the reeds above. Then, between one paddle stroke and next, we broke from the rushes and into the open.

It took a moment for me to realize what I was seeing.

Backwaters dotted the delta, spots where the current slowed or disappeared, places that seemed more like ponds than the forgotten channels of a great river. This was no pond. It was a lake. Open water stretched away for hundreds of paces in every direction. After weeks hemmed in by the walls and alleys of Dombâng, by the ranks of rushes flanking every channel, I'd forgotten the size of the sky. Instead of a fragment of cloud, a glimpse of the sun wedged between the rooftops, I could see all of it now, the huge, unbroken blue. After the dappled shadow of the rushes, the sunlight shattering off the open lake was so dazzling that for a moment I could see nothing but light and space. I shaded my eyes with a hand, and slowly shapes began to resolve from the brilliance.

Near the center, ringed by open water, was a village, if *village* is the right word for a settlement in which nothing is settled. The Vuo Ton seemed to have built everything—their homes, their barges, their walkways, even a few of their boats—from rushes. Narrow sheaves served as posts or railings. Larger bundles—waist thick, cinched with cord—took the place of beams and posts, holding up cleverly thatched roofs. At first I thought the Vuo Ton had built on one of the delta's low-lying islands, but as I stared at the settlement, I realized it was flexing, rising and falling with the water, as though the whole thing were alive, breathing.

"It floats," I said stupidly.

Chua nodded. "Every home is a boat."

Dugout canoes ringed the village, two or three tied off to each structure. Half a dozen small children were playing in one, chanting a song in a language I couldn't understand while they danced bafflingly complex steps on the gunwales, leaping from one side to the other just as the boat started to tip. In another canoe, two girls balanced on the rails as they did battle with fishing spears, stabbing and blocking, each rocking the hull in an effort to topple the other. A few old folks sat on a floating raft a few paces away, sipping something from clay cups and heckling.

Behind me, I heard the crack, then groan of a cask being opened. I turned to find Ruc tossing aside the wooden cover. His shoulders flexed as he hefted the thing up onto the rail, then dumped the contents. Gray-blue ropes of tangled intestine slopped into the water, buoyed up by pockets of gas caught inside. Blood spread in a dark slick beside the boat. Ruc watched it for a moment, eyes unreadable, then went to work with his belt knife on the second cask.

"What are you doing?" Chua asked.

"The gods want an offering," Ruc replied, pouring the second barrel into the water. "This is an offering. If the Vuo Ton love blood, here is blood. Call it a gesture of goodwill."

The fisher studied him warily, but held her peace. Overhead

the birds had already begun to gather, a dark cloud of razor-beaks and blue throats eager for the feast.

Dem Lun had stopped paddling in order to stare at the village. "They don't even seem to know we're here," he murmured.

Chua snorted, then jerked her head back the way we had come.

I turned. Immediately behind us, four canoes slid from between the reeds into the open water. The men and women in the slender boats carried short bows. They sighted down the length of arrows which were trained, as far as I could tell, directly on our throats. The arrowheads weren't steel—they seemed to be bone or, I realized after a moment, teeth. I studied the one closest to me, then followed the shaft of that arrow back to the steady eyes behind it.

The Vuo Ton looked like just about everyone else born in Dombâng: brown skin and fine black hair, high cheekbones, square jaws. Like Chua, they wore hide—crocodile or snakeskin—tight breeches, and vests that left bare their slender, muscled arms. The main difference, of course, between the people in the boats and the citizens of Dombâng was the ink: dark lines slashed across faces and down arms, streaking necks and hands, as though every bit of flesh had been raked with shadow. I recognized the man aiming at me after a moment; he was the same man who had followed me through the alleys the night I'd painted my prints all over the city. He didn't lower his bow, but to my surprise he smiled, then winked.

"I think they like us," Ela said. The priestess had finally woken up, climbed out of the bottom of the boat, and stood between the thwarts stretching lazily, leaning to one side then the next, bending forward to touch her toes.

"People who like me tend to bring fewer bows," Ruc replied. He was still holding the belt knife he'd used to open the casks, but after a few heartbeats wisely returned it to its sheath.

I hadn't quite believed we would find the Vuo Ton. Especially after Hin died, it seemed possible we might return to Dombâng empty-handed, defeated. Even moments earlier, as we'd shoved through the reeds, I couldn't really imagine discovering anything on the other side of the vegetation but another channel, another leg of the watery labyrinth. It seemed it might go on forever, that the whole world had been swallowed by the delta, that we were alone in it, six people and a corpse blundering blindly forward, relying on Chua's decades-old memories of a place and a people that might have vanished years before.

And then here they were, sliding toward us in those black canoes, smiling disconcertingly from behind their bows. The man who finally broke their silence carried a paddle rather than a bow. Unlike the others, he had remained sitting in the stern of his canoe, still as an idol as he studied us. Long lines of scar streaked his face, cross-hatching the tattoos. One of those scars had ruined an eye, leaving behind a puckered welt. The man's other eye, however, was keen, bright with the light of the sun.

"Never them, sister," he said finally, nodding to Chua, his voice quiet as the wind through the rushes.

She nodded to him in return. "Never them, Cam Hua."

He smiled, shook his head, then held a finger to the empty socket. "Cam Hua died in the delta. I am the Witness of the Vuo Ton." He spoke perfect Annurian, but an accent tugged at the edges of his words, as though the language felt strange on his tongue.

Ela raised her eyebrows speculatively at the mention of a witness. She glanced over at Kossal, who just shrugged. The title might have seemed a strange coincidence, but then, I was hardly the only creature in the world that bore watching.

Chua hadn't taken her eyes from the seated figure. "When I left, you were barely more than a boy."

"And you not much more than a girl." He shrugged. "Water flows. Channels shift. In enough time, even the lost return."

Chua shook her head. "Not to stay."

"You should not hate the place that made you what you are."

"What about the place that took the man I loved?" she countered. "May I hate that?"

"I saw him, this man you loved. He was not made to face the delta."

"Of course he wasn't. Just as you are not made to face the wide sea. And yet he braved the channels each day all the same."

The man who called himself the Witness bowed to her then, an odd ceremonial gesture that might have been a concession or an apology. It seemed utterly out of place for someone sitting in the stern of the canoe, paddle in hand, especially given all the arrows pointed at us. When he spoke again, however, he sounded sincere.

"Each heart beats its own rhythm. You have my grief. I will plant a violet for the one you loved."

Ruc, who had been watching silently, shifted at those words.

"Tell me about the violets," he said quietly.

The Witness ignored him, kept his gaze on Chua. "Here are more people who do not belong in the delta."

"They demanded to come."

"There was a transport," Ruc began grimly, "packed with Annurian soldiers—"

The Witness tapped a finger idly on his paddle, a bowstring hummed, then an arrow sprouted from the rail of our boat, inches from Ruc's leg.

"Explain to him," the older man said, "that he has not earned his voice."

Chua's face tightened. "He is not Vuo Ton."

"None of them are," the Witness replied mildly. "And yet you brought them here."

"They were persuasive."

"Perhaps you have forgotten our laws: the Vuo Ton allow children, and those who have earned their voice. None other. These," he gestured with the paddle, "are hardly children. . . ."

"They are not here to become Vuo Ton," Chua replied. "They want to talk to you." She hesitated. "About the Three."

"How will they talk with no voices?"

Chua sucked a breath between her clenched teeth. "They are made from the same stuff as my husband. They are not built to face our gods."

"Our gods?" The Witness shook his head. "I would give the rest of my sight before offering such feeble creatures to the gods. If they want to talk, they can earn their voices."

"How do we do that?" Ruc demanded.

"In the same way as the rest of our children," the older man replied with a gentle smile. "There is a test."

I found myself suddenly, massively tired of tests. The words fell out of me, tumbling through my lips before I could catch them.

"And what if we don't?"

The Witness shrugged again. "The delta is always hungry."

Ruc shook his head, furious but ready. "What's the fucking test?"

Our group made a strange procession over the rafts and bridges of the floating village. The warriors from the canoes stalked at our back, bows drawn and fixed on our shoulders, while small children ducked and darted around us, stabbing at our legs with barbed fishing spears. There seemed to be no malice in the attacks; the lithe little bastards treated the whole thing like a game, laughing and pointing, racing back and forth, poking at one another almost as much as they did at us.

"I am considering giving this entire village to the god," Kossal muttered, parrying the hundredth attack with an open hand.

"Why do you hate fun?" Ela asked. She danced and twirled her way over the bridges, knocking aside the spears, catching the stones hurled at her and throwing them back, poking kids in the nose, tugging on ears.

Ruc ignored the barbed spears entirely. Even when they drew blood, he didn't glance down, and after a short time the children tired of him. He was studying the village with a look I recognized, sizing it up, planning for a fight.

For something built entirely of rushes, the town looked surprisingly comfortable. Each house had tall windows to let in the breeze and cleverly contrived blinds to block out the brightest sun. Wide awnings overhung the fronts of the rafts, shading clusters of mats woven from the rushes. We passed a wide hall—far larger than I would have suspected possible working only with reeds. The high windows were hung with stitched tapestries of feather—red and yellow, orange and blue—through which the late-day sunlight poured its warm light, drenching the floor with color.

The line of rafts where the cooking took place looked at first to be hewn of stone. As we drew closer, however, I realized it was clay baked over the surface of the reeds beneath. Dozens of clay bowls steamed above carefully banked fires, while skewered meat smoked above steaming palm leaves. The fires washed the southern half of the town in a haze of smoke that smelled of baked fish, and fire-peppers, and sweet reeds.

"Where are we going?" Ruc asked, turning to Chua.

"To meet the Scales of the gods."

"Scales?" I asked, seizing the closest spear, blocking two others, then cracking it over the heads of my diminutive attackers. They shrieked with delight, retreated, began to regroup.

"Snakes, crocs, fish," Kossal grumbled. "Aren't there enough scales in this miserable cesspool?"

I glanced at the warriors behind us. If they took offense at Kossal's words, I couldn't see it. On the other hand, those bows were still bent, the tooth-tipped arrows still pointed directly at our backs.

"Wrong kind of scale," Chua said, as we stepped from the houses into the open. "These Scales are the kind used for measuring."

"What are we measuring?" I asked.

"*You* are not measuring anything. You will be measured. To see if you deserve a voice."

"That is incredibly sensible," Ela said. "The world would be a better place if everyone who wanted to talk had to pass a test first."

Chua snorted. "If all the world took this test, the world would be a quieter place." She nodded. "Here."

We had emerged beside a wide pool of water. I glanced over my shoulder to get my bearings, then realized a moment later that the village of rush huts and rafts formed a rough circle at the center of the lake. Inside that circle was a pond a few dozen paces across, a small lake inside the lake, ringed by the huts and boats. It might have been a pleasant place for kids to swim and adults to bathe, a sort of watery town square protected from the rest of the delta. Protected from everything, that is, aside from the three crocodiles lounging inside it.

I didn't see the creatures at first—none of us did.

It took me a moment to find the scaly tails parting the water, the eyes floating just above the surface. Each of the crocs looked at least ten feet long, all scale and tooth and claw.

Whenever a crocodile drifted into Dombâng on the river's current, a group of fishers—usually one or two dozen—would go after it with nets and spears. The hunt was part revenge—crocs killed fishers every year—and part practical city management. No one wanted to live and work within paces of a beast that could take off a leg in a single bite, that would rear up to seize its prey, drag it screaming into the water, then roll over and over until it drowned or bled out.

No one, that is, aside from the Vuo Ton.

"Here," the Witness of the Vuo Ton said, "you will worship in the Scales of the gods."

"Worship," Ela replied, frowning, "can be such a dull enterprise. A lot of mumbling and mantras."

"If a mantra helps you face the Scales," the Witness said, smiling, "you are welcome to it."

Dem Lun was staring, frozen, at the circling creatures. "Face them?" he managed, voice barely more than a charred whisper. "You mean *fight* them?"

"A less strenuous devotion would not be worth the name. Succeed, and you will earn your voices."

Chua sucked in a deep breath, then let it out. "I will worship with them."

I glanced over at her. "You didn't even want to come back here, and now you're ready to wrestle crocs?"

"If you die," the fisher replied, "my coin dies with you."

The Witness turned to consider Chua. After a moment he shook his head regretfully. "So this is why you have come back. I remember you, sister, from a time when you would not forsake your people for a handful of metal."

"I left for Tem," she said.

"And this coin?"

"The coin is so I don't ever have to come back." She tossed her spears onto the floating raft at her feet, pulled free the net coiled on her back, then spread it open with an expert toss. "Let's get this over with."

The Witness shook his head. "You earned your voice years ago."

"Then I'll earn it again."

"You know this is not the way."

"They'll be slaughtered," Chua said grimly.

The massive creatures circled the small lake as though they could sense the coming violence. I could feel my own eagerness, too, rising inside me. For more than a week I had been sneaking around the city, inciting civil war, following Ruc like a puppy, trying to fall in love. The days had been muddy, baffling. I couldn't tell from one moment to the next if I was edging closer to my goal or drowning slowly without noticing it. It seemed a long time since I had placed myself in the hand of my god. I found myself aching for the focus, the clarity.

"We'll be fine," I heard myself say.

The Witness raised his brows, but before he could respond, Dem Lun began backing away. "No," he murmured, eyes fixed on the crocodiles, then again, louder, as though a single word could hold the world at bay, *"No."*

He turned to flee, but Ruc caught him by the arm, nodded to the men and women ringing us. Some carried spears, others bows. "They will kill you if you run."

The Greenshirt rounded on him, chest heaving, eyes darting from the crocodiles to Ruc to the Vuo Ton, then back.

"The fucking *crocs* will kill us. I've seen what they do. They bite your legs off. You're still alive while they fucking *eat* you."

Ruc hit him hard in the stomach, just below the ribs. Dem Lun doubled over coughing, the words gone.

"You are a soldier," Ruc murmured, kneeling so that his head was just beside the man. "With you, there will be five of us against those beasts." He paused. "We need you."

"I'm not *sure* that we need him," Ela interjected. She draped an arm around the Greenshirt's quaking shoulders. "No offense, but you seem a little nervous."

Dem Lun turned to stare at her. "We're dead. We are all going to fucking die."

"Well, yes," Ela replied, narrowing her eyes in an effort to understand. "That's part of the deal you make when you agree to be alive."

"Not like *this,*" Dem Lun hissed.

"What's wrong with this?" Ela ran a casual eye over the crocodiles. "They look efficient. As deaths go, eaten by a crocodile seems quicker than most."

"We're not going to die," I said. "Ela, leave him alone."

The priestess shot me a wounded look. "I am *consoling* him."

"Too much speech," the Witness cut in, "for people without voices."

He waved a hand, and one of the Vuo Ton approached. She laid a brace of knives on the reeds before us, then retreated.

"You want us to fight those things with *knives*?" Dem Lun demanded.

"I was planning to bite them," Ela said. She bared her white teeth. "I can bite very hard."

Ruc was sizing up the blades. "One or two?" he asked quietly.

"One for each of you," the Witness replied. "Each child of the Vuo Ton goes naked into the water with nothing more."

"Naked?" Ela asked. She ran an appraising eye over Ruc and me. "That sounds distracting."

"The cloth will kill you," Chua said. "It is something else for the croc to bite. Another weight dragging you under."

Kossal shrugged out of his robe without a word. He wore nothing beneath, but his nakedness didn't seem to bother him.

"You could *warn* a woman," Ela said, fluttering a hand in front of her face as though for more air. For all her mock dismay, she eyed him openly. "I expected more wrinkles," she said after a moment. "And, to be honest, a little less cock."

The two of them might have been bantering at the town fair, were it not for the crocodiles waiting a few paces away, for Dem Lun staring at the creatures with wide, frozen eyes. Ruc didn't share the indifference of the priests or the terror of the soldier under his command. He stripped off his clothes in silence, taking the time to study the crocs. I should have been doing the same thing, sizing up the fight to come, but I found my eyes lingering on his stomach, the taut muscles of his thighs. I had hoped that the next time we were naked together, there would have been less of an audience—certainly I'd been hoping the situation would involve fewer predators—but hoping hadn't been working out all that well for me since arriving in Dombâng. Ruc glanced over, met my eyes. Ananshael was near—I could feel his hand cradling my heart, his fingers tracing my veins—but Ananshael was invisible. It was Ruc I looked at as my heart tested my flesh, Ruc whose eyes met mine as the excitement for the coming fight burned through my blood. He held my gaze a long time, then glanced over at Chua.

"What else can you tell us?"

"They're attracted to motion," the woman replied. "Get behind them. On their backs. Attack the eyes. If they catch you, they will roll."

"Roll?" Kossal asked.

"Crocs prefer to drown their prey. Once they have you, they roll you under, hold you there. The jaws do not kill you. The water does."

Before anyone could respond, a wild scream split the air. I spun to find Dem Lun charging naked toward the water, the knife the Vuo Ton had given him brandished in a raised hand. His terror had him. Fear does strange things to the mind. It can be easier, sometimes, to feel the teeth close down around you than to wait, wondering what it will feel like.

Ruc started after his man, but I caught him by the wrist, kicked his legs out from under him, rolled him onto his back, then wrapped an elbow in a choke hold around his neck. It shouldn't have been so easy, but he'd been paying attention to Dem Lun, not me. One of the many advantages enjoyed by the priests of Rassambur is our familiarity with death. We don't get distracted when a man is torn apart a few paces away. We don't make bad decisions.

Ruc twisted in my grip, but I had him, my legs wrapped tight around his waist. It doesn't take long to choke a man unconscious from that position.

"He's dead," I whispered into Ruc's ear. It wasn't true yet, but Dem Lun—splashing and flailing in his panic—was halfway to the crocs. They split off to close on him from three directions. "If you go in now, you die too," I murmured, tightening my grip. "And then what will become of Dombâng?"

I left out the rest: *If the crocs kill you, I won't ever have the chance*.

The largest of the beasts opened its jaws. Dem Lun, waking too late from the madness of his attack, spun in the water, realized he was alone, began to swim back. Too slow. As he stroked desperately for the shore, the crocodile caught him by the leg. The Greenshirt screamed, thrashed at the surface. The croc reared up, lifted him clear of the surface, then slammed him down. There was blood in the water. Sunlight scribbled the red, spreading stain.

Around us, the Vuo Ton watched in silence. They were witnessing the work of their gods, just as I was watching the work of mine. Ruc was rigid in my arms, his bare skin burning against my own.

Then the crocodile rolled, dragging Dem Lun under; both vanished in a furious, red-brown froth. I counted thirty heart-beats before they emerged, the man a limp puppet in the jaws. The beast slammed him against the water again, over and over until the leg of the corpse tore free at the hip. The other two were on the remains in moments, shredding the meat between them. It was over as quickly as it started.

Chua was the first to break the silence. "This is good. They will be slower with their stomachs full."

The moment I let Ruc up, he rounded on me, chest heaving, eyes ablaze. I thought he might go for the knife the Vuo Ton had given him, but he had too much of a soldier's discipline.

"When this is over," he said, the words caught in his jaws, "you will pay for that."

"When this is over," I replied quietly, wondering if I had sacrificed my only chance to win the Trial, "we may all be dead."

The water closed over me, warm as broth. Unlike the others, I had kept my own knife strapped to my thigh. The steel ballast was welcome as I felt my body go weightless, legs first, then chest, then finally arms. I might have been stepping into a dream, some other world where all the rules I knew had ceased to apply.

The crocs didn't budge as the five of us slid into the water. Chua said they were attracted to movement, and unlike Dem Lun, who had gone into the small lake screaming and flailing, we moved slowly, deliberately. I could see only their ancient eyes above the water—crocs could live for a hundred years or more—the raised scales of their backs and tails. It made sense, suddenly, that the Vuo Ton should choose these as the avatars of their gods.

"We go to the flanks," Ruc said, nodding right and left. There is a fighter's knack to putting aside everything but the fight. Now that we were in the water, he might have forgotten Dem Lun entirely.

"You go where you want," Ela replied. "I'm floating." With no more preamble, she rolled onto her back, and closed her eyes.

The three of us stared at her as she floated slowly toward the crocs.

"Is she insane?" Ruc asked.

"Yes," Kossal replied grimly.

It certainly looked like madness. The priestess had her arms stretched out to both sides, hands idly feathering the water, as though she were lounging in some lord's private pool, waiting for a servant to bring her a drink, or a towel. The sun blazed on her wet skin. She might have been afire. A contented smile played over her lips.

"What is she planning?" I asked.

"If I understood that woman's brain," Kossal said, "I would not be here now."

Ruc studied her a moment longer, then nodded toward the crocs. "Whatever she's doing, we want to be on the flanks when it happens. I'll take the left, the two of you—"

"I will take the left," Kossal said, stroking away before either of us could respond.

I looked at Ruc. "I guess that makes us a team."

He held my gaze. "Seems like we were always better at fighting *against* each other."

Off to my left, the crocs shifted, two of them tracking Kossal.

"They remind me of you," I said quietly. The words just floated up, unsummoned, strangely euphoric. If I was going to

my god, there were things I wanted Ruc to know. "Their stillness."

He watched me a while, silent, then shook his head.

"You're just as insane as the other two," he growled, then
nodded toward Ela. "Let's go. She's getting close."

We swam almost as slowly as Ela floated, circling around the
side of the smallest crocodile—small being a relative term when
discussing a beast the size of a boat—trying to betray ourselves
with as little motion as possible. The creature followed us with
those slitted eyes all the same, rotating silently in the water,
obeying some imperative bred into its flesh to keep those teeth
between it and anything moving.

"Getting behind them seemed a lot easier before we got in
the water," I murmured.

"Never mind getting on their fucking backs." Ruc nodded
incrementally toward Ela. "I hope you told your friend anything
you wanted to tell her, because she's about to die."

The priestess was barely an arm's length from the nose of the
center croc. She still hadn't opened her eyes. I watched, fascinated, as she floated closer and closer. I waited for those jaws
to open, then snap closed on her throat. The creature didn't
move, even when she bumped up against it.

"Too slow," I said, shaking my head. "They track motion,
and she's given them nothing to track."

"Unfortunately, we have to kill them," Ruc said. "Not just
float past."

Ela rolled smoothly as a log, twisting in the water to press
her naked flank against the crocodile's hide. Slowly, slowly, she
slid a hand over the creature's back, the half-drunken embrace
of a woman barely waking from sleep, searching for the lover
at her side. She smiled without opening her eyes, slid a hand
along the scales, and then, the movement so fast I saw only the
spray followed by the fountain of blood, slammed her knife into
the creature's eye.

The lake exploded.

The wounded animal thrashed, snapped its jaws furiously at the air, then rolled, tail thrashing the water to a froth. The other two crocs twisted inward, drawn by Ela's sudden attack or by the death spasms of the flailing beast. Kossal, quick as an eel, closed the distance in moments, sliding behind the closest crocodile, rolling up onto its back, clenching it between his knees like a rider on a panicked mount as he drew his knife.

I was swimming before I knew it, Ruc at my side, both of us closing on our own quarry from slightly different angles. He was near the head, the snapping jaws. I thought I had the easier approach until the tail whipped across the water, smashing me in the head, knocking me back a full body-length. When the haze cleared and I'd coughed the water out of my lungs, I found Ruc grappling with the thing, one arm caught in its jaws, the other wrapped around its neck, his face a rictus of determination.

Kossal was gone, and the croc he'd been riding, both of them transmuted into a mad boiling of the bloody water. Ela, too, had disappeared, though the croc she'd killed was still twitching, the knife standing proud from the eye. I was vaguely aware of the Vuo Ton chanting and taunting, of Chua shouting some sort of advice, but my world had narrowed to Ruc and the furious beast trying to devour him.

"Your knife," I shouted. "Stab it!"

By the time the words were out of my mouth, however, I saw it wouldn't work. The croc was thrashing viciously as a fly-maddened bull. Ruc had managed to hold on so far, but if he let go of the thing's neck with his good hand, it would toss him around like a doll until his shoulder ripped right out of the socket.

"Get on its back," Ruc growled. "Get behind—"

Before he could finish, the croc rolled, dragging him down into the muddy depths.

I hauled in a deep breath and dove. The lake was too murky with blood and kicked-up mud to see anything but my own pale hands, groping against the water's meager purchase. I debated drawing my own knife, but I needed both hands to swim. Ruc and the croc had gone down just a few paces away, but for a long time all I could see was bubbles, the slanted shafts of sunlight, the filaments of trailing reeds. Then, suddenly, I was on them, the croc like a huge rock sunk to the bottom, Ruc the vague shadow pinned beneath.

I couldn't see anything beyond the outlines, certainly not well enough to stab for the eye. For agonizing moments, I groped in the gloom. I found Ruc's chest first, warm in the warm water, muscles bunched with his struggle. He went still when he felt my hand, aware enough, even with his arm lodged in the croc's jaws, to understand that someone had come, to resist the urge to kick and scramble, to go limp while I searched for the creature's eyes. Once I found the thing's snout, the eyes were obvious enough— small, tough bulges an arm's length back from the tip of the nose. Air burning in my lungs, forcing myself to go slow, I drew the knife from the sheath at my thigh, wrapped an arm around the croc's neck, then drove the blade home, forcing my arm in and down even when I felt the knife lodge on some bone inside the head, twisting it, ripping it free, then plunging it in again.

The beast twitched, reared, then went utterly still.

Done, I thought.

Then I realized Ruc was still trapped in the jaws.

I worked my way along the serrated teeth, tried to haul them open. They wouldn't budge. In the end, Ananshael takes the strength from all creatures, but my god is patient, and Ruc didn't have time to wait. I dragged on the jaws again, failed again, forced myself to pause, to think, then found Ruc's face. Washed in the croc's warm blood, I pressed my lips to his. He stiffened at the touch, started to draw back, but I wrapped a hand behind his head and drew him close, exhaling the meager air remaining in my lungs into his own. I took his free hand in my own, squeezed it, then empty, aching for air, stroked hard for the surface.

Eight times I filled my chest to bursting. Eight times I swam back down, found him, emptied my lungs, made my breath his own, then worked at the croc's jaws with my knife. The hide was tough as tree bark, the muscles beneath knotted as old rope, but I kept at it, sawing, slicing, stabbing, rising to the surface, sucking in another breath, then going down again.

In the end, Ruc had to carry me up. I'd waited too long, spent too much time hacking through tendon, misjudged what little air I had left. The blackness closed over me like a fist. I had time for a single thought: *My god . . .* and then I was gone.

I woke to Ruc's green eyes over me.

"Wake up," he growled, then ground his bleeding palm into my stomach.

I choked, puked out the brackish water, rolled onto my side, groaned. When I rolled back, he was still there, bleeding, watching me. Something hot and violent blossomed in my heart.

Love? I wondered.

Eira, as was her way, did not respond.

20

The crocodiles watched with grave, lifeless eyes as we feasted on their flesh.

Butchers had cut off the heads, laid them on clay platters longer than my arm, then piled the fresh-carved meat around them, river garlic and boiled sweet reeds layered between the steaming slabs. All of the Vuo Ton had gathered for the feast, the adults sitting cross-legged on the wide rafts—there were no tables, no chairs—while the children made do with whatever space they could find. Surviving the day's ordeal had earned the four of us a place on the centermost barge, right beside the Witness. The women and men flanking us weren't necessarily the oldest or the most obviously strong, though they seemed to have more scars, and they carried themselves with the confidence of those who had faced their own death many times over.

Night seeped up silently from the surface of the water, from between the reeds, leaking between the floating houses until it filled the sky. Off to the west, the low moon glowed like tallow, tangled in the swaying rushes. Smoke from the cook fires smudged the stars, but fish-scale lanterns hung from the ropes overhead, swaying with the warm breeze, illuminating food and faces alike with a ruddy glow. I could feel Ruc at my side, a still form in all the motion, a fixed point in the ever-shifting delta.

I looked over to find him watching me, his green eyes nearly black in the lamplight. A tiny old woman with hands like spiders had treated the punctures on his arm with some kind of ointment, stitched them shut, then slathered the whole thing with more ointment squeezed from tubers I didn't recognize. When she insisted that he lie down, he shook his head.

"I've had worse."

The wounds didn't seem to bother him during the meal. He used his bloody left hand as often as his right, though he flexed his fingers every so often as though to check if they still worked. None of us had escaped from the water unscathed. I could feel a furious bruise bleeding beneath the skin of my cheek; it felt as though the bone might be fractured, but I couldn't tell. A pair of slices ran half the length of Kossal's leg, and even Ela, whose battle had ended almost before it started, bore a set of painful-looking welts across her bare shoulder, although like Ruc she didn't appear to notice them. All in all, it seemed a mild reckoning. Mild for us. Less so for Dem Lun, whose body the butchers had hacked out of the massive croc.

As we ate, his remains and those of Hin as well waited on a raft of floating rushes a few dozen paces out into the lake. The night's feast was both funeral and celebration. Ruc hadn't objected—he had something of my own order's practicality when it came to corpses—but once or twice throughout the meal I caught him staring at the floating shadow, as though the wrecked flesh held the answer to some unspoken question, and when the Witness finally gave the order to light the pyre ablaze, he didn't take his eyes from the tongues of flame.

As the sodden body turned to ash, the Vuo Ton sang a simple, plangent melody in their own language.

"What does it mean?" I asked Chua quietly.

"It is a celebration," she replied, "of his bravery."

"Strange practice," Ruc said, his voice sanded perfectly flat. "Murdering a man, then praising his bravery."

The Witness turned toward us. "We asked no more of him than we do of our own children."

"What kind of people feed their children to crocodiles?"

"They are not food. They are fighters."

"Not if they die."

"If they die," the Witness replied evenly, "they die with a knife in hand. What pride could they have, spending their lives in hiding?"

"More than a hundred thousand people in Dombâng," Ruc said. "Most of them live, laugh, thrive. No one throws them naked into the delta to fight crocs."

"And this is why the people of Dombâng are weak. You have forgotten your gods."

Kossal, who had been gnawing the meat from a rib, paused, wiped his face, then poked the bloody bone at the leader of the Vuo Ton.

"Tell us about the gods."

The one-eyed man nodded, as though he had expected this. "You are not from Dombâng."

"She is," Ela cut in, nodding at me. "We're Kettral."

Kossal rolled his eyes, but didn't bother responding.

"Kettral," the Witness said, drawing the word out as though studying it. "I have heard stories of these warriors. Now I start to understand how you weighed so heavy in the Scales."

He turned to the Vuo Ton seated closest, murmured a few words I couldn't understand, then said again: *Kettral.* Surprise rippled down the line, questions and exclamations. Women and men began studying us anew, eyes bright in their tattooed faces.

"And why," the Witness asked after a pause, "have the Kettral come to the Given Land?"

"To find you," Ruc said grimly, shifting languorously as an uncoiling snake.

"You are not Kettral," the chieftain said. "We have seen you in the city. Why do you want to find something you have ignored for so long?"

"Because a week ago almost two hundred men were slaughtered. Half were Annurian, half native to the city."

"Ah." The Witness paused to translate for the others, then turned back to Ruc. "A fat ship? Its decking reeked of salt?"

"More blood than salt, by the time we found it."

The Witness nodded. "A great sacrifice. Holy."

"Explain to me," Ruc said, "what is holy about two hundred men with their throats torn out, their arms ripped from their shoulders, heads severed, eyes gouged, vines planted in the empty sockets?"

"This was the work of the Three," the Witness replied, as though that explained everything.

Ruc watched him for a moment, then turned to study the mass of Vuo Ton scattered over the boats and rafts. "The Three?" he asked quietly. "Or the three thousand?"

"You think we attacked your people?"

"I've never seen a god," Ruc replied. "But I *have* seen you."

The chieftain shook his head. "You have not seen the gods because, like all in the city, you have forgotten your worship."

"Oh, worship is doing just fine in Dombâng. Kids get dragged out into the delta to die every week."

The Witness shook his head. "The Three would no more take one of your feeble city dwellers than a jaguar would a slab of rotten meat."

"I've seen the bodies," Ruc replied quietly.

"The Given Land is rich in ways to die," the Witness said. "Snakebites and spiders. Drowning. Thirst."

A hot vision seared across my mind—the eyes of a jaguar and beneath them the eyes of something else, a woman who was not a woman. Pain blazed through me. My skin had long since scarred over, but I could feel the wounds that made the scars as though they still bled. I felt dizzy suddenly. The light of the lanterns reeled in vicious orbits around me. Even the stars seemed to be on fire.

"What the priests of your city do," the Witness went on—he was still talking to Ruc, oblivious to the fact that I'd come momentarily unmoored—"is not worship."

"Says the man who tried to feed us to the crocs."

"You came to us. You demanded this."

"We demanded a conversation."

"Only those weighed in the Scales are given a voice." The one-eyed man shook his head. "You chose this," he said again.

"And what about the men on that transport?" Ruc asked. "Did they choose it, too?"

"We are bound by the oaths of our ancestors."

Ruc snorted. "What about the feebleness of city dwellers? I thought we were rotten meat, well beneath the interest of your Three?"

The Witness smiled. "Two hundred men, all armed, ready for violence. This is not a solitary soul abandoned on a mud flat. This is a prize worthy of a hunter."

Ruc fell silent. The slitted eyes of the dead crocodile surveyed the night while the feast cooled on the platter around it, grease congealing on the meat, which had gone from red-brown to gray.

"How do you know all this about the Three," I asked, "if no one has ever seen them?"

The tattooed man turned to me, seemed to look at me and through me at the same time.

"Every ten or twenty years," he replied, "they leave a warrior alive."

I shook my head. "Why?"

"To bear witness," he raised a hand to his own chest, smiled in bemusement as though surprised to find he had a body, as though surprised it had not been destroyed, "to the truth."

Dizziness washed over me again, but I forced it back, forced myself to focus through the haze of memory on the present moment, on the man sitting across from me, on the question burning like fire in my throat.

"How do they choose?" My voice was husky as it left my lips, ragged. "How do they decide who to spare?"

He shrugged. "Their ways are their own."

"Maybe," I replied, "but you've been worshipping them for

thousands of years. You must have some idea why they do what they do."

The Witness raised an eyebrow. I could feel the unreadable eyes of the Vuo Ton on me, could feel Ruc at my side, studying me. I had overstepped; a part of me knew that. I was pressing too hard for a truth I should have had no reason to want. And yet confronted with a man who claimed to have faced his gods, I needed to know.

"Why did they spare you?" I demanded.

The Witness pursed his lips, traced a scar that ran the length of his arm, as though he were following some path on a map with his finger.

"I saw myself in them," he said finally. "Perhaps they saw some fragment of themselves in me." He shook his head, as though uncertain of the words. "Perhaps they want someone who will teach the next generation."

"Teach them to die," Ruc growled.

"Teach them to live," the Witness countered. "To fight." He paused. "The Three could end us all in an afternoon. They could rise from the waters this very night and drag us to our graves. You saw your own men on that fat ship. You know what they can do."

"Then why don't they?" I demanded. "If they love hunting so much," I gestured to the dark reeds swaying at the edge of the lake, "why are we still here?"

"If we were gone, who would they hunt?"

"If this is true," Ruc said, "and I don't believe it is, you have made yourselves into prey."

"We are all prey," the Witness replied with a smile. "Life isn't in the ending, but the living."

Ruc shook his head. "Easy for you to say. You're still alive."

The smile drained off of the chieftain's face. His eyes looked suddenly hollow, as though they were holes drilled into some bottomless darkness. "There is nothing easy about living with the memory of the Three."

"How exciting," Ela cooed, laying a hand on the man's shoulder. "You really have *seen* them."

He nodded.

"What do they *look* like?"

I forced myself not to lean forward. Memory slammed into me like a fist, obliterating the present. All over again I saw the leopard coiled snare-still on the bank, saw it gather, then leap, jaws open. Felt myself raise my useless hand to fight a little longer, and then witnessed, as I had in a thousand dreams, that woman who could not have been a woman burst from the water, naked and perfect, saw her catch the cat by the neck with one effortless hand, saw the creature jerk, go limp as she snapped its neck. It had to weigh a hundred pounds, but she tossed it aside easily, almost negligently, the way a woman at the end of a long meal might toss one final, well-cleaned bone onto her plate. I could feel again my heart scrambling desperately in my chest as she leaned over me, could see those eyes, the same eyes that had haunted me ever since, cold and golden, framed in that perfect face. I could hear my voice in my ears: *Are you here to save me?* I could see her bare teeth, the sharp incisors, as she smiled, then shook her head.

"They are beautiful."

For half a heartbeat, I thought the words were my own, though I had not opened my mouth.

Then I realized it was the Witness. Slowly, my memory faded. The real world bled across my sight once more—Vuo Ton seated on the rafts of rushes, the severed head of the crocodile gazing at me with lazy eyes, Ruc, still but ready at my side, Ela's fingers lingering on the chieftain's arm, and the Witness himself, his gaze gone impossibly distant.

"Like people?" I found myself asking.

"They are to us," he replied, "as we are to the shadows we cast."

On the raft before us, the dark shape of my own shadow shifted beside Ruc's, twitching with the lantern's fire, as though something inside both of us was restless, as though something beneath or behind our bone and skin rejected the stillness of our bodies.

"That's pretty," Ela said, trailing her hand along the chieftain's arm. "I like the part about the shadows. But I don't know what it means."

"They are like us," I said, the words too hot and urgent to remain inside of me any longer. "Like us, but faster and stronger. More perfect. More full of whatever it is that makes us alive."

From across the platter of cooling food, Kossal narrowed his eyes.

"You have seen them."

It wasn't a question, and I didn't answer it. I turned instead to the leader of the Vuo Ton.

"What color were her eyes?"

He smiled at the memory. "Like the last light of the sun."

"Golden?"

He nodded.

"And the scar?" I went on, my heart thudding painfully, "right here?" I raised a hand to my cheek, traced the line down along my chin.

"So you have seen her, too."

I hesitated, then nodded. I could feel the eyes of all the Vuo Ton upon me, steady and grave. I ignored them. The only gaze that mattered belonged to Ruc, who was studying me with a mixture of anger and open disbelief. I turned to him.

"You wouldn't have believed me."

He shook his head. "I don't believe you now."

I started to object, found I could not. My whole life, I'd carried the memory of those golden eyes, the casual, awful might with which that jaguar had been tossed aside. Most of the time it seemed like a vision, a dream, the phantasm of a mind baked too long in the sun.

"Of course you don't," I replied finally. "I hardly believe it, and I'm the one who saw her."

I turned away from Ruc to find Chua leaning toward me, her weathered face intent. "When did she find you?"

I stared at her, uncertain how to relate an encounter that I'd spent almost two decades denying. The fisher stared back, hands clenched in her lap. The Witness watched me with his singular stare, as did Kossal. For once even Ela was silent. I could try to hide, to stuff the memory back into whatever part of my mind had carried it all these years, but I was tired of holding it, tired of hiding. The somber faces of the Vuo Ton twitched with the flickering lamplight. The moon had climbed free of the reeds; it hung overhead, a single, impossibly distant lantern almost lost in the immensity of the night.

It happened, I told myself, trying to feel the truth of those words. *It was real.*

Though he was the only true skeptic, perhaps *because* he was the only skeptic, I turned to Ruc, took a deep breath, then began slowly to unfold the story.

"I was eight when my mother tied my arms and legs, then paid a priest to leave me in the delta."

"You told me this story."

"Not all of it."

Ruc opened his mouth to object, then shook his head and clamped it shut. Whether that was an invitation to continue or a refusal to engage in the topic at all, I couldn't say. It didn't matter. I had thrown myself from the cliff—there was no turning back, no choice beyond the plunge.

"My mother thought that sacrificing a child to the delta might reverse my father's fortunes, might save them both, and so she gave me to the priest. He drugged me and took me to the delta.

"I woke up on a mud flat, my vision swimming, head throbbing. I couldn't see the city, couldn't even see the smoke. Just reeds all around, and the slow, brown water swirling at my feet."

I glanced over at the Witness. "The priest had untied me."

He nodded. "Scraps of the truth remain, even in the city."

"The hunt," I concluded quietly.

He nodded. "Kem Anh and her consorts would never hunt a child of eight. Those in your city who call themselves priests have forgotten that. But even they cannot forget that the Three are hunters." He cocked his head. "Did he give you a weapon?"

"Hardly a weapon," I replied quietly. "An old knife."

I could still feel it in my hands, the weight, the rough wood, the nicked steel of the dull, rust-spotted blade.

"A mockery," the Witness said, shaking his head.

"Maybe," I replied. "But that knife saved my life." I stared into the swirling currents of my memory. "For a while I didn't move. My head ached and my legs felt like lead, but the reason I didn't get up, didn't try to do something, was terror. My own blind panic pinned me to that mud better than any steel shackles. The priest might as well have left me tied. I lay there all morning, wondering when I would die, and how. The day was hot, my tongue swelled in my mouth, but I didn't dare approach the water, didn't dare twitch. I was horrified of *qirna,* of snakes, of crocodiles, of *everything.*

"In the late afternoon, a red-bill duck landed on the bank near the reeds. Just as she started pecking for bugs, a brown-back uncoiled from the reeds, caught her in a long loop of its body, and began to squeeze. I couldn't move. I just watched. The duck twitched and struggled. Her feet scrabbled at the mud. It seemed to go on forever, and then, just like that, she was dead. Still.

"I thought about killing myself then, about stabbing the knife into my stomach. It looked so much more peaceful to be dead, but the *getting* dead—that looked hard. I didn't know where I was going, but I wanted to be away from that duck, away from the snake slowly swallowing the body, and so I made my way down the mudbank. When I reached the end, I had two choices—swim to an island on the far side or go into the reeds. I swam, forcing myself to go slow, not to thrash, not to do anything that might draw a school of *qirna.* When I reached the island, I climbed partway into a low tree and fell asleep.

"I woke up lost and baffled, unable to breathe. At first I thought my father had his broad arm across my throat, choking me, then realized I wasn't in my home, that there was no stink of *quey* on the air, no cursing. A moment later I tumbled from the tree, and when I hit, I remembered: the priest, the mud bar, the island. I scrabbled at my chest and found a boa wrapped tight around me, squeezing, squeezing. It was dumb luck that I still had the knife, luck that the hand holding it was free. I went at the snake with a mad fury, stabbing over and over so viciously I cut myself in half a dozen places. Finally, just as the strength drained out of me, I felt it loosen. I dragged it off, hurled it away as well as I could, retreated shaking into the tree. I stared half the afternoon at that dead snake, then made myself climb down, skin a portion of the body, and eat the meat, which was still warm.

"I'd been on that island for three days when the jaguar came. Maybe it was the snake's blood smeared over the dirt, maybe my own blood, oozing from the cuts that broke open any time I moved, or maybe my luck was just done. It caught me standing by the bank, a makeshift spear in hand, trying to take one of the river eels. I noticed it only because everything went suddenly quiet behind me, the insects and tiny birds instantly and perfectly mute. I remember turning, seeing that mottled pelt, those wide eyes, the teeth, and thinking first, *It's beautiful* and then a moment later, *Now is when I die.*

"I managed to hold it off for a little while, my knife in one hand, my spear in the other. It was wary, but it had me trapped on the island. It was a better swimmer than I was, and I was exhausted, sick, too hot. There was nowhere to go, nowhere to flee. Each time it came at me I was a little slower, and then it got inside my guard, sliced open my arm with a claw, knocked my spear spinning into the water, darted back, circled around, then paused before the kill. When it leapt for me, I was dead, *would* have been dead except that, just as its feet left the ground, a woman who could not have been a woman, a naked woman with golden eyes, exploded from the water, caught the cat in midair, snapped its neck, then tossed it aside."

"Kem Anh," the Witness said quietly.

I looked at him a long time, then shook my head. "Why?"

He shrugged. "The ways of the goddess are strange. I cannot speak for her, but I would say she saw your future in you: a girl of eight, three days alone in the delta, who killed a constrictor, who fought a jaguar. She could see what you might become. She did not want to waste it."

"Waste *what*?"

"A woman," he answered with a smile, "who might one day be worthy of the hunt."

I shook my head. "She couldn't have known I would come back."

He spread his hands, as though to embrace me, the feast, the village, the entire night. "Yet here you are, years later, searching for her."

The drinking went on late into the night. I remembered thinking at one point, drunkenly, how strange it was that the same people who had eyed us askance then tried to feed us to crocodiles should become so welcoming, so generous, so voluble. The jugs of *quey* went around and around and, as children cleared away the remnants of the feast, people began drifting from raft to raft, leaving one conversation to join another. I couldn't understand the language, but from the fingers pointed our way and the vigorous miming, it seemed that the most popular topic was the afternoon's struggle. The old people nodded knowingly, as though they'd seen it all a thousand times. The children, those too young to have faced the crocodiles themselves, spent the night rehearsing every point, searching for some insight, some advantage, that might give them an edge when the moment came for them to swim naked into the lake.

The Vuo Ton seemed fascinated by all of us. They studied Ruc's arm, debated volubly about the welts on Ela's shoulder, and eyed Kossal with obvious, if wary, interest. A few approached Chua, women and men old enough that she might have known them before she abandoned the floating village for Dombâng. The fisher didn't seem pleased to have returned to her childhood home, and slipped away just as people began producing clay pipes, packing them with some pungent leaf I didn't recognize, inhaling smoke from the tiny glowing fires.

Most of all, the Vuo Ton seemed interested in me. When I finished my story, the Witness had spoken at length to the village. When he was done, the townsfolk turned to me, nodded their heads in deference. By the time the drinking and smoking were well underway, people were crowded around me, draping necklaces over my head, pressing pipes or bottles into my hands, urging me to drink, smoke, dance. What I wanted to do was sleep, but as the *quey* seeped into my blood, I found myself stumbling through unfamiliar steps to the pounding of a dozen hide drums set in a semicircle on the largest barge.

Ruc found me in the press of bodies, dragged me momentarily clear, to the edge of the wide raft. The water trembled with the music, each beat shattering the moonlight glazed on the surface. I had not seen him drink or smoke all night.

"You realize," he growled at me, "that drunk people are easier to kill. They sleep so much more soundly."

I stared into his dark eyes, then gestured past him, to the celebration. Kossal had vanished, but Ela was whirling from partner to partner, long limbs already fluent in the new music. Children sang with the drums and those too old to dance tapped the rhythm on their knees with gnarled hands.

"Do you really think that is what this is?" I asked.

His jaw tightened.

"Look," I said, wrapping an arm around his shoulders and turning him. "*Look.* Don't you think this would be a strange way to give us to the god?"

"What god?" he asked, narrowing his eyes.

I cursed my drunkenness, stumbled ahead. "*Any* god. They

could have killed us with their bows the moment we paddled into the lake. They could have killed us right after we fought the crocs. They could have poisoned your arm instead of healing it. They could have poisoned all of us at any point in the meal." I shook my head, drawing him close. "Instead," I went on, "they've fed us, given us a hut for the night."

Hut wasn't quite the right word. The three homes that the Witness had commandeered for us were tidier than huts—cozy domed structures of tight woven rushes, each floating on its own raft. Kossal had already claimed one, Chua the other. Ela seemed never to need to sleep, which left the third for me and Ruc. A warm wind gusted up out of the east. For just a moment, the ocean's salt tang swept aside the quieter scents of mud and human bodies. Then the rain hit, so heavy it obliterated the sight of everything but Ruc, his face lit by the smeared light of the lanterns swaying with the wind.

"Come on," I said, dragging him by the shoulder.

"Come where?" he demanded, his voice barely louder than the rain splattering the rafts, stippling the water with a million tiny splashes.

"Inside," I said, gesturing toward the dim shadowed shape of our hut. "If they've decided to kill us, we might as well be dry."

He shook himself free of my grip. I thought he intended to resist, but after a moment he nodded, then waved me ahead.

The thick rush roof muted the rain, dulled the sound of the drums that the Vuo Ton were still playing out on the largest rafts. The small space was dark, warm, redolent of smoke, sweat, some spice I didn't recognize. At first I couldn't see anything beyond Ruc's vague form and the rain draped like a silver curtain over the outline of the low door. A single lantern whirled just outside that door, flame dancing in the wind but resolute behind the shield of scales; the red light drained into the hut, and after a few moments I could make out shapes: a line of clay jars arranged neatly by the door, fishing spears racked against the wall, half a dozen baskets hung from the rushes overhead, a mattress of reeds all the way toward the back.

The two of us stood just inside. I could hear his breathing, feel the heat pouring off of him. I lifted the clay jug I was holding.

"Drink?"

He shook his head curtly, staring out into the rain.

I draped an arm around his shoulder, drawing him close. "Maybe, just once, it's all right to trust someone."

Ruc stiffened inside my arm. "They murdered Dem Lun."

"That guy," I said, knowing the words were wrong, but lost in the haze of whatever it was I'd been smoking, "was never going to make it out of the delta anyway."

"He didn't have to die in the jaws of a fucking croc."

"He didn't have to run screaming into the water like croc food." I dangled the jug in front of his face once more. "*Try this.*"

He tried to pull away, but I felt it coming and held him close.

"Let go of me," he growled.

"Nope."

I could see glimpses of the Vuo Ton, shadows dancing through the rain's soft needles. The storm slackened for half a heartbeat, and I saw Ela, whirling through the crowd. *Love isn't something you experience alone,* I reminded myself. *It's not something in your head. It's in the space between two people.*

"Listen," I said, dragging Ruc around to face me. "You want me to say I'm sorry about Dem Lun." I shook my head. "I'm not."

"Because you 'saw the goddess'?" he asked quietly. "Because you suddenly understand the truth? Because now you understand the need to sacrifice to the Given Land?"

I tucked a foot behind his ankle, slammed him down onto the rushes, my face inches from his own. "I *was* sacrificed to the delta. I spent three days out there thinking I was going to die before a boat of baffled Dombâng fishers found me."

"So now it's time for everyone to have a turn? Your father hit you, hated you, your mother gave you up, and so it's fine to feed someone else, someone who had nothing to *do* with that, straight into a croc's mouth?"

There was a fire where my heart should have been. I half expected to see Ruc's face burst into flame when I spoke. I could feel the coiled strength of his body beneath me, but for some reason he made no effort to break free.

"How did you *want* him to die?" I growled.

"Not like this."

"It is *all* like this," I said. "The stuff that comes before—the teeth or disease, the knife, the sword, the snake bite—none of that matters. None of that is death." My breath burned in my throat. I could smell his sweat. I could feel the memory of his bloody lips on my lips as I breathed into his mouth. "Death is what *stops* the suffering. Death is the *blessing*."

"Then why have you spent your life avoiding it?"

"You don't know the first thing," I growled, "about how I've spent my life."

Ruc met my glare. "No. I don't. I don't know if you're Kettral or Skullsworn or some fucking mercenary in league with the bastards trying to destroy Dombâng."

"If I'm trying to destroy Dombâng, then what am I doing here? Why am I *helping* you?"

"*Are* you? You've certainly been near me, but what have you actually done?"

"Aside from cutting you out of that croc's jaws? Aside from breathing my own breath into your mouth?"

His jaw tightened. I took his chin in my hand, pressed myself against him.

"If I wanted you dead," I went on quietly, "all I needed to do was wait." I slipped a knife out of its sheath. "I could kill you now."

Ruc caught my wrist, shook his head, flipped me over onto my back. "No," he growled. "You couldn't."

He twisted my wrist, and I let the knife go. It wasn't time for the knife, not yet.

I needed to love him first.

"I came back to Dombâng," I said, "because there were things here I could not forget. Things I needed to see again."

His breath was hot on my face. "Your goddess. The fucking myth I've spent the past five years trying to stamp out."

"She is not my goddess."

"But you believe she's real, that she's out there."

"You're real," I said, sliding a hand behind his head, drawing his face down toward mine, so close I was breathing his breath. "You're right here. That does not make you a god."

His eyes were holes in his head. "What the fuck do you want, Pyrre?"

I want you.

I couldn't say it.

Not that it wasn't true. I wanted him in that moment, wanted to feel his weight on top of mine, his skin naked against my own. I wanted him to love me and I wanted to fall in love, but that wasn't all. The things I wanted were legion—my mother's throat in my hands all over again, Ananshael's blessing, the cool air of Rassambur on my face, to see again that perfect creature that had saved me from the jaguar all those years ago—they pressed around me, beggars with hands outstretched demanding more, more.

"I want to be lighter," I said finally.

Ruc snorted—a sound halfway between a laugh and a grunt a man makes when you punch him in the stomach—then rolled off of me.

Not like that, I wanted to say. *It's my own weight I don't want.* But he was already gone, sitting in the doorway, staring at the rain as he took a long pull on the jug of *quey,* then another, then another. I sat up, retrieved my knife, then joined him, still searching for the words. The storm had slackened, and I could see Ela on the raft across the way. Most of the Vuo Ton had taken shelter, retreating to their own huts or the wide octagonal halls ringing the settlement, but a dozen men and women flouted the downpour, dancing to the thudding drums. Ela was at the center of the motion, rain streaming down her face, slicking her skin as she spun from one partner to another.

"I want to be like her."

I didn't realize the words were true until I said them.

"She seems insane," Ruc replied.

I shook my head. "She knows who she is. She understands what she wants. Nothing bothers her."

"It ought to."

"What ought to?"

Ruc took another long pull from the crock, handed it back, then waved a hand toward the rain. "Take your pick. The world is broken. Anyone who doesn't know that, who doesn't feel it right down in their bones, has to be broken, too."

"What if we're all broken?"

He chuckled grimly. "It's a possibility I've considered."

I reached over, ran a finger along the wound carved into his arm, then reached up to touch the scar on his chin.

"So what do we do?"

He shook his head. "Try to be better."

The rain picked up again, driving into the rushes, slicing silver knives across the lamplight, spattering through the open door to wet my feet, my legs. I could hear the last dancers still out there, but couldn't make out much more than shape and motion. When I turned to look at Ruc, my vision lurched. Lamplight glinted in his eyes, on the sweat beading his chest. For the rest, he was a man built out of heat, hard planes, and darkness.

"To be better," I said, testing the words. I took his face in my hands. "That's why I came back."

For once, then, something that wasn't a lie.

He touched my fingers, as though surprised to find them there, followed my bare arm back to my shoulder, his touch shockingly gentle. I could remember fighting him, fucking him, but nothing like this.

"You should have found somewhere else," he said, easing me back onto the rushes, shifting his body over me. "Someone else."

I reached down to fumble with his belt, yanked it free, slid a hand inside his pants to find him hard, ready.

"There is no one else," I said, sliding his pants down, then kicking them off his ankles with my foot. I raised my arms for him to strip away my vest. "It had to be you."

And of course, like most men, like most people, he heard the wrong thing. He heard the last word—*you*—when he should have been asking about the first, *What is it?*

21

I woke to find dawn's light smeared like wax across the eastern
sky. My head throbbed, and my body ached in a dozen places
where the crocodile had battered me the day before. I rolled
over groggily to find Ruc lying naked on his back, one arm
tossed across the rushes, the other, the one with the wound,
cradled at his chest as though he were trying to hold close
something vitally important. I watched him for a while, his
wide chest rising and falling, the twitching of his closed lids as
he lived some dream I would never see. Then I turned away,
searching for my knives.

I found them by the basket just inside the door, though I
didn't remember taking them off or placing them there. Whole
portions of the night, in fact, seemed vague or missing altogether.
I could remember Ruc's lips against mine, his fingers tracing
wonderful arcane shapes over my skin, his fingers inside me, his
tongue between my legs—but those memories were lightning
flashes—too bright, almost vicious in their precision—separated
by long, dark blanks.

I straightened, worked the kinks from my legs and back, then
bent over to strap a knife to each thigh. The weight felt good,
right. Those knives were a reminder that, no matter how much
I wanted my legs bare for Ruc's hands to explore, I was here
for a purpose. I wasn't wearing the knives for self-defense or
ornament. They were my instruments, just as I was Ananshael's.
If I could find love in the darkness of my heart, dredge it

up—strong, gleaming, writhing—into the light, those knives would be the tools with which I finished it.

I glanced back at Ruc, tried to imagine driving a blade between his ribs, forcing it past the muscle into his heart. Something inside me quailed. I stopped, half turned in the light of the doorway, naked save for the blades at my legs, trying to understand what had just happened in my mind, to chase after that fleeing emotion, haul it back out, pin it down, look at it. It had been a long time, a very long time, since death had troubled me, and yet, for just a moment, the vision of that knife parting the flesh, of the hot blood pouring forth—it made me queasy.

I watched the pulse rise and fall at Ruc's neck, traced the hard lines of his body with my eyes.

Is this love? I wondered. Could that sickness in my gut be love?

It seemed unlikely, but that's the trouble. Love is not like the things of the world—trees, sky, fire—to which you can point and affix a name. Strangers from different lands speaking different languages can teach thousands of words with no more effort than the breath spent to say them. *This is a flower. This is my hand. That is the moon.* Love, however, gives nothing to point to. All we have are a woman's words, her actions, the way she holds herself, the things she does or does not do. For most people, millions scattered the world over, love is the opposite of burying a knife inside a chest. To hear them tell it, Skullsworn are incapable of love. Ela, of course, disagreed, but who was I to say if they were right, if she was? I couldn't see inside their heads. I could barely make out what was going on inside my own.

Irritated, and vexed with my own irritation, I turned away from Ruc, pulled on my pants and vest, stepped out the door, and froze.

Everything was gone.

Not the delta, of course. The lake was still there, mud-brown water bunched by the breeze, ringed in the distance by that wall of rushes. Winebeaks darted in and out of the reeds. Half a dozen tufted ducks bobbed on the wavelets a few paces distant. The raft beneath my feet was solid enough, and the hut from which I'd just emerged. There was one just like it tethered to either side, and our own boat tied off just beyond. All *that* was as I remembered. The rest of the village of the Vuo Ton, however, the barges and boats, the scores of floating homes, the dugout canoes—all of it had vanished.

For a few heartbeats, all I could do was stare. My mind, still groggy from exhaustion, from an evening smoking and drinking, struggled to yoke my fragmented memories to the scene before me. As I stood gaping, Kossal stepped from the door of the next hut down, glanced at the vacant expanse, scowled, spat into the water, and then, before I could frame an appropriate question, disappeared back into his hut. A few moments later he emerged again, this time with Ela. The priestess had shed her soaking clothes for a light blanket draped over one shoulder, tied around her waist. She looked as bleary as I felt, spent a few moments rubbing her eyes and knuckling her back before she noticed her surroundings. Then she started laughing.

"I *thought* that *quey* tasted strange."

Kossal shook his head. "I didn't drink the *quey*."

She wagged a finger at him. "But you drank the water."

"Drugged," I said stupidly. "They drugged us."

"For which I, at least, am grateful," Ela said, shrugging. "I appreciate a good, dreamless sleep after a day fighting crocodiles and a night of dancing."

"Where did they go?"

"Somewhere else."

I turned to find Chua standing in front of her own hut, fully dressed, fishing spear in hand, studying the empty lake.

"There were a hundred buildings here at midnight," Kossal said.

The fisher shook her head. "A hundred boats. I told you the Vuo Ton do not stay in the same place."

"*You* knew where to find them," I pointed out. "We came directly here."

"No," Chua said. "I knew where to *look*. We passed half a dozen other moorings, empty moorings, before finding this place, and we only found it because they allowed us to."

"But they *did* allow it. We passed the test. They welcomed us."

"I certainly felt welcomed," Ela added with a wink, "by a lovely couple whose names now escape me."

"The Vuo Ton move," Chua said, "when they need to move. When the village is threatened."

"Where's the threat?" I asked, gesturing to the wide, empty lake.

The door to the hut behind me rustled, and a moment later Ruc stepped out, shirtless, his good hand balled into a fist. "The threat," he said grimly, "is fucking late."

Ela raised her eyebrows. "How mysterious."

I struggled for a couple heartbeats to make sense of the strange proclamation. Then it all fell into place.

"You planned an attack," I said, studying his face.

He nodded wearily. "If they were responsible for the slaughter on the transport, this was the only chance."

Ela cocked her head to the side. "I'm a little unclear on the details. Were we supposed to massacre everyone last night? Because if that was the plan, I would have done less dancing and had less sex."

"No," Ruc said. "We were just the dogs. The hunters are behind us, following our baying."

"I'll admit that I enjoyed myself," Ela said, frowning, "but it seems uncharitable to use the word *baying*. . . ."

"The chum," I realized. "Yesterday. The barrels you dumped overboard. That wasn't a sacrifice."

"Blood brings *qirna*," he said. "*Qirna* bring delta hawks. The birds have a wingspan of eight feet. With a long lens, you can see them circling from miles away, high above the rushes."

"Your men have been following us," I said.

He nodded. "The Greenshirts and the legions both. They have orders to ring the village and attack at dawn."

Chua spat in the water. "I told you already—no one finds the Vuo Ton if they do not want to be found."

"I expected a settlement," Ruc said. "Not a batch of boats tethered together." He scanned the waving rushes, searching for some break. "How far away are they?"

"Miles," Chua replied.

"Can you track them?"

She fixed him with a flat stare.

"Why all the feasting?" Kossal asked. He was picking at something caught in his teeth, squinting speculatively into the waxen sky. "Why let us in at all, if they knew about the trap?"

"The blood rush we plucked in the delta," Chua said.

Kossal frowned. "Sticking a bit of the local plant life in the front of a boat seems like a pretty meager excuse for planning an ambush."

"The Vuo Ton were never in any danger," the woman replied. She turned to Ruc. "You will have told your men to stay well back, to let us make contact before closing in."

He grimaced, nodded.

"So . . . what?" I said. "They just wanted to get to know us?"

Chua shrugged. "The Vuo Ton trust in the providence of the Given Land. It is not often a boat from Dombâng finds its way here. Those that the Three let pass are not to be ignored."

"We found them," Ruc said, "because you knew where to look. Not because the delta brought us here. Not because the Three were secretly leading the way."

"Even after what you've seen," the fisher said, "you still do not believe."

"What have I seen?" Ruc demanded, turning to face her. "A trick village built out of boats. Two of my men killed, one by a croc, one by a snake." He gestured to the rushes. "No gods. No golden-eyed women leaping out of the water."

"You have seen the Vuo Ton," Chua replied. "Do you still believe they killed the men on your transport?"

Ruc stared at the swaying reeds as though they were a script he could almost but not quite decipher. "I don't know," he admitted finally.

"Sometimes it's better," Ela suggested, "to kill everyone first and leave the details for later."

"My orders weren't to kill everyone," Ruc said, shaking his head. "Not if they didn't fight back. I just wanted the leaders, the warriors, whoever was responsible for the attack on the transport."

"And how many men," Kossal asked, "did you think it would take to subdue the leaders, the warriors?"

Ruc grimaced. "Two hundred. I would have brought more, but I didn't want to weaken the force remaining in Dombâng."

"Two hundred," Kossal said, "against thousands of Vuo Ton."

"It was a gamble," Ruc admitted. "I figured half the population would be children or men and women too old to fight. I knew they'd see the boats before the final attack, but figured that still gave us an element of surprise. We have the superior weapons—flatbows, the rest of it."

Chua shook her head. "I could have told you this was wrong."

"I didn't trust you not to warn them."

The morning was still. The sun, ruddy and reluctant, had risen a handsbreadth above the eastern rushes. I pointed to it.

"You said your men had orders to attack at dawn. So where are they?"

We still hadn't answered the question by the time we returned to Dombâng. After spending the whole day retracing our route through the delta's winding channels—the *same* channels Ruc's soldiers should have been following—we'd encountered only crocs and tufted ducks, winebeaks and tiny blue-headed rush thrushes. The sun had dropped out of the purpling sky by the time we could see the smoke rising from Dombâng's chimneys.

The first boat we spotted was a long coracle crewed by half a dozen fishers. They paused in the hauling of their nets, studied us warily, but didn't raise a hand in greeting or cry out.

Ruc and I had been rowing all afternoon, but when he noticed the fishers he shipped his oar and stood up.

"Have you seen Greenshirts?" he shouted. Like most sound in the delta, his voice didn't carry. It seemed to fade into the reeds, to sink into the mud. "War boats," he went on. "Packed with soldiers?"

The oldest of the fishers shook his head gravely, watched us a moment longer, then turned back to his nets.

"Your soldiers are probably dead," Ela announced lazily. "Just like the others. The ones on the transport."

It wasn't the first time during the long trip back that she'd made the observation, but for the first time Ruc responded. He rounded on the woman, who was reclining lazily in the bow, leveled his finger at her as though he planned to plunge it through her neck.

"The men on that transport were tricked, then ambushed. Most of them were probably drunk, finishing off the last of the journey's rum before gliding into the city. Every one of the soldiers I sent out this morning was armed with a flatbow, sword, and spear. They knew the foe and they were ready."

"No one is ready for the Given Land," Chua said. She slid onto the bench beside me, lifted the oars from my hands. "Move."

"I can finish," I said.

"Night is almost here, and you are slowing down. I do not intend to die so close to Dombâng that I can smell the smoke."

Reluctantly, I climbed aside. Ruc and I hadn't spoken all afternoon, but there had been a satisfaction, even a joy, in sitting close to him, matching my rhythm to his, listening to his breath, deep and even, as he leaned back against the oar, feeling his bare shoulder brush against mine. We'd spent so much time vying with each other, sparring, testing, distrusting; it felt good to labor at the same task, to work in concert. The oar felt honest in my hands. As long as we were silent, there could be no lies.

Chua was right, though; I was exhausted. The sooner we docked at the Shipwreck, the sooner we could find out what happened to Ruc's missing boats and the missing soldiers. More than that, I realized I wanted to be back in Dombâng. No one had died on the return trip—Chua had neatly speared the one snake that swam close to the boat—but the open delta at night brought back memories of my childhood, of huddling hungry and terrified in the low branches of that tree, knife clutched in my hand, waiting for something to emerge from the shadows to kill me. The dying part didn't bother me any longer, but not all fears are about death, and I breathed a long sigh of relief as the city buildings closed around us once more, as ruddy lanterns replaced the last light draining from the sky.

The relief didn't last.

Before we'd gone two dozen boat lengths into the city's canals, I realized something was strange. There were too few people on the docks, bridges, and causeways. Usually, the folk of Dombâng tended to congregate outside in the relative cool of the evening. Tavern terraces overlooking the canals would begin to fill. Fishers would yoke their boats together, come out from the canvas tents onto the decks. Stalls on the bridges, closed during the day's worst heat, would open, selling fruit and crushed ice, plum wine and a hundred varieties of *quey*. That, at least, was what happened on a normal night. This night felt different. At first I thought my mind was playing tricks after two days in the delta. Maybe it wasn't as late as I thought. Maybe this part of the city didn't see the same kind of traffic. As we slid noiselessly over the darkening water, however, I noticed Ruc, too, studying the walkways and bridges, a frown on his face.

Ela picked her head up from the bench where she'd been dozing, cast a sleepy eye over our surroundings. "It seems less lively than I remember."

"Something's wrong," Ruc said.

The few people who were out scuttled along the walkways, glancing furtively over their shoulders every few paces. The boats on the canal gave us a wide berth as we approached. No one hailed us. No one so much as looked our direction. We might have been ghosts drifting through the evening on an empty boat. We might have died out in the delta for all the notice anyone gave us.

"The city was skittish when we left," I pointed out. "If there was another riot . . ."

Ruc nodded. "Curfew. I gave orders for the Greenshirts to lock the city down at the first sign of violence." He cursed quietly. "That explains where the legions went."

"I thought you left enough men to deal with the city."

"So did I. But it's a big fucking city. Wouldn't be the first time I was wrong."

Despite rowing all afternoon, he picked up the tempo. Chua glanced over, then matched him, and the boat darted forward, carving through the water as though it were a living thing eager to be home. I watched the great buildings of the city slide past: the Temple of Intarra, spangled with glass; the brooding, half-collapsed custom house of Old Harbor; the water gates, built by Anho the Fat as a way to close off the city's heart from any ocean-borne attack. It looked dead, all of it. Instead of lanterns and cook fires, singing and drumming, we passed empty alehouses, empty whorehouses, boats with empty decks. I had thought a lot about killing in my life, had witnessed the life pour out of dozens of people, but I'd never imagined the death of an entire city. There was something holy about Dombâng that night. It seemed larger than I remembered, more grand, less filthy. I found myself wanting to explore the dark canals, to leave Chua, and Kossal, and Ela, take up my oar again at Ruc's side, see for the first time the city where I had grown up.

Ruc, of course, had other concerns. When we rounded the tip of First Island, the Shipwreck loomed into view. The huge, haphazard wooden fortress brooded over the canal, low towers stabbing the sky, ramparts, like rows of jagged, broken teeth, gnawing at the night. There, at least, the windows were ablaze with light, as though every candle and lantern were burning, every soldier awake. Down at the docks, too, torches and lanterns illuminated the ranks of boats. Two dozen sentries patrolled those docks, chain mail catching the light, breaking it, reflecting it back. All of them carried flatbows.

Ruc glanced over his shoulder to where I was holding the tiller. "Stay wide," he murmured, then nodded toward one of the larger vessels swinging at anchor in the center of the current. "Over there. I want some cover while we decide what to do next."

"You don't think they're your men?" Kossal asked.

"Can't tell yet," Ruc said, "and sitting still in the middle of the river doesn't seem the greatest place to find out."

One of the Greenshirts noticed us just as we slid in close to the looming hull of the double-masted carrack.

"Fishers," he called out. "You're in violation of curfew."

A few of the Greenshirts moved toward one of their own boats tied off at the dock.

"Curfew?" Ruc replied, voice barely loud enough to carry over the water. "Under whose authority?"

"Commander Lan Lac," the Greenshirt said. "There are to be no unmoored boats between sunset and sunrise."

"You've been busy," Ela murmured. "Chasing down the Vuo Ton *and* issuing orders back here in the city."

Ruc shook his head. "I left instructions." He raised a hand to his mouth. "Hoai," he called out. "Those are *my* fucking orders."

That caused a stir on the dock, Greenshirts murmuring to one another, lowering their bows, pointing into the darkness where we floated. The soldier named Hoai turned to another, shorter man, conferred for a moment in a voice too quiet to hear, then looked back to us.

"Apologies, Commander," he said. "I didn't recognize your

voice. Still, I need to ask you for the pass phrase before you approach. Your own orders, sir."

"How delightfully paranoid," Ela observed.

Ruc ignored her. I expected him to call out a word or sentence, but instead he raised his voice and began to sing the haunting opening bars to Antreem's Mass. His singing voice was deeper than his speech, a full octave lower, and the notes seemed to vibrate the very hull of the boat, to tremble the surface of the water, to shake something inside my chest, a drum-tight organ that might have been my heart. He sang for a few moments only, but the music lingered in the air, in the ear, even after he was finished. The last time I'd heard the Mass had been that night in Sia, the night we first met. Ruc glanced toward me as he fell silent, but in the darkness I couldn't see his face.

"Come on in, sir," Hoai said. "And again, my apologies."

"Stop apologizing," Ruc said. "If you'd ignored my orders I would have had you flogged."

He nodded to Chua, the two dipped their oars, and the boat shifted beneath me as we slid over the glass-black water toward the dock.

Hoai caught the painter as Ruc and Chua backed water, snugged the bow in close while another of the Greenshirts reached out to haul in the stern. Ruc was out of the vessel before it was even tied, leaping across the gap, landing easily, already asking questions.

"Riots or an organized push?"

"Organized, sir," Hoai replied. "Three coordinated attacks."

"The result?"

"We crushed two. The third we've got bottled up just south of New Harbor, although there are outbreaks of violence all over the city. Hence the curfew."

"Casualties?"

Before the Greenshirt could reply, the man behind him gasped, choked, then collapsed, clutching at a knife buried in his chest.

My knives were out of their sheaths before he hit the dock, as was Ruc's sword. The rest of the soldiers, who had lowered their flatbows as we approached, scrambled to train the weapons on us once again, some dropping to a knee to steady their aim, others spreading out, as though to block off any avenue of escape. Hoai was staring, frozen, at Ela, who spread her hands innocently.

"What have you done?" Ruc demanded, rounding on the woman.

She nodded toward the fallen soldier. His blood, slick as polished lacquer, caught the starlight, reflected it back in a score of bright pinpricks.

"I thought it might be a good idea to kill him," she said mildly, "before he killed us."

"These are *my* men," Ruc spat.

Ela pursed her lips, glanced over the Greenshirts. "I don't think so."

Ruc laid the tip of his sword against her throat.

She didn't flinch, didn't even seem to notice.

"Hoai," he said, not moving his eyes from the priestess. "Take her. Take *all* of them to a holding cell."

The Greenshirt's silence was wide and dark as the night itself. When I turned to look at him, his eyes were bleak.

"He's not on your team, love," Ela said, shaking her head.

"She's right," Hoai said. He glanced over at Ruc's men, at *his* men, two dozen of them, every flatbow aimed at one of us. At that distance, a child could put a bolt through an eyeball. "Take all of them to a holding cell," he added, then nodded to Ruc. "Including him."

Ela glanced over at Kossal. "We could make a great gift to the god."

The older priest shook his head irritably. "I want to see Pyrre's golden-eyed, unkillable goddess before I am unmade."

"Drop your sword, sir," Hoai said.

Ruc turned from Ela to his lieutenant, the sword still in his hand.

His voice was the scrape of a knife over stone when he replied. "Why?"

Hoai shook his head, as though the question were too big to answer. "Drop your sword."

"Tell me why."

"No," the younger man replied grimly. "You tell *me* why you betrayed your own city."

"Where is the betrayal in stopping centuries, millennia of bloody 'sacrifice'?"

"What of the sacrifice required by Annur? The coin stolen from our pockets? The freedom torn from our hands? What about the history scrubbed out, the pride annihilated? What about the people, *our* people, that we execute right here, in front of this very fortress?"

His voice was shook, and even when he fell silent I could see his shoulders trembling with barely suppressed rage.

"Without law," Ruc replied quietly, "there is only suffering."

Hoai shook his head. "From now on we will make our own law. As we did before Annur put her boot on the city's throat."

"You are an idiot. You won't know how easily this city breathed until these so-called priests begin choking it."

The Greenshirt started to respond, then checked himself. "This is the last time I'm going to ask you to drop your sword."

I put a hand on Ruc's arm before he could attack. If it were darker, if the range was greater, if we had any cover or flatbows of our own, we might make a fight of it. As it was, however, we stood near the center of an empty dock. The nearest escape was the water, half a dozen paces away. The men with the flatbows wouldn't even need to be fast to put bolts in our backs, and before I died I wanted to pass the Trial. When Ananshael finally untangled the stuff of my soul, I wanted him to know the full measure of my devotion.

"Not now," I murmured.

Ruc didn't look at me, but after a moment he tossed his sword contemptuously aside.

"The rest of you, too," Hoai said.

Kossal spat onto the dock. "Don't have any weapons."

"Which, at the moment," Ela added thoughtfully, "is starting to look like an oversight."

I caught a glimpse of the cell as Ruc's renegade Greenshirts shoved us inside: a narrow box ten feet by ten feet, the floor and walls carved out of the island's red-brown bedrock, ceiling built of cedar beams, each one nearly as thick as my waist. Not the perfect prison. Given a chisel, a stool to reach that ceiling, and an uninterrupted week in which to work, anyone with a brain and a little muscle could break out. Of course, no one had given us a chisel or a stool, and a week seemed optimistic. I was still scanning the space for another weakness when the door slammed shut behind us and darkness closed its unrelenting fist.

"I'll admit I'm vexed," Ela said after a few moments of silence. "I was looking forward to a bath, a bottle of plum wine, and one of those attractive young men from Anho's Dance."

"It was a mistake," Kossal said, "putting us in the same cell."

"I'll try not to take that personally," Ela replied.

The old priest snorted. "We're more dangerous together."

"To whom?" I asked. My eyes had had time to adjust and I still could see nothing, not even shadows to attach to the various voices. "We might have made a play on the docks. Now that we're in here, all they need to do is keep the door closed to kill us."

"They're not going to kill us." Ruc's voice, at the far end of the cell. In the momentary silence that followed, I could hear him dragging a hand along the rough wall. It was easy to imagine he wasn't a man, but some animal, patient and dangerous, even caged. "They want us alive. Probably for some mockery of a trial."

"I can understand why they want *you*," Ela said. "Traitor to your home, your people, all that. I'm not sure what they'll get out of putting Kossal and me on trial. He's done nothing but sit around and gripe since we arrived in the city, and unless Dombâng has some ridiculous archaic laws about who is allowed to put what inside whom, I can't imagine I've done anything wrong."

"You just put a knife in the chest of that Greenshirt on the dock," I pointed out.

"Surely a woman can be forgiven the occasional indiscretion."

"How did you know?" Ruc asked. He had paused in his circuit of the cell just behind my shoulder. He didn't touch me, but I could feel him there, a strength in the darkness.

Kossal replied instead of Ela. "They were all looking at the wrong thing."

"What does that mean?"

"Us," the old priest went on. "They had their flatbows aimed at the river, but they were watching us."

"We'd just returned from two days in the delta," Ruc pointed out. "It could have been amazement. Curiosity."

"Could have been," Kossal said. "But it wasn't."

"Why didn't you say anything?" I asked.

"If I said something, one of you fools might have done something. They had flatbows on us, which meant dying, which is fine, but I'm still keen to put a knife into whatever's out there in the delta."

From the far corner of the cell, Chua spoke. She sounded older in the darkness, more tired. "You might still have the chance."

"They're not going to put us on trial," I said, the whole thing blooming in my mind at once. "That's not why they're keeping us alive." It only made sense once I saw it. "Trials aren't native to Dombâng. They're Annurian. To anyone who worships the Three, justice and sacrifice are the same thing. Before the empire came, criminals weren't tried by courts; they were given to the delta."

No one spoke. The only sound was our breathing's whispered polyphony.

"Well, that," Ela said finally, "raises my spirits considerably. A trial sounded tedious."

Lock most people in a hot, lightless cell with only the promise of a bloody, vicious death to look forward to, and they will stay awake all night, imagining the horrors of the future in a thousand different forms. Most minds will supply their own torture well before the executioner comes with his ax, before the sticks are piled around the stake, before the furious mob hurls the first stone. History is filled with tales of women and men locked in small rooms, sane on the day they entered, raving mad by the time they emerged to face their various fates.

Kossal and Ela were not like those people.

After establishing that there was no way out, that there was no point clawing at the walls, that, in all likelihood, we would be sacrificed to the delta—a positive development as far as both of them were concerned—they chose the smoothest spots they could find on the rough floor and went promptly to sleep, Kossal's snoring the jagged bass line to Ela's deep, steady breathing. Peace is one of Ananshael's greatest gifts—when you have spent your whole life preparing to meet the god, his approach holds no terror.

Chua took longer.

"I knew this," she said after Kossal and Ela had fallen asleep.

"Knew what?" I asked.

"That I would die here."

Ruc was sitting next to me, his back to the cool rock wall. "We're not dead yet," he said.

"We will be."

"You survived the delta once," I pointed out. "Twelve days alone."

"Ten days alone," she said. "Tem was with me for the first two."

I tried to find some shape in the blackness, some human form, then gave up and closed my eyes.

"What happened to him?" I asked. "How did he die?"

"I killed him."

Ruc shifted at my side. I could imagine him, too, staring into that perfect black. For a long time, no one spoke.

"Why?" I asked finally.

"The knife seemed kind. More kind than spiders or crocs, jaguar or *qirna*. I did not expect to survive. Not him. Not me."

The next question seemed wrong to ask, and I had no idea how to pose it, but I needed the answer.

"Did he know? That it was you?"

"I stabbed him as he slept. He woke, looked into my eyes, and died."

"And you thought you could escape from that," Ruc said, "with a few hundred pieces of gold?"

"I told myself I might." Chua paused, then went on. "I knew I could not. The Given Land is inside me."

"What the fuck does that mean?" Ruc demanded. He sounded more tired than angry, despite the edge to his words.

"No one escapes. Even those who walk out walk out different. The Land makes them into something else."

All over again I could feel the boa coiling around my eight-year-old body, could feel myself slamming the knife into the snake over and over and over, then later, days later, into the chest of my father as he slept, into my mother's neck, the blood hot all over my hands, my own scream strangled in my throat.

"Save the superstition for the priests," Ruc growled.

He couldn't see my memory. With the hot darkness packed between us, he couldn't see my hands trembling. "The delta is a place like any other place. More dangerous, maybe, but still just dirt and water, plants and animals."

"And something else," Chua said quietly.

I dragged myself free of my memories. "Did you see her?"

"Not her," Chua replied. "The other two. Sinn and Hang Loc. I saw them first just as I killed Tem. They were watching, standing on a bank across the channel. I took them for men at first, called out, but what men would be standing naked on a mudbank with no boat, no spears, nothing but those beautiful, awful eyes?"

"What did they do?" I asked.

"Watched. For days they watched, followed me. I thought they were gone a dozen times only to find them around the next bend, through the next wall of rushes. They moved through the delta like shadows, like sunlight."

"For creatures that love killing," Ruc said, "these gods of yours seem to let a lot of people go."

"I was too weak to hunt," Chua replied. "After snake bites and spider bites I could barely move my left arm. Half my blood I had poured into the river. There was no sport in hunting me."

"Maybe they'll let us go this time, too," Ruc said.

"No," Chua said. "I go into the delta this time to die."

"How do you know?" I asked.

"I feel it."

"Sweet Intarra's light," Ruc burst out. "What is it about the Three that obliterates all capacity for rational thought? I'll concede there may be something out there, something unbelievable. Maybe even Csestriim. I don't understand why that means we need to abandon all reason and start speaking entirely in ominous, meaningless fragments."

"Bring your rational thought with you into the delta," Chua said. "All men should have something to cling to as they die."

During the long silence while I waited for Chua to fall asleep, my mind shuttled back and forth between two problems. The first was one of devotion. All women die, but when the moment came, I wanted to go to my god a priestess rather than a failure. I had two days left to complete my Trial, two days in which to make two offerings: a pregnant woman and the love of my fucking life. Putting aside the vexations of the latter, even the first of the two kills suddenly looked improbable. There was a dearth of mothers ripe with new life inside the cell, unless Ela had been improbably careless in her liaisons. If we'd been free, out in the city itself, I could at least have completed that part of the Trial. As it was, I expected to be dragged directly from the cell to the delta. If there were some sort of trial, some public spectacle, I might manage to kill a woman en route, but that would do nothing to solve the other, larger problem.

Love.

I lay my head back against the stone wall of the cell and closed my eyes. I could remember Ruc's hands on my skin, his mouth on mine, could remember him moving over me, inside me, those eyes, that scarred, bronze-brown skin flexing with the muscles beneath. That night with the Vuo Ton had brought us closer than we'd been when I first arrived in Dombâng, and not just because of the sex. We'd survived the delta together, fought our way free of the crocs, found the Vuo Ton. Every challenge shared, every revelation, seemed to bind us closer. On the other hand, those revelations had their limits: almost everything I'd told him, everything except the story of my childhood sacrifice, had been a lie.

Is it possible to love a person you've lied to? Possible to love a person to whom you've told almost nothing *but* lies? How could I love Ruc if he didn't know me, and how could he know me if I never told him the truth? Ela could love a man who'd never seen her before, love a man based only on the shape of his face or the work of his hands—but I was not Ela. To drop my guard, to test the full limit of my feeling for Ruc, I needed to know what he felt for *me* . . . and to know that, I needed to give him the truth.

But which truth? How much of it?

I came here to find you.

I came here to fall in love with you.

I came here to kill you.

The first two were all right, but the last statement seemed unlikely to kindle in him the unquenchable flame of desire. *The ways of my lord are obscure. Even brave men misunderstand his justice and his mercy.* Ruc's comments to the Vuo Ton were evidence enough that he saw himself as a soldier, not a sacrifice. If I had more time, I could have explained it to him, I could have shown him the truth: sacrifice is part of who we are. Without it, nothing we do—not the loving or hating, the victories or defeat—mean anything. The Csestriim and the Nevariim were immortal vessels, but hollow. Antreem's Mass would be impossible without its ending, and Ruc was a creature every bit as gorgeous and ungraspable as that mass. All true music ends. Death is no diminishment.

With more time, I might have explained this, but I didn't have more time. I had two days. I couldn't give him the whole truth of who I was or why I'd come, but maybe I could give him more. Maybe I could give him enough.

I opened my eyes, stared blankly into the dark. I could hear him breathing evenly beside me. He didn't seem to be asleep.

This is a terrible gamble, I thought, then reminded myself that everything is a gamble. Life is a gamble. The only sure bet is death. I turned my face to him, glad he could not see me when I spoke.

"I started this."

He shifted slightly. I could imagine his eyes on me. "For a short sentence, that's remarkably unclear."

I gathered myself. "The revolt." The first words were the hardest, like the first few strokes in cold water when the chest constricts and breath comes jagged and uneven. "When I arrived in the city, I was the one who left the bloody hands everywhere."

The air in the cell felt suddenly, dangerously still. I found myself tensing for a fight, turning slightly to face the coming attack, getting ready. I forced myself to stop. The whole point of the truth was to drop my guard, not to redouble it. Ruc was still as a boulder balanced at the top of a great cliff.

"Why?" he asked finally.

I hesitated. The whole point was to approach the truth, but just *how* close?

"You're not Kettral," Ruc said after a long pause.

I dragged in a long, unsteady breath. "No."

I felt the space between us shift then deform beneath the weight of that single syllable.

"What are you?"

"I was hoping you would ask *who*."

"I guess neither one of us is going to get what we'd hoped for tonight."

"I'm telling you this," I insisted, trying to seize the conversation, to hold it together, "because I want to be honest."

"And what, exactly, is it you're telling me? You're not Kettral. You came to Dombâng to start a riot, maybe a revolution." He paused, testing the various possibilities. "If you're with them, I'll kill you before we ever get to the delta. I'm about finished with betrayal for today."

Truth is like a snake. If you're vigilant, you can keep it caged. If you're brave, you can set it free. Only an idiot, however, lets half of it out hoping to keep the rest penned in.

"I am a priestess of Ananshael," I said. The words felt good, right. "Trained in Rassambur. I came here, came home, in service to my god."

Ruc was silent a long time, but when he finally spoke, he didn't sound shocked.

"Skullsworn."

"It is not a term we prefer."

"You came back to Dombâng to murder people by the boatload, and you're worried about names?" I could hear him shake his head. "I should kill you now. All of you."

"You couldn't," I said quietly. "Besides. If they really are sending us into the delta, you're going to need us. You're going to need me."

"So you can put a knife in my back?"

"So I can stand beside you."

"Is Two-Net Skullsworn, too?"

"Chua is what she says she is."

I could hear him shaking his head. "You sure? Sounds like she killed her beloved husband quick enough."

"You've seen people die of snake bites," I replied. "That knife was a kindness."

To my surprise, Ruc started laughing. The sound was hollow, rusted, mirthless. "Is that what you tell yourself? Is that how you justify it?"

"We learn early not to try to justify ourselves. Our devotion can be difficult to understand."

"Then why are you telling me?"

"I'm telling you because I want you to know the truth."

It's easy, when you've lived a long time among women and men for whom death holds no sting, to forget how the rest of the world sees Ananshael's mercy. I didn't expect Ruc to rejoice at the revelation. I expected him to be furious and confused, to demand answers, some of which I couldn't provide, some of which weren't mine to give. I expected the conversation to be difficult, but my mind was too full of the peace and beauty of Rassambur. When I thought of Ananshael's faithful, I thought of people like Kossal and Ela, men and women vibrant, full of life.

It seems stupid now, but I didn't reckon on Ruc's disgust.

I could feel whatever heat had been between us draining away. I reached out through the darkness, found his shoulder. He caught my hand in a vicious grip, and for a moment I thought everything would be all right after all. Then he let it drop. I heard the scrape of his boots on the stone as he moved to the far side of the cell.

"Ruc—" I said.

The silence swallowed his name. I could hear his breathing, heavy as though he'd been running for miles, as though he were holding some impossibly heavy weight, unable to put it down.

I began again: "Ruc—" but everything beyond his name seemed useless.

The truth was out, free. Half of it, anyway. I stared into the cage of my mind, wondering what I had done.

22

*I*nstead of flowers, here are the still-spasming corpses of a dozen traitors.

I tried, as the guards hauled open the door to our cell, as I blinked watering eyes against the dim, blinding light, to imagine saying those words to Ruc. For a heartbeat, it seemed like a plausible peace offering. These were the same men, after all, who had betrayed him, corrupted his city, and usurped his fortress.

"Who's in charge?" Ruc demanded, blinking, bulling forward even though, after a whole night locked in perfect darkness, he was just as blind as the rest of us. "Where are my men? The ones who aren't traitors, that is?"

The nearest soldier, a huge man who looked as though his muscles had been molded sloppily out of mounds of river mud, slammed a cudgel into Ruc's head. After years of bare-knuckle fighting, Ruc knew how to take a blow, but there's only so much technique to getting bashed in the skull with a length of wood. He stumbled into a wall, caught his balance with a shoulder against the rough stone, then turned back to the giant who had hit him.

"Where are my men?" he asked again.

I glanced over my shoulder. Chua, Ela, and Kossal were up. The two priests looked no less deadly than usual, although I could hardly count on them to back whatever play I made. I could take down the brute with the cudgel at least, and then go from there. A pile of bodies wasn't the most traditional romantic gift, but Ruc and I had never been too keen on roses or rubies. Maybe getting an early start on some revenge would help to heal the rift I'd hacked between us with my idiotic honesty. It would be *something,* at least; a gesture of good faith.

One heartbeat later, and I'd discarded the idea.

It wasn't practically feasible, for one thing. There had to be two dozen guards, all wearing mail, most with loaded flatbows. I'm fast with my hands, but not that fast. Even so, I might have taken the chance—except that sort of wholesale slaughter was expressly forbidden by the terms of my Trial. It would be no good finally falling in love if I'd already failed.

The huge Greenshirt—he was still wearing the uniform, although, like the rest of them, he seemed to have a flexible interpretation of the loyalties it entailed—raised his cudgel for another blow. I stepped smoothly into the gap.

"Might as well save the questions," I said, speaking to Ruc even as I met the big bastard's eye. "I have a feeling we're about to meet whoever's in charge."

The Greenshirt smiled. There is something chilling in the eyes of people who believe completely in their own rightness.

"Indeed," he replied. "Indeed you are."

One by one, they bound us at the wrists. I tried to catch Ruc's gaze as the guardsman shoved him toward the door. Tried and failed. The man who had wrapped me in his arms two nights before walked past me as though I were a doorpost—not even a person, but some architectural necessity utterly beneath his notice. I studied his straight back as he strode down the corridor, led and flanked by armed guards. It was hard to decide whether I hated that unrelenting pride or admired it. How would I have felt if he'd glanced back at me, showed some sign of confusion, of weakness? Would that have made me love him more or less? As with most matters pertaining to my heart, I had no idea.

The Greenshirts motioned to the rest of us to follow. Kossal shook his head, as though irritated at the whole thing, while Ela seemed to be making eyes at the man who'd been beating Ruc. I turned away from them both, played the docile prisoner as the soldiers marched us up the stone steps, out of the subterranean chill and damp, into the delta's midmorning swelter.

"You look tired," Ela said as we rounded the third or fourth landing.

I glanced over at the priestess. Despite the rope binding her wrists, the clothes wrinkled and scuffed with grime, she seemed blithe and well rested.

"I am," I replied after a moment.

"This is the third time I've been thrown in a dungeon," she confided. "I'm starting to develop a low opinion of them."

One of the guards shoved her roughly from behind. "Quit talking."

Ela didn't miss a step, even as she turned to cast a disapproving eye on her assailant. "What's your name?" she asked.

The man, obviously baffled by this response, glanced over at his companion.

"You don't have an unattractive face," Ela went on, "and judging from the way your uniform hangs, the body underneath might be pleasant as well." She shook her head regretfully. "Your personality, however, is deplorable."

"I told you to shut your face, bitch—" the man began.

Before he could finish, Ela slid past his loaded flatbow and slammed her bound hands into his throat. He collapsed, choking. It was a mortal blow, although it would take him some time to die. The whole thing happened so quickly, with so little noise or fuss, that only the guards closest to us noticed anything at all, at least at first. There was a moment of silence, like a rest before a new bar of music, then the Greenshirts started shouting all at once, falling over themselves either to get closer or move back, training their flatbows on Ela to the neglect of everyone else.

The priestess didn't seem to notice. She was busy fixing some imagined imperfection in her hair while the soldier choked to death at her feet.

Kossal, who had been walking one pace farther on, turned around, studied the scene, then shook his head again. "I will be vexed if you go to the god before we reach the delta. I might need you."

Ela frowned. "That almost sounds sweet." She turned to me. "I can never decide if it's better to be needed or wanted."

"Get on the *fucking ground*."

After long moments, some leadership was finally emerging out of the green-shirted chaos. The huge brute with the cudgel was pointing at Ela, alternating, in his bellowed address, between the priestess herself—*Get the fuck down*—and his men—*Get your bows* on *that bitch*.

Ela glanced at the wooden floorboards, then shook her head. "The ground is filthy. So no. Also," she added, nodding toward the twitching figure at her feet, "I don't like the word *bitch*."

In the wire-tight silence that followed, I thought I could hear my god sweeping down upon us all through the wide corridor. I measured the space between myself and Ruc, trying to decide if I could get to him in time, if I could kill him before someone else put a flatbow bolt through his chest. Not that that would be enough. I still had no idea if the feeling stalking my heart was love. Even if it was, I owed the god another death—the pregnant woman. Even if I reached Ruc, even if I choked him lifeless before the Greenshirts finished me, I failed. Still, after all this time, it seemed wrong to let someone else, someone who had no feelings for him at all, deliver him into the hands of the god.

I tensed, ready to dive through a rain of flatbow bolts.

Before anyone could attack, however, Kossal raised his bound hands.

"She won't kill anyone else," he said.

Ela raised an eyebrow. "Much as I cherish you, Kossal, I don't remember making you my prophet."

"Gods have prophets," Kossal said. "Priestesses get irritable old men who want to go to the god somewhere more interesting than a dimly lit corridor surrounded by twitchy idiots."

"He means you," Ela whispered toward the Greenshirts, lowering her voice as though she were confiding a secret. "You're the idiots."

Rage spasmed like a muscle in the face of the lead soldier, but after a moment, recalling some order or imperative momentarily forgotten in the aftermath of Ela's impromptu violence, he raised a hand.

"Everyone back," he growled. "Two paces."

"She broke Qang's neck," protested one of the men, who had set down his bow to drag the now-still soldier away from Ela. "She broke his fucking *neck*."

"And I'll break yours," the leader replied grimly, "if you don't follow orders. The high priestess wants them whole and unharmed, so we are bringing them whole and unharmed." He turned to Ruc. "Unless we can't. It's your job to keep your people in line."

For the first time Ruc glanced back at us. His eyes held mine for a moment, then he shook his head.

"They're not my people."

It looked as though half of Dombâng had turned out to see us sacrificed to the old gods. After centuries hiding their worship; praying to hidden idols; gathering in forgotten shrines; making bloody, clandestine offerings for which Annurian law would have seen them hung; the citizens of my city had finally hauled their ancient worship back into the hot, dazzling light.

We stood at the top of the wide steps fronting the Shipwreck, at least half a dozen paces above the plaza below. That plaza was filled with people, thousands upon thousands upon thousands—fishers dressed in their practical vests; merchants, women and men rich enough to afford a cordon of enormous bodyguards; beggars in their rags; children racing in feral packs through the crowd, howling to each other over the protestations of their elders; barefoot sailors with rigging knives at their belts; grand-mothers bent over canes, diminutive beneath their huge reed hats; the whole motley citizenry of Dombâng gathered to share in a vicious release centuries in the making.

Some carried effigies of Intarra mounted on fishing spears, the goddess impaled through the stomach, or chest, or eyes. Others shredded flags bearing the Annurian sun, chanting *Death to the Emperor. Death to Sanlitun. Death to the Malkeenian dogs*. Still others held up idols of their own gods; tiny clay figures small enough to fit in a palm, life-sized wooden carvings, painted and repainted in intricate detail, that must have lain waiting in attics or hidden chambers for generations. Despite the variety of those latter sculptures, there was a ferocity to all of them that I recognized, the heft of terror and death in even the smallest figure.

A wave of nausea passed over me, through me, momentarily blotting my vision. I'd known what had to happen since shortly after we were captured, but only in that moment did the know-ledge finally seep from my mind into my bones: I was going back. Once again, I would be sacrificed to the delta. My bonds chafed just as bonds had chafed my child-size wrists so many years earlier. My breath tasted sick in my mouth. I groped desperately for the words I'd learned in the intervening years:

Ananshael watches over me. His might obliterates all. In the darkest hour, his mercy remains.

Slowly, as I repeated the mantra, my vision cleared.

Cao's Canal—just beyond the plaza—was packed so tight with boats, rafts, canoes, coracles, that you could have walked straight across to the Serpentine. The women and men on the decks were drinking from jugs of plum wine and *quey*, roasting sweet-reeds, hollering to each other across the gaps. The revolu-tion had become a celebration. There was no way to tell, gazing out over the floating mass, that everyone had gathered, not just for music or feasting, but for a human sacrifice. It seemed like a holiday.

It will *be a holiday,* I realized.

The priests who had seized their city from Annurian clutches would carve this date into a new calendar. Each year, another group of prisoners would stand on these steps while the crowd howled for their blood. Annur would decry this barbarity, but at least it was honest. Most holidays, after all—the military victories, the triumphs of one family or faction over another—are watered first with blood. It's just that over the years people tend to forget.

As we stepped out of the shadow into the sun's hammer, the low grumble of the mob erupted into a roar, thousands of upraised, sweat-soaked faces, mouths wide as though they were singing, pouring their souls into the melody of some long-forgotten chorus.

"I'm impressed," Ela said, turning to Ruc. "You were holding together a city in which every single citizen hates you."

Ruc shook his head, jaw tight. "This is only a fraction of Dombâng. There will be tens of thousands hiding today, men and women loyal to Annur, or just indifferent to the old religion. Normal people hoping the fire passes over without burning them to ash. We won't be the only ones fed to the delta today, just the most famous."

"I still don't understand," Ela mused, "why they don't like *us*. There's not a single person down there who even knows who I am." She paused. "Except for a handful of young men and one singularly flexible woman, and I don't think I did anything to offend them."

"It doesn't matter who you are," Ruc growled. "You were taken with me. There will be a thousand stories already about how you're Annurian agents sent to crush the resistance. Some people will be spreading a ludicrous tale that you're Kettral." He glanced over at me, eyes hard as chips of jade. "A lie, as it turns out, but that doesn't matter. Truth doesn't matter to a mob. Justice doesn't matter. What matters is rage, having a target for that rage."

Before he could say anything else, the noise of the crowd,

which had been nearly deafening before, found a new pitch, something between shouting and screaming.

I turned to find three hooded figures emerging from the steel-banded double doors of the Shipwreck. They strode out onto the wide platform, pausing half a dozen paces behind and above us—we'd been herded down a couple of the broad steps so that we would not stand at their level—to bask in the righteous fury of the throng. Each wore a robe of a different color: storm gray, vermillion, and a brown so dark it was almost black. I'd never seen the regalia before—such robes had been outlawed in Dombâng for centuries—but I recognized it from dozens of whispered stories and songs. After a lifetime of hiding, the city's high priests had emerged into the light, had emerged to send us to our doom.

The foremost of the three, the one robed in bottomless brown, turned to the others, seemed to murmur something, and then, with a theatrical gesture, all three tossed back their hoods. I didn't recognize the two men; they might have been picked out of a Dombâng crowd at random. The woman, however, the one who led them—I recognized her immediately. Her robe was different, but it would be hard to forget that imperious face, those hawk's eyes, the way she studied us as though we were fish flopping on a deck. Even last time, when she'd been our prisoner, she had refused to bend.

"Quen," Ruc growled.

Somehow Lady Quen managed to smile without loosening her lips. "Ruc Lan Lac. You must be surprised to find yourself here, in chains, on the steps of your own fortress."

"Only an idiot expects to step into a nest of vipers and emerge unbitten."

"Vipers." The priestess raised an eyebrow. "Holy creatures."

"Legless sacks of venom," Ruc countered, "with no end beyond their own survival."

"Even here," the priestess said, shaking her head, "even defeated and in chains, you insist on your profanation."

"Let me tell you," Ruc said, "what is profane. Profane is feeding people to the delta, innocent people, all to shore up your own power."

"Innocent?" The woman glanced at her hands, as though she expected to find blood there. "I'll admit that, while the true faith of Dombâng was forced into hiding, people forgot the old ways. In their ignorance, they were forced to make . . . desperate sacrifices. Now that we have returned, however, now that we have thrown off the yoke of your empire, I will correct those mistakes."

"Meaning the only people you throw to the delta will be those who oppose you."

The woman shook her head. "Dombâng was a great city once, proud and free, before you sold it for a handful of coin."

"It wasn't sold," Ruc said. "It was invaded. And that happened twenty decades before I was born."

"Every generation has betrayed her anew. Every generation until now."

"Sending five people into the delta isn't going to rid you of Annur," Ruc said.

The priestess shrugged. "This will be the first of our sacrifices, but not the last. Great corruption requires a great purge."

Ruc spat onto the steps. "Innocent people, dead."

"Innocent?" The woman frowned as she said the word again. "The leader of the Greenshirts, three Kettral conspirators, and one of the Vuo Ton, who forsook her people for a foreign god. I would hardly say you are innocent."

"We're not Kettral," I said wearily.

"That was just something she made up," Ela added. "It seemed like a good idea at the time."

The priestess studied me a moment, then shook her head.

"Judgment is for the Three. We are only their servants. I told you last time we met: Kem Anh rises."

Before I could respond, she turned away, stepped toward the crowd, and raised a hand. The clamor, which had surged, then subsided when she first stepped out of the fortress, dropped away entirely. The only sounds were a baby crying in the distance, the hollow thudding of hulls bumping up against one another on the water, and the light breeze flapping the flags at the top of the tower behind us. I glanced up at those flags. The Annurian sun had been stripped from the pole.

"People of Dombâng," she announced, her voice louder than I expected, "today we reclaim our city."

Roaring. Rage. Ten thousand hands raised in the air, as though every one of those assembled sought to drag us down. When the mob finally fell silent once more, Quen continued.

"For centuries, rot has gnawed at the pilings of this city. Too many of us have forgotten our gods, and so those gods have turned their faces from us in disgust. Until now. *We will forget them no longer.*"

She gestured to Ruc. "This man you know. Ruc Lan Lac, this son of Dombâng who was paid in Annurian gold for every back he broke, for every neighbor betrayed. Today, he will face judgment."

Ruc studied the howling crowd as though it were a storm sweeping over the city, dangerous but not deadly.

"These four," the priestess went on, pointing to the rest of us in turn when the chaos had subsided, "are his lieutenants, his willing executioners, sent or paid for by Annur to keep Dombâng under the empire's boot. Today, they too will face the Three."

Ruc took a step forward, as though he intended to address the crowd, but the guards seized him by the shoulders, hauled him back. The priestess stepped aside, and the two priests, the men in the red and gray robes, stepped forward. They carried snakes in their hands, small, crimson vipers that they held just behind the heads, raising them up for the crowd to see.

"Heel snakes," Chua muttered.

Kossal frowned. "Deadly?"

The fisher shook her head. "Their bite will paralyze you, steal your thought for half a day."

"A ridiculous bit of theater," Ruc said. "Something else for the mob, and a way to make sure we don't kill whoever brings us to the delta."

The priest in the bloodred robe stopped in front of me. His front teeth were jagged, broken, as though someone had smashed his face into an anvil, and half a dozen scars wrapped up his cheek, behind his head. His breath smelled like rot. The serpents writhed in his hand, the yellow eyes furious, mouths stretched wide, small fangs bare and glistening. The priest reached out to me, and the creature struck so fast I didn't realize it had happened until I felt the pain bloom through my neck, the blood drain down my chest, hot as my sweat. I tried to speak, but my tongue felt suddenly huge in my mouth. The world tipped on its side, and a moment later my legs abandoned me. I lurched, then the ground slammed into my face.

Down in the plaza people were screaming again, but they sounded far away, as though they weren't there at all, as though all those thousands of voices were something I remembered, every person I'd ever spoken to or overheard calling out to me, or maybe not calling at all, but singing a loud, gleeful song, the melody of which I tried to follow, then failed.

23

Before the light came back, or the sound, or any feeling in my flesh, there was a drum. It sounded far off at first. I imagined some solitary woman at the center of a dugout canoe, wooden drum between her knees, eyes closed, pounding out the same basic rhythm over and over, unflagging, as though she'd been doing it for years without respite, as though she'd been doing it her whole life. Slowly, the sound grew louder, closer, so close that I could feel each beat reverberating inside me. The tempo quickened. Her hands, which had been so steady, grew frenzied. I watched inside my mind as the canoe approached, closer and closer, the drumming louder, faster, until the woman was barely a pace away. Lost in her rhythm, she didn't see me. I tried to move, but something restrained me.

I tried to call out—*Who are you?*—but I had no voice.

For a moment, she looked like Ela, black hair a cloud around her head. Then, though there had been no shift that I could see, she was the woman who had saved me from the jaguar all those years ago, the muscles of her bare arms flexing as she drummed, her sleek black hair soaked with sweat, whipped across her face. Then, as though for the first time hearing something other than the trembling skin of her drum, she raised her eyes. *My eyes,* I realized. My face. She smiled at me with bloody teeth, closed her hands into fists, slammed them through the drum's skin, shredding it. With a shudder that seized my entire body, I woke to the delta's darkness.

The fronds of a finger palm shifted above me. The tree was named for the shape of the leaves, which looked like human hands. They were little more than shadows now, swaying with the wind, folding and unfolding as though trying to grasp the moon, the few dozen stars unobscured by the shredded clouds. I could hear water running almost silently between the rushes, or through the branches of some downed tree. Some creature I didn't recognize shifted and chittered in the brush a few paces behind me.

When I tried to raise my head, pain lanced through my neck, as though someone had dragged a rusted knife along the inside of my spine. I swallowed the moan rising inside me—no need to call the delta creatures to me before I could fight, before I could even get up—and tried very hard not to move until the pain finally subsided.

The ground beneath me felt firm, even rocky. That and the palms meant I'd been abandoned on one of the delta's true islands. If I listened carefully, I could hear breathing: Ela's and Kossal's, Ruc's low rasping snore, a series of quick gasping spasms that had to be Chua. So we were all together. All still alive. Not that I liked our chances of staying that way if we remained paralyzed.

When I closed my eyes, I saw the Three sweeping toward us over the delta, leaping channels or diving through them, emerging glistening wet and naked to race through the reeds.

A hallucination, I told myself. *A vision kindled from fear.*

Somewhere else—seated on the deck of Anho's Dance, for instance, with people all around me and a cup of *quey* in my hand—the words might have sounded reasonable, sane. How could I see creatures leagues distant streaking through the night? It was impossible. Paralyzed in the dirt of the delta, the thought brought no comfort. I opened my eyes, and tried very hard not to close them again.

After counting out a thousand heartbeats, I tested my own body once more, rolling onto my side this time, instead of bending at the waist. I managed it, barely. The snake's venom seared my veins as I lay there, gasping for breath, ribs bruised against the rocky soil. I almost blacked out, but I knew what was waiting for me in that insensate darkness, and I clutched to consciousness like a woman to her dying child.

When the agony drained away once more, I could make out Chua lying on her back a few paces from me, mouth hanging stupidly open, still lost in her mind's own dark corridors. She'd been untied, as had I. A little beyond her, I could see a small pile of weapons—swords, spears, axes—though for the moment the discovery didn't do me much good. I tried to move my fingers, failed, tried again, felt as though I'd dragged them through a fire, then gave up, stared fixedly into the shifting reeds, tried to think of something to do next that might prove more effective than just lying there.

I needed to survive.

There were no pregnant women stranded on the island with us. Which meant even if I managed to fan my feelings for Ruc into an open flame, I would fail my Trial, fail my god. Lying there in the hot dark, unable to move, each breath a searing pain, I faced the possibility head on for the first time. I'd feared this failure all along, of course, from the moment back in Rassambur when I first heard Ela and Kossal sing the song. Fearing a thing, however, is not the same as believing it might come to pass.

God of mercy, I prayed silently. *God of justice, you saved me. You gave me a reason to keep going when my life had no reason. Please don't let me fail you now. Please, my lord, show me a way.*

Somewhere far off in the delta, a creature screamed, then screamed again, then fell suddenly, perfectly silent. Hope flowered inside me. The delta was stitched with death. Since the first serpent sank her fangs into the flesh of another creature, Ananshael had walked the mud flats, had parted the rushes with his million hands, searching for the living things of the world, holding them close in the moment of their unmaking. My god was here. He had always been here. I had decided to come home for the Trial, not just for Ruc, not just because I began my life's journey in Dombâng, but because it was a place where I could feel my god. The delta belonged to him, even more than the redstone mountains surrounding Rassambur.

And yet, if the Vuo Ton could be believed, if my own memories of a woman with golden eyes were to be trusted, there were things in the delta that mocked my god, that had been here as long as him or longer, bright, beautiful, defiantly undying. It was for the sport of these we had been captured, poisoned, dragged to the island, and they cared nothing for my Trial, for my devotion. If I wanted to complete the full measure of my offering, I would need to do it in spite of them.

I forced myself to focus on the world once more. Chua was moving now, twitching in silent pain. There was something strange about her struggle, unnatural. I squinted blearily at the shifting shadows, trying to understand. Then, between one heartbeat and the next, the wind tugged a scrap of cloud off of the moon. Milky light washed over us, and I could see. Chua wasn't moving after all. She lay sprawled motionless on the mud. The movement came from a spider the size of my open hand. It had crawled onto her stomach where it sat preening, folding and unfolding its legs, making an awful clicking noise.

I tried to call out, but pain flooded my throat, strangling the warning; the best I could manage was a whispered moan and sliver of warm drool. I forced myself up onto an elbow, but my body locked there, caught in the fist of the toxin. The muscles of my chest and shoulder trembled, quaked, then failed, dropping me back onto the dirt where I lay panting, a thousand tiny fires blazing beneath my skin.

When I could see again, the spider seemed to be digging, stabbing at Chua's stomach over and over. The fisher twitched, convulsed, but she was too lost to wake up. Again, I tried to move, to roll, and again I failed. The spider had grown furious in its exertions, frenzied, hacking at Chua's flesh with all the intensity of something fighting for its life.

Or for its spawn.

I finally recognized the creature from nightmare tales of my childhood. "Meat puppeteers" we'd called them as kids. That's what they did—they made meat dance, dance itself to death. A female would find a sick creature—a dog, a pig, anything big enough to feed her young and too feeble to fight back—hack her way into the skin, then lay her hundreds of eggs. For half a day or so, the poor beast would seem fine. Then, as the tiny spiders hatched, began to feed, the host would begin to jerk, twitch, even leap into the air as though suspended from the strings of some sadistic puppeteer. After a day of that, the final violence of the myriad spiders bursting forth seemed like a relief, a last, merciful severing of the strings.

The spider was still digging, burrowing madly into Chua's body. A thin line of blood—black in the moonlight—slipped down her side. If I could reach her before it laid the eggs, I could save her. I took an unsteady breath, then hurled myself against my own treacherous muscles once again. This time I managed to drag myself a pace, then two, pain shredding my flesh, searing each labored breath. A desperate whimper caught on the wind. I thought for a moment it was Chua, then realized the sound came from my own throat. Chest quaking, arms throbbing, I dragged my way to the woman's side.

In time.

The puppeteer was still burrowing.

I raised a weak hand to knock it aside, then stopped.

The spider's multiform eyes glittered in the moonlight like dozens of dark jewels. Her mandibles twitched, as though tasting the air. I could smell Chua's sweat, her blood—probably the same thing that had drawn the spider. I could save her, batter at the thing, keep it away until she woke. Puppeteers went after sick creatures for a reason—despite their size, they weren't dangerous enough to subdue a healthy host. I could keep Chua alive, and yet, as I lay there shaking, my arm raised to strike, a new thought blossomed in my mind: *Let her die.*

What was I, after all, if not a servant of Ananshael? What was the spider? As I lay on the hard ground, eyes clutched against my pain, I had prayed to my god; and he had answered. I imagined the hundreds of tiny eggs hatching inside the fisher, all those new-made creatures feasting in darkness on her blood, her flesh, voracious and burgeoning, all of them, straining inside the skin until finally they were strong enough to burst forth, new life crawling black and bloody from the wreckage. This too, was my god's work. It happened every day in the delta, a thousand times a day. Who was I to deny it? Especially when I could fashion it to my own end, bend it to my devotion.

Slowly, I let my arm drop.

The spider watched me. What she could see in the darkness I had no idea, but those glittering eyes remained fixed on me even as she went absolutely, perfectly still to lay her eggs. My horror had left me. She was beautiful, that spider, sleek and long-limbed, magnificent in the purity of her purpose. Like the snake that had poisoned me earlier that day, like the crocodile I had cut apart beneath the village of the Vuo Ton, like the jaguar that had come for me as a child, she was a creature of the delta, as was I, a minister of death, both humble and gorgeous. Since returning to Dombâng, I had been trying to be something I was not, to find inside myself emotions I had never known. What did the spider know of love? What did she care?

Sometimes it is enough to be only what you are.

"Go on," I murmured to her. "Go on."

I expected her to skitter away when she was finished laying. She did not. Instead, she withdrew her body from the rent she'd made in Chua's flesh, took a handful of staggering, unsteady steps, then collapsed onto the dirt. I had forgotten that part. Laying eggs was the last act of the puppeteer. She would never see her brood emerge into the sunlight, never see them grow.

I stretched out a hand to her, cupped her body in the

moonlight as she twitched herself still, as Ananshael came with his own deft, gentle hands to unmake her. I was still holding the corpse when blackness closed over me once more.

I woke the second time to Ruc's hand on my shoulder, shaking me awake. Over his head, the morning sun blazed, blinding me, casting his face into shadow.

The movement hurt, but not nearly as much as it had the first time, during the night.

The night.

I turned to find the carcass of the spider an arm's length away. Already it was buzzing with flies, crawling with ants. A few steps farther, Chua was still passed out, the wound in her side scabbed over. Ela and Kossal were gone. The space where they'd been sprawled when I first awoke was empty, the only sign that they'd been there at all some matting of the grasses. Before I could worry about their absence, however, Ruc was dragging me onto my feet.

"What's happening?" I managed, raising a hand to shield my eyes.

"Jaguars are happening," he growled. Even as he spoke, he threw something with his left hand, a stick or stone—my vision was still too blurry to make it out. "Two of them. They were wary of me at first, but I think they've figured out my secret."

"What's your secret?" I asked, blinking my eyes, scanning the tangled brush around us. My mouth tasted like ash and my head throbbed, but after a moment my vision began to steady. We were in a small clearing maybe a dozen paces across. A wide, muddy channel swept in a lazy arc behind us. Thorny shrub and reed ringed the rest.

"My secret," Ruc murmured, "is that if I take more than two steps in any direction, I fall over."

I tested a step myself, wobbled, almost toppled, then caught myself on Ruc's shoulder.

He was holding a sword, I realized, a strange, gorgeous weapon of cast bronze.

"Where'd you get a sword?" I asked stupidly, forgetting for the moment about the cache I'd noticed earlier.

"They left us with weapons," Ruc replied, pointing to the diminished pile.

"Thought they brought us out here to die."

"I think we're supposed to make the dying interesting. Here." He pressed the shaft of a spear into my hands. It was about as long as I was high, the point also of bronze. I might have spent more time admiring it if the jaguars hadn't chosen that moment to attack again, both of them flowing out of the brush from opposite sides, testing our flanks. Ruc lashed out, sunlight flashing off his blade, and I turned to face the other beast.

I hadn't seen a jaguar since the last time someone decided to make a sacrifice out of me. The cat I remembered was huge; its jaws had seemed large enough to crush my skull. Of course, I had grown since then, and had shed my childhood terror. The creature facing me now didn't weigh much more than I did. It moved with all the deadly grace that I remembered, but I had grown more graceful too. As long as I kept the spear's point between us, I could hold it at bay.

The jaguar bared its fangs, hissed, stalked side to side, searching for an opening. Its green-gold eyes were almost human as they studied me.

"Come on," I whispered to it. "Come on."

The cat lashed its tail, circled wide, swatted at the spear's point, then circled again, testing. Behind me, its companion howled in frustration.

"I can't help but notice the lack of immortal women leaping from the water to our rescue," Ruc said. "Or does that come later?"

His breathing was heavy, but even.

"I wouldn't be too eager," I said. "According to the Vuo Ton, she left me alive so I'd be more fun to kill the next time."

"Yeah, well, she'd better hurry up if she doesn't want these cats to do the job first."

I'd been so disoriented when I woke, then so focused on the jaguar stalking me, that only then did I realize that Ruc's fury from the day before, his disgust for me, his disdain—all of it seemed gone. I didn't dare turn to see his face, but his voice was the voice I remembered: wry, focused, unflappable.

"Why didn't you let them kill us?" I asked. "Kill me?"

"And fight my way out of the delta on my own?"

"You could have saved just Chua. She knows the delta better than any of us anyway."

I turned side-on to the cat, as though I'd forgotten all about it, waited for the flicker of movement out of the corner of my eye, then whipped the spear back around, knocking it from the air mid-leap. It was a long time since I'd fought with a spear, and though I nicked a gash on the jaguar's flank, most of the blow's force connected through the shaft. The creature rolled to its feet, hissed, then backed away, those molten eyes never leaving me.

"I take it you missed," Ruc said.

"It's not dead."

"Some fucking Skullsworn you are."

"Why did you save us?" I asked again. "Why did you bother to wake me up?"

Instead of answering, Ruc let out a low curse. There was a quick scramble, the sound of a blade biting into flesh, then a high, furious scream, followed by Ruc's panting.

"You still alive?" I asked.

"For now."

"Then answer the question."

Ruc spat. "I'm sure I'll have a few agonizing moments to regret my decision, but for now I'm not finished with you."

My own beast showed its teeth. I bared mine in return.

"What does that mean?"

"It means you still haven't told me the truth."

"Learning I'm a priestess of Ananshael isn't enough truth for you?"

"No. It is not. You said you came back to Dombâng, but you never said why."

"To serve my god."

"People die the same way everywhere. I watched them. I've killed them. No need for you to trudge all the way to Dombâng."

It was easier, somehow, talking about it while facing the jaguar, as though the animal were a reminder of my god's power, of the fact that, whatever we said to each other, whatever pain we inflicted or felt, death was there to take it away, to smooth it over. I raised my spear in the old Manjari crane guard, halfway above my head, then closed my eyes.

I don't know what sense it was with which I felt the jaguar leap. Maybe the wind of its attack stirred the tiny hairs on my arm. Maybe I heard it. Maybe I saw a shift in the shadows beyond my eyes' red lids. Maybe my god spoke in my bones. It didn't matter. What mattered was that I knew. With all the strength in my weakened arms, I slammed the spear down, through the pelt, through the corded muscle, through the choked feline scream, down in the sun-baked dirt. I could hear Ruc fighting behind me, locked in his own mortal contest, but I kept my eyes closed, my hands tight around my spear as the cat spasmed. When all I could feel vibrating through the wooden shaft was the last, trembling breaths, I allowed myself to look.

I had thrust the spear straight through the jaguar's back, just above the front shoulder, pinning it to the earth. It stared at me with those liquid eyes, bared its teeth, then lay its head on the dirt, a wild creature finally tamed beneath Ananshael's patient hand.

It wasn't until I'd ripped the spear free of the blood-soaked body that I realized the fight behind me was over, too. I turned to find Ruc leaning on one knee, panting above the second jaguar's corpse. Sunlight snagged on his sword's bronze, glistened in the blood slicking the edge, transforming each drop into a ruby as it fell. Sweat dripped from his face, soaked his vest, mingled with the blood leaking from his shoulder, where the cat had snuck inside his guard, and from the punctures on his arm, the remnant of our fight with the croc. He didn't seem to notice any of it. His eyes never left me. The whole world might have disappeared, might have sunk into the mud.

"Why did you come back?" he asked.

I could feel the answer inside me like a thorn snagged on my mind: *I came back to fall in love with you, then give you to the god.* Kossal could have said it. Kossal always said exactly what he meant. Ela could have said it. When I opened my mouth, however, to finally speak the truth, I found different words.

"I came back to find out what was living in the delta. I wanted to know what happened to me as a child."

Not a lie, but not the whole truth either.

Ruc studied me warily, chest heaving, but before he could press the matter further, Chua shuddered awake with a moan. For a few heartbeats she groped at the air, the ground, obviously lost.

"Chua," I said, moving toward her.

She froze at the sound of her name, then rolled onto her hands and knees, clawed a rock from the soil, and came up with the jagged stone between her fingers as though she were ready to smash my skull into splinters.

"Chua," I said again, taking a step back as I spoke. "It's Pyrre and Ruc. We're on an island. They poisoned us, then dumped us."

Her dark eyes flitted from me to Ruc, then back, focusing slowly.

"I remember," she said, voice dry and ragged. She didn't let go of the stone. "Where are the other two?"

"Disappeared," Ruc replied. "They were gone by the time I woke up."

The fisher nodded as though she expected as much. "Then they are dead."

"I wouldn't bet on it," I said.

"Your bets do not matter." She studied the river's sluggish

current for a moment, then shook her head. "We need to get farther from the water."

"Why?" Ruc asked.

"Crocs. Water snakes. We should not have survived the night. There are a hundred creatures. . . ."

She stopped, eyes fixed on the carcass of the dead spider. She dropped the stone. Her hands groped at her stomach as though following some intuition all their own, found the scabbed-over gash where the creature had laid its eggs. Slowly, in the way of a woman weary from a long day's labor anticipating rest and a warm bath, she closed her eyes. I expected her to claw at the wound, to rip it open, to try to find whatever had been left inside her and force it out. Instead, she pressed her palms to the bloody skin. The motion was slow, tender, almost protective.

Ruc glanced at me, then looked back at Chua. "What's going on?"

She opened her eyes. "I did not survive the night after all."

"Another snake bite?" Ruc asked, looking down at the woman's hands.

She shook her head. "Something slower. Something worse."

Out on the river, a fish the color of butter broke the surface to catch a low dragonfly, then disappeared into the murk, leaving behind only the slowly spreading rings. I watched it for a moment, then turned back to find Chua's eyes on me, warm and steady.

"Kill me," she said.

The spear was feather-light in my hand.

"No," I replied quietly.

"That spider," she pointed to the crabbed corpse, "has laid her eggs inside me. Soon, they will hatch, grow, begin to devour my stomach, my intestines, and then they will burst through my skin."

"I know."

"Then kill me."

"I can't."

Chua's forehead wrinkled. "You are Skullsworn. I heard you in the cell."

I could feel Ruc's gaze driving into me, as though he could see past my chest and into my heart.

"I'll give you to the god when the time comes."

"The time is *now*," the woman insisted. "By noon they will have hatched."

"Then we will wait until noon."

It felt wrong to refuse. Ananshael's beauty is exactly this: his ability to deliver us beyond our own suffering. With a quick thrust of my spear, I could spare her the hot, burrowing agony to come. She would be free before she hit the ground, released. This is what I had trained for, what I *believed* more deeply than I believed any other thing. Another day, another month—I would have opened her throat in a moment, gladly, but suddenly my days were numbered, and my work was still undone.

A woman, her stomach ripe with new life.

Had Ananshael answered my prayer? Had he sent the spider to give me one final chance to complete my Trial? Or was I deluded?

A million million mortal creatures trace their paths over the world each day, threading the air and water, walking the land. Not all of them are sent by gods. There is no special providence hidden in the death of every spider. It seemed viciously possible that Chua's fate had nothing to do with my Trial, that I was betraying the very god I had begged to serve by drawing out her agony instead of ending it. Again I considered thrusting the spear through her throat. Again I did not.

There are moments in life when reason fails, when even the greatest genius is worth nothing. All the years studying, learning, training obscure the brutal fact that there are things we cannot know. A woman could pace out the distance between Dombâng and Rassambur, but the world is filled with spaces we can never measure, effects forever severed from their causes, furious motion for which the prime mover has been lost. It was possible Anan-shael sent the spider, possible he did not. In the face of a god who resists all interrogation, the only way forward is faith.

Chua and Ruc were both watching me as I shook my head again.

"This is not the time."

The fisher spat onto the matted grass, then crossed to the small pile of bronze weapons remaining. She selected a bone-hilted dagger, ran her finger along the edge, then nodded.

"I will do it myself."

I could have disarmed her. Could have knocked her out again, tied her with her own clothes, forced her to wait, to stay alive until the spiders hatched inside her, until she was ripe. I'd given her to the puppeteer for this very reason. If she killed herself now, I was lost. I would go to my god—to the god who had delivered me from the agony of my childhood, who had given me everything good and beautiful in my life—a failure.

It didn't matter. I couldn't move.

All I could manage, as she pressed the bright point against her side, were two words: "Not yet."

Chua stared at me, knife dimpling her skin. "Why not?"

Ruc stepped forward before I could answer. "Because there's a way to stop it. You know that better than I do. Drink a couple of gallons of blackleaf tea; the eggs will die before they ever hatch."

"Blackleaf grows close to the ocean," Chua said. "Nowhere else."

"You don't know that," Ruc said.

"I've spent my life in this delta."

"You've spent the last two decades in a shack in the Weir," he shot back. "Blackleaf could have spread all through the delta by now. You stay alive," he said, shooting a glance at me, "because as long as you're alive, there's still a chance."

You stay alive, I amended silently, *because it's not yet time for me to kill you.*

Chua grimaced, then turned back to me. "Promise me that when they hatch, you will finish it."

"I promise," I said.

Chua's death would make six. Which left Ruc.

The rushes sighed, sifting the warm wind. Tiny ripples ridged the water, then subsided. Flies droned over the carcasses of the jaguars. The late morning smelled of blood and rot.

"Where are the gods?" I murmured, half to myself. The question was both practical and bottomless.

It was Ela who answered, stepping out of the brush, a bronze sickle in each hand.

"They've been here," she said brightly.

"How do you know?" I asked.

She gestured over her shoulder. "Well, it's either them, or someone else with a strong interest in stacking skulls and tending exotic flowers."

24

A chest-high wall circled the low, rocky rise near the center of the island. It looked like a stone pen for goats, though its elevated position suggested defense, some sort of fortification long abandoned. And, of course, goat pens aren't normally ringed with skulls.

Hundreds of skulls topped the circular wall, each nestled carefully in its place, the rain-washed, sun-bleached bone blindingly white. Delta violets grew from eye sockets packed with dark earth, purple flowers swaying gracefully at the ends of long green stems. Those flowering gazes had long given up all mortal sight, but I felt watched all the same, anatomized in a way that made me want to hunch, hide, slide back into the rushes and run.

"This is a bad place," Chua said. She seemed to be understating the matter.

We had stopped just inside the wide clearing, as though pinned where we stood.

The fisher glanced down at her scabbed stomach. "We are going to die here."

"At least we have company," Ela observed, nodding toward the skulls.

Ruc grimaced. "There must be what, three hundred? Four?"

Kossal shook his head. "There are thousands."

He leveled a gnarled finger at the wall beneath the skulls.

Violets grew there, too, a waterfall of purple and green cascading from the stones.

No, I realized, squinting against the light. *Not stones. More skulls.*

These were brown rather than white, streaked with the dirt from the sockets above, rank upon rank, at least five feet high and twice as wide at the wall's base. Those at the bottom had crumbled halfway to mud beneath the weight pressing down from above, finally pried apart by time's subtle levers.

"These gods take their gardening seriously," Ela observed. She pointed down the hill, toward the west. "There are two more of these down that way. One of them's basically just a ring of dirt at this point. This one seems to be the newest."

I looked over at the priestess. Mud smeared the hem of her *noc,* and her bare legs beneath. Her hair was matted down on one side, presumably where she'd been tossed against the dirt when the Greenshirts abandoned us. The snake's venom, however, didn't seem to have slowed her down any. Her smile was as bright as the sickle in her hand.

"Where have you been?" I asked.

She shrugged. "You were all sleeping so soundly, we thought we'd take a walk."

"I wanted to use you as bait," Kossal added, staring past us at the ring of skulls, as though it had offended him in some way.

"Bait?" Ruc rounded on the older priest, half raising his sword.

Kossal had selected two bronze hatchets from the cache of weapons, but he didn't bother raising them.

"Bait is something you put in a trap to attract an animal."

"Or a god," Ela added. Then she frowned thoughtfully. "Though I guess it doesn't work on gods."

I watched Ruc struggle with his anger, strangle it.

"If you believe in these things," he said slowly, "if you're so excited to kill them, don't you think you have a better chance with all five of us alive?"

Kossal squinted into the distance, considering the question, then shook his head. "Not really. Ela and I have fought together a long time. The three of you don't know the tempo." He frowned. "You'd have been better as bait."

I stared at the old priest. There had been times in the last month—during the long walk south, and even after we reached Dombâng—when Kossal had seemed almost sweet, gruff but paternal, the kind of grandfather who, in between cutting throats, might give you some good advice about life, about love. That Kossal had almost disappeared. The man who stood before me now seemed to have shed both his age and his absentminded-ness. Despite the deep lines marking his face, the slight stoop to his shoulders, he looked ready, predatory, deadly, as though he'd been waiting all his life to find this island lost in the delta grass.

"I, for one, am glad you're still alive," Ela said. "Kossal is good at giving things to the god, but he's dreadful company. And besides," she winked at me, "there's another story that I'm looking forward to seeing the end of."

"The only stories we will see the end of are our own," Chua said quietly.

Ela eyed the woman. "Well, that seems unduly pessimistic."

"This is their shrine," Chua replied, staring at the wall of flower and bone.

Kossal looked over at her sharply. "You've seen it before?"

She shook her head. "I've heard of it. People come here to die."

"Then let's leave," Ruc said, turning away.

It was a sane suggestion, as good as anything else, given the circumstances. Those skulls, however, drew me forward. I was a fish hooked through the gills and hauled inexorably in. As I crossed the open space between the edge of the scrub and the shrine, I felt myself come unmoored, as though I were moving backward through time, back toward my own childhood, toward the memories that had bloodied my dreams for so long. I'd never been to the island or seen that ring of skulls, but the space reeked—not in the nose or the back of the throat, not with the quotidian scent of mud, or blood, or anything to which a person could put a word; it reeked in the mind, in the deepest recesses of myself, of something ancient, barbed, beautiful, and undeniable—of *her*. My legs were limp beneath me, my vision hazed as I crossed the sun-baked dirt to kneel beside the wall.

The violets swayed in the light breeze. I picked up one of the shards of bone, turned it between my fingers, tried to imagine the woman it had belonged to—for some reason I thought it was a woman. I knew nothing about her, nothing of her life, nothing about her face or her fears, but I knew what she had seen in her final moments because I had seen them too—those eyes set in that horribly beautiful face.

I drove the jagged corner of the bone into my palm until my skin parted, blood welled. As the memory receded, the world coalesced around me once again: sky where the sky belonged, reeds swaying beneath it, the slight weight of the bone in my hand. I studied it.

"There are thousand-year-old skeletons in Rassambur that look newer than this."

Ela shrugged. The rest of the group had joined me at the shrine. "Rassambur is dry. This isn't."

"That's one explanation," Kossal said. "The other is that these bones are more than a thousand years old."

"And the ones down the hill?" I asked. "The older ones?"

"Are older."

I grappled with that, tried to imagine people coming to this place since before Annur was founded, before Dombâng was anything more than a few huts on stilts, people coming and dying, the sacrifice unaltered across all those millennia. It made me dizzy.

"The Three were here before Dombâng," Chua said, giving voice to my thoughts.

"A fascinating mystery," Ruc added, "but not one we're going to solve now. We have to leave. Fix what happened in the city. *Then* we come back."

"Leave how?" I asked, rising, turning to face him. "We're on an island. There's nowhere to go."

"There is an entire fucking delta," he said, gesturing with his sword.

"And how long do you think we'd last in that delta without a boat?"

He turned to Chua. "You made it once. You survived. What's the play?"

She shook her head, gestured to the skulls. "There is no play. We can fight jaguars or crocs. We might escape the snakes and spiders. If we floated still as logs in the water and tried hard not to bleed, we might even pass the *qirna*. But not the Three. *This is their den*."

"I'm staying," Kossal said.

"To do what?" Ruc demanded.

"To kill Csestriim," the old priest replied.

I stared at him. "You still think they're Csestriim? That all these years they've been hiding in the delta impersonating gods?"

"Yes."

I straightened up, plucked a skull from the top of the wall. It was heavy with packed dirt. "You think Csestriim did *this*?"

"Yes."

I stared at him. "The Csestriim were creatures of reason. I've read the chronicles. They were utterly untouched by emotion. They had no superstitions. They didn't create *shrines*."

Kossal shrugged aside the objection. "To twist an entire city to their will they could play at being gods."

Ruc shook his head. "You're even crazier than the Vuo Ton."

"And what," Kossal asked, turning to face him, "is your explanation?" He gestured to the wall of skulls. "Something piled those bones. Something has been piling them for thousands of years, and not just heaping them there and leaving, but *tending* them. Planting flowers. Replacing them when they fall. Adding to the pile."

"Some cult," Ruc said. "Another group like the Vuo Ton."

"The Three are gods," Chua murmured.

"No," Kossal replied. "They are not. Ananshael is a god. Eira is a god. Gods don't do *this*." He raised his chin toward the wall.

"What he means," Ela cut in helpfully, "is that gods don't spend thousands of years squatting in the backwater muck making towers out of skulls. They have better things to do."

"But why would the Csestriim spend millennia in the delta?" I asked, shaking my head.

"They have nowhere else to go," Kossal replied. "We defeated them, hunted them almost to extinction. In the thousands of years since the wars, the Csestriim who survived have done whatever they needed to do to continue surviving, to continue defying our god. They have posed as sailors and soldiers, peasants and priests. Maybe this is part of a larger plot. Maybe these three are the only ones left. Maybe this is just their revenge."

"The bronze weapons," Ela pointed out, angling one of her sickles so that the sunlight darted across the skulls. "The first humans didn't have steel. They would have fought with bronze."

I ran a hand along the wooden shaft of my spear. "This isn't thousands of years old."

"Of course not," Kossal snapped. "It looks like it was made last week. It's the *ritual* that's old, just like the myths. The Csestriim have been here for thousands of years, cheating Ananshael. Men and women go to the god more frequently. When they pass their stories on, they get some things right, miss others."

"It doesn't matter," Chua said.

Kossal turned to face her. "Anything that doesn't die insults my god."

"Speaking of dying," Ela said, turning to me, "aren't you cutting things a little close, Pyrre?"

I glanced furtively at Ruc, then shook my head. "I have until the end of the day."

"We may not see the day's end," Kossal said. "If you have business to settle, now is the time."

"Besides," Ela added, "it gives us something to do while we wait." She pursed her lips, studied Ruc for a long time, then turned back to me. "So. Are your body and mind singing with love?"

And just like that, it was time to face it, to confront once and for all the question that had plagued me since the moment Kossal and Ela first sang to me in the Hall of All Endings back in Rassambur. There were no more days, no more evasions.

Did I love him?

At times, during our two weeks in Dombâng, it seemed that I could almost say yes. When we'd raced through the city together, tracking the Asp in pursuit of Lady Quen, the fierce delight pounding through my veins had felt the way I thought that love should feel. When we lay in the hut of the Vuo Ton, lost in the labyrinth of each other's arms as rain tattooed the reeds of the roof—that had felt like something that a person might call love. If I'd killed him in those moments, with Ela looking on, maybe I could have claimed my victory.

In each case, however, just when the prize seemed within reach, it slipped away. I would look at Ruc, as now, and find him suddenly, impossibly distant. There were days, like the long trip back to Dombâng after the Vuo Ton had disappeared, when he seemed almost a stranger. Whatever we achieved, however close we came, whatever delicious fever seared my heart—it didn't last.

Whenever I asked myself that question—*Did I love him*—I always arrived at the same answer—*no*—the word like an iron gate barred against my entrance.

For the first time, however, lost on that island in the delta, witnessed by the gazes of the living, the undying, and the dead, I began to doubt the question itself.

I'd been treating love like a thing, an achievement, a trophy to be won and hung around my neck. People talk about it that way sometimes:

My love for you is undying.

He never knew my love.

It is an error of grammar to make love a noun.

It is not a thing you can have.

Love—like doubt or hate—is a verb. It has no fixity. Like song, its truth is in its unfolding. Language is filled with these illusions. A fist, an embrace, a blow—they are actions, not things. Action takes time, and time is the tool of my god.

I didn't love Ruc yet, but there was still time.

I turned to face him. They'd stripped away his vest before tossing us into the delta. I could see the scar etched over the muscle of his stomach and chest. Some of those scars, I'd given him. Others he had come by on his own. I wanted to touch him, to run my fingers one more time over that smooth, warm skin, but I'd touched him before, and touching hadn't been enough. If I was going to love him, really love him, I couldn't just touch him. Even the bright violence of our fighting hadn't been enough. I needed something more. I filled my lungs with the hot delta air.

"I came to Dombâng to kill you," I said.

I don't know what I expected from him. A quick retort, maybe. Scorn. Silence. He'd faced the betrayal of the Greenshirts without much more than a flicker of anger. All the time I'd known him, he'd been so cool, so ready. Even busted up, even bleeding, he never really looked hurt.

As I finally told him the truth, however, the whole truth that had been burning away inside me, the words seemed to land like a blow. He took a step back, not the tactical step of a brawler giving himself room, but the half stagger of a man who's just taken a fist to the chin. He watched me a moment, then

closed his eyes, shook his head, as though he could deny
what I'd said, as though that gesture could cancel out the whole
world.

I could have killed him then—I could feel Ela's eyes on me,
and Kossal's, his dispassionate, hers eager, curious. I could have
ended him in that moment, but I needed more. I needed him
to scream at me, or beg, or start sobbing. I needed him to deny
me, or accept me, or do anything other than rock with another
punch. I needed to see past the calm to the beating heart of
him. The surface of the man was gorgeous, but I couldn't love
a surface.

"I'm going to kill you now," I said, testing the weight of the
knife in my hand.

He opened his eyes. Sweat dripped from his face, soaked his
vest, mingled with the blood leaking from his shoulder and arm.
He didn't seem to notice any of it. His eyes never left me. The
whole world might have disappeared, might have sunk into the
mud.

I held the bronze knife in one hand, my bronze-tipped spear
between us. "Don't you want to ask why?"

"No."

"Why not?"

"You'll lie."

I shook my head. "I'm done lying."

"I liked you better when you were lying."

I closed my own eyes, searched the corners of my reluctant
heart, waited for him to strike. He didn't.

"That's what I was afraid of," I said at last.

"What, exactly, were you afraid of?"

"That you wouldn't let me get close to you."

I opened my eyes to see Ruc's face move through a series of
masks: amazement, confusion, disbelief. Then his laugh tumbled
out in great, delighted whoops. I hadn't heard him laugh like
that since Sia, since right after our first fight, our first night
together, when we lay in bed dabbing a sweet-smelling salve on

each other's wounds, passing back and forth a bottle of plum-dark wine, each ministering to the other's broken parts with the lightest of kisses.

"Yes," he managed finally. "You're right. Knowing you'd come all the way to Dombâng to slide a knife between my ribs might have made things more complicated."

"Complicated is fine. I like complicated. But you wouldn't *let* it be complicated."

"Why, in the name of your broken god, would I let it be *complicated,* when complicated, in this case, stands in for *murderous?*"

I opened my mouth, closed it, then tried again. "Because you love me? Because I thought I could love you."

He stared at me.

"Love isn't killing people, Pyrre. Killing is the *opposite* of love, you twisted bitch."

"How do you know?" The question was barely loud enough to hear, but it burned like a coal in my chest. "How do you *know?*"

"Because I was raised in a world where people value life."

"And that world told you there was one way to love, just *one.* It told you the only real love was what you hear about in the songs, what you see in the plays. It said love was flowers and gentle caresses under the moonlight."

"As opposed to what? A knife in the back and a bath full of blood?"

"Yes!" I said. "What are flowers? What is moonlight?"

"They're beautiful and gentle, for starters."

"And who said love was beautiful or gentle? Who said it was *only* those things?" I took half a stab at him with my spear. It wasn't a real attack, but it felt strange to be holding the weapon without doing something with it. He knocked it aside casually. I circled to my right, still talking. "The night I met you, I broke two of your ribs and you beat me unconscious."

He shook his head. "That was different."

"Different *how*? A bare-knuckle fight is a long way from tulips and moonlight."

"It wasn't the fight that made me—"

"Made you what?"

He tested my guard, first high, then low. "It wasn't the fight that intrigued me. It was finding someone smart, quick, tenacious. What about all the lazy days in between the fighting? What about those evenings out on the water? Those mornings drinking *ta* while we watched the sun come up? The fists and bruises were just incidental."

"Bullshit."

"You're sick, Pyrre. Your whole religion is sick."

"What's the sickness in thinking love is bigger than a few kisses, bigger than running through the same platitudes night after night? Why shouldn't love be *more* than that? Why shouldn't it be braver, more frightening?"

He lashed out with the sword. I parried, bronze grating over bronze. I pressed the attack a moment, slashing high then low, before stepping back, my breath hot in my throat. Ruc watched me warily.

"You're a killer," he said. "Just like the crocs or the vipers. A fucking animal."

"We're all animals. We're born. We fight as hard as we can to stay alive, and then, in spite of all that fighting, we die anyway." I shook my head. "The reason we think we're different from animals, better than them, is that we know how the story ends. We're in on the joke."

Ruc shook his head. "No one told me this was how it would end."

"You knew it was coming, one way or another."

"The way matters."

"Of *course* it does, you beautiful fool." I studied him, the rise and fall of his chest, the way his forearm flexed as he shifted his grip on the sword. Then I looked past his brown skin, past the lush muscles of his shoulders and stomach. They teach us this at Rassambur, to peel away each of the body's layers, to unmake what Bedisa has made and in that unmaking to *see* what it is we are. Ruc was warm flesh hung on a frame of bone. Soon, in a time counted in heartbeats rather than days, Ananshael would touch him, and he would be dirt. So would I.

What I needed, before the god unmade me, was for Ruc to see, for him to *understand*.

"Do you know what happened," I asked him, "our last night together in Sia?"

Instead of answering, he came at me with a series of quick, savage overhand blows. The earlier testing and probing was over. Any one of those, had it landed, would have split me from my throat down through my chest. I turned the first aside with the shaft of the spear, dodged the next two, thrust out with an attack of my own—deflected—and then we were circling again, eyeing each other through the light flashing off of our bronze.

"What I know," he said between heavy breaths, "is that you said you wanted to stay with me our entire lives, until one or the other died. Then the next morning, you were gone."

"I tried to kill you," I said, remembering that night, the way we made love over and over, then how he'd fallen asleep tangled in my limbs. I remembered watching his chest rise and fall, remembered the warmth in my own heart, remembered thinking, *This is a test.* As Kossal had explained to me days earlier, sometimes the god speaks in our bones. Any murderer can kill someone she hates. Ananshael requires something more of his faithful—I understood this even then, that hot, sweet night in Sia. "After you fell asleep, I took one of my knives and laid it against your throat."

"And here I thought the fact that you disappeared was bad."

"I couldn't do it."

Ruc snorted. "Obviously."

"I failed in my faith. At the time, I thought I cared about you too much."

"You'll forgive me if I don't swoon."

"Stop being an asshole. I need you to understand this."

"Understand *what*? You didn't kill me in my sleep all those years ago and here you are again, back to finish the job? All right. I understand."

This time he went for the spear, ignoring my body, trying to slice through the shaft. I knocked aside three blows, four, five, angling the wood so that the bronze glanced off rather than biting, but Ruc kept coming and coming. I had openings, moments when I could have slipped either the knife or the spearpoint past his guard, into his heart, but I couldn't kill him, not until he saw what I wanted him to see. He didn't drop back, even when I gave him space, just kept coming at me, trying to back me up against the wall of skulls. I parried, ducked, slid outside his range. I was better than him, faster, but the game I was playing gave me no room for mistakes. Which was true, also, of the game I played with myself.

As he coiled his arm to attack again, I tossed the spear aside, dropped the knife. The weapons clattered to the sun-baked dirt.

He hesitated, staring at me. My breath burned in my chest, but I forced out the words.

"Back in Sia, I thought I was in love with you. Then I thought I needed to kill you to show that my faith was stronger than my love. I was wrong on both counts. What I felt—that need to have you close, to have you near me all the time—*that wasn't love*. It was something else, something small and grasping and selfish. Love is not this stupid holding on. Love is larger."

Ruc stared at me warily, his chest heaving. "I have no fucking idea what that means."

"Yes," I said, "you do."

I reached out, took the tip of his sword between my fingers, raised it to my neck. "When I die," I said, "I want your hand behind that final cut. I want to do it looking in your eyes."

It was the truth.

I'd been scrutinizing my own mind for so long, spying on my every move, weighing each choice, second-guessing every path taken or ignored. It felt good to stand there, stripped of my last weapon, stripped of all the lies that had led to that point, and to say out loud, in plain language, one of the few things I knew to be true.

"He is waiting for me," I said. "He is waiting for all of us."

The sun ignited the delta haze, setting the world aflame. Blood and sweat burned on my tongue. Every line, every reed and rush, every angle of Ruc's face, seemed carved into being with a knife. It was beautiful, all of it—the mud, the skulls, the blood-bathed bronze—and soon, maybe before my next breath, it would be gone. I stood with my arms at my side, pinned in place by the day's heat and Ruc's unwavering gaze.

This was the man I had come to Dombâng to love, and I did not love him.

In that one moment, it didn't matter.

I could feel my own unmaking hanging in the air like the silence before a song. The silence was all.

Slowly, like a person moving through water or the depths of a dream, Ruc lowered his blade.

"No," he said.

For a moment I thought I might sob, collapse. I'd failed. I'd done everything I could to serve my god, and I had failed. I ached to have that bronze blade inside me, to feel Ananshael's final touch.

"Do it," I said.

"No." He wasn't looking at me anymore. He was looking past me, as though trying to make sense of something far off, but moving closer.

"Please."

He shook his head, took half a step back.

"I need you," he said quietly.

"No, you don't. You just said it—I'm vicious, sick, twisted."

"That's why I need you," he said again, then nodded over my shoulder. "If I'm going to live through this, I need all the vicious I can get."

Slowly, as though just in that moment reawakening to the feel of my own body, I turned.

The noon sun hung directly overhead, hammered like a bronze disc into the sky. The delta, normally so filled with the music of bird and insect, had fallen totally silent.

They were here.

As I stared, the Three stepped naked from the brush, two men and a woman, just as Dombâng's priests had claimed for centuries. They were easily the most beautiful creatures I'd ever seen, lithe as any jaguar, sweat-dappled skin shifting over the muscle beneath, eyes like liquid jewels, hair slicked back with water or sweat. The tallest of them, one of the men, was dark as midsummer midnight, each of his arms almost as wide as my waist. For all his size, however, he didn't look cumbersome or slow. He moved like flowing water, like a storm rolling over the land. The other man was shorter, slimmer, paler, built like a whip rather than a bull, constantly coiling and uncoiling, even when he seemed still.

Sinn, I thought. *That has to be Sinn.*

He caught my eyes, then smiled. His teeth were sharp as knives.

If the two men had come alone, I might have stared at them forever, lost in their perfection, but they were not alone. A woman stood between them, a woman I remembered from my childhood, bronze skin glistening in the sunlight, her flesh every bit as deadly as the weapons we held. A strip of black hair ran down the center of her shaved scalp, cascaded between her shoulder blades. Scars hatched her skin, as they did the skin of her companions. On a human body, those smooth ridges might have been blemishes; Kem Anh and her consorts wore them like priceless finery. They were naked otherwise, naked in such a way that made me feel ashamed of my clothes, ashamed to have hidden my goddess-given body beneath the skin of creatures long dead.

And then there were her eyes, golden, as I remembered, liquid and shifting as quicksand, dragging me in, down.

It seemed impossible that I had ever walked away, that I had ever had another thought in my life beyond finding her again, following her, staring into that gaze. With an effort so violent I almost cried out, I forced my own eyes closed. It felt like stepping from sunshine into frigid water, like trying to breathe ice. Even in my mind's dark I could see her, the attenuated vision more perfect than any human form.

"You're wrong, Kossal," I heard myself murmur.

The annals of Rassambur describe the Csestriim in great detail. There had been hundreds of years of war, after all, in which to compile the accounts. Those tomes all agreed on a few things: the Csestriim were inhumanly brilliant, undying, utterly emotionless, effortlessly cruel. None of the chronicles mentioned this impossible beauty. I tried to imagine setting this down in words as I am doing now. I tried to imagine overlooking that soulrending perfection in my account. I could not. Even now, years later, I could drench pages and pages in ink trying to find the right words, the fragment of a phrase that might start to describe them truly. I would be wasting my ink. There are things on this earth beyond all language.

I opened my eyes again.

"These are not Csestriim."

All three of them shifted at the word, not the reflexive jerk a human fighter might make, but a languid settling into their own power, like a cat crouching before it pounces.

Hang Loc and Sinn bared their sharpened teeth, growled, seemed ready to come for us. Then Kem Anh put a hand on each of their arms, trailed her fingers from elbow to shoulder, the gesture erotic and terrifying all at once. She shook her head slowly.

"No," Kossal agreed. I turned to find the old priest, his hatchets set momentarily aside, sliding out of his robe, that same robe he'd worn through the city for weeks. It puddled on the ground at his feet like a snake's molted skin as he took up the bronze weapons once more. "These are not Csestriim."

Again, the two men growled, and again Kem Anh held them back, draping her arms over their shoulders, sliding her flanks against them until they subsided.

"I told you," Chua murmured. "They are gods. We would not give ourselves to the Csestriim. This was our pledge: *Never them*."

I didn't look at Chua. I was staring at the creature she thought was a god, staring into her eyes until it seemed the rest of the world had fallen away. "It's not a pledge," I whispered finally, understanding settling on me like a heavy stone, almost crushing the breath from my chest.

"You have forgotten . . ." Chua began.

I shook my head. "It is the Vuo Ton who have forgotten. *Never them*. It is not a pledge. It was never a pledge."

"What are you talking about?" Ruc demanded.

I thought my heart would shatter my ribs. "It is a name."

"Strange name," Ela observed.

"Not the name of a person," I said. I was so hot I felt my skin might catch fire. "It is the name of their race. These are not Csestriim. They are the Nevariim."

Ken Anh's smile was a white, vicious sickle.

The sun was an inferno.

My own breath was flame.

"The Nevariim are a kids' tale," Ruc said.

"And how are they described," I asked quietly, "in those tales?"

No one replied, as though the weight of the words was too much to haul up out of the chest.

"They are always gorgeous," I said. "Strong. The implacable foes of the Csestriim."

"In the tales," Ruc managed finally, "they are *good*."

"Stories never get everything right."

Through this whole conversation, they just stood there—if *stood* is the right verb for creatures who seemed, even in their stillness, to gather light, to warp the whole world so that they waited at its center. They watched us with those ineluctable eyes. When Sinn growled deep in his throat, Kem Anh leaned into him, pressing her warm flesh against his, purring from between sharpened teeth into his ear. They had not spoken—maybe they never spoke—but they understood what we were saying. I was sure of it.

"Nevariim," Kossal said finally. "Maybe. It doesn't matter."

I turned to stare at him. "We found the remnants of a race that should have been extinct millennia before the Csestriim wars, a race that you believed never existed in the first place, and it doesn't *matter*?"

The old priest shrugged, shifted his weight from foot to foot, tested the heft of the twin axes in his hands. "Anything that will not die insults our god."

"On the other hand, they *have* given a lot of women and men to Ananshael," Ela observed. "And just look at them." She was almost purring. "Maybe we could be friends? Before we kill them, I mean."

Kossal shook his head. "You know as well as I do that the killing is only half of our devotion."

"And why do I feel," she asked, narrowing her eyes slyly at him, "that the other half is about to come due?"

The priest didn't respond. His eyes were fixed on the creatures who had come to add our skulls to the wall. Ruc leaned close to murmur in my ear. "This is the time. Five of us against three of them."

He seemed to have forgotten our truncated fight, forgotten the fact that I'd come to kill him. Maybe the arrival of the Three had wiped it from his mind, or maybe my surrender had convinced him I was harmless. Either way, he didn't want to fight me anymore. Instead, he wanted to fight these creatures who had walked the world for countless thousands of years.

I glanced over at Ela and Kossal, then down at the Three. They still hadn't moved. If this was a hunt, they seemed in no hurry to start hunting. On the other hand, there was nowhere for us to go. To flee was to die running. They stood with the lazy ease of predators who knew their prey could not escape.

The appearance of the Nevariim had jarred something loose inside me, broken something, some notion or belief I didn't even know I held until it shattered. They shouldn't have been real, shouldn't have been standing there, and yet there they were, waiting to slaughter us in exactly the same way that they had slaughtered so many thousands or tens of thousands before us.

That mattered, somehow, mattered in some way beyond our own imminent destruction. In that moment I could not say how, only that the whole world had shifted. Staring at that awful perfection, I knew that I knew nothing, that things I had believed in the deepest heart of myself were wrong. They would unmake us—I saw that clearly enough—but I wanted to see the world clearly before I was unmade, to know it.

I wanted, just for once, to know myself.

As I grappled with my own inchoate need, Kossal, who had locked eyes with the creatures the moment they first stepped out of the brush, turned to Ela. To my shock, he smiled, then made a low, formal bow. It should have looked ridiculous—a naked old man, bent over, baking in the noonday sun—but somehow he managed to look graceful, even elegant. He might have been a young soldier at a ball, half bedazzled by Ela's beauty, harnessing his courage to his gallantry. He straightened up, then gestured toward the Three, never taking his eyes from the woman.

"Ela Timarna, priestess of Ananshael, second, greatest, and last love of my life, will you join me in this dance?"

A quick shiver snaked up my spine. It wasn't because of the arrival of the Three, or not just that. This was something different, more. Staring at the priestess and the priest, I felt a tremor in my flesh, a new note rising, for which I had no name.

Ela smiled, stepped in, hooked the back of Kossal's neck with the flat arc of a sickle, drew him close, then pressed her lips to his. I'd seen her kiss him dozens of times during the trek south, chaste pecks on the back of the head, mocking, wet smacks on the cheek. This was altogether different. For a long time they stayed like that, the priest and the priestess, eyes closed, hands filled with their weapons, bodies pressed together. Something inside me stirred at the sight, an ache, as though some organ I didn't know I possessed were trembling after a long stillness.

When they finally broke apart, Ela studied him with sparkling eyes. "My love," she said finally.

Kossal raised an eyebrow. "Really?"

Ela laughed, spread her hands. Her sickles winked sunlight. "Of course."

Twin flowering vines of wonder and horror wrapped me, strangled me—wonder at the sight before me, horror that I would understand it all too late. Something in the way they stood, the way they looked at each other, something in Kossal's . . . no, it wasn't Kossal, it was Ela . . . There was something there, something about her, but I couldn't grasp it, not quite.

I looked over at Ruc. He was wary, ready. I turned back to the priestess and priest. I wanted to study them forever, to stare at them until I knew what it was I was seeing, but of course, I could not stare at them forever. In moments the Nevariim would tear them apart.

I stumbled forward, words tumbling from my mouth. "You can't."

The priestess and priest turned to me.

"The Trial isn't over," I pleaded, searching for the words. "You are my Witnesses. You can't die now. You can't die yet."

Kossal shook his head gently. "Everyone serves the god, Pyrre. Even those who never pass the Trial."

"And today," Ela added, winking at me, "we will make a great offering."

"I'm not done," I protested.

I wasn't supposed to feel this way. My god had come. He was waiting patiently in the rushes, floating just beneath the water's surface, lying silent on the wind. I was supposed to welcome him, to hurl myself joyfully into his embrace. I had prepared for this all my life, for the sacred moment of my own unmaking, and now that it was here . . . where was my faith?

I wasn't fit to be a priestess. I had become like any other benighted woman—some fisher or farmer—scrabbling for one last moment, then another, then another, as though my life were something I could keep, as though it were some chilly crystal in a lightless cave that would stay perfectly unchanged down the endless generations.

"There is no more time," Kossal said.

"There *is*. I have until the end of the day!"

Panic, like a rat trapped inside my chest, raked me with cold, awful claws. I had come so close. By afternoon at the latest, the spiders would hatch inside Chua. I could give her to the god, and then there would be only the question of my love, one last mystery, one final box to unlock. After a lifetime of bafflement I felt as though I finally had the key, that it was secreted on me somewhere, that I could find it if I only had the time . . . and yet that would mean nothing if my Witnesses died first.

"I'm not ready," I whispered.

"Which is why," Kossal replied quietly, "you have failed your Trial."

The words went through me like a spear. I stood like a slaughtered beast, too stupid to remember to fall. Ela gave me an unreadable smile, then pursed her lips and blew me a kiss. Before I could respond, the two of them turned away, turned toward their own ends, shoulders relaxed, bronze weapons light as laughter in their hands.

Kem Anh smiled, slid a fingernail along Sinn's neck, then nodded. He stepped forward.

I've been alive a long time and never seen a fight like the one that unfolded on that island lost in the delta. Nor do I expect to. Kossal and Ela numbered among Ananshael's finest servants. I had seen them sparring, of course, back in Rassambur. I'd gone toe-to-toe with Ela. I thought I knew just how fast she was, how dangerous. I was a fool. Whatever deadliness I thought I had witnessed before had just been sport for them, casual activity to stay warm while they searched for a fight that might be worthy. Even the crocs of the Vuo Ton hadn't tested them, not truly. As they glided down the slope toward Sinn they seemed to shed everything unnecessary, to slough off all superfluous gesture and motion. All that was left of them, when they hefted their weapons to attack, was death.

They flanked him, Kossal coming in high from the left, while Ela rolled low to the right, striking out, trying to hamstring the creature as he turned to face the priest. There was nothing unusual about the tactic, but the perfection with which they performed it made my heart ache. They might have been listening to some silent music, just the two of them, stabbing and retreating, feinting and riposting as though they could both hear the thundering rhythm, those high, staccato notes. They traded attacks like musicians passing the melody back and forth between different instruments, one, then the other, then both at once, exploring the same motif at different pitches: Kossal the drum, Ela the whip-fast fiddle played above it. There are only so many themes in a fight, but the two of them piled infinite variation on those finite notes, flipping them, slowing them, sliding echoes of earlier attacks between all the main movements.

I couldn't tear my eyes from them, but I heard Ruc exhale quietly at my side. "Sweet Intarra's light."

"They don't worship Intarra," I replied.

"No," he agreed, his voice thick with awe. "They do not."

It seemed impossible that anyone, any*thing* could survive against that attack. Sinn was naked and unarmed. They should have shredded the flesh from his bones in moments. And yet, somehow, he was still standing, fighting like the viper for which he was named—slow, almost lethargic, coiling and uncoiling, feints and counterattacks too fast to follow. He flowed between the sickles and axes as though he were not flesh, but a reflection, an apparition, something horribly gorgeous culled from a dream, impervious to all mortal instruments.

Behind him, Kem Anh and Hang Loc watched, teeth bared, eyes bright.

There is a stillness hidden in all speed. The three fought as though locked in the amber of their violence. Bronze carved gleaming lines across the day. There are moments, listening to music, when you forget to follow the intertwining lines, when you lose track of the tempo, of the counterpoint, abandon all thought and let the sound wash over you. So it was that day in the delta as my Witnesses, servants of Ananshael, fought to make their greatest offering to the god.

"We have to go in now," Ruc growled.

He was right at my shoulder, so close he could have kissed me or slipped a knife into my side. His eyes, however, were on the fight.

"We have weapons, he doesn't," he went on. "Five against one. Five against three if the other two decide to get bloody."

I turned to look at him. "We can't win."

He met my gaze. "Then we'll die. Everyone dies. You should know that—you're fucking Skullsworn."

"I'm not Skullsworn," I replied, shaking my head. "I failed."

"Because you didn't murder me?"

"Because I didn't love you."

"You are insane."

I turned away from the accusation, from those awful green eyes, to find Chua beside me. Blood leaked from the wound in her stomach, streaked her pants, dappled the dust at her feet. Pain twisted her features, but beneath that pain her strength remained, her stubbornness. This was the woman, after all, who had survived two weeks alone and boatless in the delta. Despite the spiders gestating inside her, she didn't look ready to die just yet.

Or no. That was wrong. She was ready to die, but not lying

down. Despite her wounds, she held the bronze spear steady. I hadn't noticed her picking it up.

"He is right," she said, then spat a bolus of blood and phlegm into the dirt.

I stared at her. "That we can beat them?"

"Of course not. He is right that everyone dies."

Shame washed over me, hot as a monsoon rain. Despair had stripped me so violently of my faith that it had come to this: I needed a fisher and a soldier to remind me of my god's most basic truth. I gathered my breath into my body, steadied myself, then turned back to the fight.

Ela had lost ground. Sinn had her pressed back against a patch of tangle vine. It was an even more dangerous position than it seemed; she had little room to maneuver, and worse, if a few of those thumb-long thorns snagged her clothes, she'd be held fast. Although I was staring right at it, I couldn't believe what I was seeing. It was impossible to imagine Ela defeated, Ela dead. Even knowing what I knew about her foe, I couldn't believe it.

How could the world go on being the world without her in it?

"We have to move," I said, lurching forward.

Before I'd taken two steps, however, Sinn, who had been ducking under and around Kossal's hatchets while forcing the priestess backward and still backward, attacked. The Nevariim moved so fast I couldn't see his hands. He was in one position, then another, the space between elided with terrifying ease. Ela, somehow, anticipated the attack, raised a sickle to fend him off. The creature moved back a step and Ela lunged, far off her balance, reaching, overreaching, then crying out in surprise as she stumbled forward. Sinn hissed, lashed out for her throat.

And Kossal's ax was there.

For a heartbeat everything went still.

The pale creature studied the blood welling from his skin—the rent ran finger-deep from his elbow to his wrist—turned to look at Kossal, knocked aside the flurry of attacks that followed, slapping the flats of the ax-heads with his palms, then stepped back, out of range.

Ela straightened up, glanced at Kossal. He winked at her. I'd never seen him wink. Ela shook her head ruefully.

"Ananshael," she prayed, "please take this love of mine before he begins to gloat."

"The god comes for us all," the priest replied, then turned back to Sinn.

Kem Anh stepped forward, lifted her companion's slashed limb to her lips, bared her teeth, licked the blood clear. Sinn growled low in his throat, then nodded, once to Kossal, once to Ela, an acknowledgment beyond all words. This was what they wanted, these three immortal creatures. This is why they had remained in the delta all these thousands of years, this same scene played out over and over and over. It was for this they trained the Vuo Ton, for this they had left me alive as a child, for this they lived every one of their unnumbered days.

What would it mean, I wondered, thinking with a part of my mind that calved off from the world of blood and mud and sun, *to live all those years without ever changing?*

"You lied to me," Ruc said. "You weren't even trying, back in Sia, back in the ring. I never saw you fight like that."

I shook my head, staring first at Kossal, then Ela, trying to make sense of what I'd seen.

"That's because I can't. Because I'm *not* like that."

The priestess wore a smile wide as a noonday sky, a smile that she turned on me.

"Maybe one day you will be."

"After today," I replied, "I will be dead."

She smiled wider. "Then if there's something you want to be, you'd better hurry up and start being it."

Sinn hissed, slid forward. The gash on his arm had already

stopped bleeding. He didn't look slowed or dismayed by the wound. If anything, he looked eager.

"There are five of us now, you fucking monster," Ruc spat.

I glanced past the pale creature, to where the other two Nevariim stood watching. Kem Anh had slid halfway behind Hang Loc, pressed herself up against him and wrapped one arm around his chest. With her other hand, she was stroking his massive cock. Her lips were bloody from where she'd bitten him on the shoulder. I wondered how many of those scars on his skin had been left by her. Both of them were watching us, chests rising and falling as they waited for the fight to begin once more. Neither made any move to intervene.

I edged to the left, toward Kossal, while Ruc broke right.

The old priest fixed me with a stern look. "I didn't invite you."

"Our god welcomes all," I replied, keeping my eyes on Sinn's sinuous, shifting form.

"I intend to kill this thing," he said. "To see it unmade."

"So do I."

I was surprised by my words even as I spoke them, surprised by how ardently I felt them. After a lifetime dreaming of these gods—false gods—waking to soaked sheets and my heart thudding in my chest, after a decade and a half doubting my own memory, my own mind, the very fabric of my childhood, I had finally arrived where I could bury a length of bronze in their flesh.

Kossal stared at me a moment longer, then nodded, as though that settled the matter.

We'd spread out into a rough circle, hoping to come at Sinn from four different directions at the same time. I stood off to his right-hand side, measuring the distance between us, trying to track the movement of the Nevariim against that of my allies in the fight. Our only chance, if it was a chance at all, would lie in a concerted attack. The others seemed to realize that—all except Chua, who was approaching the creature head on, her bronze spear held back behind her, arm cocked for a fisher's throw. She might have been all alone for the attention she paid us.

Sinn bared his fangs, opened his arms, inviting her to strike. Chua refused.

She crossed the intervening space at an implacable walk. There was no rush to her gait, no tension in her shoulders, nothing to suggest she was doing anything but fishing from a bank, looking to take a ploutfish or a blueback with that long, glittering spear. Out of the corner of my eye, I could see Kossal sliding closer to the Nevariim, hatchets held in the old Manjari guard—one high, one low. He was humming a tune I didn't recognize, something slow and solemn. On the other side of Sinn, Ela was saying something to Ruc, chatting like a woman in a tavern, gesturing expansively with her twin sickles even as she inched in.

Chua stopped two paces from the Nevariim. Her eyes were calm in the way the eyes of the dead are calm.

"I do not worship you," she said.

Sinn clicked his teeth together, a fast staccato rhythm, opened and closed his hands, as though flexing claws.

"You can have my skull," she went on, "but never—"

Kossal launched himself at Sinn halfway through the word, hatchets sweeping in and down even as he leapt. Ela was in motion, too, rolling low, underneath whatever guard the Nevariim might put up, lashing out for a hamstring with her sickle.

It was an impossible attack to block.

Sinn blocked it, catching one of Kossal's hatchets by the head, ripping it free of the priest's grip, then smashing it down into the arc of Ela's sickle. Ruc surged forward with a roar, swinging his sword in a great looping arc. Sinn leaped it easily, hurled the hatchet at his attacker, turned to knock away Kossal's second attack, swatting the flat of the bronze with his palm, then back-handing the priest so viciously across the chest that he fell back into the dirt, gasping. The Nevariim roared, whirled to face Ela—she was on her feet again, sickles a nimbus of bronze in the air around her—when Chua struck.

Like all good fishers, she had chosen her moment, waiting in the midst of that maelstrom for the opening, then hurling her spear. The bright bronze sank into the Nevariim's shoulder, spinning him halfway around before tearing free and clattering to the dirt. Blood welled from the wound, flowed down the arm, staining the skin red.

"Never . . ." Chua began again, then stopped, opened her eyes wide, put a hand to her stomach, and lurched into an awful, staggering dance.

The meat puppeteer.

The name of the spider was apt. She looked like a marionette jerked by some insane master, her limbs jittering and twitching as her body rocked from side to side. She opened her mouth, tried to speak again, choked on the words, then turned—with obvious and agonizing effort—to stare at me.

Pain glazed her eyes. One hand thrashed at her stomach as she tried to claw at the wound while the toxin flipped the limb back and forth like a fish dying on a deck.

I went to her, ignoring the others, ignoring the bleeding Nevariim. If he wanted to kill me while my back was turned, he was welcome to try. I had made a promise, and I intended to keep it.

I put an arm around the fisher's shoulders, whether to still her or comfort her, I couldn't say. Her skin was like fire.

"I'm here, Chua," I told her quietly. "I'm here."

She trembled in my arms as I dragged the silent knife over her throat. Her eyes fixed on mine, then slipped past me, opening wide, then wider, drinking in some final sight. Then she raised a hand halfway to her neck, sighed blood, let it fall. The body collapsed. Ananshael towered over the island, tall as the sky.

I turned away from the corpse to face Ela. The priestess stood a few paces away, chest heaving, sweat's sheen glistening on her face.

"*A mother,*" I said, "*ripe with new life.*"

She raised an eyebrow. "A little old for it."

"Hundreds of spiders have hatched in her stomach." I pointed to the wound, which was already bulging, pulsing with the creatures inside. "That makes six."

"You're still trying to pass the Trial?" she asked, cocking her head to the side. Then she smiled, a warm, luscious smile. "That's my girl."

Behind me, Sinn growled deep in his throat. I turned to find him watching me with those inhuman eyes. His chin was soaked with blood—he'd been licking the rent in his shoulder—and red stained his sharpened teeth. He bared them wide, spat onto the ground, then spread his arms in invitation. The right arm, I noticed, didn't go as high as the left. His shoulder still worked, but Chua's spear had sliced something deep inside, something important.

"I think he still wants to play," Ela said.

Ruc nodded grimly, slid off to the far flank. His bronze sword flashed sunlight, as though it were made of flame. He was trying, I realized, to blind the Nevariim. Sinn blinked as the light slid across his eyes, Kossal pounced, and the fight was on once more.

The old priest hammered implacably away with his twin hatchets—he'd reclaimed the second one from where Sinn had tossed it contemptuously in the dirt—his lined face intent on his last devotion. Ela seemed to dance, hurling her sickles in great, whirling arcs that kept the Nevariim from getting close enough to strike at her. Ruc worked like a man at an unpleasant job, mouth hanging open as he feinted, thrusted, searched for an opening.

I did nothing. I wanted to kill the creature as much as the rest of them; even if I couldn't pass my Trial, I could give my god that one final offering. There was a realization blooming inside me, however, a hot, horrifying feeling that I didn't recognize or fully understand. Not fear, exactly, though it felt like fear. Not amazement, though that was there, too. I stared at Ela as I grappled with this tremor in my chest—she was smiling, laughing as she fought, every lineament of her body bright with her delight.

I wanted to be like that, like her. I was tired of doubting the heft of my own heart, of parsing my emotions as though they were weights on some merchant's scale. I wanted to be full, and furious, and free. I ached with that need, and the ache kept me pinned in place as the priestess whirled through the ecstatic stations of her devotion. It kept me pinned in place when I could have helped.

The attack happened in the moment between heartbeats, as that indefatigable muscle gathered itself in my chest, ready to crush the blood through my veins for the millionth time, or the billionth. Even now I don't know exactly what occurred. Kossal was surging forward, driving his foe back. Sinn seemed to be collapsing. Ruc was harrying him from one side, and Ela from the other. It seemed that they had him, and then . . . faster than a bowstring's snap, the Nevariim lunged forward, twisting through the faintest lapse in the old priest's guard.

Kossal's throat exploded, blood's red spraying out across the dirt.

He stood a moment longer, holding vigil, eyes distant, as though watching the approach of his god over the waters, through the rushes and reeds. In my mind, he was still alive, still struggling, but our minds are inadequate. Ananshael came while we stared, unmade his priest without anyone seeing, then slipped away. Kossal never fell. By the time his body hit the earth, he was gone.

Ela exhaled all at once, as though someone had buried a fist in her gut. Then she straightened herself, opened her mouth wide, and poured forth the final agonizing, ecstatic bars of Antreem's Mass. It was watching the priestess in that moment, seeing her for what she was—stunning but bloody, gorgeous but mortal, bereft but joyful—that I understood, finally, about love.

She had been telling me, but I couldn't see it, couldn't *believe* it until I saw her staring at the body of the man she'd loved, standing and singing, utterly undiminished by his absence. This was the lesson I couldn't learn even from a lifetime gazing into my own heart, from a million nights fighting Ruc or feeling him move inside me: love is not some eternal state, but a delight in the paradise of the imperfect. The holding of a thing is inextricable from the letting go, and to love, you must learn both.

The world was still beautiful—Ela felt that, and as she sang, I felt the music rising inside me finally, in my flesh and mind—the music of joy in all the wonder that cannot last, of joy, not in the having, but in the passage—and I opened my mouth to sing alongside her, to pour into the world that corporeal trembling without which our lives mean nothing, nor our deaths.

My breath failed me first. When the priestess finally fell silent, she closed her eyes, nodded in response to something I would never know, then glanced back to us and raised an eyebrow. "Just because Kossal got tired is no reason for the two of you to begin loitering. He really should have set a better example."

Sinn studied Kossal's crumpled body, hissed his satisfaction, then turned to face the three of us. We had wounded him, slowed him, but two of us were gone. Over his shoulder, Kem Anh and Hang Loc looked on, beautiful as gods, eager as beasts, their bared teeth gleaming with the sun. For millennia they had trained the people of the delta to be their prey, but they could not have faced prey like us before. Even in Rassambur, there had been no one else quite like Kossal or Ela.

Ela had turned away from me, toward the Nevariim. I couldn't see her face any longer, but I could read the readiness in the set of her shoulders, in the way she flipped those sickles—one after the other—caught them, twirled them happily in her hands. Her brown skin, soaked with the light of the noonday sun, seemed to shine. She was singing again, one of the children's songs from Rassambur this time, a lilting melody that the few kids who grow up on the mesa learn to sing as they chase each other in wild summer circles. She had become a statue of bliss.

Sinn hissed and stepped forward, ready to destroy her.

A sound like a howl exploded from my chest: *"No."*

A flock of winebeaks burst from the rushes, whirled in a clamor above us, then wheeled out of sight to the south.

The world went still. I imagined it all—me, Ruc, Ela, the Three, the delta, everything beyond, the whole spherical world—hanging in a great emptiness, suspended by nothing in a great void, waiting to fall.

I said it again, screamed it this time—*"No!"*—as though that single syllable could hold at bay all the strength coiled in the flesh of that immortal creature. Sinn turned his head, twisted it toward me like a snake, held me in the coils of his gaze, then looked back at Ela, slid a step forward. At that same moment, the priestess glanced over her shoulder toward me, brow furrowed. That was when the creature struck, lashing across the empty space like a whip uncoiling to knock the sickles from her nerveless hands and seize her by the throat. Ela's face twisted. She kicked out at him as he lifted her from the ground, but his flesh didn't yield, and as he choked her, the kicks weakened. Her face purpled, lips swelled. When she tried to speak, her tongue lolled from her mouth.

Without thinking, I started in.

"Pyrre . . ." Ruc began.

I ignored him. My whole being was fixed on the priestess and the Nevariim strangling the life from her.

"You cannot have her." I hurled the words before me like spears. *"You cannot have her."*

Sinn smiled wide. Ela's arms and legs, starved of air, started to jerk. The Nevariim turned to me, opened his mouth, and roared. The sound throbbed in my heart, my lungs, as though my organs were drums, as though my skin had been stretched tight over my frame for a single purpose: to tremble when it was beaten.

"No," I said again, forcing myself to step forward, so close I could feel the heat radiating off of him. How was it possible a living thing could be so hot? My voice, when I found it again, was shredded to a whisper. "She is not yours."

The Nevariim raised a fist.

Kem Anh's growl stopped him. I glanced past Sinn to find her gliding forward, her eyes on me, curious, searching.

"I need her," I said, speaking directly to the creature of my dreams. "She is my Witness."

It couldn't have made sense. No one raised outside of Rassambur would have understood the words. I didn't even know if the Three were capable of speech. None of them had spoken since entering the clearing. It was madness, trying to explain, but my own death made me bold. I could hear my god, his million hands winnowing the air, his nimble fingers already at work in Ela's failing flesh. My whole life Ananshael had watched me, guarded me. I wasn't ready yet for him to take me, but knowing he was near annealed my will.

I put a hand against the chest of the Nevariim. It was like pressing against a wall of living stone.

He bared his teeth, but behind him Kem Anh growled again, louder this time, and finally, with a furious hiss, he tossed Ela's twitching body to the dirt.

It took the priestess a dozen heartbeats or so to open her eyes. When she did, she looked momentarily confused, as though she'd never seen the delta before, or the sky, or the reeds. Then she focused on me, on my face, and smiled as she forced herself to her feet.

"Pyrre," she said, shaking her head, "you can't save me. I have been ready to die for a very long time."

I stared at her, stared into those wide, joyful eyes, then leaned down to kiss her on the lips. Despite the pain, she raised a hand, taking me by the back of the head to pull me closer. When I finally pulled away, she was smiling, and I realized, to my shock, that I was smiling too.

"I'm not trying to save you," I murmured, then drove the knife into her still-trembling flesh. "I'm finishing my Trial."

Give to the god the one who makes your mind
And body sing with love
Who will not come again.

She doubled over the bronze blade, groaned, coughed a splatter of hot blood across my chest, raised a broken hand to her lips to wipe it away, then slowly straightened. For a moment I thought she intended to fight on somehow, despite the mortal wound. Then I saw her smile was still there, even brighter for the blood.

She put a hand on my cheek.

Her words were wet, ragged. "I didn't know . . . it would work."

I put an arm around her waist to hold her up. I was crying. The tears were hot as blood but leached of all sorrow. She was so light.

"Didn't know what would work?"

"Kossal kept saying . . . I was too old. . . . You'd never . . . love . . ."

I stared at her, stared *past* her, through her eyes into the weeks we'd shared together in Dombâng, the nights she'd insisted I stay up drinking, talking, that day on the deck in the rainstorm when I'd tried to kill her over and over and over while she laughed. I heard her whispering again in my ear: *Love is like killing. You do it with every part of you, or not at all.*

"You knew . . ." I managed weakly. "You knew it would be you, not Ruc."

She shook her head. "Didn't know . . . hoped."

"You *planned* it."

Blood seeped between her teeth as she smiled.

"Why?" I demanded.

"Thought you'd make a good priestess . . . Just needed you to stop . . . being so . . . serious all the time."

Her eyes were vague, gazing at something far away, as I lowered her to the ground.

"Live . . ." she murmured.

"We're about to die," I protested.

"Live anyway . . . Live more . . . That's the trick."

Her face was beautiful even now, even flecked with blood, but her breath rattled in her throat. Each time she inhaled, she winced. "It hurts," she whispered. "Sweet lord, it hurts."

I brushed a smear of mud from her cheek.

"Not anymore," I replied.

I cut her throat with the sacrificial knife. Blood gushed over the blade, flooded my hands, soaked the ground around me. Her body went gradually slack as the life drained out. It was impossible to say how much pain I had saved her—maybe only moments. It didn't really matter. Her whole life she had been ready for its end. That's what it is to serve the God of Death.

She was gone, utterly gone, but that didn't matter either. Love is not something you can keep. It is something you do, every day, every moment, regardless of who is dying.

I smoothed the sweat-soaked hair back from her brow. Slowly, I straightened, wiped the blade on the leg of my pants, reclaimed my spear, then turned to face the Three.

"Seven," I said quietly.

Their gazes were grave, ancient, inscrutable.

A few paces behind me, I could hear Ruc shift.

"What the fuck was that?" he demanded. The words were quiet, as though he didn't have enough breath for the question.

"I'm a priestess of Ananshael," I replied without turning to look at him.

Wind sifted the rushes.

"You're a monster," Ruc said finally.

I turned the statement over in my mind, tried to understand what it might mean.

"She was happy to go to her god."

"No one is happy to die."

"You're wrong."

Ruc stepped up beside me, put the blade of his sword against my cheek, turned me to face him.

"The only people who want to die are the ones who hate their lives."

I shook my head. The bronze sliced my cheek. I didn't mind. Ela's voice sang in my ears.

"Notes or moments—you can't hold on to them."

"So that means you give up?"

His eyes were a deep, baffled green.

I leaned forward, kissed him full on the mouth. He didn't resist.

"No," I replied, when I finally pulled away. "It means you listen. It means you play." I nodded toward Sinn, who watched us with venomous eyes. "Will you play with me, Ruc Lan Lac?"

"You're insane," he said for the second time that day.

Instead of replying, I gestured to the Nevariim once more. "You like to fight, Ruc. This is a good fight. A great fight. Will you fight it with me?"

He was silent a long time, then shook his head. "Kiss me one more time," he said quietly.

I smiled, then kissed him one more time. He tasted like blood and sorrow.

We fought that immortal creature like dreaming. If Chua, and Kossal, and Ela hadn't injured him, slowed him down, we wouldn't have had a chance, but even so, I never thought we would survive. He was too fast, too strong, too perfect in every motion. I didn't fight him because I wanted to win; I fought because I wanted to fight. I didn't love Ruc, but I liked him, I admired him, and it felt good to move my body beside his, not to be fighting *against* him for once, but with him, to be testing ourselves against something that had never been defeated. Everything felt good. The sun on my skin, the blades in my hands, the hot wind on my face, the breath in my chest. Even Ruc seemed to feel it as we fell into our rhythm, covering each other's attacks and retreats, trying to pry open the tiny cracks in the creature's guard. When I finally stole a glance at him, he had that look I recognized so well, the look of a brawler in a deadly brawl or a singer lost in a song. The world had contracted to this. There was no place else, no one else. The moment was all we wanted. I felt something new, a perfect surrender, an annihilation of whatever lifelong thought-thin membrane had separated me from everything else, from the whole glowing world.

The song of life echoing in my heart, I feinted high, low, high again, dodged a fist, ducked under a blow from the wounded arm, and slashed Sinn across the chest.

It wasn't a killing blow, shouldn't have been, but when he stepped back, Ruc roared and hurled himself forward. I barely had time to think how stupid it was, the attack of a mindless drunk in some barroom brawl, a lunge that left no reasonable defense, no chance to extricate himself if it went wrong. Sinn swatted aside the sword, and Ruc let it drop, but kept coming on, opening his arms. Even as the Nevariim shattered his chest, Ruc wrapped the creature in a huge embrace, pulled the immortal thing in tight as life seeped out of him.

"Pyrre," he managed, my name half a cough, half a moan, and I saw that he hadn't been stupid at all. His attack wasn't an attack, but a sacrifice, one last gift to me, the woman he thought was a monster. In the quarter heartbeat that the Nevariim was tangled in Ruc's arms, I stepped in and cut the creature's throat.

Ananshael is a humble god. He claimed that immortal trophy with the same quiet grace he claims all things. In the end, this creature that the people of the delta had worshipped as a god for so many thousands of years died in the same way as a bird, a fish, a lizard, any of the world's small, scuttling creatures that live their flame-quick lives, then unravel in his gentle hands.

Ruc fought the god a moment longer, long enough for me to hear him whisper in my ear as I knelt, just one word, one solitary syllable: "Love . . ."

Then, before he could finish, the light went out of those green, green eyes. I still don't know if *love* was a word he was using for me, or something he intended to explain, something he believed I still had wrong. I closed his lids. The sun would keep his skin warm until night fell. That seemed right, somehow. He'd always been warm.

I straightened, then turned to face the two remaining Nevariim.

My knives were light in my hands. The day was young. I could feel myself smiling.

"Who's next?" I asked, pointing a bronze blade at Hang Loc. "You?" I turned to Kem Anh. "You?"

The woman cocked her head to the side, as though trying to see me clearly, or to understand what she saw. I gazed into those eyes, the same eyes that had haunted me since my childhood. They were the same—liquid and inhuman—but the terror I'd felt of them for so long had vanished. How could I feel terror in a world brimming with such beauty?

"Let's fight," I murmured.

Kem Anh didn't move forward, didn't even raise a hand. She examined me a while longer, and then she smiled, shook her head, turned away, toward the brush and the thick forest beyond, Hang Loc following her as they receded toward legend once more.

I threw the knife, not because I expected to see it strike, but for the beauty of the bronze flashing in the sunlight. As I expected, Kem Anh turned, caught the blade as it spun end over end, studied the weapon for a moment, then tossed it aside. When she stepped into the brush with her consort, I didn't try to follow. The Three were Two now, gone, vanished back into the labyrinth of the Given Land.

I turned to consider the slaughter behind me. The corpses were gorgeous, even in the postures of their ending. The wind had picked up. It gusted through the rushes, half whistling—a note, a voice as wide and bright and gracious as the world, that lifted, shifted, then disappeared each time I thought I almost heard it clearly.

EPILOGUE

That is the story, my love. My story, but yours, too.

The Vuo Ton found me on the island three days later, a slender boat sliding out of the warm morning mist, tattooed figures silent as idols, even those at the oars motionless as the hull drifted toward the shore. The Witness stood near the bow, one foot on the thwart. When the boat was still a pace and a half from the sand, he leapt, landed easily, then stood watching me for a long time.

"You are alive," he said finally.

I nodded, but didn't get up from where I was sitting. I'd made no effort to escape the island. If Ananshael wanted me, he knew where to find me.

I'd spent the first day burning the bodies of the dead. I laid Kossal and Ela, Ruc and Chua on a great pyre of dry rushes, labored half the morning to kindle an ember with a dry stick in a piece of driftwood, then stood back and watched as the fire devoured the piles of bone and meat. The four warriors were gone, utterly unmade, but their bodies burned bright as anything still alive.

Sinn, I did not burn. I carved his head from his shoulders with the bronze knife, then spent the afternoon shaving away the skin from the skull, prying out the eyes, scooping clear the brain—which seemed heavier than human brains, more dense— then washing the bone in the river until it gleamed. When it was finally clean and dry, I placed it atop the wall of skulls, packed the sockets of the eyes with dirt, then planted a pair of river violets.

I spent a long time looking at the monument. To the people of Dombâng, the island is a sacred place, the abode of their gods. It is not sacred to me—no more sacred than any other place where my god has unmade a creature—but it is beautiful. I smiled, laying Sinn's skull atop the pile; he had been a gorgeous creature, and it seemed appropriate that what was left of him, too, should be gorgeous.

After that I spent the days and nights seated on the shore, listening to the birds, watching the clouds. I expected my god to gather me to him, but instead of my god, the Witness of the Vuo Ton had arrived in his long boat.

"You are alive," he said again.

I realized that I hadn't replied the first time, rose to my feet, and smiled.

"I am. The only one."

"The Three gave you back."

I considered telling him that his gods were not gods, but the remnants of a near-forgotten race, then decided against it. People worship as they will. It was not my place to take the faith of another.

"Now there are Two," I replied.

He blinked. "The gods . . ."

". . . Wanted a hunt worthy of them. They found it."

I pointed to the skull. It was larger than a human skull. Thicker, too.

The Witness crossed to it, lifted it to the sky, stared into those dirt-packed eyes for a long time, then laid it reverently back on the pile. When he turned to me, his eyes were full of tears.

"Where would you have us take you?"

I smiled. "Home."

I didn't mean Dombâng. Rassambur was my home, my true home. It had been my home even before I knew its name. I stayed in Dombâng a little more than a year, however. I knew, shortly after I'd returned to the city, while I was still healing, that I wasn't alone. I wasn't the only one to have survived the island after all.

Love sang inside my heart—Ela's last gift—and you were growing inside me, tiny but getting larger every day. You are a child of the delta, son, conceived in a hut of the Vuo Ton. Your father was a scion of your city, and you are the last of that line, the last of Goc My's lineage. What you'll do with that fact, I don't know. This story might not matter to you, but it is your story as much as mine, and you deserve to know it.

I stayed in the city long enough to see you born, then to nurse you. You were a wide-eyed, laughing child from the first. No one would have guessed at the violence of the first days of your gestation. You rarely cried, and your laughter sounded like song. It was hard to let you go, but I owed a debt for a prayer I had made, a prayer answered finally on that island in the delta. One night in autumn, just after you were weaned, just before the Annurians arrived with their legions and their blockade, I laid you on the altar of the temple of Eira, trusting to her priest-esses and priests, to the goddess herself, to raise and watch over you, my only child. I imagine you in that temple now, surrounded by white light and the smell of jasmine. The thought makes me smile.

I used to loathe your goddess. She seemed to me a player of favorites, a fickle, capricious creature, the opposite in every way of the god I serve. I was wrong. Our gods, of course, are beyond all human understanding, but I imagine Eira as the daughter of Ananshael. I imagine the two of them holding hands, her smooth fingers laced through his old, gnarled joints. The Nevariim do not die—not natural deaths—and they do not love.

We do both. We must do both.

Perhaps I will come back to the delta one day and hold you in my arms again. Perhaps not. In either case, I hope this finds you well, my son, child of my doubt and my delight, your heart full of life, and your mouth still brimming with song.

GODS AND RACES, AS UNDERSTOOD BY THE CITIZENS OF ANNUR

RACES

Nevariim—Immortal, beautiful, bucolic. Foes of the Csestriim. Extinct thousands of years before the appearance of humans. Likely apocryphal.

Csestriim—Immortal, vicious, emotionless. Responsible for the creation of civilization and the study of science and medicine. Destroyed by humans. Extinct thousands of years.

Human—Identical in appearance to the Csestriim, but mortal, subject to emotion.

THE OLD GODS, IN ORDER OF ANTIQUITY

Blank God, the—The oldest, predating creation. Venerated by the Shin monks.

Ae—Consort to the Blank God, the Goddess of Creation, responsible for all that is.

Astar'ren—Goddess of Law, Mother of Order and Structure. Called the Spider by some, although the adherents of Kaveraa also claim that title for their own goddess.

Pta—Lord of Chaos, disorder, and randomness. Believed by some to be a simple trickster, by others, a destructive and indifferent force.

Intarra—Lady of Light, Goddess of Fire, starlight, and the sun. Also the patron of the Malkeenian Emperors of Annur, who claim her as a distant ancestor.

Hull—The Owl King, the Bat, Lord of the Darkness, Lord of the Night, aegis of the Kettral, patron of thieves.

Bedisa—Goddess of Birth, she who weaves the souls of all living creatures.

Ananshael—God of Death, the Lord of Bones, who unknits the weaving of his consort, Bedisa, consigning all living creatures to oblivion. Worshipped by the Skullsworn in Rassambur.

Ciena—Goddess of Pleasure, believed by some to be the mother of the young gods.

Meshkent—The Cat, the Lord of Pain and Cries, consort of Ciena, believed by some to be the father of the young gods. Worshipped by the Urghul, some Manjari, and the jungle tribes.

THE YOUNG GODS, ALL COEVAL WITH HUMANITY

Eira—Goddess of Love and mercy.
Maat—Lord of Rage and hate.
Kaveraa—Lady of Terror, Mistress of Fear.
Heqet—God of Courage and battle.
Orella—Goddess of Hope.
Orilon—God of Despair.

Read on for an extract from

THE EMPEROR'S BLADES

Volume One in the Chronicle of the Unhewn Throne trilogy

**The circle is closing. The stakes are high.
And old truths will live again . . .**

The Emperor has been murdered, leaving the Annurian Empire in turmoil. Now his progeny must prepare to unmask a conspiracy. His son Valyn, training for the empire's deadliest fighting force, hears the news an ocean away. And after several 'accidents' and a dying soldier's warning, he realizes his life is also in danger. Yet before Valyn can act, he must survive the mercenaries' brutal final initiation.

The Emperor's daughter, Minister Adare, hunts her father's murderer in the capital. Court politics can be fatal, but she needs justice. Lastly Kaden, heir to the empire, studies in a remote monastery. Here, the Blank God's disciples teach their harsh ways, which Kaden must master to unlock ancient powers. But when an imperial delegation arrives, has he learnt enough to keep him alive, as long-hidden powers make their move?

'An enchanting union of old and new, Staveley's debut will keep you turning pages late into the night'   Pierce Brown

'Following in the footsteps of George R. R. Martin, Joe Abercrombie and the like . . . Brutal, intriguing and continuing to head toward exciting events and places unknown'
Kirkus Reviews

1

The sun hung just over the peaks, a silent, furious ember drenching the granite cliffs in a bloody red, when Kaden found the shattered carcass of the goat.

He'd been dogging the creature over the tortuous mountain trails for hours, scanning for track where the ground was soft enough, making guesses when he came to bare rock, doubling back when he guessed wrong. It was slow work and tedious, the kind of task the older monks delighted in assigning to their pupils. As the sun sank and the eastern sky purpled to a vicious bruise, he started to wonder if he would be spending the night in the high peaks with only his roughspun robe for comfort. Spring had arrived weeks earlier according to the Annurian calendar, but the monks didn't pay any heed to the calendar and neither did the weather, which remained hard and grudging. Scraps of dirty snow lingered in the long shadows, cold seeped from the stones, and the needles of the few gnarled junipers were still more gray than green.

"Come on, you old bastard," he muttered, checking another track. "You don't want to sleep out here any more than I do."

The mountains comprised a maze of cuts and canyons, washed-out gullies and rubble-strewn ledges. Kaden had already crossed three streams gorged with snowmelt, frothing at the hard walls that hemmed them in, and his robe was damp with spray. It would freeze when the sun dropped. How the goat had made its way past the rushing water, he had no idea.

"If you drag me around these peaks much longer . . . ," he began, but the words died on his lips as he spotted his quarry at last—thirty paces distant, wedged in a narrow defile, only the hindquarters visible.

Although he couldn't get a good look at the thing—it seemed to have trapped itself between a large boulder and the canyon wall—he could tell at once that something was wrong. The creature was still, too still, and there was an unnaturalness to the angle of the haunches, the stiffness in the legs.

"Come on, goat," he murmured as he approached, hoping the animal hadn't managed to hurt itself too badly. The Shin monks were not rich, and they relied on their flocks for milk and meat. If Kaden returned with an animal that was injured, or worse, dead, his *umial* would impose a severe penance.

"Come on, old fellow," he said, working his way slowly up the canyon. The goat appeared stuck, but if it *could* run, he didn't want to end up chasing it all over the Bone Mountains. "Better grazing down below. We'll walk back together."

The evening shadows hid the blood until he was nearly standing in it, the pool wide and dark and still. Something had gutted the animal, hacked a savage slice across the haunch and into the stomach, cleaving muscle and driving into the viscera. As Kaden watched, the last lingering drops of blood trickled out, turning the soft belly hair into a sodden, ropy mess, running down the stiff legs like urine.

" 'Shael take it," he cursed, vaulting over the wedged boulder. It wasn't so unusual for a crag cat to take a goat, but now he'd have to carry the carcass back to the monastery across his shoulders. "You had to go wandering," he said. "You had . . ."

The words trailed off, and his spine stiffened as he got a good look at the animal for the first time. A quick cold fear blazed over his skin. He took a breath, then extinguished the emotion. Shin training wasn't good for much, but after eight years, he *had* managed to tame his feelings; fear, envy, anger, exuberance—he still felt them, but they did not penetrate so deeply as they once had. Even within the fortress of his calm, however, he couldn't help but stare.

Whatever had gutted the goat did not stop there. Some creature—Kaden struggled in vain to think of what—had hacked the animal's head from its shoulders, severing the strong sinew and muscle with sharp, brutal strokes until only the stump of the neck remained. Crag cats would take the occasional flagging member of a herd, but not like this. These wounds were vicious, unnecessary, lacking the quotidian economy of other kills he had seen in the wild. The animal had not simply been slaughtered; it had been destroyed.

Kaden cast about, searching for the rest of the carcass. Stones and branches had washed down with the early spring floods and lodged at the choke point of the defile in a weed-matted mess of silt and skeletal wooden fingers, sun-bleached and grasping. So much detritus clogged the canyon that it took him a while to locate the head, which lay tossed on its side a few paces distant. Much of the hair had been torn away and the bone split open. The brain was gone, scooped from the trencher of the skull as though with a spoon.

Kaden's first thought was to flee. Blood still dripped from the goat's gory coat, more black than red in the fading light, and whatever had mauled it could still be in the rocks, guarding its kill. None of the local predators would be likely to attack Kaden—he was tall for his seventeen years, lean and strong from half a lifetime of labor—but then, none of the local predators would have hacked the head from the goat and eaten its brain either.

He turned toward the canyon mouth. The sun had settled below the steppe, leaving just a burnt smudge above the grasslands to the west. Already night filled the canyon like oil seeping into a bowl. Even if he left immediately, even if he ran at his fastest lope, he'd be covering the last few miles to the monastery in full dark. Though he thought he had long outgrown his fear of night in the mountains, he didn't relish the idea of stumbling along the rock-strewn path, an unknown predator following in the darkness.

He took a step away from the shattered creature, then hesitated.

"Heng's going to want a painting of this," he muttered, forcing himself to turn back to the carnage.

Anyone with a brush and a scrap of parchment could make a painting, but the Shin expected rather more of their novices and acolytes. Painting was the product of seeing, and the monks had their own way of seeing. *Saama'an,* they called it: "the carved mind." It was only an exercise, of course, a step on the long path leading to the ultimate liberation of *vaniate,* but it had its meager uses. During his eight years in the mountains, Kaden had learned to see, to *really* see the world as it was: the track of a brindled bear, the serration of a forksleaf petal, the crenellations of a distant peak. He had spent countless hours, weeks, *years* looking, seeing, memorizing. He could paint any of a thousand plants or animals down to the last finial feather, and he could internalize a new scene in heartbeats.

He took two slow breaths, clearing a space in his head, a blank slate on which to carve each minute particular. The fear remained, but the fear was an impediment, and he pared it down, focusing on the task at hand. With the slate prepared, he set to work. It took only a few breaths to etch the severed head, the pools of dark blood, the mangled carcass of the animal. The lines were sure and certain, finer than any brushstroke, and unlike normal memory, the process left him with a sharp, vivid image, durable as the stones on which he stood, one he would be able to recall and scrutinize at will. He finished the *saama'an* and let out a long, careful breath.

Fear is blindness, he muttered, repeating the old Shin aphorism. *Calmness, sight.*

The words provided cold comfort in the face of the bloody scene, but now that he had the carving, he could leave. He glanced once over his shoulder, searching the cliffs for some sign of the predator, then turned toward the opening of the defile. As the night's dark fog rolled over the peaks, he raced the darkness down the treacherous trails, sandaled feet darting past the downed limbs and ankle-breaking rocks. His legs, chill and stiff after so many hours creeping after the goat, warmed to the motion while his heart settled into a steady tempo.

You're not running away, he told himself, *just heading home.*

Still, he breathed a small sigh of relief a mile down the path when he rounded a tower of rock—the Talon, the monks called it—and could make out Ashk'lan in the distance. Thousands of feet below him, the scant stone buildings perched on a narrow ledge as though huddled away from the abyss. Warm lights glowed in some of the windows. There would be a fire in the refectory kitchen, lamps kindled in the meditation hall, the quiet hum of the Shin going about their evening ablutions and rituals. *Safe.* The word rose unbidden to his mind. It was safe down there, and despite his resolve, Kaden increased his pace, running toward those few, faint lights, fleeing whatever prowled the unknown darkness behind him.